"I shouldn't have done that," Ryland muttered, his voice sounding oddly muffled

Eleanor stared into his eyes. They seemed darker somehow—the pupils huge black pools surrounded by a blue rim. She took a deep breath, trying to force air back into her constricted lungs. "No, you shouldn't have," she agreed, confused and disconcerted by her uninhibited reaction. "It simply isn't done," she added with an attempt at firmness.

"Don't be naive. It's done all the time. What you mean is that society says we shouldn't do it. But whatever the reality, my behavior was unbecoming a gentleman, and I apologize."

"Oh? How do gentlemen kiss?" The question popped out before she realized it, and Eleanor felt a flush stain her cheeks.

Ryland chuckled. "I think that kiss comes under the heading of a little knowledge is a dangerous thing...."

Dear Reader,

When contemporary author Judith McWilliams decided to write her first historical, the result was *Suspicion*, a Regency-era historical released in April '94 by Harlequin Historicals. The book was very well received, and we are very happy to be able to now bring you Ms. McWilliams's second historical, *Betrayed*, the story of an American heiress who is forced to spy on her British relatives and finds herself in the middle of a Napoleonic scheme.

Our other titles this month include *Desire My Love* from Miranda Jarrett, the next book in the continuing saga of the irrepressible Sparhawk family of Rhode Island; *Vows*, by Margaret Moore, part of the Harlequin continuity series WEDDINGS, INC., the story of a Welsh immigrant who gets involved in the Underground Railway; and *Roarke's Folly*, the third book in Claire Delacroix's ROSE SERIES, which began with *Romance of the Rose*.

Keep an eye out for all four titles, wherever Harlequin Historicals are sold.

Sincerely,

Tracy Farrell
Senior Editor

Please address questions and book requests to:
Harlequin Reader Service
U.S.: 3010 Walden Ave., P.O. Box 1325, Buffalo, NY 14269
Canadian: P.O. Box 609, Fort Erie, Ont. L2A 5X3

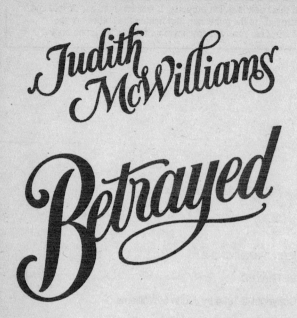

Judith McWilliams

Betrayed

Harlequin Books

TORONTO • NEW YORK • LONDON
AMSTERDAM • PARIS • SYDNEY • HAMBURG
STOCKHOLM • ATHENS • TOKYO • MILAN
MADRID • WARSAW • BUDAPEST • AUCKLAND

ISBN 0-373-28849-2

BETRAYED

This edition published by arrangement with Harlequin Enterprises B.V.

® and TM are trademarks of the publisher. Trademarks indicated with ® are registered in the United States Patent and Trademark Office, the Canadian Trade Marks Office and in other countries.

Printed in U.S.A.

JUDITH McWILLIAMS

For years, Judith has delighted readers with her entertaining contemporary romances written for the Harlequin Temptation and the Silhouette Romance lines. Now, Judith has written her second historical for the Harlequin Historicals line. The author makes her home in Texas, where she is hard at work on her next book.

Prologue

Boston—Fall 1813

"Eleanor, I have important news!" Connal Gunn's smugly self-satisfied voice invaded the quiet sanctuary of Eleanor's parlor a second before his physical presence did.

"I'm that sorry, Miss Wallace." The young maid scooted around Connal's tall, thin frame and positioned herself protectively in front of Eleanor. "I told Mr. Gunn that you said you wasn't seein' nobody no more tonight."

"And I told her that you could hardly have meant me." He glared at the girl, and she nervously inched closer to Eleanor.

Eleanor set down the knitting she'd been pretending to be working on and forced a welcoming smile. "It's all right, Betty. I'll see Mr. Gunn. You may go."

"Yes, Miss Wallace." Betty carefully skirted him as she hurried out of the room.

"Really, my dear—" Connal tossed his high-crowned beaver hat onto the mahogany table just inside the room "—you really should have reprimanded the girl for her insolence."

"Betty was not being insolent. She was merely following my instructions, Connal," Eleanor said in defense of the maid. "I told her to deny me to visitors."

"Well, you will inform her that in the future such an order does not apply to me."

Eleanor didn't argue. She simply followed the line of least resistance, as she so often seemed to do with Connal lately, and smiled noncommittally. He meant well, she told herself, trying hard to believe it. He just had an unfortunate way of expressing himself. And a bad sense of timing for social calls. She glanced at the clock on the mantel as it struck nine. It was late, and she wasn't in the mood to spend what was left of her evening serving as an appreciative audience of one while Connal regaled her with whatever business coup had created his air of barely contained triumph.

But then, how had she planned to spend the rest of her evening? As she had done every night for the past three months? By railing against a malevolent fate? By wallowing in self-pity? And Connal had always been welcome in the house before...

"Why, Mr. Gunn." Sarah Peabody feigned surprise as she rushed into the room. "What a surprise to see you here. So late," she added with an innocent smile.

Eleanor felt an unexpected flash of humor momentarily nudge aside the enveloping cloud of unhappiness that fogged her mind. No doubt Betty had told Sarah of Connal's visit and sent her in to protect Eleanor's reputation. Or perhaps Betty had done it merely to annoy Connal. She obviously didn't like him. Not that Eleanor blamed her. It would be very hard to like someone who treated you as if you were of no more importance than the furniture.

"Good evening, Sarah. As you can see, Mr. Gunn has come to visit us for a few minutes," Eleanor said, hoping it was true. She could feel the all-too-familiar tightness that presaged a violent headache beginning to wrap itself around her forehead, directly above her eyes.

"This isn't a social call. I want to speak to you privately." Connal gave the hovering Sarah an annoyed look. "I think, my dear, that considering our relationship, we can dispense with your chaperone's presence."

Eleanor started to object to his cavalier dismissal of her friend, and then thought better of it. If she knew Connal, and after two years she knew him far better than she sometimes wished, it would undoubtedly be easier in the long run to allow him to have his own way. Hopefully, once he'd told her his news, he'd go and leave her in peace. Eleanor unconsciously pressed her thin white fingers to her forehead, trying in vain to ease the escalating pain.

"I'll be in the book room if you should need me," Sarah said, pointedly leaving the parlor door open behind her when she left.

Connal promptly closed it and, turning to Eleanor, rubbed his hands together gleefully.

Eleanor felt a sense of foreboding at his expression. It reminded her of the picture in her Bible of the devil rejoicing over Adam's fall. Telling herself that she was being ridiculous, she gestured toward the yellow damask wing chair across from her, hoping to keep some distance between them. "Won't you sit down, Connal?"

To her dismay, he ignored the hint and plopped down beside her on the sofa. The heat pouring off his body seemed to crowd her, threatening her on some level that she didn't quite understand. All she knew for certain was that she wanted to retreat. But she didn't, because she also knew it would upset him, and at the moment she simply didn't feel up to the time-consuming task of soothing his hurt feelings.

"I imagine you've been wondering why I haven't arranged a wedding date for us," he began.

"No, Connal, I haven't wondered. I assumed the reason was because I told you that I had no wish to be married with my father not yet cold in his grave."

"He has been gone for three months now." Connal's even tone was at variance with his annoyed expression. "Time enough for you to have gotten over his death."

Eleanor studied him gravely, wondering how deeply Connal felt about people, if he believed that three months was sufficient time to recover from the death of the man who had been both father and mother to her all her life. If she finally did marry Connal and died in childbirth, as her own mother had done, would he mourn her for a month and then forget her? Her father had never forgotten her mother. Until the day he died, he'd grieved for her. Was Connal capable of feeling that deeply about her? It was a disquieting thought.

"Eleanor, would you please pay attention?" he said impatiently. "This is of paramount importance. I just came from the docks. A ship has just arrived from England."

"The captain's either a very brave man or a very foolhardy one, to be sailing the high seas while America's at war with England," Eleanor murmured, wondering what the captain could be carrying that would make the risk worthwhile.

"It isn't all that dangerous," Connal insisted.

"Compared to what? Fighting the Indians on the frontier?" Eleanor asked dryly.

"My dear, you really must restrain your inclination to indulge in levity," Connal said pompously. "It is a trait most unbecoming in a woman."

"Father always told me to think for myself."

"I don't object to your thinking. What I object to is your voicing your thoughts aloud." Connal smiled at her, and Eleanor wasn't sure if he was serious or not. She suppressed a sigh. That was part of her problem. She really didn't know Connal all that well. Not really. And if she were to marry him, as her father had wanted . . .

"As I was saying," Connal continued, taking her preoccupation as contrition for her outspokenness, "I met the *Merry Belle* when it docked, and you'll never guess what?" His air of triumph increased until it was an almost palpable entity vibrating between them.

Eleanor indulged him with a guess. "Someone wants to order a new ship from our boatyard?" Her father had kept her isolated from his business affairs, but even so, she couldn't help but know that this war with England was having a disastrous effect on shipbuilding. The shipyard had been virtually idle for well over a year. An order for a new ship would be welcome news indeed.

"Better than that," Connal said smugly. "I received a letter."

"Oh." Eleanor felt her brief spurt of interest drain away, making her all the more aware of the throbbing in her head. "How nice for you. From a friend back in Scotland?" she asked politely.

"No!" he announced in dramatic tones, obviously trying to prolong the suspense. But when Eleanor made no attempt to tease the information out of him, he added, "From your family in England."

Eleanor frowned uncomprehendingly at him. "What are you talking about?"

"I'm talking about your mother's family, the Bromleys."

"What?" Eleanor's apathy was consumed in a conflagration of righteous anger. "Do you mean to tell me that you actually took it upon yourself to write to those…those miscreants? My father despised them! And with good cause, too."

"All that happened long ago," Connal said with a superior smile.

"To my father it was as if it had happened yesterday. Grandmother Bromley hated him. Really hated him. She literally ran him and my poor mother out of England, and when he wrote years later to tell her that I'd been born and that her daughter had died, do you know what she wrote back? That she was glad her daughter was dead." Eleanor rushed on before Connal could say anything. "That she'd rather Emily were in her grave than to see her married to a penniless Scot with ideas above his station. My oh-so-loving grandmother ended her letter with a postscript saying that she never wanted to hear from Papa again. Nor did she wish to have any contact with me, the mongrel result of her daughter's shocking mésalliance.

"I tell you, Connal, if there were any justice in this world, she would be the one dead, instead of my parents," Eleanor finished angrily.

"Fortunately for us, she seems to have changed her mind," Connal said. "She has written, offering you a home."

"Why?" Eleanor asked bluntly. "Is the family under the hatches, and they expect me to pull them out of the River Tick?"

Connal grimaced distastefully. "Really, my dear, where do you pick up such unsuitable slang?"

"From my father, which is where I also acquired my common sense. And that common sense tells me that if my grandmother didn't relent when her own daughter died, she certainly wouldn't relent simply because the man she hated died."

"Well..." Connal got to his feet and walked over to the fireplace. He kicked at the smoldering logs with the toe of one muddied boot, absently watching as a shower of sparks danced up the chimney. Finally he turned back and studied Eleanor, his dark brown eyes narrowed speculatively.

"She didn't exactly relent," he finally admitted. "You see, in the letter I said I was your clergyman, and that I was worried about you. That your father had died and left you destitute, and I didn't know what was to become of you. I begged her in the name of Christian charity to give you a home."

Eleanor stared at him in utter disbelief. "Why?" she demanded. "You had to have known how much my father hated the Bromleys. You were his junior partner in the boatyard for the past two years. He made no secret of his feelings, and yet the minute he's dead—"

"Circumstances alter cases," Connal said with a superiority that made Eleanor long to box his ears. "If you'll remember, we are at war with England."

"I fail to see any relationship between the war and my father's hatred of the Bromleys." Eleanor eyed him consideringly. "Tell me, Connal, did you stop at Buggs' Tavern before you came here?"

"Certainly not!" Connal was plainly outraged. "This isn't common knowledge yet, but American negotiators have left for Ghent to try to forge a peace treaty with England."

Eleanor tried to hurry him up when he fell silent. "And?"

"And we are in a very poor position from which to bargain. The war has not been going well for us lately."

"Everyone knows that, but I still don't see the connection," she said, wishing he'd get to the point and leave. Her surge of anger at Connal's duplicity had increased the throbbing in her head to an excruciatingly painful level.

"We need some advantage. Some military victory. Something that would make the English willing to accept an honorable peace instead of continuing to demand a surrender. Your father was a staunch believer in the American cause," Connal pointed out. "And it's up to us who respected and loved him to carry on his fight. That's why you must go to England."

Eleanor sighed. "Connal, it's late, and I'm tired. If there is a point to what you're saying, make it."

Connal pursed his full lips together in annoyance at being rushed. "Did you know that your uncle Henry is instrumental in formulating battle plans for the English war effort in America?"

"I never even knew I had an uncle Henry." The sudden flash of interest Eleanor felt caught her by surprise.

"He was the older of your mother's two brothers," Connal elaborated. "He was already at Oxford when the family hired your father to tutor the younger one. From what your father told me, the boy was very sickly. At any rate, he died of a fever the year after your parents came to America. For some reason of his own, your father kept track of Henry's career over the years, and I was able to confirm his information with one of our diplomats before I wrote to your grandmother."

"An interesting bit of family history, but I still don't see what this hitherto-unknown uncle has to do with anything," she said, feeling hurt that her father would have told Connal about her mother's family and not her.

"That's because you aren't thinking clearly," Connal said, with a condescending air that set Eleanor's teeth on edge.

"Your grandmother Bromley lives in London, with your uncle Henry. So, when you go to stay with her, you'll be in an excellent position to discover all kinds of information about the British battle plans for their spring offensive against America. If we knew where and when they intended to attack, we would gain a tremendous advantage. Enough of an advantage to turn the tide of the war in our favor and force the English to moderate their demands for peace."

"You actually expect me to spy on my relatives?" Eleanor asked incredulously, her distaste clear in her voice.

"As you yourself pointed out, they were your father's enemies. He would have wanted you to."

Eleanor grimaced, knowing Connal was right. Her father would have relished the chance to repay the Bromleys for the appalling way they had treated him all those years ago. And it was equally true that he had passionately believed in the American cause. He would have done anything in his power to defeat the British, even spying. But she wasn't her father, and the whole idea left a nasty taste in her mouth.

"It isn't as if you'll be in your grandmother's house for any length of time," Connal told her as he sat down beside her again. "All we need is enough information to alter the course of a few battles, and the English government will be quick enough to sign a fair peace treaty."

When Eleanor didn't answer him, he reached out and captured her slender hand. Eleanor suppressed her instinctive urge to jerk away. His grasp made her feel bound in some indefinable way that panicked her.

"My poor dear," Connal murmured, oblivious of her reaction.

Eleanor held herself rigid with an effort as his short, blunt fingers stroked the back of her hand.

"This has been a very trying time for you, my dear, but it's almost over. And once you've gone to England and carried out our plans, we can be married." He offered the words like a bribe, but they merely increased Eleanor's feeling of distress.

Interpreting her silence as agreement, Connal suddenly leaned over and pressed his mouth to hers. His full lips were moist and slippery, reminding Eleanor of the frogs at the pond near the edge of town and how, long ago, her governess had told her of an old French fairy tale in which a princess had kissed a frog and he turned into a royal prince. It obviously didn't work in real life. Not only did Connal not change into anything, but she found his kiss totally repulsive. Eleanor held her breath and forced herself to remain motionless.

Finally, Connal raised his head and smiled down at her, a satisfied expression on his face. Eleanor eyed him uncertainly. What had he felt? she wondered. Had he actually liked it? Maybe men reacted differently to kisses than women did? Or was he simply better at hiding his feelings?

"I suppose I should apologize for kissing you," he said. "But, after all, one must allow a little license to engaged couples."

"We are not engaged," Eleanor hastily corrected him.

"Only because your father died so soon after his seizure!" Connal sounded peevish. "You know he wanted you to marry me."

But what about what she wanted? Eleanor thought with a flash of rebellion. She was the one who would have to live with Connal for the rest of her life if she married him. Eleanor rubbed her forehead, which was throbbing unmercifully.

"My poor dear." Connal was all sympathy now that he thought he'd convinced her to do as he wanted. "Daniel would be so proud of you for helping the American cause. Don't worry about a thing. I'll arrange all the details for your passage before I leave for New York on Friday. The *Merry Belle* will be sailing for Jamaica next week, and from there back to England. There's a lot to do before you go." He gave her a satisfied smile and, retrieving his hat from the table, left.

Eleanor leaned back against the sofa, her mind a swirling caldron of emotions. Distaste, dismay, fear, anger, grief, revulsion and a very faint sense of curiosity struggled for supremacy.

She took a deep breath and counted backward from twenty. She had to decide what she was going to do, and she didn't have much time to make the decision. Not with the ship sailing next week. Eleanor released her pent-up breath on a long sigh. Maybe going to England for a short visit wasn't such a bad idea. She tried to consider the idea unemotionally. Ever since her father's death, she'd been hiding in this house, slowly sinking deeper and deeper into a lethargic state of apathy. She'd been wallowing in her grief, she admitted with her usual lack of self-deception. Relish-

ing it. Hugging it to her for over three months now. Maybe
it was time to face the world again. To deal with life as it
was, and not hide herself away because it didn't meet her
expectations.

She had no doubt that Connal's motives for sending her
to England were entirely self-serving. He probably intended to take credit for any information she might un-
cover. But Eleanor also knew what he had said was no more
than the simple truth. The war was going badly for America, her father had been a staunch patriot, and he had hated
his wife's family. Hated them with an intensity that Eleanor
could never quite understand. But then, no one had ever
accused her of being a thief, either, she admitted.

But did the fact that her grandmother Bromley had accused her father of stealing a valuable necklace justify her
spying on her uncle? Eleanor frowned uncertainly. No matter how she looked at it, it didn't seem ethical. Rather like
claiming that visiting the sins of the father on the son was
fair. Nor did she like the idea of lying to her mother's family about her financial resources. It infuriated her that her
grandmother would think that Daniel had left his daughter
so poorly provided for that she was forced to beg shelter
from his enemies.

On the other hand, if she were to go to England, maybe
she could find out what had really happened to that necklace her father was supposed to have stolen. If her father's
theory that her grandmother had hidden it herself and just
pretended it had been stolen in an attempt to get rid of him
was correct, it should be easy to find out the truth. Twenty-
seven years was a long time to keep something hidden.
Someone would have been bound to see it during all those
years. But if her father had been wrong, and her grandmother hadn't taken it . . . Eleanor chewed thoughtfully on
her lower lip. It would be a lot more difficult to solve the
crime. But one thing was certain, she would never be able to
clear her father's name from this side of the Atlantic.

And then there was this unknown uncle named Henry.
What was he like? Did he have a family? Maybe she had
cousins. Eleanor felt a flicker of interest. She'd always
wanted a brother or a sister. A cousin would be the next-best

thing. If she went to England, she might find family members she liked and who would like her. The thought of belonging to a family again was very seductive.

And finally there was the problem of Connal. Eleanor forced herself to face the situation that she'd been avoiding for months. Connal wanted to marry her. He not only wanted to, he expected to. And he had some right to feel that way, she conceded. Her father had actively championed the match. In fact, the only reason he'd brought Connal into the shipyards as a junior partner after his first seizure two years ago was that he'd felt Connal would make an acceptable husband for her. One who would be able to safeguard both her and her inheritance.

But shouldn't marriage be more than that? Eleanor wondered wistfully. It had been for her parents. Her mother's love for her father had been strong enough that she agreed to elope with him, and Daniel's love for his Emily had been such that he'd never even considered remarriage after her tragic death. Perhaps love like that had to grow, she pondered. But if love was to grow out of the rather tepid feelings she held for Connal, shouldn't she at least like his kisses? She worried the problem around in her head.

"Don't scowl. You'll get wrinkles," Sarah told her in all seriousness as she hurried into the room.

"Sarah, you were married once, weren't you?" Eleanor asked.

"Yes, fifty years ago come July," Sarah told her as she sank down in the wing chair across from her. "He died of a fever a year later."

"I'm sorry for bringing up sad memories," Eleanor apologized.

"They aren't sad. Not really," Sarah assured her. "It was all so long ago. It's like it happened to someone else." She leaned forward, studying Eleanor's worried features. "Mr. Gunn upset you, didn't he?"

"He kissed me," Eleanor said baldly.

"I might've known he'd be one to try to take advantage," Sarah said in disgust. "Are you really going to marry him, like he says?"

"My father wanted me to."

"Your father was that worried what would happen to you after he was gone. The way you been moping around the house these three months past, maybe he had cause to be!"

A reluctant smile curved Eleanor's lips. "I do seem to have been a bit of a wet goose lately, haven't I?"

"Not that you haven't had cause," Sarah added fairly. "What with your poor father dying so sudden like, and then the miserable cold, wet fall we've had. The weather's been enough to give anyone a fit of the dismals. What you need is to get out a little more. Visit some of your friends."

"I'm thinking of going to England to visit my mother's family." Eleanor tried the words out to see how they sounded.

"England? Soon?" Sarah looked worried.

"The ship sails next week, but I would greatly appreciate it if you would remain here in the house and make sure that it runs smoothly," Eleanor hurriedly said, knowing how much Sarah hated living on the grudging charity of her brother and his pinch-penny wife. The knowledge of Sarah's uncomfortable circumstances had figured heavily in Eleanor's decision to ask the old woman to stay with her as her chaperone after the funeral.

Sarah's face brightened and then promptly fell. "Mr. Gunn won't like the idea. He'll probably want to shut the house up."

"It isn't Mr. Gunn's decision to make," Eleanor said. "Papa may have wanted me to marry him, but he left control of my inheritance in my hands."

A fact that had infuriated Connal when he'd found out. The memory suddenly surfaced from the fragments of events surrounding her father's death. Connal had tried his best to convince her to allow him to handle her investments, but she'd flatly refused, preferring to leave their management to her father's very competent man of business.

"Don't worry, Sarah. Before I leave, I'll see Papa's attorney and tell him that I want you to continue to live here. I'll make sure he understands that you are to draw on my accounts for your expenses."

"Thank you." Sarah's smile illuminated her lined face. "If there is anything I can ever do for you..."

"You can tell me..." Eleanor groped for a way to phrase her question so as not to shock her elderly friend. "I told you Connal kissed me, and...well...I found it disgusting," she finally blurted out.

"Of course you did," Sarah agreed with a promptness that depressed Eleanor. "It's frightful when men give in to their disgusting appetites. But that's the way of the world. Women have to suffer it in order to have a family. Your mother's long dead, but mine told me that it was God's judgment against women because Eve led Adam astray." Sarah got to her feet and shook out her long black skirts. "Now then, I'm going to make you a nice glass of warm milk and honey, and after you drink it, you'd best go to bed. I can see that you have the headache."

Eleanor nodded absently, her mind taken up with what Sarah had told her. Surely all wives couldn't think their husbands' kisses were disgusting. Her own mother had left her family and a comfortable way of life to follow her father to a new and unknown land. She would hardly have done that if she found his embraces repulsive. The thought made Eleanor feel slightly better, and the tight band of pain around her forehead eased somewhat.

No matter what his motives for saying it, Connal was right about one thing, Eleanor admitted. It was time she began to come to terms with her grief. And England would be an excellent place to make a start. There was nothing there to constantly remind her of her father, as there was here at home in Boston. There she would meet her uncle Henry's family, and maybe, if the gods smiled upon her, she could find out what had really happened to that necklace all those years ago.

As for the spying Connal wanted her to do... She frowned. She'd have to think about it. Think long and hard, before she agreed to do something that violated every instinct for fair play she possessed. Besides, she thought hopefully, maybe it wouldn't be necessary. Maybe the American army could win a victory on their own.

Yes, going to England was a good idea, she decided. The visit would give her time. Time to heal, mentally and physically. And time to decide what she wanted to do about Connal. Then, when the summer was over, she would come back to Boston, where she belonged, and try to reweave the ruptured threads of her life into something approaching contentment.

Chapter One

London—February 1814

"We have a problem, my friend."

The duke of Ryland ran his long fingers through his closely cropped black hair in frustration. "I'm afraid that you're going to have to be a bit more specific, Devlin. We have many problems, ranging from that egomaniac rampaging on the Continent and calling himself the emperor of France to soaring interest rates causing widespread hunger among the poor."

"Mea culpa," the marquis of Devlin murmured. "The problem concerning me most at the moment is..." He paused as he caught sight of a middle-aged woman wearing an oversize puce turban who was determinedly working her way toward them. "Actually, we have a more immediate problem. Finding a place where we can talk with some degree of privacy. Follow me. I don't want to risk being overheard."

Devlin turned and began weaving his way through the people crowding the edge of the ballroom floor. When he finally reached the French doors leading to the terrace, he pushed one open and motioned Ryland outside.

Ryland shivered as an icy blast of February air slapped him across the face. "I don't know why you couldn't have simply come to my house tomorrow," he grumbled. "Neither of us is going to be much good to England's war effort with an inflammation of the lungs."

"I have to leave London tonight, and it is imperative that I speak to you first."

Ryland's blue eyes narrowed as he studied his old friend's impassive features. "Where are you going?"

"It's best that you don't know. The point is, I don't know when I'll be back."

Or even if you'll be back, Ryland thought uneasily. He didn't have the slightest doubt that Devlin was headed for the Continent. His spying activities were a closely guarded secret that few people knew. A secret that Ryland himself had only discovered last year, when he'd come to London to help formulate battle plans for the army.

"That being the case," Devlin continued, "I need you to handle something for me."

"If I can," Ryland agreed promptly.

"You know Henry Bromley, of course."

"Yes, but not well. We've done some work together on troop movements. Although he's mostly concerned with the war in America, and I've concentrated on the Peninsula."

Devlin chuckled wickedly. "You're far too modest, my friend. I have it on excellent authority that you are about to offer for his daughter."

"Not this side of hell," Ryland said flatly. "And I'll thank you not to repeat that."

Devlin looked pained. "I never spread gossip. I simply listen to it. But in this case, I wasn't indulging in idle curiosity. I had to make sure that your loyalties weren't divided."

Ryland frowned. "What are you talking about?"

"Henry Bromley had a sister named Emily," Devlin replied obliquely.

"And I had a brother named Paul," Ryland shot back as the all-too-familiar sensations of pain and loss slashed through him.

Devlin grimaced. "Forgive me. I'm not usually so maladroit. The problem is that Henry's sister supposedly had a daughter."

"Don't they know?"

"According to Henry, twenty-seven years ago Emily eloped to America with the family's tutor."

Ryland's dark eyebrows lifted in surprise. "Somehow I would never have thought that any child of Esme Bromley would have the pluck to defy her."

"It does seem unlikely, doesn't it?"

"Why is this Emily of importance now?" Ryland asked curiously.

"She isn't. She's been dead for twenty-five years. Unfortunately, it's all happened in the Colonies. There were no witnesses to anything."

Ryland hunched his shoulders against the freezing wind. "Why do you care?" he asked.

"Because the past has a nasty way of catching up with one, Ryland. Your obsession with those ancient Greeks and Romans of yours should have told you that."

"It's a shame you weren't similarly preoccupied. Maybe then you would have learned something about the Greek method of presenting a rational argument. Complete with relevant points."

"All right." Devlin's thin face suddenly set in hard lines. "Point one, a niece no one is sure really exists is suddenly orphaned in America. She writes to Henry claiming she's penniless and in desperate need of a home. Point two, Henry accepts. Point three, some very sensitive government documents pass through Henry's hands."

"And through his home," Ryland murmured thoughtfully. "I begin to see your concern."

"Even if this Eleanor Wallace really is Henry's niece and really is penniless and really does need a home, she could still be a staunch American patriot who would be more than willing to spy on an uncle that she doesn't know."

"True," Ryland agreed. "Have you talked to Henry?"

Devlin gave him a wry look. "And what am I supposed to say to him? Henry, have you considered the possibility that this woman isn't really your niece, but a spy who's playing you for a credulous fool?"

"Yes, I can see where you might have a problem discussing specifics, when you don't seem to have any," Ryland said dryly.

"No, *you* have a problem. I bequeath the whole mess to you."

''Me?'' Ryland repeated with a sudden sense of foreboding.

''You're the logical choice, my friend. Your loyalty to England is without question, you're rich as Croesus, so you can't be bribed, you aren't into the petticoat line, so you aren't susceptible to pressures of that sort, and I trust you implicitly.''

''I see. I'll look into it for you, of course.'' Ryland gave the only response possible, even though he was not at all happy to have drawn this assignment. He had virtually no experience at spying, and even less at turning women up sweet. But as Devlin had pointed out, a lot of very sensitive material did flow through Henry's hands, and if the enemy were able to plant an operative in his house, the results could be disastrous for England.

Ryland grimaced. ''If we're lucky, I'll simply discover that Henry's niece is a hopelessly uneducated provincial with an appalling accent and an eye to the main chance.''

''Ryland, all women have an eye to the main chance. As long as the only rig she's running is to catch some poor unsuspecting male in parson's mousetrap, she has my blessing. Now, according to my operatives, her ship lands at Portsmouth late tomorrow afternoon.''

''Which means she should arrive here in London early the following afternoon.'' Ryland absently tugged on his right ear lobe, which was beginning to go numb with cold. ''It should be easy enough to find an excuse to stop by the house and meet her.''

''I'll leave the matter in your capable hands.'' Devlin headed back into the ballroom.

Ryland followed more slowly, his mind already weighing ways and means of achieving his goal.

''Here we is, miss.'' The middle-aged man brought the hansom cab to a halt. ''Bromley House, Grosvenor Square, just like ya asked fer.''

Eleanor pushed the slightly crushed brim of her black straw bonnet back and peered nervously up at the imposing limestone mansion in front of her. It rose three full stories above the street, and its gray slate roof was punctuated by a series of dormers. Freshly painted black shutters outlined the six eight-foot-high windows on either side of the entrance. A gleaming brass lion-head knocker was attached chest-high in the exact middle of the oversize black door. But despite the house's proportioned elegance, Eleanor felt repelled by it.

She shivered and pulled her warm woolen pelisse more snugly around her thin body. Perhaps it was the formality of the architecture, or the bleakness of the gray February day, or the tightly closed wine-colored drapes, which seemed to shut one out. Or perhaps it was simply that she was worried about finally meeting her mother's family, she admitted.

"This here be the address ya asked fer." The driver's impatient voice prodded her. "Has ya changed yer mind?"

It was far too late for the luxury of second thoughts, Eleanor thought with a sinking feeling in the pit of her stomach. Too late, and much too far from home.

"No." Eleanor took a deep, steadying breath. "I haven't changed my mind." She reached into her reticule and handed the driver several coins before climbing out of the carriage.

"Thankee, miss." The driver gave her a gap-toothed smile when he realized she'd added a bit extra. He pulled her trunk out of the back of the carriage and effortlessly lifted it onto his shoulder. After carrying it up the six limestone steps, he set it down to the left of the door with a thump.

"Ya gonna be the governess, miss?" He eyed curiously the salt-stained black gown that hung on her slight frame.

"No." Eleanor softened the short negative with a smile. "Goodbye, sir, and thank you for your help." She held out her hand.

The man stared at it as if he'd never seen one before. Finally he pulled his battered felt cap off his head, wiped his palm on the back of his spotted nankeen trousers and gingerly shook her hand. Then, with an encouraging nod, he hurried down the steps, vaulted into his cab and urged his bony horse forward.

Eleanor watched until he rounded the corner and disappeared from sight, and then she turned back to the door. She was actually here, she thought, not quite believing it. She had survived the perilous ocean voyage in the rough winter seas, and was about to meet what was left of her mother's family. What was left of her own family.

She clenched the carpetbag that contained the precious letters of introduction to Hoare's, her father's bank, and to his man of business a little more closely to her chest and reached for the knocker, giving it a slight rap. The sound seemed to echo in her ears, adding the final touch of unreality to the situation.

Eleanor was about to thump it again when the door suddenly opened to reveal an elderly man who looked down the length of his beaked nose at her. His eyes dropped to the carpetbag she was clutching like a shield, and, to her surprise, his harsh features relaxed into a warm, welcoming smile as he gestured her inside.

"You must be Miss Emily's daughter," he said.

When Eleanor nodded, he continued, "I'm Walker, the butler, and I wish to extend a welcome from the staff." He took her carpetbag and pelisse and handed them to the gaping footman.

Just as if I were the main exhibit at a raree show, Eleanor thought on a flash of humor.

"You, lad." Walker recalled the young man to his duty. "Take Miss Eleanor's things up to her room."

"Yes, sir." The footman bobbed his head nervously and all but ran up the wide front stairs.

Walker clicked his tongue in annoyance and pulled Eleanor's trunk into the hallway himself before closing the door. "Pray excuse Andrew, Miss Eleanor. The lad's young, and not properly trained yet," Walker said, and Eleanor swallowed a giggle. He made the poor boy sound like a puppy who hadn't been taught his manners yet.

"The family is in the salon at this time of the afternoon, having tea. You'll want to meet them."

Not yet, I wouldn't, Eleanor thought in sudden panic. What she really wanted to do was to take a hot, soothing bath in fresh water, eat food that hadn't been sitting in the musty hold of a ship for months, and then take a nap. A very long nap. But she knew that would have to wait. First, her mother's family had to be faced.

Reluctantly Eleanor followed Walker up the wide staircase, bolstering her sinking spirits by reminding herself that she didn't have to stay if her grandmother turned out to be as bad as her father had always claimed. She could simply turn around and walk out. Or she could stay just long enough to find out what had happened to the missing necklace. She wasn't at her grandmother's mercy. She had options the old woman knew nothing about. She drew strength from that fact.

"Miss Emily's daughter, Eleanor Wallace, come home from the Colonies." Walker threw the announcement into the sudden, deafening silence in the salon.

Eleanor unconsciously braced her narrow shoulders and forced herself to walk toward the two women sitting on the sofa beside the fireplace.

"Hah! Brown as an Injun! Don't look at all like our side of the family!" the older of the two women observed spitefully.

Eleanor, reminding herself of her father's oft-stated dictum that you must never allow an opponent to realize that he's managed to upset you, ignored the comment, if not the speaker.

Eleanor tilted her head to one side and studied the fat elderly woman who'd spoken. She was swaddled in yards of deep purple satin that made her complexion look sallow. Her thinning white hair had been arranged in a youthful cascade of curls—a style that paradoxically seemed to emphasize her age. Diamond earbobs the size of almonds hung from her protruding ears, while an elaborate sapphire-and-diamond necklace partially filled her deep décolletage.

The woman was undoubtedly Esme Bromley, her grandmother, Eleanor concluded.

Was that the necklace her father was supposed to have stolen? Eleanor wondered, suddenly realizing that she had absolutely no idea what it looked like. While her father had frequently dwelled at great length on the injustice of his mother-in-law's accusation, he'd never specifically described the stolen necklace. Not even to mention the type of stones in it.

"Well?" the old woman barked. "Are you dumb, as well?"

"Mother Bromley!" The thin, wispy woman seated beside her confirmed Eleanor's assumption.

Begin as you mean to go on, Eleanor thought, reminding herself of a second one of her father's sayings. Perhaps if her grandmother realized that she had no intention of allowing herself to be browbeaten, Esme would at least be civil.

"Indeed not, madame. I remained silent because the only possible response to such a patent display of bad manners would brand me as ill-bred as..." Eleanor allowed her voice to trail away.

"Why, you—" Esme sputtered. "How dare you?"

"But, madame, you asked me a question, and I wouldn't dream of being so rude as to tell you to mind your own business. Nor would I insult my upbringing by lying."

"I told you!" Esme hurled the accusation at a pudgy middle-aged man who had suddenly appeared in the doorway. "I told you no good would come of your sending her a ticket, Henry."

"Now, Mama..." he began placatingly.

"I told you, but you didn't have the sense to listen to me. Buffleheaded, you are. Always was. Always will be. All my children were fools."

Henry tried again. "But, Mama, Eleanor is Emily's daughter, and—"

"All the more reason to leave her in America with her own kind!"

"People will talk, Mother Bromley," the woman on the couch offered, and Eleanor wondered if the woman hoped they would talk or hoped that the reminder that they might would silence Esme.

"But what must you be thinking of us?" the younger woman gamely continued in the face of Esme's glowering disapproval.

Eleanor, correctly assuming that it was a rhetorical question, merely smiled faintly and waited. The woman looked far more promising than her appalling grandmother. About forty, she had a warm, if slightly nervous, smile and kind eyes. Eleanor didn't know if this woman was destined to be a friend, but she couldn't believe that she would be an enemy.

"I'm your aunt Maria, Eleanor. Your uncle Henry's wife. Please sit down." Maria gestured toward the chair across from her. "I can't tell you how happy I am to welcome you to England, even though such a sad event has precipitated your coming."

"Yes, indeed. Glad to have you." Henry hurriedly seconded his wife's words. "Was very fond of your mother. Always thought it was a shame that—"

"That her husband stole my necklace?" Esme inserted. "Did you bring it back, missy?"

"No," Eleanor said shortly as she considered the question. Apparently the necklace was still missing. Or so her grandmother claimed.

"That necklace is mine!" Esme sounded like a small, petulant child. "It belongs to me, and I want it back."

"Now, Mama..." Henry began, only to be ignored, which Eleanor was beginning to suspect was the story of his whole relationship with his mother.

Esme leaned forward, her long, pudgy fingers wrapped around the arm of the sofa like claws. "You give it back to me, missy, and I'll see about buying you a husband. We ought to be able to find a widower with a passel of brats, or a poor cleric who would welcome a small dowry."

"Cousin Eleanor, you've really come!" A soft, breathless voice spoke from the doorway, and Eleanor turned to discover the most beautiful young woman she had ever seen. She was at least two inches shorter than Eleanor's own five-three, with a slender, almost ethereal, build. Her bright golden curls emphasized the paleness of her creamy complexion, as well as the deep blue of her large eyes. A wash of pink highlighted her delicately molded cheeks and was reflected in her exquisitely formed lips. She was wearing what was obviously a very expensive gown of pale blue mulled French muslin. The color and the modest cut of the neckline labeled the girl as in her first season.

The happy, trembling smile she gave Eleanor was every bit as enchanting as the rest of her. Eleanor found herself smiling back, her anger at her grandmother's rudeness momentarily forgotten.

"This is your cousin, my daughter Drusilla," Maria announced with obvious, if forgivable, pride. "Your only cousin. At least I mean, on your mother's side of the family. I didn't know about your father's family."

"No reason why any of us should know," Esme snapped. "Now what about my offer?"

"Offer?" Eleanor repeated. She was so very tired, and her head was starting to ache. She wanted nothing so much as to hide for a while while she sorted out her impressions of her newfound relatives.

"To buy you a husband in return for my necklace, fool!"

"I'm not such a fool that I don't realize that if I really had the necklace it would make far more sense to sell it myself and buy my own husband," Eleanor couldn't resist pointing out. "I would undoubtedly get much better value for my money."

"Why, you insolent little—" Esme's complexion turned a deep and very unattractive shade of purple.

"Now, Mama, that all happened a long time ago." Henry pulled nervously at his wilted shirt points.

"Long ago?" Esme shrieked. "I'll have you know—"

"The duke of Ryland." Walker's stentorian tones sliced through Esme's diatribe.

Eleanor watched in astonishment as her grandmother's scowl was erased as if by magic, to be replaced by a coquettish smile that Eleanor wasn't sure was an improvement. Curious to see the man who had been responsible for this sudden transformation, Eleanor turned and found her gaze caught and held by a pair of keen blue eyes. For one disoriented moment, they reminded Eleanor of her father. Not the color or the shape, but the shrewdness reflected in them. The memory was unexpectedly painful, and Eleanor hastily looked away.

"Your Grace." Henry hurriedly greeted the man. "What brings you by?"

"Oh, I think we can guess," Esme simpered, and Eleanor followed her grandmother's gaze to Drusilla, who looked as if she would have welcomed instant immolation.

Now that was interesting, Eleanor thought, turning back to study more thoroughly the man Walker had called a duke. He was about five-ten, and his wide shoulders were covered by a bottle-green coat that even Eleanor recognized as having been tailored by an expert. His sparkling white linen neckcloth was immaculately clean and tied in a complicated knot totally foreign to Boston. His double-breasted waistcoat was bottle green, with horizontal cream stripes that added breadth to his already broad chest. Her gaze slipped lower, down over the fawn pantaloons that molded his muscular thighs, to land on the gleaming Hessians that covered his rather large feet.

But despite the undeniable elegance of his clothes, it was his face that she found the most fascinating. His shiny black hair was cut in a style vaguely reminiscent of Donatello's statue of Julius Caesar. The resemblance was intensified by the duke's slightly hooked nose, the tan of his leanly chiseled cheeks and his erect, almost military bearing. She had no trouble at all imagining him addressing the Roman Senate or marching at the head of his troops into battle. The man seemed to exude power. A fact that intrigued her, even as it made her faintly uneasy. She'd never met anyone quite like him before. He was totally outside her limited experience.

With a sangfroid that Eleanor could only envy, Ryland totally ignored both the tirade he'd inadvertently interrupted and Esme's cloying innuendo. Instead, he shook Henry's hand and said, "I've come tracking you. Headquarters received a communication from our North American command about the problems they're having with supply lines. It's urgent that I go over it with you at once."

"So sorry to have put you to the trouble of coming here," Henry apologized. "Your Grace, I'd like to make my niece known to you. Eleanor Wallace is m'sister Emily's only child. Come to make her home with us, now that her father is so sadly dead. Eleanor, this is James Wolfe, the Duke of Ryland."

"Good afternoon, Miss Wallace. Please accept my condolences on your loss." Ryland politely gave her his hand.

Eleanor took it, and his warm, slightly roughened fingers enveloped hers, sending tiny pinpricks of awareness skittering over her skin. She felt her mouth dry at the totally unexpected sensation. She hastily withdrew her hand, telling herself that her reaction was the result of tiredness. Tiredness and disorientation at being in a strange house in a strange country among the strangest group of people she'd ever encountered.

"Drusilla, you must tell Ryland about the new dress you have to wear to the Harringtons' rout this evening, so that he'll be able to find you," Esme ordered. "It's bound to be a sad crush."

Eleanor chuckled. "Unless all English girls are fortunate enough to look like Botticelli angels, I don't think His Grace will have any trouble recognizing Drusilla."

"Thank you, Cousin Eleanor." Drusilla smiled shyly at her. "Are the Botticellis a family you know in America?"

Eleanor glanced sharply at her cousin, but her guileless blue eyes convinced her that Drusilla really didn't know who Botticelli was. Apparently her mind had not been as elegantly tended as her face and figure.

"Botticelli was an Italian painter," she told Drusilla. Eleanor glanced up to find her gaze momentarily snagged by the wicked laughter gleaming deep in Ryland's eyes.

"Italian painters might do as friends in America, but we wouldn't have one in a polite house here," Esme stated emphatically. "We have standards in England."

"Oh, yes. Even in America we've read about your prince," Eleanor said in retaliation and then felt guilty when she saw her aunt glance nervously at Henry, who was apprehensively watching Ryland.

The insult, however, sailed right over Esme's head. She merely nodded regally. "I don't doubt that you've never met anyone like our prince," she said, with what appeared to be real pride.

"Absolutely not," Eleanor assured her.

"Um, Your Grace, you said that you wanted to talk to me?" Henry asked with another nervous glance, this one divided equally between his mother and Eleanor. "Why don't you come into my study?"

"Certainly." Ryland nodded politely to Eleanor. "It was a pleasure to meet you, Miss Wallace. Ladies." He followed Henry from the room.

The salon doors had barely closed behind them when Esme turned on Eleanor. "There'll be none of your rag manners in this house, missy!"

"I'm sorry, Grandmama. I don't know what came over me. Do you think bad manners could be contagious?" Eleanor suggested.

"So condescending of Ryland to come here to see Henry," Maria said, rushing to change the subject. "He could have easily sent a messenger requesting Henry return to Whitehall."

"Fools, that's what I'm surrounded with!" Esme said in exasperation. "Fools, the lot of you. He didn't come to see Henry. He came in the hopes that he might see Drusilla."

Curious, Eleanor glanced at her cousin. Drusilla did not look at all gratified at the idea that she'd attracted the attention of a duke. In fact, she looked petrified.

"Not that he had much chance to talk to her," Esme complained. "What with Eleanor putting herself forward in such a pert way. I tell you, Maria, bringing *that man's* daughter into the house was a grave mistake. She'll ruin her cousin's chances, you just see if she doesn't."

"I've no doubt that the duke is fully aware that Eleanor is new to England and its ways," Maria said soothingly. "She'll learn."

"Bah! What have I ever done to deserve to have my old age ruined by such a pack of gabies as my family?" Esme heaved her considerable bulk to her feet and lumbered out of the room, giving vent to her ill feelings by slamming the door behind her.

Eleanor turned to her aunt as soon as Esme was gone. "She's right about one thing," Eleanor said. "I did display shocking bad manners, and for that I apologize. I didn't mean to embarrass you in front of your intended, cousin."

Drusilla gave her a piteous look, her soft pink lips trembling pathetically. "You didn't embarrass me. I only wish...I wish..." Her voice rose to a wail, and she dashed from the room.

"Dear me." Maria's unhappy murmur did nothing to enlighten Eleanor's ignorance. "So unfortunate," Maria continued. "I don't know what you must think of us, my dear. We aren't usually quite so...volatile. But despite the paucity of my mother-in-law's welcome, my husband and I are very happy to have you here. Henry really was very fond of your mother, you know. From what he's said, she was the image of our Drusilla.

"Now then—" Maria pushed her knitting out of her lap and got to her feet "—allow me to show you to your room. I imagine that you're quite tired after that frightful voyage. And in winter, too. And it was so brave of you to travel up from Portsmouth all by yourself on the mail coach."

"I would like to rest." Eleanor eagerly grasped at the opportunity to escape for a few minutes and recoup her strength.

"Dinner isn't until eight. I'll send a maid up at 7:45 to bring you down to the dining room." Maria glanced at Eleanor's rusty black dress, which showed the effects of repeated washings in salt water. "Um, have your trunks arrived, dear?"

"One trunk." Eleanor followed her aunt's gaze, rather surprised to realize just how badly her gown did look. Ah, well, she thought. She was supposed to be playing the role of the penniless relation, and in this gown no one would question that.

"We'll have to replenish your wardrobe as quickly as possible. I think, perhaps, you should adopt half mourning. It's been long enough since...since your loss, and black is not a color which brings out your best features," Maria said diplomatically.

Eleanor chuckled. "With Drusilla in the general vicinity, I don't think anyone is going to notice me, Aunt Maria."

Maria motioned Eleanor up the stairs before she answered. "It's true that Drusilla is very beautiful." She couldn't quite hide the pride in her voice. "But she is also very young. Just barely eighteen. And I've found that there are many men who prefer a more mature woman with countenance to youthful beauty. Don't despair. I'll find you a suitable connection.

"Now then, your room is at the end of the hall." Maria briskly changed the subject before Eleanor could assure her that she didn't want a suitable connection found for her. In fact, one of her most pressing worries at the moment was what to do about the suitable connection her father had already found for her.

Maria opened the last door on the right to reveal a small, nondescript chamber that looked as if it might have been intended for use by an upper servant.

"It's a little small and . . ." Maria began uncertainly.

"It's very cozy, Aunt Maria," Eleanor assured her, detecting her grandmother's heavy hand in this. "I appreciate your putting me in the back of the house, where it'll be quieter."

To Eleanor's surprise, Maria gave her a warm hug. "Bless you, my dear. I'm so glad you've come. I hope you'll be happy with us. Not, of course, like you were with your father . . . I mean, I want you to be happy again, but . . ."

"I know," Eleanor said, rescuing her aunt from the morass of words she was floundering in.

"You rest, my dear." With one last, fluttering smile, Maria left.

Eleanor waited until she heard the sound of her aunt's footsteps receding down the uncarpeted hallway and then gently closed the door, leaning against it. She let her breath out on a long sigh. She'd actually done it. She was here in England, in her grandmother's house. In the very same house that her mother had grown up in. And not very happily, unless her grandmother had changed considerably, Eleanor thought grimly. No wonder her mother had been willing to elope. Social ostracism seemed a small price to pay to escape Esme Bromley.

Eleanor slowly walked across the room's threadbare rug and sank down on the narrow bed. She stretched out, trying to fit her tired limbs into a more comfortable position on the hard mattress.

They were certainly a strange lot, these new relatives of hers. Eleanor stared blankly at the water patch on the dingy ceiling as she tried to sort out her impressions.

One thing was certain—her father had not exaggerated in the slightest when he'd told her about her grandmother. If anything, he'd understated the case. Esme Bromley was a petty tyrant. But then, Americans had a history of defeating petty tyrants, she told herself encouragingly. And, as infuriating as Esme was, she didn't have any real power over her. She didn't need her grandmother's money or her protection. Anytime she chose, she could simply tell Esme Bromley precisely what she thought of her manners, her morals and her warped viewpoint and walk out.

But Eleanor knew that while telling the appalling old harridan exactly what she thought of her would give her a great deal of satisfaction, being able to clear her father's name of the charge of theft would give her far more. That satisfaction would be worth the temporary annoyance of having to bear Esme's rudeness.

An image of Ryland's lean, dark features popped into her head, and she frowned slightly, trying to analyze her unexpected reaction to him. She wasn't some shy young girl to be thrown into a pelter by a personable male. And as a staunch republican, she wasn't impressed by his title. But his manner . . .

Eleanor tried to pinpoint exactly why he exuded such an impression of power. Of authority. It was his eyes, she finally decided. There had been intelligence reflected in them, as well as humor. The duke of Ryland was a very unusual man. At least he would be in Boston, she thought. Here in London, she wasn't so sure. For all she knew, men like him could be common fare.

She felt a flicker of excitement at the idea of finding out, and then immediately felt guilty when she remembered Connal. If her father had lived, she might well be married to Connal by now.

But her father hadn't lived, and she wasn't certain what she wanted to do. Or with whom she wanted to do it. She needed time. Time free of Connal's constant chivying. And here in London, she'd have all the time she needed, she thought in satisfaction.

And then there was her uncle Henry and his family. It was strange that her father had never mentioned him. Especially considering the fact that he'd kept track of his career over the years. But whatever the reason for her father's silence, he hadn't seemed to bear Henry any enmity. Nor, apparently, had Henry borne any toward her father. In fact, it would seem that she had Henry to thank for her ticket, and not her grandmother. That Esme hadn't wanted her here, Eleanor could well believe. What she found harder to believe was that Henry had been willing to defy his mother to aid a niece that he didn't know. Could he be stronger than he seemed at first glance? Or had sending her passage been an impulsive kindness, regretted as soon as it was done?

There was no doubt that Maria welcomed her. Eleanor felt the tightness around her heart ease fractionally. For the first time since her father had died, she felt welcomed for what she was, not for what she possessed. As far as her aunt knew, she was a penniless orphan, and Maria had still wanted her. How could she repay that welcome by spying on them?

Eleanor closed her eyes and rubbed her forehead, which was now throbbing. But, according to Connal, if she didn't spy, America might have to accept a disastrous peace.

Eleanor sighed. Recently her life seemed to be a series of hard choices, none of them clear-cut. They were all overlaid with buts, what-ifs, maybes and perhaps.

Fortunately, she didn't have to worry about the ethics of spying at the moment. Not with Connal an ocean away. Her tension eased somewhat as she remembered this comforting fact. She'd write to him tomorrow and tell him she'd arrived safely and put him off with some platitude or other, she planned.

For the moment, she intended to concentrate on clearing her father's name by finding out what had happened to her grandmother's necklace. That and getting to know her mother's family. At least the part of it that didn't include her grandmother.

Yes, she thought with a sigh of satisfaction. There was a great deal in London to occupy her. A great deal indeed. Her eyes slowly slipped closed, and she drifted into a troubled sleep, while downstairs in her uncle's study the object of a great deal of her speculation was going over the notes he'd used as his excuse to call on Henry.

"I think your suggestion is excellent, Your Grace." Henry nodded decisively as he handed the communication back to Ryland. "As you say, we must act at once, or the results could be catastrophic to the soldier in the field."

"Yet more death." Ryland's lips momentarily tightened, his bleak expression darkening his eyes to navy. "More families to mourn."

Henry sighed. "Yes, but it doesn't take a war to cause grief."

"Your niece?" Ryland asked, quick to take advantage of the opening Henry had given him to try to find out more about her. "I believe you said that her father had died?"

"Yes, sad business, that. A seizure. His minister wrote to tell us that Eleanor had been left destitute, you know."

Ryland cautiously probed. "She didn't write to you herself?"

Henry shook his head. "No. Poor child. Her father probably told her about—" He broke off, looking flustered. "I sent her passage, and now here she is, where she belongs," he hurriedly added.

"From the looks of it, her minister wasn't exaggerating," Ryland said. "She looks half starved."

"Foreign parts, you know," Henry muttered inexplicably. "But for all that, she's a taking little thing. Pluck to the backbone, the way she stood up to m'mother."

Yes, she was an attractive woman. Ryland remembered the laughter that had momentarily lightened her brown eyes to a warm golden sherry, and the air of remote dignity that she seemed to wear like a cloak. But looks could be deceptive, and if Devlin's suspicions were right and this Eleanor Wallace really was an impostor...

Henry might have accepted her as his niece, but there was far too much at stake for him to be equally trusting. He'd be shockingly derelict in his duty if he didn't investigate further, Ryland told himself to justify his inexplicable compulsion to see her again. He'd call later in the week and take her for a drive in the park, he decided. He could dispense with his groom with perfect propriety, and once he got Miss Wallace alone he would be in a much better position to judge if she really was a penniless orphan in need of her family's protection or if she was an adventuress and her family were the ones in need of protection.

Yes, Ryland thought with an escalating sense of anticipation. He would definitely investigate this Eleanor Wallace more thoroughly.

Chapter Two

Eleanor looked up from where she was knitting in the alcove and watched sympathetically as Drusilla cautiously peeked into the salon.

"She isn't here," Eleanor said.

Drusilla jumped at the sound of her voice. "Oh, good afternoon, Cousin Eleanor. I didn't see you over there by the window. What do you mean?"

"I assumed from your furtive manner that you were reluctant to be discovered by our mutual grandmother."

"I'm sure I don't know what you mean," Drusilla said with a nervous glance over her shoulder. "One must always be glad to see her."

Eleanor lifted her russet eyebrows in patent disbelief. "One must? Why?"

"Why?" Drusilla repeated blankly.

"Yes, why?" Eleanor persisted, curious about the way Drusilla thought. If, indeed, she did think. In the four days that Eleanor had been a guest in her grandmother's house, she had never heard her cousin express a definitive opinion on anything.

Drusilla opened her mouth, closed it again and finally said, "Well, she's our grandmother."

"Undeniably. But you still haven't answered my question. Why would anyone be glad to see a domestic tyrant who seems to have no other purpose in life than to make the people around her miserable?"

Drusilla glanced frightenedly behind her into the hall. "Oh, hush, do, Cousin Eleanor. She might hear you."

"Not likely. She went out with your mother to visit someone who apparently is recuperating from a severe case of the grippe. Grandmother seemed to feel she was performing an act of charity. Personally, I think the act of charity would be if she were to leave the poor soul alone," Eleanor said reflectively.

Drusilla gave an enchanting gurgle of laughter, the first sign of humor that Eleanor had seen her cousin display.

"But the visit is an act of charity, Cousin Eleanor. To you and me, who are left in peace for a few hours."

Eleanor watched as her cousin seemed to float across the thick Aubusson carpet and gracefully sank down onto the rose damask chair across from her. Drusilla's every movement was a symphony of grace. Eleanor sighed enviously. It hardly seemed fair that the Fates had been so generous in their gifts to her cousin and so skimpy in what they had bestowed on her.

Drusilla looked up at the sound. "What's wrong?"

"I was thinking of the fickleness of the Moirai."

Drusilla looked blank. "The what?"

"Not what, who. The Fates. The daughters of Night."

Drusilla's look of confusion deepened. "The who?"

"You remember, from Greek mythology. Clotho, who spun the thread of life, Lachesis, who fixed its length, and Atropos, who used her shears to cut it at the appointed time of death. Homer wrote about them."

"Oh, that would explain why I never heard of them." Drusilla looked relieved. "I don't read. Grandmama says that learning is dangerous for the female mind."

"No wonder she and my father came to cuffs," Eleanor said dryly. "He believed that all minds should be stuffed with as much knowledge as they could hold."

"Poor Eleanor." Drusilla eyed her in real sympathy.

"Never fear," Eleanor said cheerfully. "I survived the experience unscathed."

"You won't be unscathed if Grandmama should hear you talking about the daughters of the..."

"Night," Eleanor supplied helpfully. "And I thank you for the hint, cousin. I shall take great pains to appear ignorant."

"Men don't care for women who are bluestockings," Drusilla assured her.

"How fortunate it is that I am totally ineligible for marriage. I don't have to worry about what men like."

"Don't you want to be married?" Drusilla eyed her as if she were a hitherto-unknown species.

"Not if the price is spending my life pretending to be something that I'm not. I can't think of anything more wearing. And, what's more, I don't have the slightest doubt that I'd quickly come to hate the husband who forced me into the position," she said with sudden insight.

"But, Eleanor, if you don't marry you'll be stuck here with Grandmama for the rest of your life!"

"No. For the rest of her life. The wonder is that someone hasn't murdered her yet."

"Murder?" Drusilla's eyes widened, but whether in horror or interest, Eleanor didn't know. She could hardly blame Drusilla if it were the latter. From what Eleanor had seen so far, living with Esme Bromley had all the attraction of purgatory, with no accompanying hope of eventual salvation.

Eleanor hadn't been in the house twenty-four hours before she discovered that it wasn't her grandmother who lived with Henry, but Henry who lived with his mother. What was worse, he appeared to be financially dependent on her. What Eleanor didn't know was why. From the style in which Esme lived, her husband had to have left her amply provided for, so why hadn't he done the same for his only surviving son?

"Grandmama does approve of needlework," Drusilla offered. "What is that you're knitting?"

"An infant sock." Eleanor held up the half finished piece.

"A sock? I don't think you're supposed to knit socks," Drusilla said dubiously. "When Grandmama says needlework, she means the fancy kind."

"It's for the foundling home." Eleanor bit back her opinion of what Grandmama thought. She'd already shocked her cousin enough for one day. "Charity is always proper."

"I guess so." Drusilla didn't sound any too certain. "But Grandmama always says that charity begins at home."

"Quite true—however, the rest of the quotation is that it doesn't end there."

"Really? I don't think that Grandmama knows about that part."

"Now why doesn't that surprise me?" Eleanor asked dryly.

"She—" Drusilla broke off at the sound of the door knocker. The color in her face faded, leaving it chalk white before a painful flush sent a hectic red up her cheeks.

Eleanor frowned, wondering what had produced the reaction. Surely not the fact that someone was coming to call. For the past four afternoons, she'd sat inconspicuously in a corner of the salon and watched as a steady stream of visitors had come, spent twenty minutes drinking tepid tea and either exchanging gossip with her grandmother or trying to flirt with her cousin, depending on their age, sex and inclination. Drusilla had sat unmoved through it all. So why did she look so flustered now?

"His Grace, the duke of Ryland," the butler announced.

Eleanor's sense of curiosity increased as Drusilla seemed to shrink into her chair. In disappointment?

Eleanor turned to look at the duke, but could find no cause for disappointment. From the careless elegance of his perfectly barbered hair to the tips of his shiny black Hessians, Ryland looked the picture of sartorial perfection. In fact, he looked like the answer to every young girl's prayers—wealthy, titled, and immaculately groomed.

Granted, he wasn't precisely handsome, Eleanor conceded. His chin was a little too square, his jaw a shade too determined and his nose just the slightest bit too large. But Eleanor felt that the humor and intelligence that sparkled in his eyes were far more appealing than mere physical appearance.

But then, she wasn't the one promised to him, she thought. Drusilla was. But that being the case, why didn't her cousin at least make a polite show of being glad to see him? Or was it possible that she had misunderstood her grandmother's broad hint the afternoon she arrived?

Eleanor felt a surge of exasperation. There was so much that she didn't know. But one thing she did understand was the basic good manners due a guest. They dictated that someone welcome Ryland, and since Drusilla had lapsed into tongue-tied silence, it was clearly up to her to do so.

"Good afternoon, Your Grace. Won't you join us for a cup of tea?" Eleanor said, deciding that there could be no impropriety in his staying, since she was old enough to chaperone her cousin. She found the thought vaguely depressing.

"Thank you, Miss Wallace, but there's a brisk wind blowing, and I don't want to leave my horses standing in it. I actually came to ask you to come for a ride."

"A ride?" Eleanor repeated blankly. If Ryland was courting her cousin, why was he including her in the invitation? Unless he felt that he had to ask her, since she was present?

"You do indulge in carriage rides in America, don't you?" he asked, faintly piqued at her reaction. He was used to women falling all over themselves in their eagerness to accept the few invitations he extended. And yet here was this spinster from the Colonies studying him as if he weren't quite the thing. Unless Devlin's suspicions were correct, and she really was a spy and not Henry's niece at all. Her lack of enthusiasm for his company could be caused by fear that he might discover her secret.

"Why, yes. We have both carriages and horses in Boston," Eleanor replied. "And, not only that, but we've even adopted the custom of living in houses, instead of Indian lodges."

"Um, Cousin Eleanor, this is the duke of Ryland," Drusilla mumbled.

"Yes, I know." Eleanor gave her frightened-looking cousin an encouraging smile. Really, Drusilla was going to have a miserable life if she never learned how to stand up to Ryland. "I heard him announced. We also speak tolerable English in the Colonies."

"With almost no accent at all," Ryland observed. Her perfect diction had been one of the first things about her that had bothered him. The Colonials he'd met previously had all had accents. Sometimes faint, but they never quite sounded like a true upper-class Briton, as this woman did.

"Everyone speaks with an accent," Eleanor said. "What you mean is that I speak with the same accent that you do."

Ryland ignored the strangled groan from Drusilla and concentrated on Eleanor, his interest well and truly caught. She was proving to be a far worthier opponent than her hen-witted cousin. "I stand corrected. You are right."

"I usually am," Eleanor said complacently.

"May we continue this discussion on our ride? The poor horses, you know."

Eleanor chuckled. "From what I've seen of men and their horses, I doubt that there's anything the least bit poor about the beasts. Unless, of course, it's their intelligence," she added reflectively.

"You aren't fond of horses, Miss Wallace?"

"What is there to be fond of? Horses are smelly, over-grown brutes with voracious appetites and uncertain dispositions."

"And they bite!" Drusilla blurted out, and then immediately lapsed into silence, as if amazed by her own temerity.

Eleanor laughed. "You're far braver than I, cousin. I've never gotten close enough to one to be bitten."

"You don't ride, Miss Wallace?" Ryland slipped the question in.

"No, however, we do appreciate your offer of a drive, don't we, Drusilla?" Eleanor accepted his invitation. It would be nice to escape the confines of the house for a while.

If the appalled-looking expression on Drusilla's face was any inclination, at least one of them didn't. Eleanor frowned, having the uncomfortable feeling that she'd just committed an act of cruelty, but for the life of her she didn't know what it was. Granted, Drusilla did not seem all that eager to encourage Ryland's attentions, but what could he possibly do to her in an open carriage in full view of London? He couldn't even say anything to put Drusilla to the blush with her there to chaperone.

Having already foreseen the possibility that Esme might try to make Drusilla accompany them and thus drastically limit his ability to discover anything about Miss Wallace's background, Ryland had his excuse ready. "I'm so sorry, but I'm driving my high-perch phaeton. It only seats two."

"I really don't want to go," Drusilla assured him. "I mean, I would, but... It's windy, and I felt a distinct tickle in my throat this morning, and..."

"I wouldn't dream of risking your health," Ryland said smoothly.

Eleanor eyed her cousin uncertainly. She didn't for one moment believe that nonsense about a putrid throat. What she did believe was that for reasons of her own Drusilla preferred to remain in this stuffy room to going driving in the gorgeous early-spring sunshine. Eleanor stifled a sigh and prepared to forgo the unexpected treat.

"But you must go, Cousin Eleanor," Drusilla urged.

"Thank you, but I couldn't leave you alone."

"No." Drusilla sounded unexpectedly firm. "I want you to go.

"I mean," she rushed on at Eleanor's surprised look, "I mean, I want you to have a chance to take the air. You haven't been out of the house since you arrived. Not even when we went shopping yesterday..." Drusilla's voice trailed away as she suddenly remembered that the reason Eleanor hadn't gone was that her grandmother flatly refused to allow her to accompany them, stating that she would not spend one penny on the daughter of the man who'd stolen her necklace.

"Please go, Eleanor," Drusilla hurried on. "Mama should be back shortly."

"Yes, please do go, Miss Wallace." Ryland smiled at her, and Eleanor felt her breath catch at the dimple in his left cheek.

What would be the harm? she asked herself. Drusilla would hardly urge her to go, nor would the duke have invited her if the activity was not unexceptional. And her aunt would be back soon, Eleanor thought, soothing her conscience at leaving her cousin alone.

"Thank you. I very much like to take the air." Eleanor made her decision. "I'll just be a moment."

She left the room and, once out of sight, sprinted up the stairs, intent on getting her bonnet and pelisse before something happened to prevent her from escaping. Such as her grandmother returning early.

Eleanor yanked her black pelisse out of her wardrobe and hastily buttoned it over her dress. While the pelisse was far too big for her slender frame, its material was in much better condition than the almost shapeless dress it covered.

When her father died, the dressmaker had offered her several mourning dresses that had been ordered by an elderly woman who had lost her husband and then died herself before she could take delivery of the gowns. At the time, Eleanor hadn't cared that the old woman had been five stone heavier, with no interest in fashion. She'd been so grief-stricken that she never even thought about it. And Connal had been so very insistent that she take advantage of the bargain the dressmaker was offering, pointing out that in six months she would be discarding the gowns anyway for half mourning.

Sometimes Connal showed a distinct tendency to be clutch-fisted. Eleanor frowned and then determinedly banished the disquieting thought. It was far too nice a day to be worrying about Connal, who, thankfully, was on the other side of a very large ocean.

She pushed back a few stray tendrils of hair that had come loose from the knot at the nape of her neck and then glanced quickly at her reflection in the small looking glass above the bureau. She grimaced. Since her father's death, she had fallen into the habit of pulling her hair back into a knot because it was quick, but it was not a style that became her. It made her thin face seem even thinner, and added years to her age. What she needed was a different style. Something a little more modern. She'd ask Drusilla for advice, she decided. Drusilla had impeccable fashion sense.

Retrieving her slightly battered straw bonnet from the wardrobe, Eleanor jammed it on her head and quickly tied the bedraggled ribands beneath her chin. She frowned at the way the dull black color leached out what little color there was in her cheeks, leaving them positively sallow. Ah, well, Eleanor thought as she hurried back downstairs, there was always the rouge pot.

She found Ryland waiting for her at the foot of the stairs, in uneasy conversation with Drusilla. Taking the arm he offered, she happily followed him through the door Walker held open for them.

Eleanor blinked in the bright sunlight and blinked again when she saw the two massive bay horses hitched to the strange-looking carriage sitting in front of the house. As she cautiously approached, the horse nearest her stamped his foot impatiently, and she instinctively stepped back. Straight into Ryland. It was like hitting a wall. His body was hard, with no yield to it whatsoever. And warm. The heat from his body suddenly registered in her confused senses. Warm, and vaguely scented with what she thought was sandalwood. The clean, fresh aroma flooded her mind, momentarily disrupting her thoughts.

"Zeus really won't harm you, Miss Wallace." Ryland's amused voice recalled her.

Hastily she stepped away from him. "If he's anything like his namesake, then I'm in a lot more trouble than I originally thought!" she said as she scrambled up onto the seat with more speed than finesse.

Ryland rounded the front of the carriage and effortlessly vaulted into the seat with a lithe grace that bespoke a well-conditioned body. Apparently he was more than just one of the idle aristocrats that her father had so vocally despised, Eleanor thought.

Pulling a coin out of his pocket, Ryland tossed it to his groom, who was holding the horses' heads. It glittered brightly in the sunlight for a moment before the man neatly caught it in his tanned fingers.

"I won't be needing you any more this afternoon, Wells," he told him. "Take a hansom home."

"Yes, sir." Wells grinned at the duke, obviously relishing the thought of a free afternoon and money to brighten it. He released the horses' reins, tipped his hat to Eleanor and stepped out of the way.

Ryland tightened the reins, and the fidgety horses moved out into the street's light traffic. He glanced curiously at Eleanor and asked, "What do you know about Zeus?"

Eleanor looked up from her nervous contemplation of just how far she would have to fall before she hit the road if she were to tumble out of the seat and muttered, "Just that you said he was safe."

"Not the horse, the other one."

"The other one?" Eleanor stared blankly at the other animal. He didn't appear to be doing anything unusual. "What's his name, Jupiter?"

"How did you know that?"

"I don't, but it's certainly a reasonable guess."

"What do you know about Latin and Greek mythology?" Ryland persisted.

Eleanor sighed. "Far more than I ever wanted to. My father believed in education. Lots of education."

"For females?" Ryland asked sceptically, finding it hard to believe that anyone related in any manner to Esme Bromley could value the classics. Or any other type of learning, for that matter.

"For young minds. He didn't believe in differentiating..." Her voice trailed away unhappily as a wave of longing for her father unexpectedly washed over her.

"I'm sorry," Ryland said. He wondered if her sad expression was real or assumed for his benefit. "I didn't mean to remind you of your loss."

Eleanor gave him a wan smile. "Sometimes it seems as if everything reminds me of him."

"I know," he said, deciding that her grief was real. She couldn't be that good an actress. "My only brother, Paul, was killed over a year ago on the Peninsula, and I still miss him. Sometimes I forget he's dead, and I make a mental note to tell him something, and then when I remember that I can't ever share anything with him again..."

Eleanor nodded sympathetically, understanding perfectly how he felt. But even knowing that he empathized with her, she still didn't want to talk about her loss. She wanted to enjoy the present for a brief moment without dwelling on the past.

"The day is thoroughly delightful," she said, redirecting the conversation along less emotionally fraught lines.

"And the air is unexceptional," he countered. "But to return to the point, exactly how much have you studied the classics?"

"Enough to know that the Greeks were a pack of xenophobic egotists, and the Romans were a bloodthirsty flock of vultures who were a plague on their poor neighbors."

"What?" Ryland gasped. "You can't have much knowledge of the ancients, if that's what you think."

"On the contrary. I am fluent in both Latin and Greek, and I suffered through every major writer in both languages, as well as most of the minor ones. I told you. My father believed in education, and to him education consisted of the classics and mathematics."

"But... but that was the golden age of man," Ryland protested. "The flowering of reason. The zenith of civilization."

"Nonsense!" she said briskly. "The present is far more interesting than a horde of long-dead barbarians."

"Barbarians!" Ryland howled, and then hastily lowered his voice when a passing dowager in an ancient laudet frowned at him. "The Greeks were the epitome of reason."

"You mean like the Athenian Council that convicted Socrates on some trumped-up charges and sentenced the poor man to death?" she asked innocently.

"So you do approve of Socrates, then?"

"Certainly. He didn't write books. Would that Plato and Xenophon had shown the same restraint," she added tartly.

Ryland closed his eyes in disbelief at such comprehensive heresy. How could she have had the honor of studying the classics and reached such heretical ideas? Perhaps the problem was that she had never really understood the significance of what the Greeks and Romans had given to the world?

"The Romans brought civilization to the world," he began.

"If by that you mean they united the known world by killing off everyone who resisted their rule, then I suppose I'd have to agree."

"But the Roman civilization was superior," Ryland argued.

"Their form of government was certainly more efficient," Eleanor conceded, "but efficiency and superiority are not the same thing."

"But they had literature and ethics—"

"Ethics! They had very convenient ethics, if you ask me. What about Caesar deciding to bring his troops back across the Rubicon and conquering Rome? He certainly didn't do it for any ethical reasons. He did it for his own personal glory. Not only that, but the early Romans were so frightful that no woman in her right mind would have anything to do with them. Why, they even had to steal brides from the Sabines."

Ryland took a deep breath and said, "All right, forget the Romans for a minute . . ."

"Personally, I'm willing to consign them to permanent oblivion."

He ignored the interruption. "And let's consider the Greeks."

"Let's not. I found them an immoral lot."

"Immoral?" Ryland eyed her in frustration.

"Certainly. What about Paris? If he hadn't coveted his neighbor's wife, then a lot of people wouldn't have died. And then there's—"

"You simply don't understand," Ryland said.

"On the contrary, I understand the ancients all too well. What I don't understand is why it should bother you. After all, they're all thankfully dead.

"What's that?" Eleanor, having disposed of a subject that had never held much appeal to her, pointed to the large grassy area to their right.

"Green Park," Ryland answered absently, his mind taken up with the best way to convince her that she was mistaken. He wasn't any too clear even in his own mind why he wanted to, but he did. For some reason, it was important to him that she realize the error of her ways.

Ryland glanced sideways at Eleanor as he drove around a slow-moving laudet. Her thin face was alight with interest as she drank in the sights and sounds of the teeming city, and he felt a strange twist in his chest. She was such an incongruous mixture of knowledge and enthusiasm and naïveté. She either didn't know or didn't care that no English lady would ever admit to being a classics scholar. Nor that any woman of marriageable age ever disagreed with him. But what he found even more intriguing was that she had put out absolutely no lures to capture his interest. He had the lowering feeling that she'd come driving with him to escape the tedium of her sitting room, and that she'd have been as happy to go if he were an octogenarian.

Unless she really was a spy and her behavior was all part of an elaborate ruse to present herself as... As what? he wondered. One of the first rules of spying was to be inconspicuous. To blend in with one's surroundings. There was nothing inconspicuous about Eleanor Wallace. From her bright mind to her unconventional views, she was unique. But did that mean that she wasn't a spy, or that the person who'd recruited her wasn't very clever?

Ryland didn't know, but he did know that he intended to explore the matter in much greater detail. Starting with her totally erroneous view of the classics. But how—

A book! The idea suddenly struck him. He'd give her one of Millsaps' books to read. The one in which he explained how much Western civilization had benefited from the Greek and Roman cultures. Millsaps' conclusions were brilliantly drawn and totally inescapable. More than likely her dislike of the classics was nothing more than a childish reaction to being forced to study them when she would no doubt rather have been doing something else.

Doing what? he suddenly wondered. What did she do in her free time? He tried to imagine her sketching or dabbling in watercolors and failed miserably. She seemed too vital and alive for such passive activities.

Yes, he decided. He'd get a copy of Millsaps' book at Hatchards, since his own well-worn copy was at his principal estate in Cumberland, and give it to Miss Wallace to read. The sooner the better.

He turned the horses sharply to the right, onto Piccadilly Street.

"Where are we going?" Eleanor eyed the shops with interest. Since the start of the war, manufactured goods had been in very short supply in Boston. London obviously had suffered no such lack.

"Hatchards."

"Hatchards?" She tried to place the name, and failed.

"It's a bookstore where one may borrow books. I should be able to get a copy of Millsaps' *History of the Ancients* for you there."

Eleanor studied him for a moment and finally asked, "Why would I want a copy of his book?"

"It will give you a proper appreciation for the Greek and Roman cultures." He pulled the carriage up in front of a store with a large bowfront window and tossed a coin to an urchin standing near the curb. "Hold their reins, lad, and there'll be another one for you when we come out."

"Right, gov'nor." The boy wiped his runny nose on his ragged shirt sleeve and reverently took the horses' reins.

Eleanor gave the boy a warm smile as she cautiously stood up on the dangerously high seat. The warm strength of Ryland's fingers closing around her forearm as he helped her down disconcerted her, and she stumbled. Ryland steadied her, momentarily bracing her against his side, which only added to her sense of confusion. Telling herself not to be a fool, she hastily stepped away.

To her relief, Ryland didn't seem to notice her reaction. He merely offered her his arm.

Eleanor placed her hand on the smooth material of his blue coat, trying to appear totally self-possessed. Her pride demanded that she not allow him to realize how his touch had disconcerted her. It was too humiliating.

There was a faint jingle of a bell above the door as they entered, and Eleanor looked around the crowded shop with interest. There were quite a few fashionably dressed people browsing among the bookshelves. Apparently Drusilla was wrong. Some of the ton did read.

"I think the book we want is in the history section," Ryland said.

"No, the book *you* want," Eleanor corrected him. "I have read all the history books I ever wish to."

"You just haven't read the right history book yet," Ryland insisted.

Eleanor eyed him wryly, knowing the absolute futility of trying to argue with fanatics. They simply weren't open to reason. Experience with her father had long since taught her that her best course of action would be to accept Ryland's book and then hide it behind her wardrobe.

"Perhaps," she murmured soothingly. "Why don't you go find the book you have in mind, while I see what else they have."

Ryland nodded and headed toward the back of the store.

Eleanor looked around a moment to get her bearings and then decided to investigate the shelves that seemed to have the most people in front of them. She squeezed past an overweight dowager and positioned herself between a young matron dressed in what Eleanor recognized as the first stare of fashion and a girl of about sixteen who kept glancing warily over her shoulder at a plainly dressed, hatchet-faced woman who appeared to be her governess.

Eleanor peered down at the titles, assuming that the poetry was located here. Lord Byron's fame had penetrated even to Boston, although her father had flatly refused to have his works in the house, claiming that they were an affront to all decent-minded people. But, since he'd similarly condemned the Psalms, Eleanor had not given much weight to his opinion.

The Wicked Uncle, The Duke's Revenge, Virtue's Reward. Eleanor read the titles curiously. They certainly didn't sound like any poetry she'd ever heard.

"This is her best one," the girl murmured, pointing to a black marbled book titled *The Guillotine.* "It was absolutely horrifying." The girl shivered in remembered delight.

Eleanor grinned at her. "Now that's a recommendation not to be taken lightly."

"My particular friend, Miss Warburton, liked it excessively, too," the girl continued.

"Then it is a treat not to be missed," Eleanor assured her, taking the book off the shelf.

"And this one, too." The girl handed one to Eleanor. "It was—"

"Are you talking to a stranger, Miss Julia?" her governess demanded, glaring at Eleanor.

"Certainly not." Eleanor looked down her nose at the pugnacious woman, wondering what the woman thought she was going to do to her charge in the middle of the bookstore. "I know exactly who I am. What I don't know is who you are."

The woman blinked uncertainly at Eleanor, obviously taken aback by her manner. She had evidently judged Eleanor to be a not-too-prosperous member of the merchant class by her ill-fitting clothes, but Eleanor's manner clearly belonged to the aristocracy.

The woman decided to retreat. "Come along, Miss Julia." She grabbed Julia by the arm and dragged her away.

Eleanor watched them leave as a wave of homesickness washed over her. England seemed to have such rigid, restrictive rules of proper behavior. She wrinkled her nose in disgust. Probably too much Roman influence.

She looked around for Ryland and finally saw him at the end of a row of books, deep in conversation with an elderly man. Not wanting to interrupt, Eleanor moved away from the crowded shelves and, opening one of her books, began to read, curious as to what a book entitled *The Guillotine* was about. Two minutes later she was deep in the catacombs beneath a castle in northern Wales. Miss Julia was absolutely right, Eleanor thought happily. This book was terrifying. In fact, it was without a doubt the best book she'd ever read in her entire life. It put Plutarch and that crowd to shame. Noticing that it was labeled Volume One, she hurried back to get Volume Two and, as it turned out, Volumes Three and Four, as well.

She was busily trying to find any other books by the same author when she glanced up and felt a sense of disorientation sweep over her that made her feel giddy. She looked down at the floor, counted to ten and looked back. The dizzying sensation had disappeared, but not what had caused it. She could still see Connal standing at the end of the aisle, reading a book.

Eleanor stared at him incredulously, her mind not believing what her eyes were telling her. It couldn't be Connal, she thought in confusion. Connal had gone to New York, trying to find business for their shipyard, the Saturday before she sailed. And he certainly hadn't mentioned that he intended to come to England, too. That she would have remembered.

She focused on the white-painted shelf directly in front of her as she probed her reaction to his unexpected appearance. She should be happy, she told herself. Not only was Connal a familiar face from home, but she was seriously considering marrying him. At the very least, she should be mildly pleased to see him.

So why wasn't she? The question nagged at her. Why was her overwhelming feeling one of dismay? She didn't know. All she knew for certain was that she most emphatically was not glad to see Connal, and the fact made her feel guilty.

Why was Connal here in London? Had he missed her when he returned to Boston, and come to find her? Somehow, Connal in the role of impatient lover didn't quite ring true. It was far more likely that he still wanted her to spy and was here to try to pester her into doing it.

Whatever the truth was, she was never going to find out by hiding behind the shelves. Connal was the only one who could enlighten her. Telling herself that even if she wasn't sure she wanted to marry him, she still owed him the loyalty of a friend, as well as that of a fellow American, Eleanor pasted what she hoped was a welcoming smile on her face and walked over to him.

"Good morning, Connal. I didn't know you planned to come to England."

"Don't look at me!" Connal gave her a fulminating glance and then furtively peered around the bookstore. To his obvious relief, no one was paying them the slightest attention.

Eleanor eyed him uncertainly, wondering if the old German folktale about everyone having a twin somewhere really could be true. Maybe this rude individual really was a stranger. Her spirits soared for a second before common sense shot them down. This had to be Connal.

She took a deep breath and tried again. "Why not?" she asked.

Connal inched closer to her, pretending to be studying the books not far from her. "Because," he hissed out of the side of his mouth, "I don't want anyone to see us talking. Pretend to be looking at the books."

Eleanor felt a surge of exasperation at his melodrama, but decided that it would be easier in the long run to agree. She opened one of her books and, feeling like an actress in a French farce, muttered, "I didn't know you were planning on coming to London."

"I decided I should be on hand to see to the details myself. Since your ship stopped in Jamaica, I found a faster passage, on the *Mary Jane,* out of New York. I arrived almost two weeks ago.

"I've been watching the Bromley house, hoping for a chance to talk to you."

"You could have come to the door and pulled the knocker," she suggested impatiently.

"Don't be stupid. I don't want anyone to know that we're acquainted."

Why? Eleanor wondered, but before she could ask, he changed the subject.

"What have you found out about your uncle?" Connal demanded in an undertone.

"That he's totally under my grandmother's thumb."

Connal glowered at her. "I meant about his position in the Horse Guards. The plans he makes."

"Nothing," Eleanor said truthfully. "I only arrived a few days ago."

"We don't have much time. The peace talks have already begun in Ghent."

"I'll pray for them."

"God helps them who help themselves," Connal replied. "It's your duty."

When Eleanor didn't reply, he continued, "Who is the man you came in here with?"

Eleanor glanced toward Ryland. He was still talking to the old man. "Just a friend of the family."

"And does this friend of the family have a name?"

Eleanor bit back a nasty retort. Had Connal always been this overbearing, or had his attitude developed since her father had died? She tried to remember the weeks following his death, but she couldn't clearly recall Connal's manner. She'd been too grief-stricken to notice anything.

"Eleanor!"

"The duke of Ryland." She supplied his name in the interest of peace.

"A duke, you say?" His eyes narrowed thoughtfully.

"So he claims, and since everyone else seems to accept it, who am I to cavil?" she asked dryly.

"Keep your voice down! What is his importance in the scheme of things?"

"I've only seen him twice in my life. All I know is that he's a reasonably polite gentleman with a totally inexplicable love of things classical."

"What does that—" Connal broke off as Ryland turned around and caught sight of them. With a quick word to the elderly man, Ryland started toward her.

"Damn!" Connal muttered. "I don't want him to see me. Not yet. One of my contacts put me in touch with a man who might be willing to sponsor me in society. I'll call you later."

Eleanor frowned as he slipped around the end of the aisle. Why didn't Connal want Ryland to see him, and why did Connal want to be sponsored in society? He'd never been interested in the social round before.

"Was that man bothering you?" Ryland watched Connal as he hurriedly left the bookstore.

"No," Eleanor lied. "He was looking for a book for his mother, and asked me for a recommendation, that's all."

Ryland studied her for a long moment, and Eleanor held his clear gaze with an effort. It was proving harder to lie to Ryland than she would have thought. But Connal was an old friend, and her father's choice of husband for her. She owed him some loyalty, she told herself in an attempt to salve her guilty conscience.

"Did you find the history book you were looking for?" She changed the subject. To her relief, he followed her lead.

"Yes." He handed her a depressingly thick tome. "What did you get?" He peered closer at them. *The Guillotine?* he read incredulously. "Those are Gothics! The worst of the

Minerva Press. My mother reads those . . . those . . ." Words failed him.

"Your mother is to be commended on her taste in literature." Eleanor refused to take umbrage.

"My mother didn't have the advantage of your education!"

Eleanor smiled at him. "She sounds charming."

"You aren't really going to read those, are you?" he demanded as she handed her choices to the clerk.

"As soon as I get home. I already started *The Guillotine,* and it's absolutely delicious." She shivered. "Only six pages, and so far the heroine has been locked in the dungeons and chased by a murderer brandishing a knife."

"How can you pollute your mind with such trash?"

"Easily." Eleanor smiled into his frustrated face. "But I will agree to at least try to read your history."

Ryland stifled a protest as he followed her outside. Once she started Millsaps' work, she'd be fascinated, he assured himself. He'd found the book absolutely spellbinding. He hadn't been able to put it down. With her intelligence and education, surely she'd feel the same. If not... He began to consider other schemes as he helped her into the carriage.

Chapter Three

"Cousin Eleanor! Are you back already?" Drusilla blurted out as Eleanor paused in the doorway of the salon.

Eleanor chuckled. "Would you believe me if I said no?"

"But I thought you were going for a drive with Ryland."

Eleanor studied Drusilla's flushed face curiously. "I did, but everything must come to an end sometime. Even drives with dukes."

"I know what you mean." Drusilla sounded strained. "Every time I have to dance with him, it seems to last forever."

Eleanor frowned. That didn't sound like the kind of a thing a girl would say about the man she wanted to marry. Nor did Drusilla's assessment of an outing with Ryland tally with her own. She'd enjoyed herself enormously. At least, she had until she'd discovered Connal.

Eleanor walked into the salon wishing that her grandmother wasn't so convinced that opening the heavy lace inner curtains would spell the instant ruin of all the room's furnishings. After the bright sunlight outside, she felt as if she were in a cave.

Eleanor set her books down on the marquetry table in front of the sofa and then let out a startled squeak when a stocky young man suddenly heaved himself out of one of the chairs in the window alcove.

"Forgive me. Didn't mean t'startle you." He gave her an uncertain smile. "I was waiting for Drusilla t'introduce us before I spoke."

"I was going to," Drusilla rushed into speech. "Eleanor, this is Bertrem Arylesworth. He's a very old friend, which was why I allowed him to stay, even though I was by myself. I mean, no one could possibly object to my visiting with Bertrem, whom I've known all my life and who's just today arrived in London—"

"By no one, I take it you refer to our mutual grandmother?" Eleanor said, cutting to the heart of the matter.

"Grandmama doesn't think..." Drusilla trailed off into silence.

And therein lies the crux of the matter, Eleanor thought wryly. Although in this case, Esme might well be right. Even in the freer society of Boston, a young girl of eighteen did not entertain a man by herself. Even in her own salon. Such behavior would brand her as fast. But whether Drusilla's actions were proper or not, they weren't any bread and butter of hers, Eleanor told herself. She had enough problems of her own to worry about.

"There can be no impropriety in my calling," Bertrem offered, although not with a great deal of conviction.

"Certainly not in my eyes," Eleanor agreed promptly. "You say you've also just arrived in London, Mr. Arylesworth?"

"Yes." Bertrem bobbed his head nervously. "On the mail coach, a few hours ago."

"Bertrem's father's estate marches next to Papa's on the northern boundary of Linton Gates," Drusilla told her.

"Uncle Henry has an estate?" Eleanor asked curiously. From various comments that had been made, she had assumed that he was completely dependent on his mother for financial support.

"Papa inherited it ages ago, when Grandpapa Bromley died. It's been in the family since Elizabeth gave it to one of our ancestors," Drusilla said. "I like it far better than London."

"Me too," Bertrem agreed. "Don't much care for all the hustle and bustle of the city."

"Then what brings you to London during its busiest season?" Eleanor asked, more in an attempt to keep the conversation alive than from any real desire to know.

Unfortunately, her question had the opposite effect. Drusilla flushed vividly and looked as if she were about to burst into tears, while Bertrem shot a nervous glance toward the door. Eleanor couldn't decide if he was looking for a rescuer or contemplating escape.

"Everyone comes to London during the Season," Drusilla finally offered into the uneasy silence.

"Quite true. Even I came," Eleanor agreed.

"Yes, indeed." Bertrem gave an overhearty laugh at her faint attempt at humor.

Eleanor searched her mind for a topic that wouldn't produce any more unexpected reactions from either Bertrem or her cousin. But since she didn't know why they had reacted the way they had in the first place, she didn't know what might set them off again. The weather, she finally decided. As a topic of conversation, it was absolutely neutral.

"It was a lovely afternoon for a drive," she said, mentally wincing at the inane brightness of her voice.

"Where did you go, Cousin Eleanor?" Drusilla asked politely.

"To a bookstore called Hatchards." Eleanor forced herself to continue, because while the conversation might be pointless, her presence wasn't. If Esme were to come back and find Drusilla alone with a young man...Eleanor barely suppressed a shudder at the thought of the resultant scene.

"Jolly good idea, reading," Bertrem observed. "Read a book m'self once, when I was at Harrow. Read several, as a matter of fact." He beamed at Eleanor.

"Grandmama doesn't approve of being bookish," Drusilla said uncertainly.

"Oh, don't read now," Bertrem assured her. "'Cept, of course, farm journals. Couldn't object t'that, could she? Mean t'say, I'm a farmer and all."

"Grandmama objects to everything," Drusilla muttered, then lapsed into silence.

Eleanor glanced longingly toward the door, wishing the tea tray would arrive. Not only was she parched, but serving the tea would take up several minutes, and if there were biscuits to munch on, too... Unfortunately, the doorway remained empty.

Taking a deep breath, Eleanor tried again. "Is your estate far from London, Mr. Arylesworth?"

"Well, now." He scratched the side of his nose reflectively. "Not too far. Leastwise, not if you got good horses. Took me about two days' steady travel on the mail coach."

"It took Grandmama five days the last time we went home," Drusilla offered. "But then the vicar's wife made her mad as fire because she wouldn't give her precedence over some visiting baron's wife, and Grandmama said she'd never go back again. She hasn't, either."

Eleanor waited a moment, hoping one of them would feel obligated to offer a subject for discussion. When they didn't, she gamely tried again. "Are your parents joining you in town, Mr. Arylesworth?"

"No, m'father says the cost of a London Season is ruinously expensive, and what with the price of agricultural products . . ." Bertrem heaved a sigh that seemed to come from the tips of his well-polished boots.

"Yes, agricultural markets in time of war tend to be very volatile, which is why it is important to diversify your holdings," Eleanor quoted her father.

"Don't have enough holdings t'diversify." Bertrem heaved another sigh. "The way things are going, not going t'have no holdings at all, unless I . . ."

"Oh, Bertrem!" Drusilla wailed unhappily. She gave Eleanor a reproachful look as Bertrem got to his feet.

"Really must be going," he said. "Mustn't outstay m'welcome. Good afternoon, Miss Wallace. It was a pleasure t'meet you." With a jerky bow to Eleanor and a pleading glance at Drusilla, he left.

Drusilla watched him go, her soft pink lips trembling under the strength of her emotions. "Oh, Eleanor, how could you?" she cried, and then ran from the room.

"How could I what?" Eleanor muttered, having no doubt that she was responsible for Bertrem's hasty exit. What she didn't know was what she had said to cause it. Eleanor grimaced. There were so many things she didn't know. Such as who exactly was Bertrem, besides just a neighbor from the country? And what was his relationship to Drusilla? Her cousin seemed very fond of him, but how fond, and what kind of fondness was it? And if it was, as Eleanor suspected, a romantic fondness, then why was Drusilla allowing her grandmother to engineer a wedding with Ryland? After all, it was her father's permission Drusilla needed to get married, not Esme's.

Although, she had found out one thing. Uncle Henry had an estate in the country. And had had it since his father's death over twenty-five years ago. But if Henry had his own estate, why was he living here in town, under his mother's thumb? Even if he preferred living in London to rusticating in the country, why didn't he use the proceeds from his estate to maintain his own establishment, which would free him from his mother's constant interference?

Eleanor didn't know. Nor could she find out without inquiring into her hosts' financial position which would be the height of ill manners. Honestly, Eleanor thought in exasperation, this family had more twists and turns to it than one of those interminable Greek plays her father had so inexplicably loved.

Although, collecting a myriad assortment of problems seemed to be a family failing, she thought as she remembered Connal's unexpected appearance at the bookstore. What was she going to do about him? The problem nagged at her. She'd counted on having the whole summer in which to decide which role, if any, she wanted Connal to play in her future. And now those months had suddenly evaporated. And what was worse was that Connal was still determined that she spy on her uncle. Something she was even more reluctant to do now that she'd met Henry. The poor man didn't deserve such treachery.

But her father hadn't deserved the treatment he received from Esme, either, she conceded. And now her father was dead, and nothing could ever make up the past for him. A sense of profound loss washed over her, chilling her skin. She rubbed her hands over her arms, ineffectually trying to warm herself. But the cold was of her spirit, not her body.

Her father's cause wasn't dead, though, she reminded herself. Even if she couldn't ever again do anything for him, she could do something for the cause he'd believed in.

Too upset to sit still, Eleanor got to her feet and walked over to the window. She twitched aside the heavy lace curtains and stared blindly down into the peaceful square. The street didn't look all that different from her home in Boston. There was nothing visible that would account for the hatred her father had felt for the English and all things English. In fact, with the exception of her grandmother and Ryland, she hadn't found the English to be that much different from the Americans she'd known all her life. Some were good, some were bad, and most were simply trying to survive in an uncertain world.

Feeling guilty and confused, she let the curtain fall and turned her back on the pleasant scene. Try as she might, she simply couldn't hate the English as her father had. Nor could she quite bring herself to agree to marry her father's choice of husband for her. At least not yet, she thought, feeling pressured by Connal's sudden appearance.

Why didn't he want anyone to know that they'd already met? And why did he want to be sponsored in society? And far more importantly, why couldn't he have stayed in America, where he belonged? She rubbed her forehead, which was beginning to ache again. So many questions, and so few answers.

Eleanor picked up her books, deciding to forgo a cup of tea in favor of the privacy of her bedroom. She would read for a while, she decided. She'd lose herself in someone else's problems. Later, she'd worry about her own. Clutching her precious Gothics to her chest, Eleanor sprinted up the stairs to the haven of her bedroom, sending up a silent prayer that she wouldn't be disturbed.

To her relief, she wasn't. She spent the rest of the afternoon and the early evening lost in the adventures of an intrepid heroine who was foiling the villain's every attempt to force her into marriage so that he could get his hands on her enormous fortune in order to pay off his outrageous gambling debts. It was with real reluctance that she put the book down when she heard the dinner gong.

She wasn't really hungry, but she was a guest, she reminded herself. And guests appeared punctually for meals. If she were lucky, the family would go out after dinner to some social event, as they had every evening since she arrived, and there'd be plenty of time for her to finish her book. Maybe even to start Volume Two. She shivered in anticipation.

Eleanor got to her feet and carefully shook out the full skirt of her black bombazine dress, trying to erase the wrinkles. It didn't work. She looked a quiz, she admitted, studying her wavy reflection in the looking glass above her bureau. Her dress hung on her, emphasizing her skinniness, and its dusty black hue made her complexion look like that of a recovering plague victim.

If there were company tonight... An image of Ryland's bright blue eyes, gleaming with laughter, floated through her mind, and unconsciously an answering smile curved her soft lips. What had the duke thought of her appalling gown? she wondered dispiritedly. The women in his world all were impeccably turned out.

Her aunt had made some mention when she first arrived about new gowns, but Eleanor didn't really expect anything to come of it. For one thing, Maria did not seem to have much money. And for another, Esme would be bound to object. Loudly and in as vulgar terms as she could. No, if her wardrobe were to be replenished, she was undoubtedly the one who would have to do it. But if she did that, her grandmother would want to know where she'd gotten the money.

Eleanor grimaced. She could always say she'd sold the necklace. Her grandmother would certainly believe that. Or she'd claim to believe it. Had the necklace really been stolen? Eleanor wondered in frustration. What she needed were some hard facts, if she was ever going to find out what had really happened to it. Beginning with a description.

Perhaps her aunt knew what it looked like? Although perhaps not. Henry hadn't been married when the necklace was stolen. So Maria hadn't been living here at the time.

"Miss Eleanor?" The call was accompanied by a knock on the door. "Mrs. Bromley sent me up t'tell ya that dinner's ready," the young maid told her.

"Thank you, Daisy. I'm coming." Eleanor hastily picked up a thin lawn handkerchief and pushed it in her pocket before going downstairs.

Eleanor found the family about to be seated at the dinner table. With a quick smile at her aunt, she slipped into her seat. Eleanor turned to politely greet her grandmother and then blinked as she got a good look at her. Esme seemed to glow with the reflected light from her huge diamond necklace, her dangling diamond earbobs and the three oversize brooches pinned to the front of her pea-green satin gown. It was a very impressive—and totally tasteless—display of wealth.

"You're late! Where have you been?" Esme demanded.

"My bedroom." Eleanor forced herself to respond to the question and ignore the tone in which it was asked.

"All afternoon?" Esme persisted. "You weren't in the salon when we returned."

"I was there earlier," Eleanor said, and paused as she caught the look of mute appeal Drusilla sent her. Appeal for what? Eleanor asked herself. Did her cousin want her to say something or not say something? Probably not, she finally decided. And the *not* undoubtedly had to do with Bertrem's visit.

"Hiding in your room seems like mighty strange behavior for a young girl," Esme said suspiciously.

"And so it might be, if I were a young girl," Eleanor replied calmly. "But since I am a mature woman of five-and-twenty—"

"It seems like only yesterday that I was that age," Maria offered hopefully.

As usual, Esme ignored her. "And you, missy." Esme pinned Drusilla with her gimlet gaze. "Did you wait in the salon for Ryland to come by, as I told you?"

Drusilla stared at Esme, her mouth slightly parted and her eyes fixed. Eleanor was forcibly reminded of a mouse she'd once seen cornered by the kitchen cat. It, too, had been frozen into immobility, as it had waited for certain death. Now, as then, she rushed to the rescue.

"The duke was very nice," Eleanor said. "So kind too. To drive to Hatchards as he did."

"Hatchards!" Esme glared at Drusilla. "Have your wits gone begging, missy? I've told you and told you. Gentlemen don't like bookish women."

"Oh, Drusilla didn't get any books," Eleanor carefully skirted the truth. "I was the one who got some. Four Gothics."

"Everyone reads Gothics, Mother Bromley," Maria hurriedly explained. "Why, Sally Jersey gave me one just yesterday and Maria Sefton has read every book Mrs. Radcliffe has ever written."

"What's suitable for the patroness of Almacks is hardly suitable for her." Esme gave Eleanor a disparaging look before turning her attention back to Drusilla. "Did you see anyone while you were out this afternoon?"

"We came straight home from Hatchards," Eleanor said before Drusilla could inadvertently blurt out the truth. "Although several people did bow as we passed on the street."

"Bowed at Ryland, not you," Esme snapped. "See that you don't make a fool of yourself over the duke. He's not for the likes of you."

"Somehow I doubt that he's for our Drusilla, either." Henry unexpectedly looked up from his dinner. "Not to say that you're not a fetching little thing." He smiled fondly at his daughter. "But the truth of the matter is, you're not in his style. Ryland's always been more interested in those ruins of his than in females. Fact is, most of us at Whitehall were that surprised when he agreed to help with the war effort. Didn't think he'd ever leave his diggings. We figure it must've been because of his brother's death. Ryland fair doted on him. Pity, that." Henry shook his head and turned his attention back to his food.

Eleanor was caught off guard by the relief she felt at her uncle's words. So a match between her cousin and Ryland was not a settled thing. And from the skittish way Drusilla reacted to him, it wasn't likely to be. Although... Eleanor bit uncertainly on the inside of her lip. If the duke were to offer for her, Drusilla might not be given the option of refusing. Esme certainly wouldn't allow her to. But what about Henry? Eleanor glanced speculatively at her uncle.

He might not expect an offer from Ryland, but that wasn't to say that he wouldn't be delighted to align himself with a wealthy dukedom if given the chance. Her own father had opted for security and stability when choosing a husband for her. Who was to say Henry might not do the same?

"You are a bobbing block, Henry Bromley!" Esme threw at her son. "You always were and you always will be. Just you wait. By the time the season's over, Drusilla's engagement to Ryland will be puffed up in all the papers, and we'll be spending the summer at a ducal seat." Esme glared around the table, defying anyone to deny it.

No one was so fool-hardy as to try. Drusilla bent her head over her plate so that only her blond curls were visible, Henry continued to eat, Maria studied the pattern on the wallpaper, and Eleanor simply wanted the whole subject dropped.

Satisfied that she had cowed her family into acceptance, Esme turned to Henry and said, "Did Ryland tell you which of the engagements he'd be attending this evening?"

"Me? Dash it all, why would the man tell me?" Henry asked in honest confusion.

"You could have asked," Esme retorted.

"Why? I'm no social secretary," Henry muttered.

Esme gave him a withering look and turned her attention to her daughter-in-law. "Maria, what cards do we have for this evening?"

Maria frowned, trying to remember. "The Sefton do, and the rout at the Wallingsfords'..."

"You forgot the Almstons' ball," Esme said.

Maria looked pained. "We weren't sent an invitation. Jane Almston is still in the boughs about the things you said about her youngest daughter last season."

"Well!" Esme looked furious. "A fine state of affairs it is when some jumped-up country squire's wife takes exception to my telling her the truth. You must have simply missed the card. She wouldn't have dared not invite me," Esme declared with absolute conviction. "Eleanor, make yourself useful and go down to the salon and go through the invitations. Bring up any for this evening."

"But, Mama, Eleanor hasn't finished her dinner yet," Henry began.

"It's my food, and she eats it at my pleasure," Esme snapped. "And right now I don't please. You heard me, missy."

"Mother Bromley," Maria began.

"That's all right, Aunt Maria. I don't mind." Eleanor hurriedly made her escape. She could always eat a snack later. Now, she was only too happy to escape Esme's hectoring.

She found all the invitations thrown together in a cut-glass bowl in the salon. Grabbing a handful, she began to sort through them, putting the ones that were outdated to one side to be disposed of. It seemed incredible to her that so many people had nothing better to do with their time than to entertain to this extent. Didn't families ever simply stay home and pass a pleasant evening talking to one another? She frowned as the thought of trying to converse with her grandmother for an entire evening suddenly struck her. If all of these people had a family member like her grandmother, it was no wonder they surrounded themselves with other people to serve as buffers.

Eleanor was about half finished with the task when she heard the front knocker. She looked toward the door, wondering who would be calling at this unfashionable hour. She didn't have to wonder long.

"The duke of Ryland," Walker announced a second before Ryland strode into the salon.

Eleanor stared at him, her eyes widening at the tailored perfection of his black evening coat and pantaloons, which contrasted with the snowy perfection of his elaborately tied cravat. The huge sapphire nestled in its intricate folds and the single fob that hung from his white waistcoat were his only jewelry. He looked starkly authoritarian, very elegant and totally inaccessible.

Until a smile curved his lips at her absorbed expression and he suddenly became something else. But what else? she wondered uneasily.

Ryland felt a curious twisting, tightening sensation curl around his heart as she tentatively returned his smile. Her brown eyes, which seemed too big for her thin face, suddenly sparkled with life. Eleanor Wallace was one of the very few women he knew whose smile was reflected in her eyes, he realized.

"The rest of the family is at dinner, Your Grace," Walker murmured.

"Don't disturb them yet, Walker. I fear I lost track of the time, but I must give Mr. Bromley a communiqué that arrived at Whitehall after he had left," Ryland said, hoping that they'd assume that he'd been asked to deliver the note instead of realizing that he'd seized on it as an excuse to see Miss Wallace again. His all-too-brief outing with her this afternoon had merely whetted his interest in her.

"I'll talk to Miss Wallace for a few minutes." He waited until the butler had left and then asked, "If the family is at dinner, why are you here?"

Could she have been searching for something? But what could she hope to find in the salon? Henry was far too experienced to leave sensitive memoranda out here where any chance visitor might stumble across them.

"I'm looking for invitations."

"Invitations?" Surely she wasn't planning to go out in that appalling excuse for a dress she was wearing? He eyed the shapeless black sack with disfavor. Neither the color nor the style became her. There wasn't much she could do about the color, considering her bereavement, but the style... His eyes lingered on the slight swell of her breasts beneath the bagging bodice. She should wear a classical style, he decided. Maybe a draped Greek gown with a gold ribbon threaded through her hair and gold sandals on her small feet? Her arms should be bare, and—

"Here, you may help." Eleanor's prosaic words interrupted his thoughts, and he regretfully allowed the enticing vision to melt away.

She handed him a stack of invitations. "I need the ones for this evening."

"Why?" Ryland obediently began to sort through the cards. "Good Lord," he muttered. "I thought old Gassingham was dead."

Eleanor leaned over his shoulder to read the card, and a wave of perfume redolent with the scent of roses teased his nostrils and drifted into his lungs. The air in his chest seemed to heat, sending a flush of desire along his cheekbones. It was an interesting choice of perfume. He struggled to think rationally. Definitely not the type of scent favored by a young girl in her first season. But something that a matron of several years' standing who was secure in her place in the world might wear.

He glanced down at Eleanor's soft cheek, his eyes lingering on its paleness. Her skin seemed translucent, and the urge to touch it, to find out if it really was as silky as it looked, was almost overpowering.

"Who is Gassingham, and why should you think he's dead?" Eleanor asked.

"A friend of my grandfather's. Perhaps this card is from his son."

"Perhaps," Eleanor agreed, not really caring. She had enough things to worry about, and Gassingham's mortality wasn't one of them.

With Ryland helping her, it only took a few minutes for her to finish the task. She slowly gathered up the evening's invitations to give to Esme. She didn't want to leave the salon, she admitted. She wanted to stay and talk to Ryland. But she couldn't. She knew she had to return to the dining room before Esme came looking for her. She'd be well and truly in the basket if her grandmother were to find her talking to Ryland.

"Good night, Your Grace," Eleanor said. "I'll have Walker announce you in about five minutes."

"Fine."

Pausing long enough to have a quick word with Walker, Eleanor hurried back to the dining room and handed Esme the invitations.

"Ha! Took you long enough." Esme glared at the few cards. "Where's the rest, missy?"

"That's all there were for this evening," Eleanor said.

Maria picked up one of the cards. "The Wallingfords' do will be the best attended," she hurriedly said. "The patroness of Almacks will be there."

"Prinny mentioned something about putting in an appearance," Henry offered.

"He did?" Esme's face took on a calculating expression. "Then probably most of the really important people will be there. That's where we'll go first. We can try one of the other parties if the evening seems flat."

"The duke of Ryland is here to see you, Mr. Bromley," Walker announced from the doorway.

"Ryland?" Henry looked surprised. "Here? Now?"

"That's what he said."

Esme gave the appalled-looking Drusilla a speculative glance.

"He said it was a matter of some import," Walker said.

"You didn't leave him in the hall, did you?" Esme demanded.

"Certainly not, madame," Walker returned woodenly. "He is in the salon."

Henry tossed his napkin on his plate and stood. "Best go see what it is he wants. Probably more bad news about supply lines." He shook his head in frustration.

Esme watched him go and then said, "I don't believe Ryland came to see Henry. I think he came in the hopes of seeing you, Drusilla. We'll stay home tonight and entertain Ryland ourselves," she decided.

Eleanor watched as Drusilla's face fell in dismay, wondering why she should want to go out with her grandmother. Personally, Eleanor could think of few ways she would less rather spend an evening than with their overbearing grandparent. Unless... Could Drusilla have hoped to see Bertrem at the Wallingsfords' party this evening? Could her cousin really prefer the youthful Bertrem to Ryland? On the surface, it seemed inconceivable, but then, as her old nurse had been so fond of saying, there was no accounting for tastes.

"But if the prince is going to be at the Wallingfords', then the duke will undoubtedly go, too," Maria pointed out.

"True." Esme looked uncertain for once. "And he did ask to see Henry, and it is a very strange time to come calling...."

"And the duke has excellent manners." Maria pressed her point. "He would never interrupt someone's dinner unless it were a matter of utmost urgency."

Esme grimaced. "It probably really is something to do with that infernal war. How annoying. Very well. Drusilla and I will go on to the Wallingfords'. You stay here, Maria, and if you're wrong and he really did come to see Drusilla, then tell him where he can find us."

Esme heaved her not-inconsiderable bulk to her feet. "I shall be ready to leave in fifteen minutes, Drusilla. See that you don't keep me waiting."

"But what about Eleanor?" Drusilla asked with a look at her cousin. "You always leave her behind."

"She's in mourning," Esme stated.

"She should be in half mourning by now," Maria said. "And in that case it's perfectly proper for her to attend social events, just not to dance."

"In that gown?" Esme said scathingly. "She looks a disgrace."

"Yes, she does rather look as if the family is in the basket, doesn't she?" Maria said slyly. "Don't worry, dear." She smiled warmly at Eleanor. "I gave your measurements to the dressmaker when I was there day before yesterday, and she promised to have something ready for you by week's end."

"And who do you expect to pay for this 'something'?" Esme asked ominously. "I've already told her that when she returns my necklace—"

"I will pay for Eleanor's gowns. This is a critical time for Drusilla, and I don't want any malicious gossip circulating about how we treat poor Emily's daughter." Maria offered the one argument that she thought might silence Esme. "Many people still remember Emily with a great deal of fondness."

Esme glared at Maria, who stared back at her, her amiability seemingly unimpaired. "Oh, do as you please, but on your head be it," she muttered, and stomped out of the room.

Eleanor glanced down at her cold dinner, feeling both touched and guilty. Did her aunt but know it, the niece she was trying to befriend was rich enough to buy an abbey.

"Don't mind your grandmother, Eleanor." Maria stood up. "We all try not to."

Eleanor choked on an unexpected giggle. There was a lot more to her aunt than she'd originally thought.

"Do you mind not going to the party tonight?" Drusilla asked after Maria left.

"No," Eleanor said honestly. "I'd much rather finish reading my book."

"Eleanor . . . I want to thank you for not telling Grandmama about . . ."

"Don't mention it. I couldn't do any less for my favorite cousin."

"How many cousins do you have?" Drusilla asked curiously.

Eleanor chuckled. "Just you."

"Eleanor . . ." Drusilla paused, and then blurted out, "Eleanor, why don't you just give Grandmama back her necklace, and then she'll find you a husband and you can be credibly established too."

"Unfortunately, I don't have it. I don't even know what it looks like."

"Ugly" was Drusilla's assessment. "There's a picture of Grandmama wearing it in the small salon."

Eleanor felt a burst of excitement heat her skin. At last, a solid fact about the necklace.

"Would you show it to me?" Eleanor hurriedly got to her feet.

"If you want." Drusilla's tone expressed doubt as to why anyone would. "It's this way." She led the way toward the back of the house. "No one uses the small salon, because it's so cold all the time."

Eleanor followed, her steps instinctively slowing as they passed her uncle's study. Inside, she could hear the indistinct murmur of voices, but that was all. Telling herself not to be ridiculous, that Ryland had no more come to see her than he had come to see Drusilla, she forced herself to catch up with her cousin.

Drusilla took one of the argand lamps from the break-front at the end of the hallway and carried it into the small room to her right. As she had warned, it was cold. Very cold. Eleanor shivered as a current of icy air curled around her ankles.

"There." Drusilla walked across the room and held up the lamp to illuminate a large oil painting of a fleshy woman. Her grandmother. Eleanor had no trouble recognizing the subject, but it was the necklace that caught and held her attention. It consisted of a tight collar made up of six rows of good-size diamonds, and suspended from the center of it was a huge ruby.

"Ugly—" Eleanor agreed with Drusilla's assessment "—but impressive for all that. And probably worth a small fortune, if it's real and not paste." Eleanor frowned. Could the necklace have been nothing more than strass glass? She took the lamp from Drusilla and, holding it up, peered closer, but it was impossible to tell in a painting.

"Drusilla, was the necklace insured?"

"I don't know."

"That ruby in particular is very distinctive," Eleanor said slowly. "I've never seen one quite that big."

"Bertrem said it was all fudge." Drusilla sounded disappointed.

Eleanor blinked. "What was?"

"That you had the necklace. I mean, like he said, you'd never come here to live with Grandmama if you had any money. No one would," she said simply.

"Drusilla, was Grandmama always so—?" Eleanor gestured ineffectually.

Drusilla grimaced. "Mean? As long as I've known her. I know one shouldn't speak ill of her, but..."

"That's the dead," Eleanor said, "and my personal feeling is that someone ought to speak ill of her to her face and that they should have done it years ago."

"According to Mama, your father did, and look what happened to him. He died penniless in the wilderness."

Eleanor opened her mouth and then closed it when she found that she couldn't enlighten Drusilla without giving away far more than she wanted to. For the time being, at least, it was far better that they all believed that she really was a penniless orphan.

"Miss Drusilla." Walker spoke from the doorway, and Eleanor jumped, almost dropping the lamp. "Your grandmama is ready to leave."

"Thank you, Walker. I'll be right there." Drusilla gave Eleanor a quick hug. "I wish you were coming. I like you. You're so... You don't seem afraid of any of them. Not Grandmama, or the duke..."

"Ryland?" Eleanor was startled. "Why ever would I be afraid of him?"

"He's the duke of Ryland," Drusilla said reverently.

"I keep telling you, I know who he is, and I fail to see why the fact that an ancestor of his once earned or bought a title should impress me."

Drusilla stared at Eleanor in trepidation. "Eleanor, are you a Jacobin?"

Eleanor chuckled. "No. I have not the slightest desire to chop off anyone's head, even Grandmama's. I simply don't believe in toadying to someone just because he happens to have had an able ancestor."

"But it's more than that. He's frightfully clever, you know. Why, sometimes, I can't even tell what he's talking about."

"Some of his ideas are certainly frightful," Eleanor agreed, remembering the thick tome he'd burdened her with. "But you'd better hurry, before Grandmama decides to stay home after all."

Drusilla paled at the thought and rushed from the room.

Eleanor turned back to study the portrait more closely. That center ruby was definitely unique. Surely someone would have noticed if it had been reset into another piece of jewelry. Unless her father had been right and Esme had hidden it away all those years ago. Eleanor frowned. It would be very difficult to keep something that valuable hidden for that long. Someone, sometime, would have been bound to accidentally stumble across it. And there was also the matter of her grandmother's personality. Esme didn't seem to be able to resist making a show of something she owned. Eleanor couldn't believe that she would have been able to resist wearing the necklace if she had it in her possession. Esme was too much of an exhibitionist, and the necklace would have been far too tempting for her to have put it in a drawer and forgotten it, even for revenge against a hated son-in-law. Besides, there wouldn't have been any point in Esme's continuing to hide it once her daughter had died.

What she needed to do was to find some way to casually show the portrait to people and then try to discover if they recognized either the whole necklace or the central stone. But how? Eleanor nibbled on her thumbnail. How did you casually lure visitors into a small, icy room in the back of the house, show them a painting and ask questions without any of them becoming suspicious?

You couldn't, she decided. So the other alternative would be to bring the painting to the visitors. And visitors were normally received in the front salon. She'd ask one of the servants to exchange this picture for the Turner landscape hanging over the fireplace one afternoon when her grandmother was out visiting. And if Esme noticed, she'd empty the butter boat over her. She didn't have the slightest doubt that Esme would believe any flattery, no matter how outrageous.

Then all she would have to do would be to draw the picture to people's attention and lead the conversation around to the necklace. She knew it wasn't an infallible plan, but she was making progress. She now knew what the necklace looked like, and was reasonably certain that her grandmother didn't have it in her possession. Two facts she hadn't known before she'd come to England. It should be a short step to finding out what had really happened to the necklace, she thought, trying to encourage herself.

Chapter Four

"**M**iss?" The sibilant was followed by a muffled knock on Eleanor's bedroom door.

Distracted, Eleanor stared blankly at the door, her mind still deep in the trials and tribulations of the much-put-upon heroine of the Gothic she was reading.

"Miss?" The young maid's voice wavered between desperation and determination. "Is ya in there?"

"No," Eleanor said, and went back to reading.

"Miss, please!" Daisy's voice rose on a wail.

Reluctantly Eleanor put her book down and got to her feet. No doubt Daisy had a message from her grandmother and was terrified of not delivering it.

Eleanor opened the door and smiled at the young girl standing there.

"Good morning, Daisy. What is it you want?"

"I wants..." She paused and peered nervously down the empty hall. Eleanor followed her glance, wondering what Daisy expected to find. Or feared to find might be more accurate, considering her apprehensive manner. The chilly hallway was deserted.

"You have a message?" Eleanor prodded.

"Got two of 'em, miss," Daisy said importantly. "One's from Mrs. Bromley, the nice'un, she says t'tell ya that peoples'll be comin' fer social calls now. An' I gots another message." Daisy paused as if to give added importance to her words.

"And it is?" Eleanor contained her sense of impatience.

"It's from him," Daisy announced.

"Him who?"

Daisy frowned, obviously disappointed in Eleanor's prosaic reaction. "You know, him what's your beau."

Eleanor's eyes widened as for a moment an image of Ryland's lean face, his eyes gleaming with intelligence, superimposed itself on her mind. And just as quickly as it had appeared, common sense erased it. By no stretch of the imagination could he be called her beau. What was more, even if he were, he'd hardly be sending her clandestine messages. He had no need to. If he wanted to talk to her, he'd come to call.

A feeling of disquiet feathered over her skin as she suddenly remembered yet another man she knew in London. Connal Gunn. And Connal hadn't wanted anyone to know that they were acquainted, she remembered. Could he be sending her messages through the servants?

"Which beau might that be?" Eleanor asked slowly.

"The one what was outside the kitchen door last night when I took the garbage out. He done gave me a note fer you, and sixpence to deliver it, secret like."

Botheration! Eleanor thought angrily. How could Connal involve this credulous girl in what she obviously thought was a case of thwarted love, and all for sixpence. Had he given no thought to the possible consequences of what he was asking Daisy to do? If Esme ever found out that one of her maids had carried clandestine messages, the girl would find herself on the streets with no references.

"Ain't he yer beau?" Daisy looked uncertain. "Did I do wrong t'take the money? I wanted t'give the sixpence to m'mum."

"It isn't so much that you did wrong, Daisy." Eleanor tried to make her understand. "It's that you did stupid."

Daisy frowned in confusion. "Stupid, miss?"

"Daisy, think. What would my grandmother do if she were to find out that you'd taken a message from a strange man and brought it to me?"

Daisy's eyes widened into huge pools of stark black fear in her white face. "Oh, miss, you wouldn't tell her? Please, no, miss. M'mum, she needs m'wages, and—"

"I don't have the slightest intention of telling my grandmother anything," Eleanor hurriedly reassured her. "But I can't guarantee that someone else might not."

Daisy gulped fearfully. "No one else saw me. I was real careful, just like he said."

"Perhaps, but I want your word that you won't even talk to this man again, let alone carry messages for him."

"Yes, miss. I won't no more, miss." Daisy looked wistful. "But do ya think I could keep the sixpence, just this once?"

"Yes." Eleanor smiled at her. "Just this once. And the message . . ."

Daisy reached into her pocket and shoved a dingy sealed envelope at her. "Here it be."

"Thank you. Please tell my aunt that I'll be down in a moment. And Daisy," she called after the girl, "if there should be any trouble about this, you tell me. Promise?"

"Bless ya, miss, what could ya do? You ain't even got sixpence like me."

"Nonetheless, tell me," Eleanor insisted.

"Yes, miss, I promise." Daisy scurried away.

Eleanor shut her bedroom door and, leaning up against the scratched wood, slowly broke the mud-brown wax seal on the envelope. She pulled out the single sheet of thin paper and squinted down at the crabbed handwriting. The message was short, succinct and bordered on a command.

Meet me at Hatchards tomorrow at two, Connal had written.

Eleanor crumpled the sheet in annoyance. She really didn't need the added complication of Connal's presence in London. Especially not if he were going to persist in trying to convince her to do something that ran counter to her own sense of right and wrong. Eleanor was fast coming to the conclusion that in order to be a spy one needed to be either single-minded to the point of fanaticism or totally lacking in scruples. Unfortunately, she didn't fall into either category.

But Connal did. To him, the validity of his goal justified whatever means he had to use to reach it. Eleanor chewed uncertainly on the inside of her lip. Her father had felt that way, too, she remembered. To him, no sacrifice was too great to ensure America's continued freedom.

Eleanor carefully hid the note away in the bottom of her bureau drawer, wishing she could dispose of the problem as easily. It wasn't that she didn't believe in the American cause. The problem was that she couldn't seem to keep focused on the overall picture. The individual people who made up that picture kept getting in the way. She kept seeing their problems and what her spying might do to them. But did she have the right to sacrifice her father's dream so as not to cause problems for her uncle, when her father had hated the Bromleys?

She didn't know the answer. Nor did she know anyone she could discuss it with. A rueful smile teased her lips as she remembered Ryland and his fascination with the Greeks. It was too bad she couldn't talk to him about the problem. It was just the kind of a moral dilemma a Grecophile would relish.

Unfortunately, the duke was first and foremost an Englishman. An Englishman who'd lost a brother to the war. Which would make it as hard for him to be objective as it was for her.

Perhaps there was no such thing as a truly objective viewpoint, she thought in frustration. But be that as it may, this wasn't the time to consider it. Now she needed to go down to the salon and make polite, boring conversation with an assortment of polite, boring people. Eleanor chuckled. What a lot of time society would save if they would all be honest with each other.

Perhaps Ryland would call this afternoon, Eleanor thought on a flash of anticipation. He was definitely interesting.

To her disappointment, Ryland was not in her grandmother's salon. Unfortunately, her grandmother was. Esme was seated in her favorite chair by the fireplace, glaring at the young man who'd been there yesterday with Drusilla. Esme looked up as Eleanor tried to silently slip into the room.

"Ha! So it's you, is it?" Esme transferred her glare to Eleanor.

Eleanor was about to respond in kind, but the look of mute appeal Drusilla sent her, as well as Maria's harassed expression, stifled the impulse. Instead, she forced a polite nod at Esme, walked over to the sofa and sat down beside her aunt.

"Eleanor, allow me to make known to you Bertrem Arylesworth. His estate marches next to ours in Lincolnshire." Drusilla fixed a pleading eye on her cousin.

"How do you do, Mr. Arylesworth?" Eleanor went along with the pretense of not having already met him. Obviously Drusilla didn't want Esme to know that Bertrem had come to call yesterday. But why not? He certainly seemed an unexceptional young man, and he was a neighbor. Maybe Drusilla didn't want Esme to know that she'd entertained him without a chaperone present.

Eleanor stifled a sigh. She was certainly getting plenty of practice if she should decide to become a spy. She was positively dripping in half-truths, innuendos and outright lies. She just hoped she didn't forget what she'd told to whom. That was the trouble with lying. It took an excellent memory to be successful at it. Probably better than she possessed.

"Pleased to meet you, Miss Wallace," Bertrem said with a nervous glance at Esme, and Eleanor felt a sense of exasperation mingled with pity. Someone should tell her relatives that pandering to tyrants never served. It only encouraged the tyrants to believe they were invincible. One needed to face them down. As she intended to do with her grandmother, just as soon as she found out what had really happened to that necklace. Then, after she'd indulged in the pleasure of telling Esme exactly what she thought of her, she'd go home to Boston.

Although... Eleanor watched as Maria ineffectually tried to deflect Esme's ill humor. She'd miss her uncle's family. They might be lacking in backbone, but they had been kind to her. Very kind.

"...why you've come." Eleanor caught the tail end of the diatribe Esme had flung at Bertrem.

"Papa thought it was time I acquired a little town bronze," he offered with a look at Drusilla. "Thought I

should make my bow at St. James' now that I'm down from
Oxford.''

"Did you enjoy your studies, Mr. Arylesworth?" Eleanor
introduced what seemed to her to be an innocuous subject.
After all, Esme might deplore a female being bookish, but
surely that stricture wouldn't apply to a man.

"No," Bertrem said simply. "Didn't want to go, but Papa
said that going to Oxford was the thing to do. Said all the
young men do it."

"And so they do," Maria offered placatingly. "And now
you're finished."

As was the conversation, Eleanor thought ruefully as an
uneasy silence fell on the group. If only there was some way
to get rid of her grandmother. Esme was enough to put a
damper on the most vibrant personality, which Bertrem
definitely wasn't.

"You should go back to Lincolnshire instead of aping
your betters in London," Esme sniped at Bertrem.

Bertrem flushed to the tips of his overlarge ears, but he
didn't respond to the provocation.

"Now, Mother Bromley, you know that the Arylesworths have been in Lincolnshire as long as the Bromleys,"
Maria reminded her peaceably.

"Longer," Bertrem muttered.

"Ha!" Esme snapped, leaving her audience uncertain of
her meaning. "He'll not be getting many invitations here.
London's not the provinces."

Bertrem spoke up. "Been invited to the Jerseys' ball.
Mama gave me a letter of introduction."

"Well, you needn't think you'll be invited to our rout
party," Esme said. "I can fill my rooms with the tip of the
ton. I don't need to clutter them up with provincials."

"Esme!" Maria gasped. "Surely we will invite our
neighbor's son?"

"No! I don't want him. Besides, he wouldn't know nobody."

"Then he must definitely come and talk to me, as I won't
know anyone, either," Eleanor said, embarrassed and angry. It was bad enough that Esme afforded the family such

Turkish treatment. That she should abuse a guest in such a scaly fashion was inexcusable.

"I would consider it a pleasure to introduce both of you to the other guests."

Eleanor swung around at the sound of the deep voice behind her to find Ryland standing in the doorway. Avidly her eyes skimmed over his closely fitted biscuit pantaloons, up past his buff-and-white-striped kerseymere waistcoat, to linger on the shoulders of his well-fitted coat of blue superfine. The color of the material seemed to deepen his eyes to lapis lazuli.

His sharply chiseled features were impassive, but the tight compression of his lips hinted that his emotions weren't quite so sanguine. He was annoyed about something, but exactly what, she didn't know. Probably something that had occurred before he'd arrived, she decided.

"The duke of Ryland," Walker announced a second later.

"Your Grace." Esme gave Ryland a simpering smile that exasperated Eleanor. How could the woman toadeat him so? Had she no pride? "It's kind of you to offer, but our young neighbor will undoubtedly be returning home before Friday—"

"No, I won't," Bertrem said, ignoring the searing glare Esme sent him.

Esme ignored the interruption. "And my granddaughter can't possibly come, because she's in mourning."

"I have it on excellent authority that I may attend social affairs if I don't dance," Eleanor said, absolutely determined to attend the rout. It would be the best chance she was likely to get to ask lots of people about the missing necklace.

"Who said that?" Esme's simpering manner cracked somewhat.

"Why, I did, Mother Bromley," Maria said. "Don't you remember? That was what you told me was the proper thing to do when Cousin Waldo died last year and you wanted to go to Prinny's ball. And that was two days after we buried the poor old soul, not six months, like in Eleanor's case," she added reflectively.

Eleanor glanced at Ryland, surprised to see a glint of laughter in his eyes at Esme's expression of impotent frustration. She felt an answering spark of humor curl through her, dissolving some of her annoyance.

"What is that you have there, Your Grace?" Maria, to the relief of at least four occupants of the room, changed the subject.

"A book." He showed Maria the thick tome he was carrying. "I found a copy of Smithton's *Influence of the Roman Culture on Modern Society* last night in my library." He handed it to Eleanor. "It's even better than Millsaps."

"That's not saying a great deal." Eleanor reluctantly accepted it.

"What kind of book is it?" Esme demanded suspiciously.

"An improving book," Eleanor said.

"A fascinating book," Ryland countered. "Smithton gives an excellent recounting of the influence of the Romans on our present civilization. After you've read it—"

"All of it?" Eleanor opened it, gazing in dismay at the tiny print on the thin pages. She started to close it and then noticed the inscription on the inside cover. "To James from Paul, with love if no comprehension," it read.

Ryland noticed her interest. "My brother. He gave it to me the Christmas before he was killed." The muscles of his jaw clenched, as if he were forcibly holding his emotions in check.

"Such a tragedy," Maria said sympathetically.

"Yes," Ryland said shortly.

"Are you interested in the Romans, Eleanor?" Maria asked.

"No," Eleanor said honestly. "I find the whole lot of them dead bores."

Ryland suddenly backed away from her, and Eleanor looked at him in surprise.

He gave her a lopsided grin that seemed to squeeze her heart. "A comment like that is just tempting Zeus to throw one of his thunderbolts. And I, for one, don't want to be too close when disaster strikes."

"Oh, Your Grace, what a jokesmith you are." Esme tittered.

"He isn't joking, Grandmama," Eleanor said dryly.

"Studied them old Romans at Harrow," Bertrem threw in. "Never saw much sense in 'em myself. Mean to say, them bein' dead and all."

"Mr. Arylesworth, allow me to congratulate you on your common sense." Eleanor decided she liked Bertrem. His understanding might not be all that quick, but he arrived at the proper conclusion in the end.

"Philistines, the lot of you," Ryland said mournfully.

"Would you care for a cup of tea, Your Grace?" Maria asked, with a nervous glance at Esme.

"Thank you, Mrs. Bromley, but I can't remain. I'm due at Whitehall shortly. I merely stopped by to give Miss Wallace the book. You may tell me what you think of his conclusions at your grandmother's rout party tomorrow evening, Miss Wallace."

Eleanor grimaced. "I could tell you now and save you the suspense of waiting and me the bother of reading it."

"You'll be fascinated," he insisted. "Goodbye." With a nod to the others, he left.

Bertrem jumped to his feet. "Must go, too." He sketched a nervous bow and hurried out after the duke.

The minute the front door closed behind them, Esme turned to Eleanor and snapped, "Well, what have you to say for yourself, missy?"

Eleanor studied her grandmother's red face, wondering if Esme had any idea how unattractive she looked when she lost her temper.

"I asked you something, missy," Esme bit out.

"Oh. I thought it was a rhetorical question," Eleanor said.

"What?" Esme glared at her. "Never mind your break-jaw words. I want to know what you mean by taking the duke's book."

"I thought I was displaying good manners," Eleanor said.

"How dare you pretend to be interested in his dreary old ruins?"

"You weren't listening, Grandmama," Eleanor said tightly. "He gave me the book because I said *I wasn't* interested in his dreary old ruins."

"I won't have you putting yourself forward."

"Do you wish me to be rude to him?" Eleanor asked. "If you prefer, I can tell Ryland that my grandmother doesn't approve of my talking to him."

"Why, you impudent—" Esme heaved herself to her feet. "I give you fair warning, missy. I'll have none of your sauce. Ryland is going to marry Drusilla, and he's only being nice to you because you're her penniless, orphaned cousin."

"If his idea of being nice to me is to make me read several thousand pages of a boring history, then I'd just as soon he weren't," Eleanor snapped as Esme's barb struck a nerve. For some reason that she didn't want to examine too closely, the thought that Ryland saw her only as an extension of her cousin grated.

"You remember what I said, missy, or you'll find yourself out in the gutter, where mongrels like you belong." Esme stomped out of the room.

"Don't worry, Eleanor." Maria patted her hand soothingly. "Your uncle and I won't let that happen. But, dear...it might be better if, perhaps...you didn't..."

"Didn't what?" Eleanor asked in exasperation. "I certainly didn't ask Ryland to bring me a book. In fact, I clearly told him I wasn't interested in the Romans. Several times. That woman has to be the most unreasonable person the good Lord ever created!"

"Oh, hush, Eleanor." Drusilla glanced apprehensively toward the door, clearly worried that Esme might return. "She's always like that."

"And no one has seen fit to murder her yet?" Eleanor marveled. "I begin to see why the English lost the Colonies. You lack resolution to do what any sensible person can see must be done."

Drusilla heaved a heartfelt sigh. "Even if we had the resolution, how could we go about it?"

"Murder is highly improper." Maria tried to sound severe.

Eleanor chuckled. "Not according to Machiavelli. He said that a good end justifies evil methods. Although perhaps we could try placating her instead," Eleanor said as she suddenly realized that Drusilla's words gave her an excellent opening to suggest moving Esme's portrait into this room.

"We do that all the time, dear," Maria said. "Mostly, it doesn't answer."

"Then we need to try something different," Eleanor said with seeming casualness. "Something like taking that picture of her out of the back parlor and hanging it over the mantel in here."

Maria looked up at the perfectly unexceptional Turner landscape hanging there and said, "Why would we want to do that, dear?"

"To flatter her," Eleanor said. "Everyone at the party would see it."

"Do you really think it would turn her up sweet?" Maria looked hopeful.

Eleanor stifled a guilty feeling that she was using her aunt to further her own ends. She was doing this for a good cause, she assured herself. She needed to find out if anyone recognized the necklace in the portrait, and she couldn't do that if it were hidden away in a room in the back of the house.

"Well, I don't know if it'll sweeten her mood, but on the other hand, it shouldn't make it any worse," she said.

"Probably not," Maria agreed after a moment's reflection. "But you know, dear, I've noticed that lately the strangest things seem to annoy her. I mean, as you pointed out, it is hardly your fault that Ryland brought you a book. And the Turkish treatment she meted out to poor Bertrem..." Maria sighed. "How I'm supposed to face his mother..."

"Don't worry, Aunt Maria, chances are that he'll never tell her." Eleanor tried to comfort her. "Men don't set the same store by these things as women do."

Eleanor got to her feet and ineffectually shook out her wrinkled black skirts. "I think I'll go find Walker and ask him to have that painting cleaned and ready to hang in here by Friday."

"I hope your idea works," Maria said, without much conviction.

"We could pray that it works," Drusilla offered helpfully. "The minister said that prayer works miracles."

"You could try," Eleanor said dubiously, "but I've often noticed that heaven never seems to grant a miracle when you really need one."

Heaven ran true to form. Not only did it not moderate Esme's vile temper, but it also didn't provide Eleanor with an opportunity to keep the appointment the following afternoon at Hatchards that Connal had forced on her. Even though she deeply resented his order, she had nonetheless intended to go. She felt she owed him that much. Not only was she still engaged in business with him, but he'd been a staunch friend to her father. Added to which, both she and Connal shared similar views on the importance of America winning the present conflict, even if they were at odds over how to accomplish that goal.

But her good intentions came to naught. When she asked her aunt to go to Hatchards with her, Maria told her that not only was she too busy with the preparations for the rout party to go anywhere, but that Esme had taken the carriage to the dressmaker's, leaving them without transportation. Maria had then driven all thought of the tiresome Connal out of Eleanor's mind with the news that Monsieur Pierre had arrived to style Drusilla's hair and had time to do hers while he was there.

Eleanor eagerly accepted her aunt's offer, stilling her guilty conscience by reminding herself that she hadn't made the appointment with Connal in the first place, or even agreed to it. And she had tried to keep it. It wasn't her fault if the Fates were conspiring against her.

Monsieur Pierre turned out to be a dour, taciturn individual who squinted at Eleanor's long, fine hair as if he found the sight personally painful. After giving vent to his lacerated feelings in a flood of incomprehensible French, he snatched up his scissors and proceeded to snip off most of her hair.

Eleanor forced herself to sit silently, trying hard not to think in terms of hostile Indians and scalpings. She succeeded only by reminding herself over and over again what a masterful job he'd done on her cousin's hair.

Her confidence was not misplaced. When Pierre finally pronounced himself satisfied, her long hair had been reduced to a feathery cap of nut-brown hair that curled softly around her face. Eleanor was enormously pleased with the effect. She hadn't needed Drusilla's enthusiastic praise to know just how becoming the style was.

Her pleasure increased tenfold when the gowns her aunt had ordered for her arrived from the dressmaker's later that afternoon. While Eleanor was perfectly aware that lavender was not a color that became her overmuch, it was still an enormous improvement over the rusty black gowns she had been wearing. And the fashionable new Empire styling was very flattering to her thin figure.

It was with a feeling of eager anticipation that Eleanor dressed for her grandmother's rout party that evening. She smiled as she smoothed her hand down over her sleek silk skirt. It felt so soft and luxurious after the rough woolen dresses she'd been wearing. Her smile faded slightly as she focused on the gown's deep décolletage, and she ineffectually tried to rearrange the profusion of narrow lace ruffles that had been sewn around the neckline to hide the swell of her small breasts. Even though her aunt had assured her that the gown would not be thought immodest by London standards, she still felt uncomfortable. Nothing she had ever worn back in Boston had prepared her for it.

Maria had said it was unexceptional, she reassured herself for at least the fifth time, and her aunt was certainly more familiar with the prevailing fashions than she was.

Carefully she brushed her short hair, positioning a few curls so that they caressed her cheeks. Perfect, she thought with satisfaction as she bit on her lips to give them a little more color.

If only the evening went as well. She sent up a silent prayer for success. One thing she had long ago discovered was that most people loved to talk. Surely among the over one hundred and fifty guests invited this evening, she'd find someone who remembered something about the necklace. Anything that might help her with her quest.

Eleanor opened her bedroom door and stepped out into the hall, pausing as the sounds of a string quartet tuning up drifted up the stairwell. A feeling of sadness tore at her composure. Her father had loved music so. She swallowed the huge lump in her throat. If only...

Stop it, Eleanor Wallace, she ordered herself, taking a deep gulp of air and opening her eyes wide against the tears that glittered on her thick lashes. She stiffened her shoulders and forced herself to continue down the hallway, when what she really wanted to do was to retreat to her room and sob her heart out. To rail at the fickleness of a fate that took her father, who had been a good, kind man, and left her grandmother, who had not uttered one kind word to anyone in the entire time Eleanor had been here.

The music grew louder as she reached the first floor, and Eleanor immediately headed to the front salon, intent on making sure that the painting was still where the footman had so carefully hung it earlier.

To Eleanor's relief, it was still there above the mantel.

"It's a beautiful gold frame, isn't it?" Drusilla slipped into the room behind her, and Eleanor turned, her eyes widening at the sight of her cousin. Drusilla was wearing a gown of the palest pink crepe with a spangled scarf casually draped around her slender white arms. Her golden hair had been arranged into a Psyche knot on top of her head. A small faggot of pink silk rosebuds circled the knot, adding a touch of color.

Eleanor sighed, wondering what it would be like to be so beautiful that conversations stopped when you entered a room.

"I like your gown," Drusilla said, with every evidence of sincerity.

Eleanor chuckled. "I don't think it matters what I wear, cousin. With you in the room, everyone will be looking at you."

"I know." Drusilla wrinkled her small nose unhappily. "And I wish they wouldn't."

"You do?" Eleanor asked in surprise. While she'd never known anyone quite as beautiful as her cousin, all the pretty girls she had known had seemed to relish their looks.

"People stare so," Drusilla confided, "and it makes me uncomfortable. And my looks don't really have anything to do with me. I mean, I'm me. Not what I look like. And if I weren't beautiful, then Ryland..."

Then Ryland what, Eleanor wondered. Ryland wouldn't want to marry her? But did he? Her uncle didn't seem to think he did.

"Drusilla..." Eleanor began, only to come to a halt as her grandmother sailed into the room trailed by her aunt and uncle. Esme stopped short when she saw the picture of herself over the mantel.

"Who put that there?" she demanded.

"I did," Eleanor replied promptly.

"Ha!" Esme gave Eleanor a nasty smile. "Won't do you no good to toady to me, missy. I told you. I won't give none of my money to a schoolteacher's brat with ideas above her station."

Eleanor clenched her teeth and counted to ten, afraid that if she opened her mouth what she really thought might pop out. This was not the time to make Esme mad. Her grandmother might take her revenge by banishing her from the party. And if that should happen, Eleanor would miss the best chance she'd had to date of finding a clue to the missing necklace. Clearing her father's name was far more important than swallowing a few insults, she told herself. Revenge would be all the sweeter when it finally came. And it would come, she assured herself, refusing to even consider the possibility of failure.

Satisfied that Eleanor was suitably chastised, Esme walked over to the portrait and studied it with a self-satisfied smile on her thick lips. "I'd forgotten how handsome it looks. That Reynolds painted a fine portrait. Not that he didn't charge the earth to do it. Two hundred I gave him, and it only took a week. Did you ever hear the like?"

"You were buying his talent, not his time," Henry said, pointing out the obvious.

"Fool, what would you know about talent?" Esme glared at him, and Henry subsided into silence.

"You look very nice, Eleanor, dear." Maria, ever the peacemaker, rushed to fill the void. All she accomplished was to redirect Esme's ire.

"Mutton dressed for lamb," Esme said snidely.

"Really?" Eleanor gave her grandmother a genuine smile. "I've always fancied being an older woman. Thank you, Grandmama. You've quite made my evening."

"Bah! Fools, the lot of you. I've—"

"Lord and Lady Jersey." Walker's calm voice cut into her tirade, and Esme quickly rearranged her lips into a smile and went to greet their first guests. Eleanor watched her aunt and uncle hurry after her, feeling sorry for Maria. Her lot in life seemed to be following in the wake of her abusive mother-in-law, trying to soothe the feathers Esme ruffled.

"You really do look very nice, Eleanor, and you'll look even nicer in a few months, when you can wear colors again. Grandmama was simply being..." Drusilla looked over at Esme.

"Her normal self?" Eleanor said dryly. "Would that we knew a cure for it."

Drusilla giggled enchantingly and then suddenly paled and scooted behind Eleanor.

"What's wrong?" Eleanor looked up, and a shiver of excitement exploded in her mind as she caught sight of Ryland waiting to greet his hosts. Compulsively her eyes skimmed over the stark simplicity of his black coat and pantaloons, lingering on the flash of green fire emanating from his emerald tie pin. Somehow, he made every other man look overdressed. But it couldn't be the duke who had frightened Drusilla, could it? She'd seen absolutely no evidence that he'd ever done anything to make anyone fear him. She forced her gaze to move beyond Ryland's elegant figure to study the other arrivals. She didn't recognize any of them, although they looked rather typical of what she'd seen of the English aristocracy to date—overdressed and overweight.

"What's wrong, Drusilla?" Eleanor finally asked.

"Wrong?" Drusilla gave her a wobbly smile. "Why, whatever do you mean?"

"Cut line, cousin," Eleanor said impatiently. "You looked at the door and turned white. What did you see?"

"I was just surprised that Ryland had accepted Grandmama's invitation, that's all," Drusilla said. "He's never come to one of her parties before."

"He hasn't?" Eleanor looked back at him. Esme was telling him something, and very emphatically, too, if the way her double chins were bouncing was any indication.

"From what Grandmama said, I thought he visited here quite often," Eleanor probed.

"Not all that often, and then only to see Papa. Ryland's not a very social person. That's why Grandmama was ever so pleased when his brother died."

Eleanor's eyes widened in disbelief.

"Oh, not that the French killed him," Drusilla rushed to explain. "She didn't care about that."

"That doesn't surprise me," Eleanor muttered.

"What made Grandmama happy was that the duke was so upset he gave up digging for ruins on his estate in Cumberland and came to London to help with the war effort."

"Which made him available to be hunted in the marriage stakes," Eleanor concluded.

"Yes, he…" Drusilla gulped nervously. "Um, excuse me, Cousin Eleanor, but my particular friend Sophy just arrived, and I want to make her welcome." She scurried away.

Eleanor turned and found her field of vision limited to an expanse of crisp white neckcloth. She tilted her head back slightly and looked up. Her gaze was caught and held by Ryland's gleaming blue eyes. A feeling of pleasure that he had immediately sought her out washed over her, only to fade when she realized that he could have been coming to talk to her cousin and, when Drusilla so precipitately left, he'd been too polite to also leave.

"Why are you looking so pensive?" Ryland asked.

"I was thinking," she hedged, wondering how much of his relationship with her cousin was real and how much of it was the product of her grandmother's imagination.

"About the book I gave you to read?" He moved closer, and the faint aroma of sandalwood that she was coming to associate with him drifted into her nostrils, seeming to isolate them from the other people around them.

"No," she said honestly. "I did start to read it, but it was so boring that—"

"Boring!" He looked down his nose at her. "It's fascinating reading."

"Boring," she repeated. "And even then I might have persisted, because my nanny used to say that one should practice self-denial every once in a while, and reading that book would certainly qualify. But you see, I found *The Evil Duke* in the library, and..."

Ryland frowned. "Evil? I can think of several dukes who would come under the heading of foolish, or simply stupid, but hardly evil."

"Not a real one. It's the title of a book."

"You aren't still reading those Gothics, are you?" he asked in disbelief.

"I would be, except that I finished the last one this morning."

"Good. Now, perhaps, you'll read something of value."

Eleanor was about to give him her opinion of what was of value when she saw her grandmother scowling at her. Unless she was mistaken, Esme would be over to capture Ryland as soon as she could escape from the portly gentleman talking to her.

Eleanor glanced up at the portrait. If she were going to find out if Ryland recognized the necklace, she'd have to do it now and not worry about trying to gracefully lead up to it.

"Isn't that a lovely painting?" she asked.

Ryland blinked. "What painting?"

"The one over the fireplace." She gestured toward it. "I discovered it in the back parlor yesterday. It's of my grandmother, you know. She sat for it before I was born."

"She hasn't really changed all that much over the years." Ryland eyed it critically. "The technique is excellent. Reynolds, isn't it?"

"Yes, he certainly was a dab hand at painting jewelry. You can almost see the gleam on that ruby."

"If it's really as big as it is in the portrait, that's hardly a surprise," Ryland said dryly.

"I don't know. I've never seen it. Have you?"

Ryland looked back at the painting, this time studying it more closely. "No, I don't remember ever having seen it. And that's not the kind of bauble one is likely to forget."

Eleanor stifled a sigh, not having realized until this moment just how much she'd been counting on him saying that he had indeed seen it. Around her grandmother's pudgy neck.

"Really, Your Grace—" Esme bore down on them "—you must not allow my granddaughter to monopolize you. Being new to England, she hasn't as yet learned the rules that govern polite society."

"You mistake the matter, Mrs. Bromley," Ryland said, in a level voice that revealed none of the anger he felt at the disparaging way she had spoken of Eleanor. Much as he wanted to tell the old harridan exactly what he thought of her vulgar manners, he knew that if he did, Eleanor would be the one to bear the brunt of Esme's anger. "It was I who saw Miss Wallace and took the opportunity to talk to her. She has been showing me the Reynolds portrait of you."

"Yes, I had it painted right before my daughter...left." She shot Eleanor a venomous glance. "But you're standing too close to view it properly, Your Grace. Come back a ways." She maneuvered him toward Drusilla, who was standing with her friend Sophy by the window.

With a feeling of loss, Ryland allowed himself to be led away. He watched out of the corner of his eye as Eleanor nervously twitched the ruffles around the neckline of her new gown, and a slight smile curved the edge of his firm mouth. He'd been right. She did look much better in color, although that lavender wasn't exactly right. He considered the matter as Mrs. Bromley launched into a monologue that required nothing more than that he nod from time to time. Eleanor should wear vivid colors, he finally decided. Bright colors that reflected the intensity of her vibrant personality and the sharpness of her mind.

He frowned slightly as he watched her approach old Fielding. Why was she talking to that loose screw? His frown deepened as Fielding laughed uproariously at something she had said. Fielding was no fit companion for a green girl who wasn't up to snuff. She'd never recognize him for what he was. Someone should warn her. His frown became a scowl.

"I'm pleased that you agree with me." Esme nodded complacently. "I was horrified, too."

Ryland stared blankly down at her, having not heard a word she'd said.

"Quite," he muttered. "Simply shocking. But I think that Henry is trying to attract your attention." Ryland noticed Henry's frantic glances at his mother with relief.

Esme glared at her hapless son. "I'll have to see what he wants. You talk to Drusilla," she ordered, pointing toward the window. "She's over there with that butter-toothed daughter of the Wilkens'."

Ryland nodded noncommittally, having no intention of allowing himself to be trapped into trying to carry on both ends of a conversation with Drusilla. When Esme moved away, he moved with seeming casualness toward a group of men who were standing directly behind Eleanor.

By the simple expedient of looking enthralled with Denby's account of the brilliance of his last speech in Parliament, Ryland was able to eavesdrop on Eleanor's conversation with Fielding. To his relief, Fielding wasn't subjecting her to his usual heavy-handed gallantry. He was talking about the picture Eleanor had pointed out to him a few minutes ago. Ryland strained to hear their conversation over the growing number of voices in the Bromley salon. Why did hostesses have to try to squeeze in as many people as their rooms would hold? he wondered in exasperation. When he married, he was going to limit his wife to half a dozen guests at a time.

He leaned forward slightly as he caught Eleanor's question about the necklace in the portrait. Why was she fascinated by it? It was as ugly a piece as he'd ever seen, although the stones themselves could possibly be reset into something more modern.

Ryland's curiosity grew as the interminable evening passed and he heard her question at least half of the guests about the necklace. What was the lure of that particular necklace? He didn't know, but he was certain that she had a reason for her questions. A reason he intended to discover. As soon as possible.

Chapter Five

"And Lady Jersey was so kind as to tell me what a delightful time she had at our party last night." Maria recounted her moment of triumph to Eleanor the following afternoon. "Do have some tea, dear."

"Thank you." Eleanor accepted the cup and sniffed the fragrant steam rising above the delicate china.

"Yes," Maria sighed happily. "It was definitively a sad squeeze. I can't tell you how gratified I am."

Would that her evening had been as successful, Eleanor thought glumly. Despite her having asked as many of the guests as she could about the necklace in Esme's portrait, not a single one of them had recognized either it or the principal stones. There had to be someone who knew something. But who would it be, and where could she find them?

"The duke of Ryland." Walker's announcement scattered her thoughts like dry leaves before a brisk autumn wind.

Eleanor's heart seemed to skip a beat at the sight of Ryland's lean face. His lips were lifted in a warm smile, and his eyes sparkled with life. Suddenly, the world seemed filled with exciting possibilities that had somehow been lacking just seconds ago.

"Good morning, Mrs. Bromley. Miss Wallace." He glanced around the room, and Eleanor assumed he was looking for Drusilla, since no one in full possession of his faculties would want to find her grandmother. She ignored her feeling of pique as being small-minded and, as a penance, forced herself to ask, "Where is Drusilla, Aunt Maria?"

"I insisted she rest in her room this afternoon after her late night." Maria smiled proudly. "She is very delicate, you know. Like a fairy princess come to earth.

"Won't you have a cup of tea, Your Grace?" Maria turned to Ryland.

"No, thank you. I merely came by to thank you for a delightful evening last night."

Eleanor watched in affectionate amusement as her aunt seemed to visibly swell with pleasure at his tribute.

"And to invite your daughter and Miss Wallace for a drive. Since Miss Bromley isn't available, perhaps you would like to return your books to Hatchards, Miss Wallace," he said with a feeling of satisfaction. He'd been afraid that Esme would be holding court in her salon this afternoon and he wouldn't be able to escape including Drusilla in the invitation. Something that would have severely hampered his efforts to find out what Eleanor's fascination with that necklace was.

About to eagerly agree, Eleanor paused when she remembered the note Connal had sent ordering her to meet him at Hatchards yesterday. He was bound to be angry that she hadn't gone. But even so, he'd hardly still be there waiting for her.

Though it might not be a bad idea if he were, she decided militantly. Then she could tell him to stop sending messages through the servants, as if there were something unsavory about their acquaintance. She might not be sure how she felt about Connal as a husband, but one thing she was certain of. If her father had approved of their friendship, there was nothing improper about it.

"All that thought for a simple visit to Hatchards?" Ryland's voice broke into her convoluted thoughts.

"Ryland's invitation is unexceptional, dear," Maria assured her.

Her aunt was wrong, Eleanor thought ruefully. There was absolutely nothing about Ryland that was unexceptional. She was fast coming to the conclusion that he was unique. Even in English society.

"I was just trying to decide which books I would get," Eleanor lied. "I'd very much like to go.

"I'll be back in a moment," she told Ryland, and walked sedately from the room. Once out of sight, she sprinted up the stairs to her bedroom, where she jammed her new gray poke bonnet on her head and grabbed her white cashmere shawl, and then rushed back downstairs. She arrived back in the salon with a becoming flush on her thin cheeks and slightly out of breath.

"Have a nice time, dear." Maria smiled benevolently at her. "And if you should find any more books by the author of *The Wicked Duke,* please get them."

"I will," Eleanor promised as she took Ryland's arm.

"Why is it always peers who get cast as wicked?" Ryland complained. "Why not a wicked miller or a wicked confectioner?"

Eleanor chuckled at his aggrieved expression. "Because peers have more free time to devote to perfecting the state of wickedness. A miller's opportunities are far more limited."

She automatically gave his horses a wide berth as she allowed Ryland to hand her up into his carriage. The seat on this one was much lower than the high-perch phaeton he'd driven on their first outing. Lower, roomier, and much more sedate. It would easily seat three people. Had he brought this vehicle because he wanted to invite her cousin, too, or because he feared he might have to invite Drusilla?

Ryland vaulted up beside her and took the reins from his groom, who was perched on the seat behind them.

"How did you like your first ton party?" Ryland asked with seeming casualness.

"My aunt was very gratified with it," Eleanor hedged.

"That was quite obvious," he said dryly. "But it wasn't what I asked."

Eleanor studied him out of the corner of her eye as he expertly guided the restive horses through the street's heavy traffic.

"Well?" he persisted.

"The truth is that with a few exceptions I found the whole affair a dead bore." She opted for the truth.

"I hope I was one of the exceptions?"

Eleanor smiled. "Oh, yes. You only mentioned history once. And I was interested in several of Uncle Henry's friends, who were very taken up with the need for agrarian reform, but as for the rest...they didn't seem..." She frowned, struggling to find the right word. "Real," she finally said. "Most of the ton seems to live in its own little world, and it doesn't bear much resemblance to my perception of reality."

Ryland blinked at her observation. "And you were deprecating the Greek philosophers? You must have absorbed more than you thought, if you noticed that."

Eleanor looked down her nose at him. "I see no reason to be insulting."

"Is London society so different from American?" Ryland slipped in the question in the hopes that he might find out something more about her background.

Eleanor studied a ragged-looking urchin running along the flagstones for a long moment and then said, "Yes. Although it's not easy to explain. For one thing, London society feels different. In Boston, being a part of society depended more on what you were than who your family was."

"Family isn't important in Boston?" Ryland asked skeptically.

"Yes, but not in the same way." She tried to make him understand. "Virtually all our society leaders in Boston either made or significantly enlarged their fortunes in trade, so there isn't the sharp class distinction between the landed gentry and the merchants that you have here. Perhaps it's because we're a newer country that we're so much less rigid in our beliefs."

"Maybe," Ryland said noncommittally, wondering if what she was telling him was true. He didn't know enough about America to know, and to continue to question her about it would be bound to make her suspicious, if she really was spying.

Ryland shot her a quick sideways glance. She was watching the people on Piccadilly Street with a fascinated interest. She couldn't be a spy, he thought, mentally refuting Devlin's suspicions as he expertly pulled his team up in front of Hatchards. After waiting until the groom had reached the horses' heads, he jumped down and walked around the wagon to give Eleanor his hand.

Eleanor grasped his warm fingers, feeling his latent strength as they closed around hers. A shiver of awareness slithered through her, and she found her attention drawn to the firm line of his lips. He had fascinating lips. The unexpected thought popped into her mind. Not too thin, like the villain's in *The Guillotine*, nor too full, like the villain's in *The Deserted Priory*, but just right. What would they feel like pressed against her own? The fugitive thought momentarily disconcerted her.

Ryland reached around her to get her books from the seat, and the tantalizingly musky scent of his warm body teased her senses.

"Thank you." Eleanor took his arm and accompanied him into the bookstore. London was changing her, she thought uneasily. She was discovering completely unexpected facets of her personality.

Eleanor stole a quick sideways glance at Ryland. And a lot of her self-discovery seemed to be centered around the duke—a man who was totally beyond her reach. It was a sobering realization.

With a supreme effort, she banished her disquieting thoughts and returned her books to the smiling clerk before heading toward the shelves of Gothics. Ryland followed her.

"Those things are a waste of good paper," he said in disgust.

"That is an opinion," she muttered, eagerly scanning the shelves for new titles.

"Of an informed mind."

"Sounds more misinformed to me."

Ryland chuckled. "That's giving me the word with no bark on it. Enjoy your atrocious taste in literature while I elevate the order of my mind. I'll be over in the biographies. I want to see if they have that new book about Nelson."

Surreptitiously Eleanor watched him walk away, her attention focused on his graceful stride. As he rounded the end of the stack and disappeared from sight, she mentally shook free of her fascination with the man and turned back to her Gothics, only to let out a startled squeak when Connal seemed to materialize at her side. Bother the man, anyway, she thought in exasperation. Why must he creep around like that and startle her out of her wits?

"Be quiet," Connal muttered out of the corner of his mouth. He jerked a book off the shelf and, opening it, pretended to be reading it.

Under cover of choosing a book, Eleanor probed her reaction to seeing Connal. Exasperation, unease and a sense of foreboding were all mixed up in it, along with several other, less easily defined emotions. What wasn't there was a sense of pleasure. She wasn't the least bit glad to see him, she realized, and squarely faced the fact.

But was her reluctance caused by not wanting to see Connal or by not wanting to hear about his plans to spy? If he had simply come to the house for a social call, would she have been happy to see him then? she wondered.

"I told you to meet me here yesterday." His aggrieved voice interrupted her thoughts. "Where were you?"

"At home," Eleanor answered in the interests of peace, even though she felt he had no right whatsoever to question her movements. "This is London, not Boston. Things are far more formal here. I can't just leave the house whenever I wish. I need an escort and a reason for going and permission to go. I'm not my own mistress here."

Connal grimaced. "I'm sorry," he said grudgingly. "I should have realized that."

"You should have also realized that sending notes by way of a servant was a good way to land us all in the basket. If someone had seen you, Daisy could have found herself on the street without references, and I could have been sent back to America on the first boat."

Connal looked worried. "Is anyone suspicious of you?"

About to say no, Eleanor paused as she suddenly remembered Ryland's repeated questions about her background. He was probably simply curious about America, she thought, trying to reassure herself. He had a very inquisitive mind. All kinds of unexpected things seemed to fascinate him.

"My uncle's family seem to have accepted me at face value," she finally said.

"They really believe you're a destitute orphan?"

Eleanor nodded. "As far as I can tell, they do. My aunt even bought me some new gowns." She gestured toward the French gray jaconet morning dress she was wearing.

Connal never even glanced at it. "What have you found out?"

She deliberately misunderstood him. "That the ton are a group of hedonists."

Connal audibly ground his teeth. "I meant about the military plans your uncle is working on."

"Nothing. He's never mentioned his work, and I can hardly ask."

Connal grimaced. "No, I suppose not. But there's no reason why you can't look."

"At what?"

"His papers." Connal bit off the words as if exasperated beyond belief by her denseness. "Have you been in his study?"

"No. There's no valid reason for me to be there."

"The only valid reason you need is that your country is in sad straits," Connal replied. "The peace talks are going even worse than we'd originally thought. These damn English think they've got us cornered, now that Napoleon is on his last legs."

Eleanor sighed. She didn't want to hear this. Even less did she want to deal with it. But even so, she didn't doubt for a moment that Connal was telling her the truth. If England's negotiators were anything like the Englishmen she'd met in her grandmother's drawing room, then they'd be arrogant enough to demand virtually anything. Or everything.

"You must do as your father would have wanted," Connal urged. "You are the only person that we have in a position to find out anything."

"Connal, I just don't feel right about spying—"

"Hush! Don't use that word."

"I don't care what word you use, I still don't feel that it's honorable."

"You must allow yourself to be guided by me in this," Connal said. "I have your best interests at heart, after all." He gave her a wide smile that showed his gleaming white teeth to perfection. But the smile wasn't reflected in his eyes, Eleanor noticed. His dark brown eyes had no glimmer of humor in them. None at all. They were watchful, waiting. For what? she wondered. For her capitulation?

"My poor honey," he murmured soothingly. "You haven't yet recovered from your father's death. You'll be able to rest much easier in your mind when you know that you've done as he would have wanted you to."

"Possibly," Eleanor muttered, knowing that in that at least Connal was entirely right. Her father would have applauded her spying on the English. But if he'd wanted her to blindly follow his wishes, then he shouldn't have taught her to think for herself, she thought. Because of her own sense of honor she had serious reservations about the morality of what Connal wanted her to do.

"And London must seem so very strange for you," Connal continued, in that same soothing tone that she mistrusted. "Take heart. As soon as I've appeared at a few social functions, I'll be in a position to call on you at your uncle's home. We'll be able to make plans without all this subterfuge."

Eleanor felt herself stiffening in dismay at his news. She didn't want more contact with him. She wanted less. In fact, that was one of the major reasons she had braved the trip across the Atlantic in the first place. To put distance between them while she decided how she felt about Connal and where he fit into her future.

"Who is this person you've found to sponsor you?" she asked.

"Never mind about that." Connal smiled at her, and Eleanor's sense of unease intensified. Something in his smile made her very nervous. As if he knew something she didn't, and should. "All you need to worry about is discovering what your uncle is planning.

"And there's one other thing," he said slowly. "I've found out something about the duke of Ryland."

"Found out what?" she asked curiously.

"He's very important to the war effort. He's one of the men formulating the plans for the final offensive against Napoleon."

Eleanor nodded, not really surprised by Connal's news. She already knew that Ryland was involved in the effort to defeat Napoleon. She simply hadn't known exactly how.

"Being a woman, you've undoubtedly missed the implication," Connal said smugly.

Eleanor bit back an acid retort and, instead, asked the question he clearly wanted her to. "What does it matter if the duke plans troop movements on the Continent?"

"That's where the real gain is." Connal's eyes took on a covetous gleam. "Everyone knows that Napoleon is teetering on the brink of defeat. He would pay a fortune to know what the English are planning next."

"Papa hated Napoleon," Eleanor reminded him. "He called him a Corsican upstart with no pretensions to brains or breeding."

"Circumstances alter sentiments," Connal said. "You must allow me to be the judge of what your father would have wanted if he'd been in possession of all the facts."

"What facts?" she asked, trying to make sense out of his words.

"The only fact that matters is that Ryland has information that we can make very good use of, and I want you to find out what it is."

Eleanor's mouth fell open, and she stared at Connal, not believing what she'd just heard.

"Is it so hard to understand?" he asked roughly. "I want you to find out what the English are planning to do on the Peninsula."

Eleanor closed her eyes on a feeling of unreality. Her role as a spy seemed to be expanding by the moment. Expanding to the point where it was ridiculous.

"I—" she began.

"Shh." Connal turned away from her as two young women moved toward them. "Pretend to be reading until they're gone," he muttered over his shoulder.

Eleanor peered down the aisle past the browsing women, looking for Ryland, with the vague hope that he might rescue her from a situation that was becoming more untenable by the moment. She didn't see him.

Stifling a sigh, she began to pull Gothics off the shelves at random. She could rescue herself, she told herself stoutly. She was a capable woman of independent means, and Connal didn't have the power to force her to do anything against her will. The only hold he had on her was that of affection. And that affection derived from the love she'd had for her father. But as for affection for Connal himself . . .

Eleanor was beginning to wonder if she had ever really known him. Somehow he seemed different here in London from the way he had in Boston. Or, perhaps, it was simply that she hadn't paid much attention to him there, she considered. While her father was alive, her contact with Connal had been minimal. Mostly she'd simply listened to her father singing his praises. That and entertaining him at dinner occasionally. And then, when her father died, she'd been so grief-stricken that Connal as a distinct personality barely registered. All she'd wanted was to be left alone, and Connal had seen that she was. He'd handled all the aspects of the business so that she could mourn her father without interruption. And he'd done a good job of it, too, she admitted. An impeccable job. He really was every bit as good a businessman as her father had claimed. But did that mean that he'd be as good a husband for her as her father had also claimed?

Eleanor peered around again, this time finding Ryland. He was standing at the end of the aisle, talking to a very old lady. She tried to listen, but they were too far away for her to hear their conversation.

"The Life of Nelson?" The old lady peered nearsightedly at the book Ryland was carrying. "Sounds dull as ditchwater."

Ryland smiled at the outspoken old woman, wondering what Eleanor would make of her.

"Good morning, Mrs. Symington. You're looking particularly well."

"Bah! Don't try your flummery on me, Ryland." She poked him in the ribs with her book. "How's your dear mother?"

Ryland sighed. "She hasn't left Cumberland since Paul died. Sometimes I think she misses him more with each passing month, not less."

"Needs a new direction for her thoughts," Mrs. Symington pronounced. "You ought to get married and fill up a nursery for her to dote on. Nothing like a passel of brats to pull one out of the mopes. 'Specially if they take after you."

Ryland chuckled. "I was an unexceptional child."

"Unexceptionably horrendous!" the old lady retorted. "Always up to some mischief or other. 'Course, I will admit there wasn't no vice in you. Like that time at your grandfather's, when you wanted to see if you could fly if you stuck all those feathers to your jacket."

Ryland's laugh reverberated down the aisle, causing several heads to turn and stare. "You were just mad because it was your mattress I took the feathers out of."

"Perhaps," she conceded. "But what about the time you were looking for ghosts and blamed near frightened poor old Foxton into a fit of apoplexy. He was never the same. Took up strong drink."

Ryland opened his mouth to point out that Foxton had been a confirmed tippler fifty years before that ill-fated event, but then paused as something suddenly occurred to him. Mrs. Symington was nearly ninety, with an insatiable love of gossip and a memory like a mantrap. If anyone in London remembered anything about Eleanor's father, it would be her.

"Mrs. Symington," he said slowly, "could you tell me something?"

"Could tell you lots of things. Whether they'd be what you want to hear is another matter."

"It's about an old scandal."

"Yes?" She leaned forward eagerly. "Which one?"

"You remember Mrs. Bromley?"

Mrs. Symington snorted. "She's not the kind of woman one forgets. No matter how hard you try."

"Well, this time try to remember. About twenty-seven years back, she had a daughter who had just made her bows."

"Hmm..." Mrs. Symington squinted contemplatively at the row of books in front of her. "I recall. Emily was her name. An Incomparable she was. Took the ton by storm. Fact is, Ryland, she looked a lot like the granddaughter... um..."

"Drusilla?"

"That's the one. Same golden hair, blue eyes, perfect complexion."

"Same moderate understanding?" Ryland asked.

"If by that you mean was Emily fly to the time of day, then the answer is no. She was every bit as hen-witted as this Drusilla seems to be."

"What happened to Emily?"

"As I remember, she fell in love with a tutor the Bromleys had hired to prepare the younger boy for Oxford. Old Mrs. Bromley was fit to be tied. Rumor had it that she was all set to sell the girl to an old roué with a minor title." Mrs. Symington lapsed into a contemplative silence.

"And..." Ryland prodded.

"And the young lovers eloped. To foreign parts. Old Mrs. Bromley was mad as fire. Disowned the gel and wouldn't have her name mentioned in the house. She must have changed her mind, though, because I heard from Lady Jersey that she's giving a home to Emily's daughter. Although, knowing Esme Bromley, it's more likely she's only letting the gel live with her so's she can make her life miserable. Esme Bromley is a mean-spirited, old tartar! Always was and always will be."

"And the man Emily married..."

"Daniel... Daniel Wallace was his name. Scotch, I believe. Some country family from near..." She frowned. "I can't remember, but I do know that as far as I was concerned, his family was more than good enough for the likes of Esme Bromley."

"Did you ever hear anything more about them after they eloped?"

"Just that poor Emily died a few years later in childbed. Then, of course, Daniel died this last year. Other than that, I never heard anything."

And if Mrs. Symington hadn't heard it, it hadn't been said, Ryland conceded. Which didn't tell him much more about Eleanor than he already knew.

"Why the interest in old scandals?" Her voice sharpened. "There ain't no truth to the rumor I heard that you was dangling after the Bromley chit, is there?"

"Absolutely not!" His voice was emphatic. "I simply see her from time to time because I work with her father on policy matters. That's where I met Eleanor Wallace."

"Oh?" Mrs. Symington gave him a shrewd look. "And if this Eleanor Wallace raised enough interest for you to ask questions, she must take after her father. You never was one to fall victim to a pretty face hiding an empty cockloft."

"I feel for her uncomfortable position in the household," Ryland said, hedging.

"Any good Christian would feel sorry for another human being dependent on Esme Bromley's goodwill. Hah! There's my coachman pulling up." She gestured toward the window. "Must go."

Ryland thoughtfully watched her leave as he considered what she'd told him. Daniel Wallace really had had a daughter. If Eleanor was that daughter, it would explain several things about her. Such as her unusual education, her impeccable accent and her excellent manners. And, having grown up without a mother, she would have served as her father's hostess, which would also account for her self-assured manner. Yes, Ryland thought, it was beginning to appear that the woman who'd shown up at Henry's really was his niece and not an impostor. If he could just find someone who had actually met her and her father in Boston, he'd know for sure.

He felt a sudden, inexplicable urge to talk to Eleanor, and he started toward the Gothics, pausing when he saw her talking to a man. No, Ryland realized with a sense of disquiet. Not just a man, but the same man she'd been talking to the first time he brought her here.

Ryland cautiously inched closer to them, trying to look engrossed in the titles in front of him while he continued to watch them out of the corner of his eye.

They were definitely talking. At least the man was talking. Eleanor was listening. And none too happily, judging from the exasperated expression on her face. She looked... harassed, he finally decided. As if she wanted to get rid of the man and didn't quite know how to do it.

Ryland frowned. It was possible. Eleanor Wallace was a very strange mixture of intelligence and naïveté. She might not know how to send the man about his business without causing a scene. Something no well-bred lady, even one newly arrived from the Americas, would want to do.

The man could have seen Eleanor arrive with him both times and assumed that her acquaintance was worth cultivating, Ryland considered. From the provincial cut of the man's jacket, he appeared to be a stranger to London. Perhaps he was an adventurer who spent his afternoons in Hatchards trying to strike up acquaintances with women who might be able to offer him social advancement?

It was hardly likely that the man spent his afternoons at Hatchards waiting to talk just to Eleanor, Ryland conceded. No, if there really was something between them, there were far better ways to arrange meetings than this. The man was undoubtedly a cit looking for an entrée into polite society. But that entrée most assuredly wouldn't be Eleanor, Ryland thought as he started to move toward them.

"The devil!" Connal exclaimed in annoyance as he caught sight of Ryland. "I want to meet the duke first in a social setting. You remember what I told you." He set the book he'd been holding back on the shelf and began to move away, trying to make his retreat appear casual.

"Who was that?" Ryland frowned at Connal's disappearing back.

"He didn't introduce himself," Eleanor said in perfect truth. "He was changing his mother's books, and he wanted to thank me for recommending Gothics to him last time." Eleanor did her best to sound disinterested. To her relief, Ryland didn't pursue the matter. A fact for which she was very grateful. Maintaining a network of lies was a strenuous undertaking.

"If you're finished, I'll drive you back home," Ryland said.

"Yes, thank you," Eleanor replied promptly, refusing to allow her disappointment that their outing was over show. It was just that she so seldom got to go anywhere, she told herself. She wanted to savor the sense of freedom escaping the house gave her.

The ride back was over far too quickly for Eleanor, but Ryland appeared preoccupied. He refused her invitation to come in for tea, citing a meeting at Whitehall as an excuse.

He couldn't be all that taken with her cousin, or he would have taken advantage of her invitation and come inside to see if she was downstairs yet, Eleanor thought. Or perhaps he really did have an important meeting. Perhaps his hurrying away was a reflection neither on how much he'd enjoyed himself with her nor on how much he might want to see Drusilla, Eleanor considered as she hurried up the steps to her grandmother's front door. That was the trouble with a guilty conscience, she thought ruefully. Because you know you're hiding secrets, you begin to assume that everyone else is.

"Good afternoon, Miss Eleanor." Walker opened the door for her and took her books. "Did you have a pleasant outing?"

"Yes, thank you." She smiled at him. "And profitable, too, as you can see." She nodded towards the books.

"Yes, Miss Eleanor." Walker looked uncertain. "I shall have the footman take them up to your room."

Where her grandmother wouldn't see them and be outraged that someone in her family was actually reading, Eleanor thought in exasperation. Someone needed to do something about that woman. But what, that was the question. What could anyone do that was both moral and legal? And who was going to do it? Her uncle Henry? Not if he really was dependent financially on his mother.

"Is something the matter, Miss Eleanor?" Walker broke into her circular thoughts.

Yes, Eleanor thought. What's wrong is my total lack of knowledge about the family. But she could hardly question the servants.

"No, nothing, thank you." Eleanor gave him the only possible answer. "I'm just going to have a cup of tea in the salon." She started up the stairs, hoping that Esme wouldn't be there. Having to deal with her vitriolic grandmother on top of Connal would simply be too much to cope with in one afternoon.

For once, luck was on her side. The only inhabitants of the salon were Drusilla, her aunt and Bertrem Arylesworth.

"Good afternoon." Eleanor gave them a warm smile. Only her aunt returned the smile. Drusilla turned a becoming shade of pink, and Bertrem nervously bounded to his feet.

"Afternoon, Miss Wallace." He made her an awkward leg.

"Good afternoon." Eleanor sat down beside her aunt, beginning to feel like the specter at the feast. It was obvious that she was making both her cousin and Bertrem uncomfortable. What she didn't know was why. She glanced over at her aunt, who was placidly pouring out the tea. They could hardly have been doing anything they shouldn't, with Maria in the room.

"Ryland was kind enough to take me to Hatchards to exchange my books," Eleanor offered.

Drusilla stared at her in dismay while Bertrem cleared his throat and mumbled, "Marvelous things, books."

So's conversation, Eleanor thought wryly. Not that she was likely to find any here.

"Here you are, dear." Maria handed Eleanor a cup of tea. "Drink it while it's still hot."

Eleanor took a reviving sip, surreptitiously watching Drusilla as she whispered something to Bertrem. A minute later he jumped up and said, "Must go. Been twenty minutes."

"It has been the better part of an hour, Bertrem," Maria observed without rancor, "but if you must go..."

"Yes, she'll be back soon." He nodded emphatically, and Eleanor had no doubt who the she who was expected back soon was. She didn't blame him one bit for escaping while he had the chance.

"I'll walk you to the door, Bertrem," Drusilla said.

Eleanor watched them leave and then turned to her aunt, curious about their relationship.

"Bertrem seems like a nice young man," she said, probing.

"He is. There's not an ounce of vice in him." Maria sighed despondently.

"Is that a reason to be mournful?"

"Esme does not approve of him."

"Is his family..." Eleanor gestured expressively.

"Not at all. They're a good country family. But Esme is determined that Drusilla marry Ryland. And I must say it would be by far the better thing."

Eleanor frowned. "Why must you say it?"

"Because Ryland is so very rich, don't you see?" Maria said earnestly. "And while Bertrem's family isn't exactly poor, the agricultural problems have hit them hard. Bertrem's dear mother confided in a letter to me just last month that she was going to have to wait a year to present Bertrem's sister because of funds being so low."

"I see," Eleanor said slowly.

"Drusilla may not think so now, dear, but, believe me, it is so much more pleasant to be beforehand with the world. Having to always pinch and scrape and make do..." Maria glanced apprehensively at the door. "Even putting aside Esme's plans, and I'm not sure just how we could, Ryland would make a much better husband. He'd be so much more supportive of all her little fears."

But what did Ryland think about being cast in the role of prop to Drusilla's inadequacies, Eleanor wondered. Somehow, for all his politeness, she didn't think he'd be an easy man to maneuver into anything. She shivered as she remembered Connal's blithe instructions to find out what Ryland knew.

No. It wasn't Connal's or her grandmother's wishes that would prevail in the end, Eleanor thought. It would be Ryland's. The only question was, what was it that he wanted?

Chapter Six

Aha, success! Ryland felt a flash of triumph as he finally located his quarry in the far corner of White's reading room. It had taken him most of the morning to find someone in the Foreign Office who could remember the name of a trade delegate who had been in Boston before the current war had broken out. And then it had taken him another two hours to run Lord Talbort to earth at his club. Perhaps now he could get some firsthand information about Eleanor and her father.

Ignoring the glare he was receiving from the octogenarian reading his paper by the roaring fire, Ryland walked across the room and sat down beside a portly old man of about seventy who was gently snoring into his crumpled neckcloth.

Ryland tried softly clearing his throat. The only result was another glare from the elderly reader. So he gently shook Lord Talbort by his padded jacket shoulder.

"Hmm?" Lord Talbort opened his eyes, blinked and looked around in confusion. "Who are you, lad?" he muttered.

"Ryland, sir. The Foreign Office thought you might be able to help me."

Talbort studied him from beneath his bushy eyebrows. "Did, eh? Might I ask why?"

"Harrumph!" The old man by the fire rattled his paper and scowled at them.

"Oh, be quiet, Archie." Lord Talbort was plainly unimpressed. "Stands to reason His Grace's got something of importance to say, or he wouldn't be wasting his time chasing after an old man like me.''

"Not important to me," Archie snapped, and retreated behind his paper.

"Now, Your Grace, what is it you want?" Talbort asked.

"Information. You were in Boston on a trade mission a few years ago?"

Talbort nodded. "Before this demmed war broke out. Most ill-advised action the American Congress ever took."

"Yes, sir," Ryland agreed. "But about Boston. While you were there, did you meet a man named Daniel Wallace?"

"Wallace...Wallace..." Talbort squinted, his eyes fixed on some distant vision. "I was only in Boston a few days. Most of the negotiating was done in Philadelphia. My memory isn't what it used to be," he muttered. "I can't quite... Wait a minute. Boston, you say? I remember now." He smiled widely.

Ryland bit back his sense of impatience and prodded, "You remember Daniel Wallace?"

"Yes, as I recall he owned a shipyard that built trading vessels and fishing boats. Or, at least, he owned part of it." Talbort frowned. "Seems to me there was a partner. An arrogant young fire-eater. Don't recollect his name, though. Wallace did most of the talking. Understood the problems of tariffs real well. Also didn't seem to be in prime twig," Talbort said reflectively. "The delegation had dinner at his house one evening, and he looked kind of gray and short of breath."

"At his house," Ryland asked eagerly. "Did he have a wife?"

"No," Talbort said slowly. "Don't remember a wife. Remember a daughter. I remember her because of how worried she was about him. She watched him all the time."

"What did she look like?"

"Kind."

"Kind?" Ryland repeated impatiently. He needed to know if the Eleanor Wallace who'd appeared at Henry's house matched the description of the Eleanor Wallace who'd lived in Boston, and the only person he'd found who could verify her identity only remembered "kind." What sort of description was that?

"Kind," Talbort repeated stubbornly. "She had warm brown eyes that seemed to smile at you."

"But what did she look like?" Ryland persisted.

"She wasn't an Incomparable, if that's what you're getting at," Talbort said. "I vaguely remember brown hair. Long, it was." He pursed his lips together consideringly. "She wasn't too big. About seven stone, and as tall as your shoulder. Maybe an inch more. But I tell you, it wasn't her looks you remembered, it was her kindness."

Talbort's description of that Eleanor Wallace tallied with the Eleanor Wallace who'd arrived at Henry's, Ryland conceded. And his Eleanor did smile with her eyes. He felt an unexpected warmth slowly unfurl in his chest as his mind obligingly recalled the exact tilt of her soft pink lips and the sparkling glimmer of laughter that always seemed to lurk in the back of her eyes, inviting one to share the humor of the situation.

"You say Daniel Wallace had the delegation to dinner?" Ryland persisted.

"Yes, he said it," Archie grumbled from behind his paper. "Heard him myself. Clear over here."

Ryland ignored him. "Then Daniel Wallace must have been a man of some substance?"

"Well...as to that...not sure how much substance," Talbort said slowly. "Like I said, there was that young man who was introduced as his partner, and a partner cuts into profits. The house was big, but that's not to say that it wasn't mortgaged to the hilt. No need to tell you how hard the shipbuilding industry's been hit by this demmed war. And Wallace being so sick and all..." Talbort shrugged. "Could well have lost the business to the bank or the moneylenders. Or his partner could've cheated him out of it. Seemed the type."

"I see. Thank you very much for your information, sir." Ryland got to his feet. "You've been a great help."

"Glad to be of service," Talbort said earnestly. "Don't get much chance to be of service to anyone at my age. Come again."

"Hummph!" Archie gave his opinion of the invitation in no uncertain terms.

"I may need to do that, sir," Ryland said as he left the reading room. He collected his high-crowned beaver hat from the butler and slowly walked down the steps into the bright sunshine as he considered what Talbort had told him. It would appear that Eleanor Wallace was exactly who she said she was. As for her reasons for coming to England . . .

Ryland automatically skirted a street vendor selling meat pies. Talbort was right about the precarious state of shipping since the war. Her father could have lost everything. Eleanor could have found herself without a feather to fly with when her father died. It could have been a choice of risking an ocean crossing in the middle of a war or staying in Boston and quite literally starving. It all fit together very neatly. Talbort's limited physical description of her matched, and her dire financial circumstances were explained. As well as the fact that she didn't act like any penniless relation he'd ever known. She simply wasn't used to the role.

Even if she had managed to salvage a few pounds from her father's business after his death, she could still have wanted to be with what family she had left. Or she could have decided to see if she could find a husband on this side of the Atlantic, since she hadn't managed to do so on the other.

Ryland frowned as he absently hailed a passing hackney coach and climbed in. Why hadn't she married before now? Granted, she wasn't an Incomparable like her cousin, but she had countenance. And she was certainly intelligent enough. Perhaps her father had been ill for some time, and she hadn't wanted to leave him alone? Or perhaps her father's business had not been prospering even before the war, and he hadn't been able to provide her with a dowry? Few men had the luxury of being able to ignore their bride's financial position when they considered marriage.

He had that luxury, Ryland thought as he stared blankly at the passing landscape. He could afford to marry where he chose. His eyes narrowed thoughtfully as in his mind's eye he saw Eleanor sitting at the foot of his table. He swallowed hard as suddenly, unbidden, a tantalizing image of her lying in his huge bed at Ryland House flooded his thoughts. Of her turning to him and holding out her arms welcomingly. Of her small white breasts visible through a thin, almost transparent silk negligee in a soft pink to match the flush of desire riding her cheeks. Unconsciously his fingers curled into fists. He could almost feel Eleanor's soft flesh. Her skin would smell of roses. Roses and fresh air and love. His body hardened at the thought.

"Whitehall," the driver announced, pulling the carriage to a stop.

Ryland shook his head slightly, forcibly banishing the seductive images that were playing havoc with his self-control. Tossing a coin to the man, he climbed out onto the flagstones.

Although, just because his preliminary findings pointed to the conclusion that Eleanor Wallace was who she claimed to be didn't mean that she was necessarily harmless, he conceded. Even if she really was Henry's niece from Boston, she could still be a spy. Despite her English roots, she had been born and raised in America. He should continue to keep an eye on her, he decided. A very close eye.

He squinted up at the clear blue of the afternoon sky. It was a beautiful day for a drive. Sunshiny and not too cold. After he'd concluded his business at Whitehall, he'd call on Eleanor. If he were lucky enough to find her grandmother from home, he would take Eleanor out alone in the carriage. But he'd keep the conversation away from any political slant. If she really was spying, it might make her suspicious. Instead, he'd talk about other things and occasionally slip in questions about her background.

In fact, he'd use the opportunity to talk to her about Plutarch's view of the Trojan War. He found it inconceivable that someone as well educated as she was could have dismissed the whole affair as merely an immoral rampage on Paris' part. He'd explain the historical significance to her so that she had a more comprehensive view, he decided with a sense of happy anticipation. He'd also suggest a few books for her to read. She was probably spending her afternoon reading those appalling Gothics.

Ryland was wrong. Eleanor wasn't reading her Gothics. She was sitting in her grandmother's salon, practicing restraint in the face of extreme provocation.

"What does she need another new dress for?" Esme eyed the deep flounce around the hem of Eleanor's simply cut violet Indian muslin gown with distaste.

"Four day dresses, three evening gowns and one ball gown can hardly be thought excessive," Maria offered from her spot beside the fireplace. "Why, you yourself have—"

"I pay for my own clothes!" Esme snapped. "I'm not a pauper living on other people's charity."

"Grandmama!" Drusilla gasped with an apologetic glance at Eleanor, who was forcing herself to conjugate Latin irregular verbs. Something she did when she was in imminent danger of losing her temper.

"You didn't pay for Eleanor's gowns," Maria murmured. "I bought them out of my allowance."

"And who pays for that allowance?" Esme cackled nastily. "I suppose the fact that you bought her a ball gown means that you intend for her to come to the Jerseys' ball tonight."

"Everyone knows that she is here, and everyone also knows that she is only in half mourning," Maria pointed out. "And she was at our own rout party. Indeed, it would look very strange if you were to try to keep her hidden away now."

"I've told her and I'll tell you—when she returns my necklace, I'll find her a husband. A cleric."

"I thought I got to choose between a widower and a cleric," Eleanor said, entering the fray.

"Don't give me none of your sauce, missy!" Esme snapped. "I want my necklace."

Esme couldn't want it any more than she wanted to give it to her, Eleanor thought grimly. Nothing would give her greater satisfaction than to be able to fling that barbaric piece of jewelry into Esme's fat red face.

"I hardly think Eleanor could have it, Mother Bromley," Maria said. "After all, she wasn't even born when it disappeared."

"I know that!" Esme yelled. "Her father took it! But that's not to say that he didn't give it to her when he died!"

Drusilla tried to help. "You don't know that, Grandmama."

"Bah! You're all a pack of fools, and I have no intention of sitting here and listening to your ravings. Come, Drusilla." She heaved herself to her feet. "I wish to make several calls this afternoon. You may accompany me."

"But, Grandmama." Drusilla glanced furtively toward the door. "Someone might come."

Which undoubtedly meant that Drusilla had planned to meet Bertrem this afternoon, Eleanor thought, feeling sorry for her cousin. But inconvenient or not, Drusilla might as well give in and accompany her grandmother, because even if they stayed home, Esme would be appallingly rude to poor Bertrem. He'd be routed in minutes.

Esme pursed her lips consideringly. "Possibly. I've noticed that Ryland has started visiting with gratifying frequency." She gave Drusilla an approving look.

"Oh, no!" Drusilla looked appalled. "He comes to see Papa about the war."

Esme nodded knowingly. "That's his excuse to call. But then he stays to visit. Just you make sure that you don't do anything to give the duke a disgust of you, missy," Esme warned. "I'll see you married to him if it's the last thing I ever do."

"Drusilla is incapable of giving anyone a disgust of her," Eleanor hurriedly said, afraid that Drusilla might inadvertently tell Esme that she wasn't the one that Ryland talked to. That it was Eleanor.

"That's because Drusilla has had the advantage of being raised in my household," Esme said smugly, and Eleanor went back to conjugating irregular verbs.

"Come, Drusilla, I wish to call on the countess Lieven." Esme stalked out of the room, trailed by the dispirited Drusilla.

Eleanor waited until she heard the front door close behind them and then turned to her aunt.

"Aunt Maria, may I ask you a question?" she said, deciding that, good manners notwithstanding, there were some things she needed to know about the family finances.

"Certainly, dear, not that I know much."

Eleanor cut straight to the heart of the matter. "Is Uncle Henry financially dependent on his mother?"

Maria sighed. "Unfortunately, yes. All he owns is the family estate, which is sadly depleted."

"But why did Grandfather Bromley not make adequate provisions for Uncle Henry? I mean, his other son and daughter were already dead. Why would he leave everything except the run-down family estate to Grandmother? He must have known what she was like."

"None better. She didn't treat him any differently than she treats us. But he did his best by Henry. He left him everything he had to leave."

"But—"

"The money wasn't his," Maria told her. "It always was Esme's. You see, your Grandfather Bromley came into his inheritance at far too young an age, and proceeded to squander it. I think deep basset was his weakness, or was it faro?" She looked thoughtful. "But no matter. The end result was that by the time he was thirty he was left without a feather to fly with. Not only that, but he was deeply in debt. He was faced with either marrying an heiress or being rolled up." Maria sighed. "Father Bromley used to say that he should have tried the fleet. That it couldn't have been any worse. Unfortunately, he didn't. He opted for an heiress, and the only heiress who would have him was Esme. So he married her. Then he found out that her father had tied up her funds so that he couldn't touch them. Esme had complete control."

"And proceeded to exercise it," Eleanor observed.

"Quite true, dear. It is very hard to live with someone who threatens to throw you out if you don't cater to her every whim. That's why I want Drusilla to marry Ryland. If she does, then she won't ever have to dance attendance on her grandmother again. She'll be safe, don't you see?"

"I see the logic, but, Aunt Maria, marriage is more than just being safe."

"If you mean love, dear, believe me it's vastly overrated. Why, I was fathoms deep in love with my father's second footman when I married Henry, and I have been very happy. At least I would be, if it weren't for..." Maria glanced furtively at the door.

What this family needed was a stiff dose of gumption, Eleanor thought. Or money. But her father would turn over in his grave if she were to spend so much as a farthing of his hard-earned blunt on his wife's family. What was more, she was certain that he would have had very little sympathy for Henry's plight. Her father had been a man of action. When he found himself in a similar situation to her grandfather Bromley's, he'd rolled up his sleeves and earned his own fortune. Not tried to marry an heiress. No, Eleanor conceded. Her father would have dismissed his wife's family as a gormless lot and never given them or their plight a second thought.

"Don't look so sad, dear." Maria smiled gently at her. "The situation isn't entirely hopeless. Henry has his work, and I have Drusilla, and we'll find you a nice husband. You see if we don't."

"I guess," Eleanor said slowly. "If you'll excuse me, I think I'll go to my room for a while. I want to finish my latest Gothic."

"Certainly, dear. It would never do to be caught reading down here. Esme would rant for days." Maria smiled conspiratorially at her. "And could I have it when you're finished? I absolutely adored *The Guillotine.*" Her eyes gleamed with the pleasure of remembered terror.

Eleanor giggled at her aunt's expression. "Why, Aunt Maria, I hope you aren't being corrupted."

Maria sighed, looking wistful. "I think it would be nice to be corrupted. Just once. Don't you?"

"I'm not sure. It might be interesting, with the right hero."

"Oh, no, dear. With the villain," Maria said seriously. "Haven't you noticed that all of Mrs. Radcliffe's heroes bear a striking resemblance to those thoroughly boring, sickeningly good men the minister extols every Sunday?" She shook her head emphatically. "No, I want a villain."

"I'll try to remember that." Eleanor got to her feet. "But I have the lowering feeling a villain would be very wearing to live with."

"Probably. But just once it would be nice to try. Be sure to come back down in an hour or so. Your grandmother will be back by then," Maria called after her.

Poor Aunt Maria, Eleanor thought as she headed toward the back stairs. How sad to have such a boring life that she hungered for the excitement of a villain. But was Maria's life really all that different from those of most women of her class? They all seemed to be so . . .

Eleanor lost her train of thought as she passed her uncle's study and noticed the door was ajar. She stopped and, trying to appear casual, quickly glanced up and down the hall. It was empty. Walker was nowhere to be seen, and the footman had no doubt gone with her grandmother.

She stared at the opening for a long moment. Connal wanted her to find out what information her uncle had. It wouldn't hurt to look, she finally decided. She didn't have to take anything. All she had to do was to look. And if there was nothing to look at, she could tell Connal that she couldn't find anything with a perfectly clear conscience.

With a last furtive glance around the deserted hallway, Eleanor silently eased the door open. She slipped inside and carefully closed the door behind her, then leaned against the wooden panels and took a deep breath. She felt as if the whole world must know what she was doing.

Telling herself that this was no time for thinking, this was time for acting, she hurried across the thick carpet toward the oversize Sheraton desk to one side of the fireplace. It was littered with stacks of papers. They covered every square inch of the surface.

Eleanor sighed in dismay. Where did one begin to look for information in that mess, and how would she know when she found something worthwhile? She picked up a sheet from the stack nearest her and squinted down at the crabbed handwriting.

"Gulong cakes?" she muttered, trying to decipher it. It was hopeless. She set it down and picked up another. It consisted of rows and rows of numbers unaccompanied by any identifying symbols. The numbers could have represented anything from troop supplies to farm animals to flowers.

Eleanor grimaced. If these papers were a sample of military planning, then her uncle must be serving in the cryptology department. She rounded the desk and opened the top drawer. It was stuffed with yet more papers. Papers whose ink had faded. Older, she decided. Much older. They couldn't be of any interest to Connal. She shoved the drawer closed and opened another. The papers in it looked slightly more promising. She was riffling through them when she suddenly heard the sound of her uncle's voice in the hallway outside. An icy trickle of fear bubbled through her mind, momentarily freezing her thought processes.

Please, Lord, don't let him come in... Eleanor sent up the distraught prayer while her gaze skittered frantically around the small room. There was a large leather chair on the other side of the fireplace and a globe in a stand beneath the room's lone window. There were no doors other than the one that led into the hallway.

Eleanor sped over to the window and tugged on the sash, but it refused to budge. Which was probably for the best, she conceded. It was a fifteen-foot drop to the flagstones below. She might as well try explaining what she was doing snooping in her uncle's study as to try explaining why she was lying with a broken limb or two on the street below.

But what possible explanation could she give for being in her uncle's study, other than the truth? And she could hardly do that. Unless...

Feverishly, she ran around the desk and jerked open the middle drawer. To her relief, it held some blank paper. Yanking out several sheets, she waited with a sense of impending doom for her uncle to appear.

There was a strange buzzing in her ears as the door slowly opened and Henry's bulky frame filled it.

"Eleanor!" He looked surprised to see her. "What are you doing in here?"

"Umm, I'm so sorry, Uncle Henry. I hope you don't mind, but I wanted to write to friends back in Boston and tell them that I've arrived safely, and I didn't have any paper, and..." She didn't have to fake the nervous, guilty note in her voice. It was all too real.

"Oh, my dear. I'm so sorry." Henry dropped the stack of papers he was carrying on the already overloaded desk. "I didn't even think to provide you with pocket money. I've just been that busy, what with the trouble in the Colonies and that monster rampaging all over Europe... Not that that's an excuse. I'll speak to my man of business about giving you an allowance so that you won't have to go foraging again." He smiled warmly at her.

"Thank you very much, Uncle Henry," Eleanor muttered, feeling like the greatest villain unhanged. She'd been trying to spy on him, and he was castigating himself for not remembering to give her money. And not only that, but she was relatively certain that in order to give her an allowance, he was going to have to first give up something himself.

"That's all right, Eleanor. You take what you want."

Eleanor took the paper she'd been clutching and all but ran from the room. What she couldn't run from was the oppressive feeling of guilt that weighed on her mind. Her poor uncle trusted her, and he shouldn't. Because she wasn't trustworthy. At least not when it came to a choice between his best interests and her father's.

Eleanor let out her breath on a long, shaky sigh as she fled up the back stairway to her bedroom. Things were so complicated. She envied Connal his black-and-white view of the situation. America was his country, and its interests came first. No matter who got hurt, America's interests had to prevail. Unfortunately, she was not so clear-sighted. Her feelings for her mother's family kept getting in the way. Life as she saw it wasn't painted in stark shades of black and white, but in a variety of muted grays.

Eleanor knew that she was attempting to rationalize her indecision. She also knew she couldn't sit on the fence forever. Sooner or later, she was going to have to decide where she belonged. It was not a choice she relished making, because no matter which side she chose, someone was going to be hurt.

But it wasn't a choice she had to make now, she told herself. Now she could escape into a Gothic, where choices were easy. Where good was clearly defined and evil entirely black. In an hour or so, she'd worry about the real world. With luck, she wouldn't have to see Connal for days. And if she were really lucky, Ryland might come to call this afternoon. She plopped down on her bed and picked up her book, hoping it would soothe her frazzled nerves.

"We goin' straight home, Your Grace?" Wells gave Ryland a hopeful look as he picked him up at Whitehall.

"Home?" Ryland considered the question. He'd just spent a wearying two hours trying to convince a bunch of shortsighted government ministers that it was in England's best long-term interests to adequately support the troops for the final assault against Napoleon. He was tired and out of sorts. But he didn't want to go back to his empty mansion in Berkeley Square. He wanted to see Eleanor, he admitted. He wanted to talk to her. To listen to her practical observations, which would be so welcome after the idiotic theories he'd just endured. And, while it was too late to take her for a drive, as he'd hoped to do, it wasn't too late for a social call.

Giving in to the compulsion to see her, he turned his curricle toward Grosvenor Square, and Wells stifled a sigh at the delay in getting his cold pint.

Ten minutes later, Ryland pulled up in front of Esme's house and, handing the reins to Wells, said, "Walk them around the square. I shouldn't be more than twenty minutes."

"Yes, Your Grace." Wells gave silent thanks for the time limits polite society set on social calls as he urged the horses forward.

Ryland self-consciously tugged the front of his blue-and-white-striped waistcoat and then mocked himself when he realized what he was doing. He was checking on a potential information leak, he told himself. It wasn't necessary that he look his best. Not that Eleanor was likely to be impressed if he was, he admitted ruefully. Even his title hadn't impressed her. In fact, she seemed to set even less store by it than he did.

"Afternoon, Your Grace?" The voice didn't sound any too certain of the fact, and Ryland turned to find a young man standing on the flagstones near the street.

Ryland's memory obligingly supplied a name. Bertrem Arylesworth. A country neighbor of the Bromleys in Lincolnshire. A place that Esme Bromley quite obviously wished Bertrem would return to—and, unless he was very much mistaken, Drusilla didn't. But why was Arylesworth lurking out here? Had Esme refused him the door? Or was he afraid to put his luck to the touch?

"Good afternoon," Ryland replied. "Are you calling on the Bromleys?"

"If you are . . ." Bertrem looked for all the world like the hopeful spaniel Ryland had had when he was just a boy.

"Certainly, come along." Ryland rapped on the lion-head knocker. The door was opened almost immediately by Walker, who greeted the duke with the reverence due his title and then smiled benevolently at Bertrem.

"All of the ladies are receiving in the salon," Walker said.

Ryland handed his curled beaver hat to the butler and, unable to restrain his eagerness a second longer, sprinted up the stairs to the salon. Bertrem, clearly happy to bring up the rear, trailed along behind.

When Ryland reached the salon, he paused in the doorway, his eyes quickly scanning the room. He located Eleanor immediately. She was sitting by herself on the sofa, knitting a black something or other and ignoring the hectoring sound of her grandmother's voice complaining about the cost of georgette.

"His Grace, the duke of Ryland." Walker finally reached the door, out of breath and puffing slightly. "And Mr. Bertrem," he added.

Ryland watched in satisfaction as Eleanor's head quickly swung around and her deep brown eyes immediately focused on him, not even bothering to look for Bertrem. A slight pink washed over her prominent cheekbones, adding some much-needed color to her face. She was still far too thin, he thought in dissatisfaction. She needed to be cosseted. Something that clearly wasn't likely to happen in her grandmother's house.

"Your Grace." Esme fawned on him. "How good of you to favor us with a visit. Although I imagine we all know that you didn't come to see an old woman like me." She smiled archly at Drusilla, who flushed a brilliant scarlet and looked around the room as if seeking a place to hide.

Ryland ignored the comment and made an elegant leg.

"Actually, I came to see your son, madame," Ryland said, knowing full well that Henry was still at the ministry. But at least it gave him an excuse for coming that wouldn't raise expectations about his intentions toward Drusilla.

"My husband is still at Whitehall." Maria gave him a gentle smile. "But since you're here, won't you join us for a cup of tea?"

"Thank you." Ryland sat down beside Eleanor, to Esme's obvious annoyance.

Esme glared significantly at Drusilla, who didn't notice. She was too busy smiling at Bertrem.

"Bah, the tea's cold! Maria, ring for more." Esme took her annoyance out on her daughter-in-law.

Eleanor surreptitiously studied Ryland out of the corner of her eye as he politely listened to her grandmother's fulsome compliments. His tanned skin seemed pale, and there were corded muscles visible along his taut jawline. As if he'd had a very trying afternoon.

When Esme turned to eavesdrop on what Drusilla and Bertrem were saying, Ryland caught Eleanor studying him. He raised his dark brows inquiringly. "Yes?" he asked.

"I was simply noticing that you looked . . ." Her eyes lingered on the tightness around his mouth and the cloudiness of his normally bright eyes. "Tired," she finally said, even though that didn't exactly describe her impression.

"Tired of the pigheaded stupidity of so many of our government ministers!" His frustration unexpectedly boiled over. "That's the trouble with political hacks, they have no vision. They expect the troops to live off the land, and never mind that it's spring and the crops haven't even been planted yet and the retreating French troops long ago stole all the livestock. Even a civilian should know better."

"Even I know better," Eleanor agreed. "What's the maxim? An army travels on its stomach?"

"That's an old Roman maxim," Ryland said in satisfaction.

"They should have known. They always seemed to have their armies out somewhere killing someone. A more bloodthirsty pack of predators I never saw."

"You can't make an omelet without breaking a few eggs," Ryland insisted.

Eleanor frowned at him. "Your precious Romans weren't the least bit interested in cuisine. What they wanted to make were orphans and widows!"

Ryland grinned at her. "Not always. Remember the Sabine women."

"Sabines?" Esme turned back in time to hear the last comment. "Maria, do we know any Sabines?"

Eleanor pressed her lips together to keep back the laughter that threatened to bubble out and gave Ryland a reproachful look. If her grandmother ever found out just who the Sabines were . . .

"I don't think so, Mother Bromley," Maria said doubtfully.

"They are dear friends of mine. Very exemplary females. I hope to copy their behavior," Ryland said outrageously.

Eleanor choked and tried to turn it into a coughing fit.

"Sabines?" Bertrem looked confused. "The only Sabines I ever heard about was in that book—"

"I don't doubt that the Sabines were in a book." Ryland gave him a quelling look. "They were very laudatory women. But we mustn't bore the company."

"Indeed not," Eleanor hurriedly said. "Comparisons are odious."

"There can be no comparison to His Grace!" Esme stated flatly. "If the duke admires their behavior, then everyone must admire them."

How could her grandmother toady to the man like that? Eleanor thought in disgust. It was enough to make any self-respecting republican bilious.

"We are going to the Jerseys' ball this evening," Esme told Ryland.

"I have an invitation, too," Bertrem offered, and then fell silent when Esme glared at him. "Do," he muttered under his breath.

"You may escort us to the ball, Your Grace," Esme said. "Henry will be unable to accompany us, and I feel much safer with a man in attendance."

"But the Jerseys just live across the square," Bertrem reminded her.

"Unfortunately, Mrs. Bromley, I don't know at what time I will be free to attend." Ryland declined for fear that Drusilla might read more into an acceptance than mere politeness.

"Be glad to lend my support, Mrs. Bromley," Bertrem blurted out in response to Drusilla's pleading glance.

"How kind of you to offer," Eleanor hurriedly interjected as her grandmother opened her mouth—no doubt to annihilate poor Bertrem.

Maria seconded Eleanor's efforts. "So kind of you, dear boy."

"Pleased to." Bertrem nodded happily.

"But the duke—" Esme wasn't one to accept defeat gracefully.

"We are very busy planning troop movements just now," Ryland improvised.

"Hope you manage to send that monster to grass right and proper this time," Bertrem said. "Your brother was one of the heroes of the war, wasn't he, Your Grace?"

"Yes." Ryland's features tightened under the force of his memories.

And now he was spending all his time trying to defeat his brother's enemies, Eleanor thought. Trying to further his brother's cause. And what was she doing to further her father's cause? The question popped into her mind, bringing a sense of guilt in its wake.

Nothing, was the answer that inexorably followed. Absolutely nothing. And that despite the fact that Connal had shown her exactly how she could accomplish it.

Did that mean that Ryland had loved his brother more than she'd loved her father? The appalling thought nagged at her.

Chapter Seven

"It's like a fairy tale, Mama." Drusilla gazed around the Jerseys' ballroom in wide-eyed wonder. "I've never seen anything so lovely. Just look at all that blue muslin hung from the ceiling. It looks just like the summer sky."

"Sally really outdid herself this time," Maria agreed.

"I wonder what would happen if it came down?" Bertrem eyed the gently swaying material nervously. "Mean to say, we'd all be scrambling around underneath it, bumping into each other."

Eleanor giggled at the image his words provoked.

"We'll have no levity out of you, missy," Esme ordered. "It's not seemly, what with you in mourning."

"Yes, Grandmama." Eleanor refused to let her grandmother's perpetual bad humor spoil what promised to be a delightful evening. The decorations were spectacular, huge bowls of cut roses perfumed the air with their heady fragrance, and everywhere women in brightly colored gowns dipped and swayed to the hypnotic music of the waltz.

"Disgraceful! Simply disgraceful!" Esme proclaimed as she watched a couple glide by. "Holding a woman in public like that! Whatever is the world coming to? Why, in my day, we would never have made such a vulgar display of ourselves."

"The duke of Ryland is very fond of the waltz," Eleanor, responding to Drusilla's worried expression, said, having no idea if it was true or not. It probably was, she told herself. He was a prominent member of the ton, and the waltz was a very social dance.

"True," Bertrem added. "I saw him dancing with Lady Sefton t'other night." He sighed enviously. "It looked so easy when Ryland did it, but . . ."

"You can practice on me," Drusilla offered. "Come on."

Bertrem, with a happy smile, took Drusilla's arm and led her out onto the floor.

"Maria Bromley, I won't have my plans for that girl upset." Esme glared at her daughter-in-law.

"Man proposes and God disposes," Maria replied with a vague smile.

"Bah! I'm surrounded by fools, but it makes no difference. You remember that, Maria. I'll be in the card room. As for you— " Esme turned to Eleanor "—no dancing and no levity."

"Yes, Grandmama," Eleanor muttered at Esme's departing back.

Maria merely shook her head and, catching sight of a middle-aged woman sitting in one of the chairs against the wall that had been set up for the chaperones, said, "Come along, dear. I see an old friend of mine I'd like you to meet."

Obediently Eleanor followed her aunt over to the woman.

"Bertha, this is Henry's niece from America, Eleanor Wallace," Maria said. "Eleanor, my very oldest friend, Mrs. Armstrong."

Eleanor smiled at the plump little woman and politely answered all the usual questions about how she liked England. Once the amenities had been observed, the two older women fell into a comfortable coze while Eleanor turned to study the scene in front of her.

Her eyes moved over the crowd, lingering here and there as a particularly colorful gown caught her attention. The women looked like a field of wildflowers swaying in a gentle breeze, she thought fancifully. And the men, in their more somber hues of evening dress, were like bumblebees swarming around their petals.

She continued to peruse the crowd, wondering if Ryland were there yet. She was surreptitiously studying the men clustered around the edge of the dance floor when her sense of delightful anticipation was abruptly shattered at the sight

of Connal Gunn dancing. How had he gotten an invitation
to the Jerseys' ball?

She frowned as she remembered him saying something
about having found someone to sponsor him. Apparently
his sponsor had gotten him the ticket.

Botheration! she thought in annoyance. She didn't want
to cope with Connal on a regular basis. It was more than
enough having to deal with his occasional whispered conversations behind the bookshelves at Hatchards.

As she watched, the music ended and Connal smiled
down at his petite blond partner. He'd never smiled at her
like that, she realized. He didn't waste his company manners on her, but did that mean that their relationship was
less artificial, or that he simply didn't care to make the effort? Eleanor didn't know. Probably because she didn't really know Connal all that well, she admitted.

And, what was worse, she had absolutely no desire to get
to know him better. And that despite the fact that she was
seriously considering honoring her father's last wish and
marrying him. Warily she watched as he approached Lady
Sefton and bowed over her hand. He said something to her,
and to Eleanor's dismay they both turned and looked directly at her.

Eleanor unconsciously straightened her shoulders as they
approached, reminding herself that there was very little that
Connal could do in such a public place. Unfortunately, there
was plenty he could say. Plenty he undoubtedly *would* say,
she thought in resignation as Connal and Lady Sefton
reached her.

"Good evening, Miss Wallace," Lady Sefton said. "This
gentleman has begged an introduction." She gave Connal an
arch smile. "Miss Wallace, may I present Lord Gunn."

"Lord Gunn?" Eleanor's voice rose questioningly.

"From Scotland," Lady Sefton elaborated. "Come to
London to expand his horizons, he says."

"Oh, I see," Eleanor muttered, wondering what her next
move was supposed to be. Connal was no more a member
of the nobility than she was. But she couldn't expose him
without also revealing that she already knew him. And she
didn't want to expose him, she realized in some confusion.

Connal was fighting for what he believed in. For what her father had believed in. She couldn't betray him. It would be tantamount to betraying her father.

"And I see the prettiest woman in the room," Connal said with a heavy-handed gallantry that inexplicably annoyed Eleanor. Somehow she felt cheapened by the glib, insincere compliment.

"And everyone always says the Scotch are dour." Lady Sefton playfully tapped his forearm with her fan.

Connal responded with a flirtatious smile. "Ah, my lady, but the women in Scotland do not inspire a man to the heights that you do."

"I'd watch this one, Miss Wallace," Lady Sefton said before drifting away to talk to Maria, who had been watching the exchange from her seat.

"Immoral bitch," Connal muttered, shedding his ingratiating manners like a jacket. He held out an imperious hand to Eleanor. "Come. We'll dance while we talk."

For the first time, Eleanor was glad that her mourning proscribed dancing. "I can't," she told him.

"I'll show you the steps," he said impatiently.

"That's not why I can't. I'm still in mourning."

"Damn!" He glanced around the room as if seeking a hidden spot.

"And hiding in an alcove would be bound to bring censure down on our heads." Eleanor was trying to forestall being alone with him. "To say nothing of my grandmother."

"Damn!" Connal repeated. "Very well. We'll have to talk here." He glanced around to make sure that no one was close enough to overhear.

"What have you found out?" he demanded.

"Nothing," she whispered back, smiling at her aunt, who was covertly watching her. "And I suggest you try to look more like a Scottish lord—" her voice took on a caustic edge "—and less like a member of the Spanish Inquisition, or my aunt will be over here directly to see what you're about."

"The English set great store by titles." He tugged at his elaborately tied neckcloth in embarrassment. "De Selignac suggested I adopt one to help grease my way in society."

"De Selignac?" Eleanor asked, not recognizing the name.

"The man who's sponsoring me in society. He's here. I'll introduce you later. But never mind that now. Tell me why you haven't found out anything."

"I tried," she defended herself. "I snuck into Uncle Henry's study and looked around."

"And?"

"And I almost got caught. I was going through some of the papers on his desk when he came back unexpectedly and walked in on me." Eleanor shivered at the memory.

Connal frowned. "He didn't realize what you were doing, did he?"

"No." Eleanor grimaced in self-disgust. "I lied and told him that I was looking for some paper to write a letter."

"And he believed you?"

"Oh, yes, and castigated himself for not remembering to give me pocket money."

"Good."

"I certainly didn't feel good," Eleanor muttered. "I felt awful."

"Your uncle Henry is the enemy," Connal said with absolute conviction. "What he stands for is the death of America's dreams of independence. You've got to find out where Whitehall plans to attack."

"Connal, I tried."

"Try harder. It's vitally important to our cause. The English are now demanding that we return the entire Northeast to them as part of the price of peace."

Eleanor stared at him in disbelief. "Why would they do that?" she finally asked.

Connal gave her a look of exasperation. "Because they are strong enough to demand it, of course. I tell you, Eleanor, we are in bad trouble. And it's going to get worse. If the English do manage to put an end to Napoleon any time soon, as everyone expects, it will allow them to reassign seasoned Peninsular troops to America."

Eleanor sighed. "It makes sense."

"What doesn't make sense is your refusal to help us."

"But I'm a guest here, and—"

"The social conventions don't hold during times of war. Besides, you don't even know your English relatives. All of your friends are Americans, and I'm the man you're going to marry, and I'm American."

"I haven't agreed to marry you yet." Eleanor latched on to the one point that bothered her the most.

Connal waved her qualification away. "This is not the time to be missish, Eleanor. You know full well that your father wanted you to marry me."

Eleanor studied his dark, craggy features for a long moment and then asked, "What about what I want?"

"You don't have the experience to know what you want. You must allow yourself to be guided by older and wiser heads. And smile," he ordered. "Your aunt is watching us."

"I wish I had Lady Sefton's fan," she muttered through a tight smile. "It would be easier to carry on a whispered conversation with something to hide behind."

"This is no time for levity. Do you remember anything at all from looking through your uncle's papers?"

Eleanor tried to think of something, anything, that might appease him. "Not really, although he was carrying a blue folder when he came in. It said something about the summer offensive in . . ."

"In where?" Connal leaned toward her eagerly.

"I couldn't read all of it, but I think it said something about Canada."

"That's it!" His eyes gleamed with excitement. "We'd heard that they planned to launch an offensive through Canada. We have to get our hands on that folder."

"But I don't know what he did with it. He could well have put it in the safe. Or at the very least a safe spot. How am I supposed to steal something I can't find?"

"It's a pity he caught you in the study," Connal said slowly. "It might make him suspicious enough to take extra precautions."

"He caught me in the study because you were hounding me to be there," Eleanor said, with a great deal of asperity.

"I don't want to steal the folder," he continued.

"You don't want . . ." Eleanor stared at him in confusion.

"I don't expect you to understand the procedures," he said loftily. "After all, you're just a woman."

"And you are obviously a very perceptive man," she sniped.

To her annoyance, Connal took her words at face value and smiled smugly.

"However, this dance can't last forever, and it will cause talk if you remain past it. So would you please get to the point?" she said.

"Think. If you steal the plans, the English will know they're gone and change them. But if you copy them, they won't know. Now do you see?"

"Yes." Eleanor nodded. "Now I see."

"I've already spoken to my American contact, and he's authorized to act, just as soon as I can present him with something concrete."

"You mean as soon as I can steal something," Eleanor said.

"Call it what you like, but America could well be doomed if you don't do something. Cutting the Northeast out of the country would destroy it."

Along with a great many people, Eleanor thought bleakly. The majority of people she knew would hate being British subjects again. They'd fight it to the last man. The loss of life would be horrendous. And she might be able to prevent it. If she did as Connal wanted.

"You will try, won't you, Eleanor?" Connal urged.

Eleanor looked into his dark eyes, which glowed with emotion. Emotion for a cause, not for her, she acknowledged. But it had been her father's cause, too. What more fitting memorial could she give to him than to make sure that his dream of a free and united America endured?

And as Connal had pointed out, if she copied the plans, the English probably would never know where the information leak had occurred. No one would blame her uncle for it. He wouldn't be hurt. Not really, she tried to convince herself.

Taking a deep breath, she gave the only answer she felt she could. "I'll try, Connal, but I can't promise that I'll be successful."

"You will," Connal assured her. "I'll drive down to see my contact at Dover tomorrow and make sure that he's ready to send the information on."

"Tomorrow?" Eleanor frowned. "There's no way I can get the information by then."

"I know." The warm smile he gave her annoyed her. She was perfectly aware that the only reason he was smiling at her now was that she'd agreed to do what he wanted. It made her feel like a not-too-bright kitten he was trying to teach manners to.

"I'll call on you after I return. I want to make sure we've agreed on terms before we pass on the information."

Terms? But before Eleanor could ask what he was talking about, her aunt, obviously curious about their long conversation, joined them, and the talk became general.

As Maria began to gently quiz Connal about his background, Eleanor allowed her gaze to wander over the ballroom. It was even more crowded than it had been just minutes before. She saw her cousin Drusilla dancing with Bertrem near the bank of French doors that led out onto the terrace. Eleanor winced in sympathy as Bertrem landed on Drusilla's small foot, almost oversetting her. No, Eleanor thought ruefully, Drusilla was dancing; Bertrem was creating havoc.

Eleanor nodded absently in response to something her aunt said and continued her survey of the room. She tensed as she thought she caught sight of Ryland partially hidden behind one of the huge marble supporting columns on the right side of the room. Impatiently she waited until an oversize matron in a bright green gown finally moved and then leaned forward ever so slightly in an attempt to see more clearly.

It was Ryland. Excitement sizzled through her as she recognized the proud tilt of his dark head. The almost monastic simplicity of his superbly cut black coat and pantaloons, the stark simplicity of his white marcella waistcoat and snowy white neckcloth seemed to set him apart, contrasting with the brighter colors around him.

Surreptitiously she tried to see who he was talking to. A man. A fair-headed man of about forty, who was casually leaning against one of the marble columns, looking utterly bored.

A rueful smile teased her lips. Was Ryland lecturing the poor man about his beloved Romans?

Fearful that someone might notice her staring, she forced herself to turn back to Connal. He was pumping her aunt for information. He'd catch cold at that, Eleanor thought in amusement. Her aunt was basically a very kindhearted woman who didn't have the vaguest idea of what was going on around her. Let alone what was going on at Whitehall.

Compulsively Eleanor's eyes were drawn back to Ryland. To her embarrassment, her gaze was momentarily captured by the man with him. Hastily she looked away.

"Our Miss Wallace has seen you, Ryland," the man drawled.

"My Miss Wallace, Devlin."

"Pity," Devlin said reflectively. "Miss Wallace is looking much better than she did when she first arrived. Far less like a drowned kitten."

Unable to resist the impulse, Ryland turned and looked at her, taking in the soft line of her thin cheek and the fashionable low cut of her bodice, which gave him a tantalizing glimpse of her soft breasts. "The dress is an improvement...." he said, frowning as he suddenly recognized the man standing between her and her aunt as the one who had spoken to her in Hatchards.

"But?" Devlin asked.

Ryland turned, looking blankly at his friend.

"If the dress is an improvement, and I'll concede that virtually anything would be an improvement on those shapeless black bombazine sacks she was wearing when she arrived, why are you frowning? Actually, Miss Wallace pays for dressing. I begin to regret I didn't decide to keep an eye on her myself."

Ryland ignored the jagged flash of dark emotion that sliced through him and asked, "What do you know about the man she's talking to?"

"Virtually nothing. According to our host, De Selignac asked if he might bring a friend with him."

"De Selignac!" Ryland glanced back at Connal.

"Just so," Devlin agreed. "And any friend of De Selignac's is almost certain to be no friend to England."

"The man's French, too?"

"No, he was introduced as a Scottish baron named Connal Gunn. I ran Argyll to earth in the card room half an hour ago, and he's never heard of him."

"Suspicious, but then the duke can hardly know every minor twig of nobility in the whole of Scotland."

"True, and Gunn does sound Scotch. Acts it, too," Devlin said meditatively.

"Oh? And how do the Scotch act?"

"Dour and canny with their money. He's staying with De Selignac."

"He's not so canny that he wasn't willing to buy a new wardrobe," Ryland said slowly, studying the line of Connal's dark blue jacket. "That coat is from Stultz, yet when he approached Eleanor he was wearing a coat of a very provincial cut."

"And when was this?"

"The first time was the day after you asked me to watch her. I took her to Hatchards."

Devlin stared at him. "Hatchards?"

"I wanted to get her a book about the Romans," Ryland muttered defensively. "But why we were there isn't important. What's important is that this Gunn accosted her behind the stacks. He was there again a few days later, when I took her back."

"Hmm..." Devlin slowly stroked his long forefinger over the scar on his thin cheek. "Interesting. Could Gunn be hanging about Hatchards hoping to strike up an acquaintance with an impressionable female? Hatchards would certainly be a prime hunting ground for a fortune hunter. But if that was his motive, why waste his time on Miss Wallace? Her dress at the time didn't proclaim her as either wealthy or fashionable."

"Miss Wallace is very interesting to talk to," Ryland said in her defense.

Devlin gave him a wry look. "Fortune hunters aren't interested in conversation. They're interested in money. Although he could have thought that, since she came with you, she had some."

"And he could be exactly what he said he is," Ryland countered. "A minor baron come to London for some town bronze. Or he could be a Scottish adventurer who is willing to make himself useful to De Selignac in order to gain entrée into polite society...."

"Or he could have his own plans, which have nothing to do with either Miss Wallace or De Selignac, and he's simply making use of them to further his own ends." Devlin frowned. "Unfortunately, they're all possibilities, but I still don't like it."

"I can't say as I do, either, but I don't think Miss Wallace is a risk to Henry's security," Ryland insisted. "She has a very clear grasp of ethics. Better than most men."

Devlin raised his eyebrows in surprise. "Does she now, Your Grace?"

"Don't 'Your Grace' me, and yes, she does. She reads Latin and Greek."

Devlin stared at him a moment and then said, "Her unexpected skills notwithstanding, I would still prefer you to keep her under close surveillance. I want to know if this Gunn continues to sniff round her skirts. You might also see if she'll talk about him. Most women like to boast of their conquests."

"Miss Wallace isn't most women," Ryland said flatly. "And I'll watch her, but you stay away from her." His voice had hardened.

Devlin held up his hand, as if to ward off a blow. "Acquit me of any desire to harm your ewe lamb. My only concern is England's safety."

"And mine is in defeating Napoleon." Ryland moderated his voice, with an effort. "But I won't have Miss Wallace worried needlessly. She's had a bad time of it lately."

"She's bound to have, if she's living with Esme Bromley," Devlin said. "Ah, our quarry is leaving." They watched as Connal walked away from the two women. "Why don't I dance with the cousin and try to discover if Miss Wallace has mentioned this Connal Gunn to her, while you see what you can find out from Miss Wallace herself?"

Ryland chuckled. "I'm definitely getting the better of this exchange. I should also warn you that her grandmother considers any man who so much as smiles at the fair Drusilla as a potential husband."

"Ah, but how can I, a mere marquis, and one who's reached the advanced age of thirty-nine at that, possibly compare to a duke in his prime?"

"You can't, of course." Ryland grinned at his friend. "But since I'd rather see the dukedom pass to my Irish cousin than spend the rest of my life leg-shackled to a vapid female who never reads anything more challenging than the social column, the old tartar may decide to make do with you."

Devlin grinned back. "I appreciate the warning. And now to battle stations."

Ryland watched as Devlin slowly made his way across the ballroom floor and approached Drusilla. A wry smile curved his mouth. He could see her blush from here. Surreptitiously Ryland began to work his way toward Eleanor, pausing to speak first to one person and then another as he went.

Perhaps he should give her a hint that Gunn wasn't quite the thing, Ryland considered, before rejecting the idea. She might inadvertently repeat his warning to Gunn and, if he really was involved in spying, it would alert him to the fact that they were suspicious. Then, too, her sympathy might well be roused for someone she saw as an outsider. Much as she herself was.

"Oh, look, Eleanor. Ryland is here." Maria hastily scanned the ballroom floor, looking for her daughter. "And there's Drusilla, standing up with Devlin. How vexatious."

Eleanor tried to ignore the way her heartbeat accelerated as Ryland approached them, but the sparkle in her eye was hard to hide. Suddenly the evening seemed brighter, clearer and in sharper focus. As if Ryland's presence added some dimension that had been lacking.

"Good evening, Mrs. Bromley, Miss Wallace." Ryland bowed.

"Drusilla is dancing," Maria offered.

"One would expect such a lovely girl as your daughter to be in great demand," he said.

Unanswerable, Eleanor thought, wondering what Ryland's intentions toward Drusilla were. He certainly didn't seem to be concerned that she was enjoying herself with another man. In fact, he hadn't even turned to see who she was dancing with. Almost as if he didn't care.

"And since you can't dance, Miss Wallace, may I show you our host's collection of Greek statuary in the conservatory?" He held out his hand to Eleanor.

Eleanor stared down at it, fascinated by the supple strength evident in his long, lean fingers. His hand looked capable of taking what he wanted and holding on to it. A sudden premonition shivered through her mind. Connal might be sanguine about the English being a group of effete hedonists who would be easy to dupe, but Eleanor had doubts. Serious doubts.

"It is an unexceptional entertainment," Maria said, when Eleanor didn't reply.

"If you happen to be enamored of Greek bits and pieces," Eleanor said.

"Oh, no, dear," Maria assured her. "Greek statues are all the crack. Everyone must admire them, whether you see any sense to it or not."

Eleanor looked up into the gleam of laughter lighting Ryland's eyes and swallowed an urge to giggle.

"How perceptive of you, Aunt Maria," she choked out.

Maria smiled complacently. "I should hope I'm not behind the fashions. Now go look at the statues, dear, before your grandmother comes out and..." Maria glanced nervously toward the card room door.

It was all the urging Eleanor needed. She hurriedly placed her hand on Ryland's arm and followed him around the crowded edge of the ballroom toward the conservatory. Tentatively she flexed her fingers. The smooth material of his black coat felt warm and sleek, and the forearm beneath it hard and unyielding.

"Ah, an island of sanity in a sea of bedlam," Ryland muttered when they reached the relative quiet of the conservatory.

"The party seems to be a great success," she offered tentatively, curious about his comment. Most of the ton that she'd met had seemed to positively relish these overheated, overcrowded affairs.

"So were the Punic Wars, but that doesn't mean that any rational person wanted to be a part of them."

"Don't you like balls?" Eleanor persisted.

"No," he said succinctly. "Ah, here's one of Lord Jersey's more famous pieces. I think it's a Polyclitus." Ryland stopped in front of a tall marble statue.

Eleanor gave it a cursory look and went back to what really interested her. "Why?"

"Well, the lines of the torso suggest—"

"No, not that," she said impatiently. "Why don't you like balls?"

"Do you?" he countered.

Eleanor looked back toward the crowded room they'd just left. The din was muffled in here, but still audible. "I don't like that many people squashed together, but that's not to say that I might not like to entertain a more reasonable number."

"Yes, a small number of friends would be nice. At an affair like this, one finds so many strangers. Such as that man you were talking to when I came in?" Ryland took advantage of the opening she'd given him. "I don't think I've ever seen him. Is he a fellow American?"

Eleanor felt the muscles in her shoulders tense at his unexpected question. Why had he asked about Connal? Did he suspect something? But what could he suspect? Maybe he was jealous? A spark of excitement skittered through her mind, until sanity extinguished it. If Ryland had tender feelings about anyone in her family, it was her cousin, Drusilla. But did he? She shot him a surreptitious glance to find him intently watching her. Like a cat watching a mousehole. The image popped into her mind, only to dissolve into nothingness when he smiled at her.

Connal, she reminded herself. Ryland had asked about Connal, and she'd better tell him something, but what? A lie as close to the truth as possible, she finally decided. It would be easier to remember.

"Lady Sefton introduced him as a Scottish baron, and he certainly talked about Scotland as if it were paradise." Boring memory gave her words an authentic ring. "What's that?" She purposefully changed the subject, moving toward a large ruby-backed plate displayed in a glass case. Her interest wasn't assumed. The piece was beautiful. Its red color glowed in the reflected light.

"It's Chinese," Ryland said. "From the Yung-Cheng dynasty, I believe. Lord Jersey's grandfather was an avid collector of Chinese pottery."

"Oh, look." Eleanor pointed to the small bowl next to it. "That Vincennes blue is almost exactly the color of Drusilla's eyes," she added with seeming casualness, hoping to find out something about his feelings for her cousin. If Ryland did intend to offer for her, then he ought to do so before her cousin broke her heart over Bertrem.

"Hmm..." Ryland barely gave it a glance.

"Drusilla is so beautiful," Eleanor continued. "When I first saw her, I thought that she looked like an angel."

"Have you ever wondered why angels are always portrayed as beautiful blond beings, when most of us are no such thing?" he asked.

Eleanor gritted her teeth in frustration. Was the man being deliberately obtuse, or was he simply being his normal self? She studied him. He was looking at a piece of broken statuary with a covetous expression of the sort men usually reserved for women or money.

"The man who marries Drusilla will be gaining a diamond of the first water," she persisted doggedly.

Ryland tore his fascinated gaze away from the artifact and gave her a long, thoughtful look. Finally he asked, "What are you trying to say?"

Eleanor almost gave up, but concern for her cousin and something else, something she refused to examine more closely, drove her on. Taking a deep breath, she blurted out, "I am trying, in my direct Colonial manner, to ask you what your intentions toward my cousin are."

Ryland blinked in surprise. "That certainly is direct."

"More direct than your answer," she said, deciding that having gone this far, she might as well see it through to the bitter end.

"You want a direct statement?"

Eleanor nodded.

"Very well. I do not now entertain, nor have I ever entertained for one single second, the slightest desire to make your cousin my wife."

Eleanor frowned at such a comprehensive statement, finding it hard to believe that he wouldn't have been tempted by such beauty. At least a little. Otherwise, why would her grandmother be so certain that he did intend to marry Drusilla?

"Not ever?"

"Never," he said flatly.

"But she's so beautiful." Eleanor unconsciously sounded wistful.

Ryland looked down into Eleanor's confused features, uncertain of his ground. He felt it was imperative that he convince her that he meant what he said. But to do that, he would have to be frank. Far franker than society considered acceptable between a man and an unmarried woman. Society be damned, he finally decided. Eleanor's feelings were far more important than any conventions.

"Yes, Drusilla is beautiful, but hardly unique. A man with money who wants to can find any one of a number of mistresses every bit as beautiful and a lot more entertaining," he said bluntly. "It isn't necessary for him to sacrifice his freedom."

"Are you opposed to the married state?" Eleanor asked cautiously.

"I am with a female who cringes and blushes every time I approach her. Marriage is for a long time, and I very much fear, if I were to marry your cousin, it would begin to approach eternity."

"Then why does Grandmama think you're going to marry her?"

"Does your grandmother think?" he asked caustically. "From what I've observed, she forms an opinion based on heaven only knows what, and then acts on it as if it were an established fact."

"True." Eleanor had to concede the truth of the charge. "But why don't you make your lack of interest in Drusilla clear?"

He gave her a wry look. "And how do you propose that I do that? Tell Henry that I have no interest in marrying his daughter? Perhaps while I'm about it I can visit the home of every marriageable female in London and tell their fathers that I have no interest in marrying them, either."

"There is no need to be snide." Eleanor looked down her nose at him. "I'm concerned about Drusilla. She is my cousin."

"And she's fast becoming the bane of my life," Ryland answered.

"Not true. It's my grandmother who's the bane. Wolfbane, I think." She giggled. "It's like the book I read yesterday, where—"

Eleanor's words were cut off when Ryland leaned forward and covered her lips with his. Surprise held her motionless as his mouth pressed gently against hers. His lips were smooth and warm, and the musky scent of his body teased her nostrils. The smell seeped into her lungs, shortening her breathing and accelerating her heartbeat. She could feel it pounding against her rib cage as if trying to break free. Sensation shuddered through her, making her skin tingle with a sudden awareness of her basic femininity. She wanted . . . But before she could decide exactly what it was she wanted and, more importantly, how to get it, Ryland raised his head.

"I shouldn't have done that," he muttered, his voice sounding oddly muffled.

Eleanor stared into his eyes. They seemed darker somehow, the pupils huge black pools surrounded by a blue rim. She took a deep breath, trying to force air back into her constricted lungs. "No, you shouldn't have," she agreed, confused and disconcerted by her uninhibited reaction. "It simply isn't done," she added with an attempt at firmness.

"Don't be naive. It's done all the time. What you mean is that society says we shouldn't do it. But whatever the reality, my behavior was unbecoming a gentleman, and I apologize."

"Oh? How do gentlemen kiss?" The question popped out before she realized it, and Eleanor felt a flush stain her cheeks.

Ryland chuckled. "I think that kiss comes under the heading of a little knowledge is a dangerous thing."

It might also become an addictive thing, Eleanor thought. But Connal's kiss hadn't, she suddenly recalled. Quite the opposite, in fact. Why should one man's kisses be so different from another's? She sighed. Nothing was turning out the way she'd expected.

"Ah, Your Grace, what brings you into the conservatory?" a bluff voice belonging to a middle-aged man hailed him.

Eleanor turned, glad of the interruption. Unfortunately, her pleasure didn't last past the man's next words.

"Oho! So it's a pretty young chit who's lured you out here." He poked Ryland in the ribs. "Ha! Must be more of your father in you than we all thought."

"Lord Charleton, may I make known to you Miss Wallace." Ryland ignored the innuendo.

Eleanor politely held out her hand. "How do you do, my lord?"

"Fine, fine." He pumped her hand with a vigor Eleanor found painful. "So you're Henry's niece from the Colonies. Nasty situation, that." He shook his head mournfully. "Never did understand them demmed Colonists. Complaining about a few taxes, when we was paying more than that right here in England."

"I don't think they understand you English, either," Eleanor said dryly.

"Well, you're safely out of it now. In fact, from what Prinny was saying just this afternoon, England will be getting the northeastern Colonies back when they ratify the peace treaty of Ghent."

Lord Charleton turned to Ryland. "Your Grace, do you really think we've got Napoleon on the run this time, like everyone is saying?"

Ryland's reply swirled meaninglessly through her confused mind. All Eleanor could think about was what Lord Charleton had said. It was confirmation of everything Connal had claimed. He hadn't been exaggerating to get her to do as he wanted. Eleanor chewed on her inner lip.

Tomorrow she'd have to try to find a way to copy the notes Connal wanted. Really try. A feeling of dread engulfed her, but she pushed it to the back of her mind. She had to do it. Not for herself, and not for Connal, but for her father.

Chapter Eight

"You're late!" Esme glared at Eleanor as she entered the breakfast room. "And I abhor lateness!"

It would probably be easier if her grandmother would simply list the things she did like, Eleanor thought as she stared at Esme through eyes that felt gritty from lack of sleep. From what she'd seen so far, the list would be limited to two or three items.

"Good morning, dear." Maria smiled warmly at Eleanor. "Did you have a restless night?"

"Yes, Aunt Maria," Eleanor said. She'd tossed and turned for what had remained of the night after the Jerseys' ball, dreading the necessity of spying and trying to justify it in her own mind. She had not been successful. No matter from what angle she examined her moral dilemma, she knew that spying on her uncle was wrong. The only comfort she'd been able to find—and it was slim comfort at that—was that it was the lesser of two wrongs.

"I won't have you giving yourself airs by pretending to be delicate," Esme pronounced. "Since you are late, you may not come to the dressmaker's with us this morning."

"But, Grandmama," Drusilla looked confused, "you never let Eleanor come shopping with us."

"I'll have none of your sauce, missy! After your behavior last night..." She took a deep breath and continued with her grievance. "You only danced with Ryland once."

"But he only asked me once," Drusilla mumbled.

"Perhaps you should have asked him?" Eleanor whispered to her cousin, and Drusilla's eyes widened in horror at the thought of such hurly-burly behavior.

Maria tried to deflect her mother-in-law's anger. "She did dance twice with the marquis of Devlin."

"Bah! Devlin's past praying for. Besides, I've told you and told you. I have decided on Ryland."

"Perhaps you should try telling the duke," Eleanor muttered, and Drusilla choked on her tea.

"What did you say, missy?" Esme demanded incredulously.

"The carriage is waiting, Mrs. Bromley." Walker provided a timely diversion.

Esme rose, brushed the muffin crumbs from her ample bosom and said, "Don't dawdle, Maria. I want to visit the Parthenon Bazaar afterwards. Come, Drusilla, we shall order you a dress that will be sure to catch Ryland's eye." With that, she sailed out of the room.

Maria hastily jumped up, dabbed her mouth with her spotless white damask napkin and urged Drusilla to her feet. "Hurry, dear. You know how she hates to be kept waiting. Eleanor, I...I'll bring you back something from the bazaar," she finally said.

"Thank you, Aunt Maria." Eleanor smiled gently at her, feeling very sorry for her aunt. Her role in life was not an enviable one.

"Don't feel badly about being left behind," Drusilla told Eleanor. "I'd much rather stay here than trail after Grandmama while she abuses shopkeepers. Eleanor, if I should have a visitor..."

"You mean when Bertrem calls?" Eleanor asked.

Drusilla flushed painfully, but she didn't deny it. "Would you please tell him that I'll be back as soon as I can?"

"Certainly," Eleanor agreed. "I'll even give him tea."

"Drusilla!" Esme's bellow rolled down the hallway and barged into the breakfast room.

"Oh, dear, now she's mad," Drusilla muttered and rushed out. A minute later, the front door slammed behind them.

Eleanor poured herself a cup of tea from the almost empty pot, wishing that the English favored coffee, as her father had. She needed something strong to fortify herself for the task ahead.

She glanced at the empty place at the head of the table. Her uncle was undoubtedly gone. He always left the house as soon as he finished his breakfast.

Distractedly Eleanor rubbed her aching forehead as she sipped the tepid tea. She'd promised Connal that she'd try to copy what had been in that folder her uncle had brought home, and she fully intended to. But Connal had said that he was going out of town this morning, so if she copied the information today, then she'd have to keep it hidden until he returned to London. And someone might find it and . . .

And you are procrastinating, she told herself. She knew full well that no one was going to find anything she secreted in her room. The only servant who ever came near it was Daisy, and she barely bothered to clean on the surface of things, let alone inside them. And the family wouldn't snoop in her possessions. Esme because she didn't think Eleanor had anything worth looking for, and the others because they were too well mannered. No, Eleanor squarely faced her reluctance. She was simply trying to postpone doing what she knew had to be done.

She sighed despondently. Her father had been all too right when he said that declaring war against the English was an idiotic thing to do. A thing they would all come to regret. And while she couldn't speak for the American Congress, she certainly regretted it.

Eleanor drained the rest of the tea and carefully set the empty cup down in the exact center of the saucer. It was time. She bolstered her flagging spirits. She'd copy the plans and give them to Connal when he returned to London, and then she'd be free. Free to pursue her own dreams.

But what did she want? The question nagged at her. To marry Connal? Eleanor frowned. With each passing day, she felt less inclined to marry him, but she didn't have a good, logical reason, and that bothered her. Especially since she knew that Connal had a great many fine qualities. He was well-favored physically; he wasn't a spendthrift; he cared about the cause her father had loved; he was an astute businessman; he attended church on Sunday. And her father had wanted the marriage. She ran her fingers through her short, silky hair in frustration. Always it came back to her father's wishes.

"Would you like a fresh pot of tea, Miss Eleanor?" Walker's soft voice made her jump, and she spun around to find him standing in the doorway.

"No, thank you." She forced a smile. "I've had enough."

"If you should change your mind, just ring," he said as he left.

It was too late to change her mind, Eleanor thought bleakly. Far too late. With a feeling of impending doom, she got to her feet and trailed out into the hall. One glance was enough to assure her that it was empty. Slowly she walked toward her uncle's study, carefully listening for the sounds of someone coming. But there was nothing to hear. A funereal silence hung over the house. The only noises were the muted clip-clopping sound of the horses' hooves from the street outside.

Finally, after what seemed like an eternity to her tautly stretched nerves, Eleanor reached the study door. She stared at the dark mahogany wood, wishing that she could see through it. Her gaze dropped to the shiny brass knob in morbid fascination. Just do it and be done with it, she urged her reluctant muscles.

Taking a deep breath, Eleanor reached for the knob, only to freeze as she suddenly heard the sound of china rattling from behind the green baize-covered door to her right. She jumped back and hastily retreated ten feet up the hall, stopping beneath a truly hideous painting. She stared blindly at the picture of a rabbit dripping blood into chartreuse grass as Walker shouldered open the door from the kitchens. He was carrying a silver tray with a steaming pot of tea on it.

She watched in horrified disbelief as he knocked softly on the study door and entered when her Uncle Henry answered. Eleanor swallowed against the sudden knot of fear that twisted through her. A cold, clammy sensation iced her skin as she realized what would have happened if she had opened that door and crept in. She sagged limply against the wall, feeling dizzy. Her uncle might be trusting, but he wasn't stupid. He would never have believed that she needed writing supplies again.

She'd just learned lesson number one of the spy's modus operandi, she thought on a rising sense of hysteria. Never, but never, assume anything. A competent spy would never have presupposed that simply because her uncle was in the habit of leaving the house immediately after breakfast he had done so today. A real spy would have somehow found out.

For a brief, tantalizing moment, she considered forgetting the whole thing. Considered telling Connal that she wouldn't do it. That she couldn't do it. But only for a moment. There was far too much at stake for her to give in to her own fears, and she knew it. She had to do her part for America. But not right this moment. The thought steadied her shaky nerves somewhat. She had a reprieve until her uncle left the house.

"Is there some way I may help you, Miss Eleanor?" Walker emerged from the study, softly closing the door behind him.

"Umm, no. I was just admiring the painting," she lied.

Walker looked at the bloody corpse a moment and then looked back at Eleanor, disbelief written all over his elderly face.

"Actually, there is something you can do," she rushed to say, hoping to distract him. "If Mr. Arylesworth should call asking for my cousin, would you put him in the salon and tell me."

"And where shall you be, Miss Eleanor?"

"In the library."

Walker nodded regally and disappeared through the green baize door to the kitchens.

Eleanor retreated down the hall to the library, being careful to leave the door open so that she could see when her uncle left. Wearily she sank down onto the soft leather chair by the fireplace.

Eleanor frowned at the ornate carving of an angel in the marble mantel. Somehow, its delicate features reminded her of her cousin, and her cousin reminded her of what she'd discovered last night. Ryland had said that he had no intention of marrying Drusilla. She ignored the spurt of pleasure she felt, telling herself that whoever he eventually married was no bread and butter of hers. Even if she decided against marrying Connal, she couldn't marry Ryland. Her father would turn over in his grave at the very thought of his only daughter married to one of the despised English aristocracy.

Besides, she thought, chance would be a fine thing. Simply because Ryland didn't want to marry her cousin, that didn't mean that he wanted to marry her. Although, he had kissed her. The enchanting memory of the feel of his warm lips against her own bubbled up out of her troubled thoughts. She felt a hectic flush scald her pale cheeks. She'd liked it, she admitted honestly. Far from sending her into strong hysterics, which she suspected would have been the reaction of any properly bred Englishwoman, she'd only wanted to repeat the experience. To enlarge on it. To thoroughly explore the totally unexpected sensations she'd glimpsed.

But one thing still bothered her. Why had she responded so mindlessly to Ryland's kiss, when she'd felt nothing but revulsion when Connal kissed her? Her eyes narrowed in concentration as she made a supreme effort to analyze Ryland's kiss. She found it very difficult. Her impressions were all jumbled up. She vaguely remembered the glow of his eyes, the faint scent of sandalwood, the strength of his fingers holding her...

He hadn't seemed shocked at her uninhibited response, though, she remembered. He'd seemed more...bemused. As if he'd been caught off guard. But why would that be? He'd been the one who kissed her. She hadn't instigated that kiss. At least she hadn't done it consciously.

"Oh, botheration!" she muttered. She'd wanted something to take her mind off her father's death, but, somehow, she hadn't quite expected to find so many new problems to worry about.

Eleanor frowned as the wall paneling that she'd been blindly staring at suddenly registered in her mind. It looked exactly like the description of the paneling in the villain's book room in the Gothic she'd just finished. The heroine had escaped the villain's clutches by hiding in a priest's hole.

Eleanor glanced around the room consideringly. Could there possibly be a priest's hole hidden behind the paneling in this room, too? Even if there wasn't anything as elaborate as a priest's hole, perhaps there was a hiding place for valuables secreted behind the paneling? Eleanor felt a quick sizzle of excitement. Valuables such as the stolen necklace?

Eleanor carefully began to examine the paneling around the fireplace, looking for cracks or joints that didn't quite match. There was nothing readily apparent, but that didn't discourage her. A hiding place should be hard to find, she told herself.

She gently ran her fingers down over the seams of the individual panels, and when she didn't feel anything unusual she started tapping on the panels themselves. Meticulously she tapped her way entirely around the fireplace, closing her eyes to better evaluate the echoes.

"What are you doing?" The unexpected sound of Ryland's voice poured through her mind, fragmenting her concentration into a thousand tiny pieces.

Eleanor whirled around to find him standing in the doorway, watching her. Uncertainly her eyes flew to his face, looking for some indication of a difference in how he now regarded her after the kiss they'd shared last night. She couldn't see anything. He looked exactly the same. Unconsciously she relaxed.

Ryland rephrased his question. "Why are you pounding on the woodwork?"

"I am not pounding. I was tapping."

"All right. Why are you tapping on the woodwork? Are you looking for bugs?"

"Bugs?" Eleanor's eyes widened, and she scooted back from the wall, cautiously studying the baseboard. "Does this house have bugs?"

"Not that I've ever noticed." Ryland carelessly tossed the blue folder he was carrying onto the table to the right of the doorway as he walked into the room.

"What's that?" Eleanor looked at the folder.

"Nothing that would interest you," Ryland said dismissively, hoping it was true. "It's for your uncle. We're deciding which troops to ship to America once we finally defeat Napoleon."

"Oh," Eleanor muttered, forcing herself not to stare at the folder. She might not want to know what was in it, but she didn't doubt for a moment that Connal would. "Are you looking for Uncle Henry?"

"I know where Henry is. Walker told me when I came in. What I don't know is what you're doing."

"Looking for a priest's hole."

Ryland frowned. "Why would you want to find a priest's hole?"

"Why would you want to spend your time digging in the ground for a few broken bits of Roman pottery?" she countered.

"That's different," he said defensively. "The Romans had a great civilization, while Oliver Cromwell merely had a fanatical belief in his own view of right and wrong."

"In common with a great many men," she said tartly, thinking of Connal. "The only difference I can see is that Oliver Cromwell commanded an army."

"You still haven't answered my question. Why are you looking for a priest's hole?"

Eleanor glanced down at the carpet, her eyes tracing over the pattern as she tried to think. Maybe she should tell Ryland about the necklace? He had a very logical mind. Perhaps he would have some ideas as to what might have happened to the necklace all those years ago? One thing was certain, she was having no success trying to find it on her own. And Connal had told her to play up to Ryland. To get close to him. A flush warmed her skin as she remembered the kiss they'd shared in the conservatory last night. Would Connal have wanted her to go that far to involve Ryland? She felt a frisson of distaste as she remembered the hard glint in Connal's dark eyes. He might well consider the prize worth a few kisses.

"Eleanor?" Ryland took her hand.

She stared down at her fingers lying in his much larger, much browner ones. His hand closed around hers. She could

feel his latent strength, but it didn't frighten her. In some
strange way, she found his strength comforting. And very
exciting, she admitted honestly.

"Is something wrong?" Ryland asked.

"Not exactly." Eleanor gently tugged her hand free. She
found it extremely difficult to think clearly when he was
touching her. She'd tell him, she made up her mind. The
worst thing that could happen was that he'd dismiss the
whole thing as a product of her father's imagination. But,
if she were lucky, Ryland might prove to be a useful ally.

"You see, a long time ago, when my parents wanted to get
married, my grandmother was against it."

"Of course she was," Ryland said dryly. "Your grandmother measures a husband's worth by first his title and
then his bank account."

"Yes, well..." Eleanor cleared her throat, remembering
that Ryland had good reason to know about Esme's values.
"A valuable necklace disappeared, and Grandmama
claimed that my father had stolen it. She threatened to have
him arrested for theft. My parents eloped and emigrated to
America, but that necklace weighed on my father's mind all
his life. I must have been about five the first time he told me
about it."

Eleanor frowned, remembering her father's indignant
face. "He felt that my grandmother had taken the necklace
herself to get rid of him."

"She's certainly capable of it."

"So I decided when I came to England to see if I couldn't
find out what had happened to it."

"That's why you were so interested in that appalling picture of Mrs. Bromley in the front salon, wasn't it?" Ryland
suddenly realized. "The necklace in the portrait is the one
that disappeared."

Eleanor nodded dispiritedly. "And it really seems to have
disappeared. No one I asked about it could even remember
having seen it. At least, not in the last quarter century."

"And you think your grandmother has it."

Eleanor grimaced. "I did, originally, but having met
her..."

"Personally, having met your grandmother, I wouldn't put anything past her," Ryland said succinctly.

"Yes, but she's vain," Eleanor tried to explain. "I mean, look at the way she drapes herself with every brooch, necklace and bracelet in her jewelry box."

"And she's never worn the necklace?"

"No one remembers seeing it, and I don't believe she has the willpower to possess it and not wear it in public. She doesn't seem to know the meaning of the word *discretion.*"

"No, but she's pretty good at teaching it to those around her! Which leaves us where?"

Eleanor heard the "us" with a sense of relief coupled with an unexpected tinge of uneasiness. If Ryland were willing to help, she had a better chance of solving the mystery. But on the other hand, he was beginning to dominate her thoughts and that could be a problem. Sooner or later, probably sooner—provided she wasn't arrested for spying first—she'd have to leave England. And him. And if she allowed herself to become too fond of Ryland, the leaving would be that much harder.

"Why don't you review what you know for my benefit?" he said, interrupting her confused thoughts.

Eleanor forced herself to push her worries to the back of her mind and concentrate on his question. "I know there really was such a necklace. My father told me about it, and my grandmother mentions it. Constantly. And I know what it looks like from the painting."

"Could it have been paste?" Ryland asked thoughtfully.

"I considered that, but my grandmother doesn't seem like the type to be taken in by a fake."

"Probably not," he conceded.

"We know that my father didn't take it." Eleanor gave him a challenging stare, but Ryland merely nodded, and she felt her tension ease somewhat. "And I honestly believe that my grandmother didn't take it."

"Which leaves . . . who?"

"I don't know. Grandfather Bromley suffered a seizure and died very shortly after it disappeared, so if he took it he would have had to dispose of it very quickly."

"Or he could have hidden it away and then died before he could retrieve it." Ryland's eyes wandered thoughtfully over the paneled walls she'd been tapping when he entered.

"Or hidden it," Eleanor agreed. "My mother could have taken it, but..."

"What was she like?" Ryland asked, wondering if Eleanor's description would match Mrs. Symington's. To his relief, it did.

Eleanor shrugged. "She died three hours after I was born, but from what my father said, she must have been very like my cousin Drusilla in looks and temperament."

"Which hardly makes her a likely candidate to do something like stealing her mother's jewels. On the other hand, it also makes her an unlikely candidate to defy her mother and marry your father."

"True," Eleanor conceded, remembering Drusilla's inability to stand up to her grandmother. "Besides which, if Mama had taken it, my father would have known."

"Not if she hid it to get even with her mother, and then eloped before she could give it back."

"Possibly," Eleanor agreed. "Which brings us back to it being hidden in the house."

"Who else was living here at the time? Henry?"

"I believe he was up at Oxford, and only visited London a couple of times."

"It would have only taken once."

"But if Uncle Henry took it, what did he do with it?" she asked. "Selling it would have given him a great deal of money, and he doesn't seem to have any. Doesn't seem to have ever had any."

"A man can gamble away three fortunes in a night."

"Yes, but not without occasioning comment. Wouldn't someone have noticed losses like that, and said something to his mother?"

Ryland grimaced. "Undoubtedly. There's always someone to gossip. Besides which, in all the time I've known Henry I've never known him to gamble for more than chicken stakes. But it almost has to have been stolen by someone in the family," he continued. "And, if either your mother or grandfather took it, it should still be here. Have you searched anywhere else?"

"No. I just remembered reading about priest's holes, and that gave me the idea of a hidden panel."

Ryland eyed her narrowly. "You aren't still reading those..."

"Books?" she offered helpfully.

"Fanciful ravings of a deranged mind?"

"How can anyone who reads about Zeus and Hercules and that lot possibly stigmatize anyone else's reading matter as the ravings of a deranged mind?" she asked self-righteously.

"I don't believe them," he said defensively.

"Well, I don't believe my Gothics, either. Even though they're proving very helpful. I would never have thought of a hidden panel without them. And, if I ever get kidnapped, I'll know just what to do."

"What— No, don't tell me. I don't want to know. Come on, I'll help you look." He dragged a chair over to the fireplace.

"What are you doing?"

"I'm taller than you." He shoved the chair up against the wall.

"So?"

"I'll tap on the top of the wall, and you tap on the bottom. Then we'll both do the spaces under the bookcases."

Eleanor nodded in agreement. "That sounds logical."

"I am very logical," Ryland said smugly. "It's the result of a classical education. We'll need to hurry. I do have to talk to Henry about those plans before he leaves for Whitehall."

Yes, those blasted plans. Eleanor glanced over at the harmless-looking blue folder on the sofa table. For a moment, she'd forgotten her role as spy. She'd been enjoying her role as detective. And she'd enjoy it a little longer, she told herself, determinedly turning her back on the incriminating folder.

Crouching down, she began to softly tap her way across the bottom half of the wall while Ryland did the same thing above her. It wasn't until she'd worked her way almost entirely around the room that she discovered anything that sounded out of the ordinary. She was rapping on the paneling behind the large sofa when the sound was suddenly different.

"Ryland, listen!" she said excitedly.

He broke off his examination of the paneling around one of the bookcases and looked up. "Listen to what?"

"The sound. It's different."

He hurried across the room and squeezed in beside her. "Different how?"

"Listen." Eleanor gently tapped on the spot, and the sound seemed to echo.

"You're right!" He eagerly tried it himself.

"It's hollow. Listen how it sounds over here." She tapped about two feet to his right, and the sound was different, more solid.

"It could be a hidden compartment!"

"Hmm..." He continued tapping, defining the perimeters of the hole. "It doesn't appear to be very big. Just about twelve inches on a side."

"Big enough to hide a necklace," Eleanor insisted. "How do we find out what's behind it?"

"Just a minute." He crawled out from behind the sofa and hurried over to the desk. He returned a few seconds later, carrying a wicked-looking brass letter opener. Squeezing back in beside her, he used the sharp point to pry the paneling away from the baseboard. Eleanor winced at the high-pitched squeaking sound the wood made as it separated from the wall. She peeked up over the top of the sofa and then ducked back down as she heard a noise from the hall outside.

She grabbed Ryland's arm, shook her head and gestured toward the door. *Someone is coming.* She mouthed the words, praying whoever it was wouldn't come into the room. She didn't want to try explaining why she was hiding behind the sofa with the duke of Ryland, stripping the paneling off the walls. The first offense flew in the face of what was considered acceptable behavior for an unmarried woman, and the second violated the laws of hospitality.

Ryland nodded, carefully holding the letter opener steady as they waited.

"Anybody here?" Eleanor recognized Daisy's voice, and she scrunched her shoulders together, willing the girl to go away.

"What are you doing in here, girl?" To Eleanor's relief, she heard Walker's voice. "You don't belong in the front of the house."

"I's just goin' down the back stairs t'the kitchen when I heard a sound like...like...creakin'," Daisy said, defending herself. "So I stuck m'head in t'see what 'twas."

"And as you can see, there is nothing here," Walker said. "Now be about your business, girl, before I find it necessary to discuss your behavior with the housekeeper."

"Old puffguts," Eleanor heard Daisy mutter and then there was silence.

Eleanor closed her eyes, counted to twenty and then opened them to find Ryland's face scant inches from hers. This close, she could see the shimmering flecks of deeper color swirling in his eyes and the thin laugh lines that radiated from their corners. As if he were a man who found much in the world to amuse him. He blinked, and Eleanor watched in bemusement as his thick black eyelashes brushed against his tanned cheeks.

Eleanor swallowed uneasily as she found herself wanting to touch those luxuriant lashes. To see if they were as strong as they looked. Her gaze dropped lower, down over the strong blade of his nose, to land on his lips. They were slightly parted, as if in anticipation, and their dusky pink color seemed to entice her closer. Unconsciously she swayed toward him.

Ryland's response was swift. His hand grasped the back of her neck, holding her steady as his mouth eagerly covered hers, exerting a firm pressure that made her exquisitely aware of his masculinity. After a moment, the pressure eased slightly, and his lips began to slowly move from side to side with a tantalizing, teasing lightness that hinted to her of untold delights.

Intense excitement chased over her skin, raising goose bumps as it traveled. An ache of longing sparked to life deep in her chest and quickly became a raging torrent of need. It forced her breathing into a ragged cadence and sent a tingle of anticipation through her breasts. Eleanor trembled under the force of the sensual onslaught that gripped her.

Daringly her hand crept up to touch his cheek. The sudden tremor that racked his body encouraged her, and she blindly rubbed her palm along his jawline. His emerging beard gave his skin the texture of rough silk, and her palm greedily absorbed the abrasiveness, delighting in the physical difference between them.

Eleanor shuddered convulsively. His kiss blatantly foreshadowed something. Something that would forever change her conception of who and what she was. The knowledge both frightened and exhilarated her.

Ryland's grip tightened at her movement, pulling her body yet closer as his mouth seemed to devour hers. The overwhelming urgency of his kiss intensified her feeling of anticipation, as well as her fears.

She shouldn't be allowing this familiarity. Reality briefly surfaced through the fantasy his kiss had created, only to die unlamented as the tip of his tongue darted out to trace over her lower lip. A small, soft yearning sound escaped her.

To her intense disappointment, he drew back. His eyes seemed to burn with the force of the emotion driving him, and he reached out to gently brush his fingertips against her soft cheek. Eleanor shivered as his touch tightened the skin on her cheeks. She saw the very faint trembling in his fingers with a sense of wonder. Had she caused that reaction? Or would any woman's kiss have done it?

"I think she's gone," Ryland muttered.

"Yes." Eleanor made a monumental effort to match his self-control. "We'd better hurry before someone comes back."

"I'll do that while you go watch the door," Ryland ordered, his sense of acute sexual frustration making his words terse.

"I'll do it, and you watch the door," Eleanor objected. "It was my idea to look for panels."

"Oh, for heaven's sake! Will you do as you're told?"

"No," Eleanor said succinctly.

"Then we'll both do it." Ryland pushed the letter opener back into the crack, levered it upward. The paneling ripped free.

"What's there?" Eleanor leaned over his shoulder, eager to see what they'd uncovered.

"A small, empty hole, and..." He used the blade of the letter opener to pull something out onto the floor.

"What is that?" Eleanor poked the gray thing, thinking it might be a leather pouch. "It's..." She picked up what she thought was a string and then squeaked in horror when she realized it wasn't a string, it was a tail. The tail of a mummified mouse.

Eleanor hastily dropped it and scrambled out from behind the sofa, rubbing her fingers on her pale mauve muslin skirt.

"It's a mouse!" she squawked. "And it's dead."

"Would you prefer it to be alive?" Ryland pushed it back into the hole and pounded the paneling back in place with the end of the letter opener.

"I would prefer it to have never been there at all."

"It appears that the builder pieced the bit of paneling down here." Ryland's voice sounded muffled as he peered into the small opening. "And that's why it sounded different from the rest of it."

"Fudge!" Eleanor muttered in acute disappointment. "And I thought we'd found something."

Ryland chuckled. "We did. You just didn't like what we found." He emerged from behind the sofa and tossed the letter opener on the desk. "I think it's safe to say that there isn't anything hidden in the paneling in this room, at least."

"True," Eleanor conceded. "I suppose I ought to search the attics and the basement."

"I'd offer to help, but it would occasion talk if—"

"Your Grace." Henry hurried into the room. "I didn't realize that you were here. Thank you for entertaining His Grace, Eleanor."

"You're welcome." Eleanor hoped that her uncle never found out just how thoroughly she'd entertained him.

"Henry, I need to talk to you," Ryland said.

"Come into the study. If you'll excuse us, Eleanor?"

"Of course." Eleanor watched them leave, her eyes lingering on Ryland's broad shoulders. As she turned, she saw the blue folder he had been carrying with him when he came.

She stared at it, knowing that Connal would want her to look. It might well contain important information for the American cause. Taking a deep breath, she crept over to the door and cautiously peered out into the hall. Ryland and her uncle had disappeared into his study, and the servants were nowhere to be seen.

After hastily closing the door, she opened the folder and squinted down at the florid handwriting. It was not easy to read. It seemed to be just a list of numbers and regiments.

A sound from the hall outside startled her, and she quickly replaced the folder, sprinted to the sofa and dropped into it. She took several deep gulps of air, trying to control her erratic breathing.

She watched with a sense of burgeoning guilt as Ryland opened the door. He studied her flushed features for a long moment, and Eleanor forced herself to meet his speculative gaze, hoping that he would put her flushed appearance down to embarrassment over the kiss they'd just shared and not to guilt over trying to spy on him.

"Let me know if you find anything in your search besides spiders and mice," he said as he picked up the folder.

"Spiders?" she squeaked, suddenly having something new to add to her list of worries.

Chapter Nine

Eleanor hastily shoved the paper on which she'd just finished scribbling down what she could remember from Ryland's folder in her pocket when she heard the sound of the door opening. Mindful of her promise to Drusilla, she stuck her head out of the library to see if it was Bertrem. It was, but to her surprise he was accompanied by Drusilla.

Eleanor weighed the necessity of hiding the stolen notes in her room against her curiosity over why Drusilla had returned so early and decided that the notes would be safe in her pocket.

"Drusilla, I thought you were going to be gone for hours," Eleanor said.

"I was, but I got the most frightful headache at the dressmaker's so Mama sent me home in the carriage, and then I met Bertrem at the door," Drusilla explained, with a happy smile at him. "And I feel much better now. The fresh air, you know."

"Yes, I do know," Eleanor said, surprised that her cousin had found the backbone to lie to Esme, because she didn't have the slightest doubt that that was what the headache had been. A lie concocted to escape her grandmother's restrictive presence.

"How do you do, Mr. Arylesworth?" Eleanor smiled at the nervous-looking Bertrem.

"Fine, thank you," he mumbled.

"Ummm, Eleanor..." Drusilla peered nervously around the hall. "Is that Ryland's carriage outside?"

"I presume so, since he's inside."

"Here?" Drusilla's eyes widened apprehensively, and she shrank closer to Bertrem.

"In the study with your father," Eleanor said soothingly.

"Ah, military matters." Bertrem nodded sagely. "Told you it was all a hum, Drusilla. He's not here to see you."

"But he'll see me if he comes out," Drusilla moaned.

And what did Drusilla think Ryland was going to do to her if he did see her? Eleanor wondered in exasperation.

"We could go for a drive in the park," Bertrem suggested helpfully. "Have a carriage."

"Grandmama wouldn't like it," Drusilla said doubtfully.

"Grandmama doesn't like anything," Eleanor pointed out. "What's one more thing?"

"She's right, you know." Bertrem nodded vigorously. "Your grandmama's always one to nab the rust. Positive tartar. Everyone says so."

"And I'll come along to play propriety," Eleanor offered.

"Kind of you, Miss Wallace." Bertrem beamed at her. "Very kind."

"I'm not sure. . . ." Drusilla hesitated.

"Don't forget the duke lurking in the study," Eleanor reminded her. "Besides, Grandmama will probably be hours yet. We'll be back long before her."

"Yes, that's true." Drusilla brightened visibly at the thought.

"Settles it." Bertrem opened the front door with a flourish. "We'll tool around the park and admire the posies."

And she could tell Drusilla that there wasn't any impediment to her marriage to Bertrem, because Ryland didn't intend to marry her, Eleanor realized, relishing the thought of their excitement.

Bertrem's carriage turned out to be a shabby, rented affair with a pair of dispirited job horses that looked as if they hadn't moved above a walk in the past ten years. Eleanor surreptitiously ran her hand over the cracked leather seat to remove at least some of the dust before she gingerly sat down, being careful to avoid the broken spring in the middle. She glanced enviously at Ryland's immaculately clean curricle as Bertrem carefully pulled around it into the road.

"How clever of you to find a way to get a carriage." Drusilla smiled appreciatively at him.

Would that he could have found one that didn't smell quite so badly. Eleanor gamely tried to ignore the pervasive aroma of mildew.

"Rented it so's I could take you driving," Bertrem told Drusilla as he slapped the reins in an unsuccessful attempt to increase the horses' gait.

"Drusilla." Eleanor decided not to waste any time imparting her news. "Last night at the ball, I sat out one of the dances with Ryland."

"Yes, I know." Drusilla smiled commiseratingly at her. "I saw you while I was dancing with the marquis of Devlin. In fact, he pointed you out. He said he was curious about the lady talking to Ryland."

"He did?" Eleanor frowned, momentarily distracted.

"Yes. He asked who you were and how long you'd been with us," Drusilla said.

"I see," Eleanor murmured, wondering if the man's curiosity had been on his own behalf, or Ryland's—or could it have a more sinister meaning? She shivered in sudden foreboding. Could the marquis somehow be connected with the government and suspect her? But why would he? She hadn't done anything. She swallowed uneasily as the paper in her pocket crackled. Not really.

"Is this marquis in the Foreign Office, like your father, Drusilla?" Eleanor asked.

Drusilla shook her head. "Oh, no. Devlin is a very social man. He doesn't do anything."

"Gives nasty setdowns," Bertrem offered.

Eleanor breathed a sigh of relief. If the marquis was nothing more than yet one more bored aristocrat, then he was no danger to her. Or her father's cause. His interest had undoubtedly been no more than a passing curiosity.

"About Ryland, Drusilla..." Eleanor returned to the original subject. "Last night at the ball, he said that he had no intention of marrying you."

Drusilla stared at her, hope warring with disbelief in her tense features. "But how do you know? Did you ask him?"

"Not exactly," Eleanor hedged. "He was showing me Lord Jersey's statuary..."

"Some of it ain't at all the thing. Got no clothes on," Bertrem whispered in hushed tones.

"Be that as it may, what the duke showed me was unexceptional. Boring, not unexceptional. Anyway, the subject of marriage came up—" Eleanor glossed over the particulars "—and he was quite clear about the fact that he has absolutely no intention of marrying you, Drusilla."

"Grandmama says that no man ever has the intention of getting leg-shackled until he finds himself caught in parson's mousetrap," Drusilla said doubtfully.

"You can't force a man to the altar," Eleanor insisted.

"Not a duke, you can't, but other men..." Bertrem heaved a gigantic sigh.

"I don't quite understand," Eleanor said, confused by their reaction. "I thought the problem was that Ryland was a better matrimonial prospect than your Bertrem—"

"He is not!" Drusilla protested.

"In the eyes of the world," Eleanor added.

"She's right, you know," Bertrem said. "Ryland's swimming in lard, and he has a position few can offer."

"So does the czar of the Russias," Eleanor pointed out impatiently. "But neither of them wants to marry Drusilla, and you do."

"I do, but m'father, he don't." Bertrem heaved another sigh, and Drusilla sniffed disconsolately.

Eleanor took a deep breath, counted to ten and tried again. "Why does it matter who your father wants you to marry?"

"'Cause of the price of corn, don't you see?" Bertrem sawed on the reins, guiding the plodding animals into Hyde Park.

"No, I don't see," Eleanor said in exasperation. She was beginning to think that this pair didn't have a coherent thought between them. "I'll ask questions and you provide the answers. If you don't mind," she added.

"I know you want to help, Eleanor," Drusilla said sadly, "but I very much fear that our situation is past praying for."

"God helps them who help themselves," Eleanor countered.

"She's right, you know, Drusilla," Bertrem said, much struck. "Heard the minister say that very thing one Sunday."

"There is another impediment to your marriage besides Ryland, correct?" Eleanor asked.

Drusilla nodded.

"And it has to do with Bertrem's father?" Eleanor guessed.

Drusilla nodded again.

"He's opposed to the marriage?" Eleanor continued.

"Told me to put all thoughts of marrying Drusilla right out of my mind. Said I had to marry money."

"Because of the price of corn?" Eleanor had finally connected the two points.

"Uh-huh. It being so low these past few years, Papa had to take out a mortgage on the estate. A big mortgage," Bertrem related gloomily. "Got no way to pay it off unless I marry someone with a big enough dowry."

"But Grandmama has already said she'll give you a dowry, Drusilla," Eleanor said. "It's me she refuses to frank."

"Only if I marry Ryland." Drusilla sniffed unhappily. "She says if I marry to disoblige her, she'll cut me off without a shilling."

"Old tartar would, too," Bertrem muttered.

"Yes, I rather think she might," Eleanor conceded.

"For myself, I'd marry Drusilla and the devil take the mortgages," Bertrem burst out. "But m'mama, she just cries when Papa says that they'll have to leave the estate and live in a pokey little rented cottage in the village. And m'sister says she'll drown herself in the duck pond if'n she don't get her season next year. And it's not like she'll form an eligible connection unless m'father comes down heavy for her dowry. Very restless sort of female, m'sister is. Branfaced, too."

Eleanor grimaced, feeling a great deal of sympathy for Bertrem. The tyranny of affection could be very hard to resist—as she well knew.

"What's worse, got a letter from m'father today," Bertrem continued woefully. "Said he'd asked Mr. Potter, our man of business, to see if'n he could locate a bride from the merchant classes whose papa would be willing to pay handsomely to marry her into the ton."

"Eleanor, what are we going to do?" Drusilla wailed. "There'll be scores of girls who'll want a handsome, well-set-up young man like Bertrem."

Maybe love really is blind, Eleanor thought with a quick look at Bertrem. Where Drusilla saw perfection, she only saw a nondescript young man unable to withstand emotional blackmail.

She could provide the dowry Drusilla needed to marry Bertrem, Eleanor knew, although she couldn't do it until she was ready to leave England, because it would lead to all sorts of awkward questions. Ten thousand pounds or so would mean very little to her, but it could mean a new life for her cousin. And Bertrem would probably make Drusilla an excellent husband. He wouldn't be likely to overset her delicate nerves or be impatient with her seemingly innumerable fears.

"If you had a dowry—" Eleanor began.

"It isn't just the dowry, it's Grandmama's permission," Drusilla explained morosely. "She'd never give her consent. She'd rather I dwindled to an old maid like...I mean..."

"But why would you need her consent?" Eleanor ignored Drusilla's unintentional slur on her single state. "It's your father who's your guardian."

"But it's the old tartar who pays the piper," Bertrem said.

Drusilla nodded in agreement. "I already asked her to let me marry where my heart was, and she said hearts change. That the only things that matter in the long run are money and position. And that if I married to disoblige her, I'd best be prepared to support Mama and Papa, too, because she wouldn't. And she said that she'd leave her money away from the family."

"I see," Eleanor said slowly. Which meant that if she gave Drusilla a dowry, she would also be assuming the financial responsibility for her uncle and aunt. Eleanor chewed on her lower lip as she considered the situation.

Financially, it presented no problem, but emotionally... Making her uncle her pensioner could well lead to resentment on his part. A far better plan would be for her to reclaim his estate so that it would generate enough rents to support them. But how much would that cost? And would her uncle be willing to take the necessary funds from her? Men had some very strange ideas where their pride was concerned.

What she should do was visit her uncle's man of business, she decided. The same Mr. Potter who handled Bertrem's father's affairs, if she remembered correctly. He should be able to tell her what she needed to know.

"Oh, look, Bertrem, that man on the walkway is waving at us." Drusilla pointed to her left. "I think I met him last night at the ball. Isn't he a Scottish lord or something?"

Eleanor turned and, to her dismay, found herself staring at Connal. She frowned, wondering what he was doing in Hyde Park. She distinctly remembered him telling her that he would be out of London today.

Bertrem jerked on the horses' reins, yanking them to a stop.

"Good afternoon, Miss Bromley, Mr. Arylesworth." Connal greeted them with a seeming good humor that Eleanor instinctively distrusted. "And what a pleasure it is to see you again, Miss Wallace. I did so enjoy our conversation last evening."

Eleanor's gaze moved from his polite smile to his dark eyes. His dark, watchful eyes. There was no hint of reflected humor in them. Only impatience, and something else. But what else? she wondered uneasily.

"Good afternoon, my lord," Eleanor replied cautiously.

"You could get down and walk beside the carriage for a space, Eleanor," Drusilla suggested when Connal made no effort to move away.

"These slugs aren't likely to outpace you," Bertrem said.

Eleanor's first impulse was to refuse to leave the sanctuary of the carriage. She had more than enough on her plate to worry about at the moment. She didn't need Connal to add something else, which was what he always seemed to do. But she stifled the impulse. Refusing such a commonplace invitation would be bound to make Drusilla curious, and she didn't want anyone curious about Connal. Besides, Eleanor suddenly remembered the note in her pocket. She could give it to him now. Perhaps that would satisfy him for the time being.

Eleanor carefully slipped past the smiling Drusilla, who thought she was giving her old-maid cousin a treat, and allowed Connal to help her out of the carriage. His fingers were warm, dry and strong, but she felt none of the sense of breathless anticipation she had when Ryland took her hand in his. Why? Why was Ryland's touch so different from Connal's? she wondered as Connal placed her hand on his forearm and moved away from the carriage.

"Pay attention," Connal ordered.

Eleanor broke off her musings and looked up into his impatient face. Impatience seemed to be the emotion he displayed the most around her, she realized. Was it just she who roused the emotion in him, or was it all women? Or was it the situation? Eleanor didn't know, but she did know that she intended to find out before she made up her mind about marrying him.

"I thought you said that you were going out of London today," she said, taking the offensive.

"The trip was postponed. De Selignac received an urgent message that necessitated his staying here."

"I see," Eleanor muttered, seeing nothing of the sort. Why were Connal's movements dictated by the Frenchman's?

"Were you able to get to that folder?"

"No, Uncle Henry is working at home this morning."

"Damn!" Connal bit out. "Is he going out this afternoon?"

"I wouldn't know. He doesn't keep me apprised of his movements."

"Did you manage to find out anything?"

"Yes," Eleanor said, watching as his face lit up with anticipation. He'd never looked at her like that, she realized.

"Well, what?"

"The duke of Ryland came by to see Uncle Henry, and he noticed me in the library looking for a hidden panel—"

"A hidden panel?" Connal eyed her narrowly. "Why were you looking for a hidden panel?"

She shrugged. "Why not? Lots of old English houses had hiding places built into them, and I was hoping that I might find the necklace."

Connal frowned at her. "What necklace?"

"Didn't my father ever mention the necklace to you?" she asked, stalling as she tried to decide if telling Connal was a good idea or not.

"No, you tell me," he ordered.

There couldn't be any harm in telling him, she finally decided. He might even have an idea to offer. "Years ago when he was courting my mother, a necklace belonging to my grandmother was stolen. At least she claimed it was stolen. She blamed my father, and since I'm here, I thought I'd try to find out who really took it."

Connal shook his head at her apparent gullibility. "You can save yourself the effort. Your father undoubtedly took it."

"My father wasn't a thief!" Eleanor declared.

"Hush." Connal shot a quick glance at Bertrem's team, which was slightly ahead of them. "I wasn't suggesting that there was anything wrong with your father taking that necklace, Eleanor. He was certainly entitled to it. Your mother should have brought far more to the marriage than the five-thousand-pound dowry she did."

"Papa loved her," Eleanor said tightly. "He didn't care about some trumpery necklace, or her dowry."

"All men care about money," Connal said cynically. "Even that duke your grandmother is determined your cousin is going to marry. You think he'd consider for a moment marrying a dowerless female?"

Eleanor bit back the urge to defend Ryland, telling herself that what he would or wouldn't do was irrelevant. What was relevant was the way Connal viewed marriage. As little

more than a business arrangement. But even as disquieting
as she found that fact, it still didn't invalidate Connal's de-
votion to America's cause, she reminded herself.

"Ryland left his folder in the library alone with me for a
few moments. I only had time to glance at the first few
pages, but I copied down what I could remember."

Connal glanced around at the almost empty roadway and,
placing his body between her and Bertrem's carriage, demanded, "Give it to me."

Eleanor resisted the impulse to remind him of his manners and surreptitiously handed him the note, feeling hor-
rendously guilty as she did so. She shouldn't feel guilty, she
tried to convince herself. It was what her father would have
wanted.

Connal glanced over the sheet. "This is all you have?"

"I didn't have much time."

"Hmm . . ." Connal slipped the paper into the pocket of
his green-and-yellow-striped waistcoat. "I'm not sure just
how valuable this is. I'll show it to De Selignac and see what
he thinks. In the meantime, I want you to continue trying to
get the information about the Canadian offensive. There's
no saying when your uncle might take the folder back to
Whitehall. We simply don't have the luxury of waiting for
the perfect moment."

"I'll try," Eleanor agreed reluctantly, knowing Connal
was right, but wishing with all her heart that he wasn't.

"I shouldn't worry about that. The English are stupid,"
Connal said scathingly. "Look at how trusting your uncle
is."

Eleanor winced. "I'd rather not. It makes it all the harder
to violate that trust."

"And Ryland. Leaving a top-secret folder lying out in
plain sight. I tell you, the English are stupid," he insisted.

"Whatever else Ryland is, he isn't stupid, Connal. In fact,
he's quite one of the smartest men I've ever met. I wonder
if he didn't leave that folder alone with me on purpose,"
Eleanor said as a shiver of apprehension slithered through
her.

"Bah! What have we to fear from a classical scholar, of
all things? I found out plenty about him last night, and do

you know he's normally to be found on his estate in Cumberland, digging for Roman artifacts?''

"Until his brother was killed on the Continent," Eleanor reminded him. "He wants revenge, Connal, and a man who's looking for revenge is a dangerous enemy."

Connal frowned, looking uncertain for a moment.

"I don't like it, Connal," she blurted out. "I don't like any of this. It's too dangerous."

Connal's lips tightened, and he forced a soothing note into his voice. "You're simply nervous, because you're a gently nurtured female, and all of this has overset your nerves. But we don't have any choice." His voice hardened. "I told you. The negotiations are at a critical point. We must gain some kind of leverage, or America is doomed.

"It's only for a little while." He moderated his voice. "Just a few more weeks, and then we can return to Boston and be married, and you'll never have to do anything like this again."

Eleanor bit back her instinctive denial of their marriage. This was hardly the time to argue about it, she told herself. Not with the situation already so confused by the necessity of her spying. First she'd do what she could for the American cause, then she'd weigh what she felt for Connal, and then she would make a rational decision.

"Come on." Connal took her arm and hurried her toward the carriage. "I want to get the paper you gave me over to De Selignac. I'll see you later."

"Yes," Eleanor murmured, wishing that his words didn't strike her more as a threat than as a promise.

"Ryland, you're harder to run to earth than a virtuous woman. White's is the fifth place I've tried." Devlin sank into the chair beside him. "And let me tell you, the book room is a devilish dull place at this hour of the afternoon." He glanced disparagingly at the few old men reading their papers.

"Were you looking for a virtuous woman?" Ryland ignored the rest.

"No, the other kind are far more rewarding."

"Only in the short term."

Devlin's dark brows shot up. "Ryland, my friend, you're beginning to sound like a Methodist. Or, even worse, like a man who's in danger of losing his head over a woman."

An image of Eleanor's laughing features floated through Ryland's mind. He might well have already passed the danger point, he considered. Eleanor was beginning to dominate his thoughts of the present, as well as the future. But whether he had or not, he had no intention of exposing his feelings to Devlin's cynical tongue.

"I'm quite certain you didn't track me down to discuss my amorous impulses," Ryland said.

"Quite right, old boy. I want to discuss treasonous impulses."

Ryland grinned. "Not mine, I know. And I hope not yours. I'd hate to see you hang. Or would they behead someone of your rank?"

"A moot point. Dead is dead. Pay attention. I don't have much time. It's about that Scotsman who was at the Jerseys' ball last night."

Ryland felt a sudden tension invade his muscles. "What about the Scotsman?"

"That, my friend, is the problem. No one seems to know anything about your ewe lamb's Scotsman."

"That demmed Scotsman isn't hers. Simply because she isn't sufficiently up to snuff to know how to cut a man trying to strike up an acquaintance in a public place—"

"Mea culpa." Devlin held up his hand in a fencing gesture of defeat. "Perhaps I phrased that poorly. But be that as it may, I've had my operatives asking discreet questions of everyone who has any connection whatsoever to Scotland, and no one can recall a Baron Gunn."

"Disquieting," Ryland conceded.

"Especially when allied to the fact that his sponsor is a French émigré of questionable loyalties. Tell me, has Miss Wallace ever mentioned De Selignac?"

Ryland ran his finger over his jaw thoughtfully. "No, although she doesn't seem to like Napoleon at all."

"I see." Devlin gazed off into space for a long moment.

"Which is more than I can say," Ryland said dryly. "This all seems to be pure supposition on your part. Even if you're right and this baron is a fraud, it still doesn't make him a spy.''

"True, but it does make him worth watching. And if I were you, Ryland, I'd keep a sharp eye on Miss Wallace. If she were to get herself mixed up in anything—''

"She isn't mixed up in anything,'' Ryland insisted, hoping it was true. "And if you upset her—''

"Peace, my friend. I'm simply delivering a word of warning. Our spurious baron did rather make a point of seeking her out at the ball last night. Perhaps he thinks she could be of use to him.''

"I think that having my brother restored to me would be a good idea, too,'' Ryland said harshly, "but it doesn't mean that it'll happen this side of heaven.''

Devlin sighed. "No, it doesn't. All I meant was that English society is new to Miss Wallace, and she doesn't seem to have led a very social life in America. In fact, from what Mrs. Bromley says, she was living in direst poverty.''

"Mrs. Bromley also says that I'm going to marry Drusilla. From the excellence of Miss Wallace's manners and the depths of her education, it is far more likely that she and her father lived in genteel poverty.''

"Possibly, but it has been my experience that the older a woman gets, the more susceptible to flattery she becomes.'' He shrugged. "Miss Wallace wouldn't be the first woman taken in by a charming rogue.''

"Is he?'' Ryland asked curiously.

Devlin blinked. "Is he what?''

"Charming?''

"I don't know. What's more, I don't care.'' He got to his feet. "And, having delivered my warning, I'll go.''

Devlin was wrong, Ryland assured himself as he watched him leave. Eleanor had too much sense to be taken in by a plausible rogue. Far too much. Although ... A shimmer of uncertainty slithered through him. She could be surprisingly naive about some things. But if it came to that, he was more than capable of dealing with this Baron Gunn. In fact, he thought with anticipation, he'd rather enjoy the task.

Chapter Ten

It is my most earnest wish, my precious daughter, that you marry Connal as soon as a suitable period of mourning has been observed. In that way I will be able to rest easy, knowing that you will be safe. Eleanor reread the letter her father had written and left with his lawyer to be given to her after his death.

Her meeting with Connal that afternoon had thoroughly unsettled her, and the first thing she'd done when she returned home was to seek the privacy of her own room to try to think. As always, her thoughts of Connal were inexorably tied up with what her father had wanted.

She stared down at the shaky handwriting, wishing she could convince herself that it wasn't her father's hand, but she couldn't. She knew it was. Despite the weakened slant of the letters, his writing was unmistakable. As was the message it conveyed. Marry Connal Gunn as soon as the proprieties had been observed. Marry Connal and be safe. But safe from what?

Eleanor grimaced. Connal was the one who'd involved her in the most dangerous activities of her life. It was at Connal's urging that she'd braved a dangerous ocean voyage while America was at war with England. It was at Connal's insistence—no, his demand—that she was about to spy on her uncle. An act she had yet to complete.

Eleanor stared blindly out the one tiny window her small bedroom boasted, trying to decide when would be the best time to rifle her uncle's study. During the day was exceedingly risky. Not only were there invariably servants about, but her uncle's schedule was too erratic, as well. She shuddered as she remembered how she'd almost walked in on him that morning. So when would be the best time to copy the folder? She nibbled thoughtfully on her thumbnail. Probably the middle of the night, when everyone was in their beds. But if she was discovered, there would be no way she could explain it away. The second best time would be in the evening, she finally decided. After the family had finished its dinner, and while the servants were still busy with their own.

Eleanor frowned at the brown stain on her ceiling. It might be the best time to copy her uncle's notes, but it was also the time it would be hardest for her to be alone. Immediately after dinner was when her grandmother dragged them from one interminable social function to another. And while her grandmother would be only too happy to leave her behind, her aunt would object. For some inexplicable reason, Maria actually thought she enjoyed spending her evenings listening to malicious gossip being exchanged and watching other people dance.

Although... A slow flush washed up under Eleanor's pale skin as she remembered her interlude with Ryland in Lord Jersey's conservatory. Maybe her aunt did have a point. That kiss had certainly been an enlightening experience, and one that not even the most jaded partygoer could have called boring.

"Miss Eleanor," Daisy hissed from the other side of the door. "Dinner's 'bout t'be served, and you'll be wantin' t'hurry, or yer grandma, she's liable..." The young maid's voice trailed away, but Eleanor didn't need the sentence finished. She knew perfectly well that being late would put her grandmother sadly out of curl.

Perhaps she should be late, Eleanor considered as she carefully replaced her letter in the drawer, beneath her underwear. It might make her grandmother angry enough to refuse to take her along to whichever social functions she'd chosen to attend. Then she could copy her uncle's notes and be finished with it.

"Miss Eleanor, Walker told me t'fetch ya." Daisy sounded desperate. "It's m'off night, and I gets t'go visit m'mum soon as the family's t'dinner."

"I'm coming." Eleanor abandoned her half-formed plan. It might accomplish her goal, but it might also get poor Daisy into trouble, since she'd been charged with getting her down on time.

Eleanor hastily straightened the profusion of pale violet ruffles around her deeply cut neckline and ran her palm down over her narrow muslin skirt to smooth out the wrinkles before going down to dinner. She'd think of some other way of escaping the evening's entertainment, she decided. Some way that wouldn't rebound on anyone else.

But as the dinner wore on, Eleanor's thoughts were of murder, not escape. She was fast coming to the conclusion that Machiavelli had been right after all. The ends really did justify the means. In this case, simply disposing of her grandmother would make virtually everyone else in the household ecstatically happy. From Walker, who'd been subjected to a scathing denunciation of his skill as a butler during the first remove, to her cousin, who'd been reduced to tears during the second remove by Esme's order that Drusilla dance twice with the duke of Ryland and that she snub poor Bertrem.

"You understand me, missy?" Esme glared at Drusilla. "I won't have you speaking to that mushroom."

"Oh, I say, Mama," Henry objected. "The boy's not a mushroom. Been Arylesworths at the Grange forever."

"When I want an opinion from you, I'll ask for it," Esme snapped.

Eleanor studied her grandmother thoughtfully over the yellow-and-white floral arrangement in the middle of the table. Esme Bromley was the most consummate bully Eleanor had ever encountered. Anywhere. Esme seemed to have only one way of dealing with her family. She tore their characters to shreds and then barked out orders. Any failure to immediately comply with her wishes only brought more recriminations down on her hapless victim's head. And they endured it because they had no choice. They were dependent on her financially.

What would her grandmother do if they were to stand up to her? Eleanor wondered. If they were to refuse to allow her to bully them? If they were to insist that she treat them with the respect Eleanor had been taught all human beings deserved? Would Esme moderate her demands? Would she learn new ways of dealing with her family? Or would she continue to try to bend them to her will, and in the end be left with no one?

Eleanor didn't know. She'd never met anyone quite like her grandmother before. And, God willing, she never would again. But Eleanor was now convinced that she was going to have to rescue her uncle's family from Esme's malevolent domination. She might owe it to her father's memory to spy for America, but surely she also owed her mother's memory something. And what more fitting tribute could she give her unknown mother than to thwart Esme's spite? A smile curved her soft lips.

"Ha! So you think it's funny do you, missy?" Esme glared at Eleanor.

Eleanor blinked and looked up into her grandmother's furious features, wondering what she'd missed. She glanced around the table searching for a clue, but her uncle Henry looked his normal harassed self, her aunt was obviously worried—also a normal state of affairs—while Drusilla was sniffling into her wine goblet.

Botheration! Eleanor thought in exasperation. It was a miracle that the whole family didn't suffer from bilious stomachs, considering the tension they endured at every meal.

"I asked you a question, missy," Esme snapped.

"Forgive me, Grandmama, but I wasn't paying any attention to the . . . conversation, so I haven't the vaguest idea what it was that you said. Although, allow me to assure you that in all probability I would not have found it funny." Eleanor smiled blandly at her. "Since I have not found anything you've said to date to be humorous."

Henry choked on his wine, while Esme turned an unbecoming shade of scarlet.

"How dare you! You . . . you . . ."

"Granddaughter?" Eleanor purposely fanned her grandmother's anger. With a little luck, she could wind up banished to her room for the night, while everyone else went out.

"I'm at a loss, Grandmama. Did you intend to be funny? If so, perhaps it's just that in America our sense of the ridiculous does not include such things as terrorizing the servants or abusing one's family."

"Why—" Esme's face passed from red to purple.

"Not exactly terrorizing the family, Eleanor." Maria automatically tried to smooth things over. "Mother Bromley tries to—" She broke off in confusion.

"Just so," Eleanor said levelly.

"You may leave the table, you ungrateful whelp!" Esme shrieked. "And for your insolence, you may not attend the Nesbitts' ball this evening, and you can forget what I said about finding you a husband."

"I already had, Grandmama." Eleanor got to her feet, well pleased with the results of her insolence. With just a little more luck, she would be able to copy her uncle's notes after the family left. And once that was done, she would have fulfilled her obligation to her father's cause and she would be free of its burden.

"Don't worry, miss. You hide in the library, and I'll bring you a pot of tea and a bite to eat in a moment," Walker whispered to her as she passed him in the hall.

Eleanor smiled at the old man, touched by his gesture. All the more so because he had to know how her grandmother would react if she were to find out.

Eleanor slipped into the library to wait. For her purposes, it was an excellent choice. From its vantage point near the front door, she would be able to hear when the family left.

The wait seemed interminable. She'd long since demolished the snack that Walker had snuck in to her before she finally heard the sound of her uncle's voice in the hallway outside. She pressed her ear against the library door, and her enterprise was rewarded by hearing him tell Walker not to wait up for him. That he was going to Carlton House and didn't expect to be home much before dawn. That took care of her uncle. Eleanor mentally crossed one worry off her list.

Ten minutes later, Eleanor watched through a small gap in the heavy red velvet drapes as her grandmother, trailed by a dispirited-looking Maria and Drusilla, who appeared to be still sniffling, climbed into the closed carriage and were driven away.

They were barely out of sight when Walker opened the door and said, "If you should want me, Miss Eleanor, I'll be in the kitchen at dinner."

"I'm fine, thank you," Eleanor said. "I won't need anything else tonight."

"Nonetheless, I'll check on you later," Walker said before withdrawing.

Eleanor carefully picked up the pen and paper from the library desk and crept across the thick Chinese carpet to the door. She forced herself to count backward from fifty before she cracked it open and peered out into the hallway. It was deserted.

Her reasoning appeared to be correct. She felt a sense of satisfaction, heavily tinged with guilty fear. She had the front of the house to herself. At least until the servants had finished their well-earned dinner. Wasting no time, she raced down the hall and slipped into her uncle's study. She hurried over to his desk, breathing a sigh of relief when she found the folder that Connal was so interested in, lying on top of one of the piles.

Sitting down, she began to copy the six sheets inside. Her hand trembled with the need for haste, leaving ink splotches all over the paper, but she didn't care. Along with the blots was all the relevant information. If Connal didn't like her penmanship, he could do his own spying!

Forty-five minutes later, she copied the final directive. It had been almost too easy, she thought nervously. Surely something as serious as spying should be more difficult? She didn't know, but she did know that this wasn't the time or the place to consider the question. Right now, her first priority had to be to get out of the study and secrete the notes away.

Stealthily she inched open the study door and peered out. The hall was still deserted. Eleanor sagged against the frame, feeling light-headed with relief. She'd done it. She'd gotten what Connal wanted, and now she was free.

Eleanor quietly closed the study door behind her. She was crossing the hall when the emphatic sound of the knocker momentarily froze her to the black marble tile floor. She gulped and, instinctively, turned back toward the study. No, not back in there, she thought, bringing herself up short. If that was her uncle, ringing because he'd forgotten his key again, the study would be the first place he'd go.

She glanced longingly up the wide staircase, knowing that there wasn't time to reach the safety of the upper floor before Walker got there. Where, then? Her frantic gaze swung around the hallway. To the library, she decided hurriedly. She'd hide the papers she'd copied in there. She sprinted across the hall and into the library, managing to close the door behind her just as she heard the sound of Walker opening the green baize door from the kitchens.

Eleanor's glance swept the room, looking for a hiding place. Not the desk. Someone might conceivably use it. A book. That was it. She hurried over to the shelves, with their outdated titles. Grabbing one at random, she stuffed the sheets inside and hastily shoved it back in the row. Then she dropped the pen and leftover paper into a drawer. Satisfied that she'd removed all the incriminating evidence, she ran over to the sofa and plopped down.

She was taking deep breaths in an attempt to control her erratic breathing when she heard a soft knock on the door above the pounding of her heart.

"Ye—" her voice broke from sheer nervousness. It was a good thing her career as a spy was to be short-lived, she thought ruefully. She simply didn't have the pluck to sustain it. "Yes?" she tried again. This time merely sounding breathless.

The door opened to reveal Walker, who announced in a faintly disapproving voice, "His Grace, the duke of Ryland."

Ryland? What had brought him here tonight? she wondered, shocked by the strength of the pleasure she felt.

Pleasure that was quickly drowned out in a tidal wave of guilt at what she'd just done. But her actions really hadn't hurt Ryland, she tried to tell herself. Ryland wanted revenge against the French for his brother's death. He had no quarrel with the Colonies.

"Would you like me to ask Daisy to sit with you, Miss Eleanor?" Walker asked.

"No, she wouldn't," Ryland answered him impatiently. "I came to see if Miss Wallace's headache was any better, not to compromise her."

"It's all right, Walker," Eleanor said. "I'll be fine. Besides, have you forgotten, this is the night Daisy sees her family?"

"Very well, Miss Eleanor." Walker withdrew, carefully leaving the door ajar.

Ryland grimaced at his action. "I can't decide if I should be complimented or annoyed that he thinks I'm such a dashing blade that your reputation won't survive my sick visit."

Eleanor looked at him, more touched than she would have thought possible by his concern. She wasn't used to people worrying about her. Her father never had. Not until he'd had his first seizure and it had suddenly struck him that he'd failed to provide his daughter with a husband. And Connal certainly didn't worry about her. In fact, he seemed to spend his time thinking up actions guaranteed to put her in a position where she needed to be worried about.

"You do look a slight bit flushed." Ryland studied her. "Did you take some headache powders? The Romans used them with great success."

"Your precious Romans stole the idea from the ancient Egyptians. And I don't like headache powders. They taste frightful. Besides which, I don't have the headache."

Ryland sat down beside her and placed the back of his hand against her cheek. "You're hot," he accused.

"It's warm in here." And I've been busily spying, she thought as she scooted away from the unsettling feel of his hard knuckles pressing into her skin.

"If you haven't the headache, why did your grandmother say you did?" Ryland persisted.

Eleanor shrugged. "If you want to know why she lied, ask her. I didn't attend the ball tonight because I was forbidden to go."

"Forbidden?" Ryland's dark brows shot up in disbelief. "It sounds like she's the one who's been reading those appalling Gothics you favor. Why did she forbid you?"

"I annoyed her." Eleanor massively understated the case.

"Which hardly distinguishes you from anyone or anything else in this world," he said dryly. "Your grandmother, to give you the word with no bark on it, is a viper-tongued old tartar. Although in this case, she's done us a favor."

"She has?" Eleanor felt a shaft of fear rip through her composure before common sense came to her rescue. Ryland couldn't possibly know that she'd used the opportunity to spy.

"Instead of standing around a boring ball making inane conversation with a bunch of chuckleheaded fools, we can be comfortable here."

Eleanor smiled. "My idea of comfort does not include Walker hovering outside the door, waiting to dash to my rescue."

"Forget Walker. I wanted to talk to you about the necklace. Have you finished searching the house?"

"Yes." Eleanor shuddered. "And the things I found . . . One of the spiders in the basement was so big that I thought it was one of the kitchen cat's litter who'd gotten lost, and I almost picked it up."

Ryland's eyes gleamed with sudden interest. "Did you save it?"

She wrinkled her nose in disgust at the idea. "No, I squashed it with a wine bottle. Fortunately, I'd already searched them."

Ryland eyed her with unfeigned horror. "You moved the wine bottles?"

"Of course I moved them. How else could I look behind them?" she asked reasonably.

"I wouldn't tell your uncle what you did," Ryland said. "He has enough on his plate, what with his mother and the intransigent fools at Whitehall."

"Umm, yes," Eleanor muttered, having no desire to discuss Whitehall. "Anyway, I didn't find the necklace in the basement or the attics or in any of the spare rooms." She shrugged in discouragement. "I doubt very much if it is in the house."

"So do I."

Eleanor stared at him. "Then why did you set me to looking for it in those frightful places?"

"If you'll remember, you were the one who had the idea of searching first. I simply wanted to do a thorough job of it."

"I was the one who did the thorough job," Eleanor said, still a little upset about the huge spider.

"Since you haven't been able to find it in the house, I think we should consider the possibility that it might have been taken by an outsider who sold it."

"You could be right, but if you are, what can we do about it?"

"We can make a sketch of the necklace and show it to a few prominent jewelers. If the piece was sold and then reset, they might recognize it. Even if we can't recover it, you'll at least be able to clear your father's name."

"That's true," Eleanor felt slightly more hopeful.

"Let's get the drawing made." He glanced down at her ink-stained fingers. "Since you appear fond of drawing, you can do it."

"Me?" she repeated blankly.

"You must have been doing a pen-and-ink drawing. You've ink all over your fingers."

"Umm, actually, I was writing when you came, and the point on the pen needed sharpening, and I didn't have a penknife. I'll get what we need," she rushed on, not wanting him to ask any more questions that would necessitate more lies. She rummaged around in the middle desk drawer and found the pen she'd hurriedly stashed in there, as well as some more paper. Carefully picking up the ink well, she followed Ryland into the salon. "Do you have any talent for sketching?" she asked.

"I sketch the artifacts I find."

"Good enough." Eleanor set the paper and ink well down on a small end table and dragged it in front of the sofa. The pen she handed to him, wincing when it dripped black ink on the carpet.

"Botheration," she muttered, rubbing at it with her handkerchief, succeeding in staining both of them.

Ryland sat down on the sofa and studied the portrait for a long moment. Then he flexed his fingers and, picking up the pen, carefully began to drawn an excellent representation of the necklace.

"That's rather good," she said, admiringly.

"Quiet," he said, squinting up at the necklace. "I'm concentrating."

Eleanor felt a warm sensation squeeze her heart at his intense expression. He looked so serious, so absorbed in his work. His eyes were narrowed in concentration, and a tiny fan of lines radiated out from the corners. His full lower lip was caught in his firm white teeth, and she found herself studying it. Remembering the feel of it against her mouth. The taste of his wine-flavored breath.

Eleanor shifted restlessly, brushing up against the smooth hardness of his black jacket. It scraped abrasively over her bare arm, making her skin tingle in response. She resisted the impulse to rub the spot.

What was the matter with her? she wondered uneasily. Why was she so fascinated by Ryland? And just him. Connal, whom she was seriously considering marrying, generated no such interest. And never had. Not at any point of their relationship.

What was the lure that Ryland held for her? It certainly wasn't his title. She was enough of her father's daughter that a title didn't predispose her to like the man who held it. It wasn't his wealth, because she really had more money than she could ever spend.

Ryland added a final stroke to his drawing and turned to find her studying him. He smiled, and Eleanor felt an answering warmth unfurl in her chest.

One thing about him she knew she liked was his ready sense of humor, she decided. Ryland did not take himself anywhere near as seriously as those around him did.

Eleanor took a deep breath and forced herself to look down at his drawing. "That looks very good. When can we show it to the jewelers?"

"Tomorrow," he suggested, with a promptness she found gratifying. "We ought to be able to see several in one afternoon."

But that would mean that she wouldn't be at home to give the plans she'd copied to Connal, she suddenly realized with a sinking heart.

She wanted those plans out of the house before someone accidentally stumbled across them. But she had no guarantee that Connal would come tomorrow afternoon, she told herself. He could be otherwise occupied. Or he could come in the morning.

Maybe she should take the notes with her in her reticule and give them to Connal if she should happen to see him. She considered the idea before abandoning it. Slipping Connal a note while her cousin and Bertrem were with her was one thing. Trying to do it in front of Ryland would be quite another. He had a very sharp eye, and if he were to see her trying to surreptitiously give something to Connal... No. She shuddered at the thought of the possible consequences. It was too risky by far.

She refused to sit home waiting for Connal to appear, she decided. She'd go with Ryland tomorrow to try to track down the necklace, and she'd give the notes to Connal when she had a chance.

"If you think your grandmother would object to your coming with me, we could take your cousin with us," Ryland reluctantly offered when she remained silent, lost in worried thought.

"Drusilla wouldn't thank us for separating her from Bertrem. If we leave early, Grandmama won't be downstairs yet." Eleanor firmly consigned Connal and his spying to the back of her mind. She'd done her part for patriotism. Surely she was entitled to follow her own pursuits now.

Chapter Eleven

"The family is in the salon, Miss Eleanor," Walker told her as Eleanor hesitated on the bottom step.

Yes, but the stolen plans are in the library, Eleanor thought nervously. And her first order of business this morning had best be to make sure that they hadn't been disturbed. It wasn't likely that anyone had accidentally stumbled across them, but then, she would have said that her spying on her uncle wasn't any too likely, either.

"Thank you, Walker. I want to get a book first," she lied. Once she had given the stolen notes to Connal, she could go back to telling the truth, she told herself, trying to appease her guilty conscience.

Eleanor slipped inside the library and closed the door behind her. She hurried across the room, and yanked the book with the secreted notes off the shelf, expelling her breath on a long, relieved sigh as she saw the ink-splotched sheets still squashed between the pages. Hastily she shoved it back.

Her role as a spy was almost over. Soon she'd be free to concentrate on her own problems. Such as who had stolen her grandmother's necklace.

A feeling of excited anticipation nudged aside her worry about the stolen notes. Ryland would be here shortly to begin their search for the necklace among the jewelers of London. If she were lucky, she just might pick up a clue concerning its whereabouts.

At least she would be able to go with Ryland as long as nothing happened to upset their plans. Such as her grandmother's rising early. She'd best go see if her grandmother was among the family in the salon, Eleanor decided fatalistically.

She wasn't. Eleanor's tense muscles sagged in relief as she looked around the spacious salon. Her grandmother appeared to have adhered to her normal schedule of sleeping very late after a night of socializing. As had her aunt, although not so comfortably. Eleanor smiled at Maria, who was sitting by herself near the fireplace, gently snoring. Her cousin was over by the window deep in conversation with Bertrem.

Eleanor's soft leather slippers made no sound on the thick carpet as she walked across the room.

"Good morning," Eleanor said.

"Good morning, Eleanor." Drusilla's mournful voice gave the lie to the sentiment.

"Miss Wallace." Bertrem lurched to his feet and glanced nervously at the door.

"I think Grandmama's still asleep." Eleanor had had no trouble interpreting his look. "At least I certainly hope so."

"Me too!" Drusilla sounded as emphatic as Eleanor had ever heard her. "Her Turkish treatment of you last night was positively Gothic."

Eleanor swallowed the sharp, metallic taste of guilt that filled her mouth as she sat down across from them. While Drusilla had been worried about her having been left behind, she'd been spying on her father. But she'd make it up to him, Eleanor thought, trying to soothe her conscience. She'd free him from his mother's dominance before she returned to America.

"What are your plans today?" Eleanor opted for a subject that didn't make her feel guilty.

"Plans?" Drusilla's eyes widened nervously, and she glanced at Bertrem, as if seeking guidance. "Why do you ask?"

"Out of politeness," Eleanor said dryly. "Certainly not out of vulgar curiosity."

"Beg pardon, Miss Wallace," Bertrem said. "It's just that we've been worried."

"Yes, I know."

"You don't know about the note Bertrem got last night," Drusilla said tragically. "From his papa."

Bertrem nodded gloomily. "He's gone and done it."

"And I take it he shouldn't have?" Eleanor probed.

"Oh, Eleanor," Drusilla moaned. "Bertrem's papa writes that his man of business has found a candlemaker with an eligible daughter that he wants to marry into the ton—and he's willing to pay twenty thousand pounds," she finished in a hushed whisper.

"A handsome dowry, but candlemaking is passé. Gaslight is the future," Eleanor said, quoting her father.

"What?" Bertrem looked confused.

"You might find your heiress's papa hanging on your sleeve before too many years have passed," Eleanor explained.

"No, I won't," Bertrem burst out. "Cause I'll put a period to my existence before I let myself be leg-shackled to her."

Drusilla nodded vehemently, obviously agreeing with this sentiment.

"You'd do better to put a period to Grandmama's existence," Eleanor said practically. "That way Uncle Henry could inherit, and there'd be no impediment to your marrying Drusilla."

"True," Drusilla agreed. "If Grandmama were dead, then we'd all be comfortable."

"Well, perhaps not exactly all of us. I doubt that Grandmama would appreciate being dead," Eleanor felt obligated to point out.

"But if she's dead, she won't know anything about it," Drusilla argued.

"She's right, you know." Bertrem defended his love. "Mrs. Bromley'd be in heaven, or..." His voice trailed away, and he glanced down at the floor.

Eleanor finished the thought. "Hell, which is far more likely."

"That's up to the Lord," Drusilla said piously.

"If I remember my theology correctly, so's the time of her demise," Eleanor said.

"Yes, but—" Drusilla began stubbornly.

"And if the morality of the situation doesn't stop you, and I can well understand why it might not," Eleanor added honestly, "consider the consequences. Murder is a hanging offense."

"Only if they catch you." Bertrem wasn't ready to abandon what was plainly the best idea he'd heard to date.

"That's true." Drusilla gave him an approving smile. "What is needed is a little care."

"What is needed is a little common sense," Eleanor said.

"We can't shoot her," Drusilla decided.

"Certainly not. It would make such an awful mess on the carpet," Eleanor said, wondering uneasily if her cousin was serious. Such bloodthirstiness seemed entirely out of character. But then, her father always used to say that when a timid man finally got his back up, he could be extremely dangerous. Eleanor glanced over at her aunt, but she was still snuffling in her sleep.

"No, that's not the problem," Drusilla continued. "The servants would be bound to hear the shot and discover what had happened." Drusilla pursed her lips together consideringly. "I rather think that poison would work the best."

"What kind?" Bertrem asked.

"Actually, the very best way would be if she were to eat oysters that had gone off. Remember that friend of your papa's who ate oysters at that inn in Harrowgate a few years ago and died?" Drusilla said.

"It went out of business," Bertrem said. "But mayhap we could discover some off oysters right here in London."

"Might I point out to you two that if you were to go around asking vendors if they just happened to have any bad oysters, someone just might become suspicious when Grandmama suddenly died from eating them," Eleanor said tartly. "Besides, how would you get Cook to prepare them? Surely she'd notice?"

Drusilla sighed. "You're probably right, Cousin Eleanor."

Bertrem echoed her sigh. "There's a lot more to this murder business than first meets the eye. I don't suppose you'd care to help us, Miss Wallace?"

"Absolutely not," Eleanor said unequivocally. "And I want your word that you won't, either," she continued.

"No!" Drusilla's beautiful features took on a decidedly mulish cast.

Eleanor eyed her cousin in frustration. If she had thought for one moment that this idiotic pair would ever take her seriously... And she didn't dare risk telling Drusilla that she would give her a dowry. Not yet. Drusilla would never be able to keep the news to herself. She'd blurt the whole thing out, and there was no telling what her grandmother might do. No, Eleanor decided, she would announce her intentions of providing Drusilla with a dowry in her own time. After she found out what had happened to the necklace, and after she decided what she wanted to do about Connal as a husband.

"Then will you promise me that you won't do anything until after the Season is over?" Eleanor asked.

Drusilla looked at Bertrem, who shrugged and then nodded. "All right," she said.

"But what am I to do about this candlemaker's daughter that Papa wants me to marry?" Bertrem asked uncertainly.

Eleanor stared blindly at the Meissen china shepherdess on the mantel as she considered the problem. Finally, she said, "I think your best course of action would be passive resistance. If you were to flatly refuse to go along with the plan, your papa might come to London to try and force the issue. And we don't want that."

Bertrem tugged at his elaborately tied neckcloth and gulped. "No, we don't!" he agreed fervently. "He'll go on and on about how we'll all be living in a tumbledown cottage and how m'sisters'll dwindle t'old maids and how m'mother'll waste away... Fair gives me a turn to hear him go on like he does."

"I can imagine," Eleanor said in genuine sympathy. Connal produced much the same reaction in her.

"But he can't agree to marry this girl!" Drusilla wailed.

"Of course not. But the poor girl probably wants the marriage as little as Bertrem does."

"Not want to marry my Bertrem?" Drusilla looked at Eleanor as if she'd taken leave of her senses.

"I meant her affections are probably already engaged," Eleanor said soothingly. "What I would suggest, Mr.—"

"Call me Bertrem, if you like," he offered shyly.

"Bertrem," Eleanor repeated, "is that you stall. Tell your father you're not sure you can't do better. Or that you don't think she would settle into life in the country."

"Much m'father'd care about what she wants," Bertrem muttered. "But I'll try it."

"His Grace, the duke of Ryland," Walker intoned from the door.

Eleanor was quite clearly the only person glad to see him. Bertrem seemed to shrink in on himself, and Drusilla paled dramatically. Her aunt jerked up at the sound of Walker's voice and peered around the room in confusion.

"Good morning, Aunt Maria." It was Eleanor who broke the silence. "His Grace is here."

"How nice." Maria looked uncertainly at her shrinking daughter. "Won't you sit down, Your Grace?"

"No, thank you, Mrs. Bromley," he said, and Eleanor was hard-pressed to keep from giggling at Drusilla's relieved expression.

"I came to take Miss Wallace for a drive. I thought I'd show her a few of the sights of London."

"I'd like that." Eleanor hurriedly got to her feet, intent on escaping before her grandmother came downstairs.

"Goodbye." Eleanor smiled brightly at her still-groggy aunt and, taking Ryland's arm, hustled him out of the house, stopping only long enough to tie on her bonnet.

"Are we escaping?" Ryland asked as Walker closed the door behind them.

"Would that it were that easy," she muttered, carefully skirting his restless horses.

"They won't hurt you." Ryland took exception to her caution.

"Ha! It won't surprise me at all to find out that horses are really carnivores. Good morning." Eleanor smiled at the groom who was holding the beasts' heads.

"Mornin', miss." Wells bobbed his head.

Eleanor's breath caught in her throat as Ryland's strong fingers closed over her arm in order to help her into the carriage. She ran the tip of her tongue over her suddenly dry lips at the prickly sensation that chased over her skin. Her response to him seemed to be becoming more intense each time she touched him. Settling herself on the narrow seat, she made a pretense of straightening her soft muslin skirts to take her mind off her intense reaction to his touch. She wasn't successful. She could still feel the heat from his hand burning into her skin.

She watched with mesmerized fascination as he swung himself up onto the seat. He moved with a lithe grace that fascinated her. As he leaned forward to pick up the reins, his hard thigh pressed against her much softer one, heightening her awareness of him as a virile entity. Eleanor swallowed uneasily and, surreptitiously, inched away from him.

"I thought we'd try three jewelry shops that were in business at the time the necklace was stolen." Ryland's matter-of-fact tones helped her to submerge her confused emotions. "The first one is Addison and Henchly. It caters mainly to the merchant class."

He guided his restless team through the heavy traffic for about a mile and then turned into a quieter side street. Halfway down the block, he stopped in front of a smallish shop with a bow-fronted window. The name of Addison and Henchly was painted in gold on a white sign hanging above the gleaming black door, the windowpanes sparkled in the sunlight, and the flagstones had been freshly swept. The shop exuded a self-satisfaction that spoke discreetly of prosperity.

Eleanor allowed Ryland to help her down, trying to keep her mind firmly on the problem at hand and not on the feel of his skin pressing against hers. Worry about one thing at a time, she told herself.

The proprietor hurried over to them as they entered.

"Welcome to my humble establishment, Your Grace. I'm Addison. How may I be of service to you?"

"We're looking for a particular necklace." Ryland pulled the sketch out of his pocket and handed it to him. "The central jewel is a ruby, and the other stones are diamonds."

Addison raised his eyebrows as he studied the drawing. "A bit heavy for modern tastes," he finally said, with a speculative look at Eleanor. "Perhaps the young woman would care to see something more in keeping with the times?"

"The *lady*—" Ryland's voice hardened ever so slightly "—is only interested in this piece. It is of historical interest to her family."

"Hmm ... I see." Addison pulled on his lower lip as he studied the picture again. He shook his head. "I'm sure I've never seen it before. That one stone is very distinctive. Rubies are very hard to cut."

"Would there be anyone else in the shop who might recognize the necklace?" Ryland asked.

"Well ..." Addison tugged on his lower lip again. "There's old Jonas, in the workshop upstairs. He makes a great many of the pieces for our customers. Been doing it for almost fifty years now. I could ask him."

"Thank you. We'd appreciate it." Eleanor smiled warmly at Addison, and he seemed to swell under her admiring gaze.

"Certainly, m'lady. Be glad to oblige. I'll be right back."

Eleanor watched as he disappeared into the back of the shop and asked Ryland, "How did he know you were a duke?"

Ryland chuckled. "My fame has gone before me? More practically, he probably looked out the window when we drove up and saw the crest on the curricle. Since I'm the only member of the house of Wolfe left in England, it was a reasonable assumption."

"Ah, Your Grace, sorry to keep you waiting." Addison emerged from the back room. "But I didn't want to rush Jonas."

"And?" Eleanor asked eagerly.

Addison looked crestfallen at having to disappoint her. "He never saw either the stone or the setting before."

Eleanor bit back her sense of frustration and forced a smile. "It was kind of you to take the time to try to help us, Mr. Addison. I shall remember your establishment in the future."

"Thank you, m'lady." He beamed at her, evidently visualizing hordes of fashionably dressed, well-inlaid society

matrons patronizing his shop. "If I should find out anything more about the necklace, I'll be sure to let you know."

"Thank you," Ryland said. "Simply send word to Ryland House."

"Good day, Mr. Addison." Eleanor followed Ryland out
of the store. Hoping to forestall her growing reaction to his
touch, she scrambled into the carriage herself.

"You aren't discouraged yet, are you?" Ryland checked
the reins and urged the horses into motion.

She grimaced. "A little. I know that it wasn't likely that
he'd recognize it, but..."

"But you hoped he would, anyway," Ryland concluded.
"Take heart. We still have two more shops to try. One of
them might remember something."

Their second stop, at the establishment of Price and Sons,
was equally fruitless. The proprietor was quite obviously
overwhelmed to see Ryland, and was all eagerness to please.
Unfortunately, he couldn't tell them anything about the
necklace.

However, their third stop proved far more profitable. It
was at Rundell and Bridge, which, according to Ryland, was
the city's leading purveyor of jewels to the aristocracy and
had been as long as he knew.

Their arrival was greeted with restrained but unmistakable enthusiasm. An enthusiasm that didn't wane one bit
when Ryland told the head clerk that he had come for information, not jewelry.

They were discreetly ushered back to the office of Mr.
Bridge and invited to be seated while the clerk discovered the
whereabouts of the proprietor.

Eleanor's interest was caught by a curio cabinet under the
window that held an impressive collection of carved jade.
Her father had been an avid collector, too, and she felt a
sudden lump in her throat at the thought of how much he
would have enjoyed examining this one.

"What is it?" Ryland leaned over her shoulder and stared
at the small pieces.

"The past. While your precious Romans were out
slaughtering the Gauls, the Chinese were carving these.
Look at the intricacy of the carving of that whale."

"Ah, are you a devotee of jade sculpture, Your Grace?" Mr. Bridge spoke from the open doorway.

"No, it is Miss Wallace here who has the interest," Ryland said. "Miss Wallace, may I make known to you Mr. Bridge."

"How do you do, Miss Wallace. I read of your arrival in *The Morning Post.* Allow me to extend you a welcome to England, and to hope that you will continue your family's long tradition of patronizing my establishment."

"Thank you, Mr. Bridge," Eleanor said.

"Now, how is it that I might be of service to you?"

"By telling us if you recognize this necklace." Ryland handed the drawing to him.

Mr. Bridge took the sketch over to the large window and held it up to the light, where he carefully studied it. Finally, he asked, "What is it you wished to know?"

"Have you ever seen it before?" Eleanor asked eagerly.

"Yes." He nodded his head with a slow deliberation that made Eleanor want to shake him to hurry him up. "My, it must have been . . ." He squinted thoughtfully, as if looking down a long corridor of years. "My, yes. It was the summer my grandfather died."

"You actually saw it?" Ryland demanded.

"Why, yes. Right after your grandfather won it, Miss Wallace."

"Won it?" Eleanor repeated in confusion. "I thought it was a family heirloom?"

"Oh, my, no." Mr. Bridge put the tips of his fingers together and stared thoughtfully at them. "It isn't possible. I mean, the circumstances being what they were, and all," he said delicately.

Eleanor looked at Ryland, who raised his eyebrows as if disclaiming all knowledge of what Mr. Bridge was talking about. Finally, Eleanor simply asked, "What circumstances?"

"I was merely referring to the fact that, since your grandmother's father made his fortune in trade, and since your Grandfather Bromley ran through his inheritance before marriage . . ." Mr. Bridge shrugged.

Eleanor stared at him in shock, having a hard time believing what she was hearing. Her snobbish grandmother was herself one of the cits that she was forever stigmatizing?

"Yes, your grandfather won that particular piece from a man who'd just returned from India after having made a considerable fortune," Mr. Bridge continued. "As I recall, the man died shortly thereafter of a fever he'd picked up out there. Beastly climate, that." He shook his head mournfully.

"And my Grandfather Bromley brought the piece to you?"

"Yes, for an appraisal to have it insured."

"You appraised it?" Ryland asked.

"My father did the actual appraisal," Mr. Bridge corrected. "I merely helped. I remember that he was struck by the particular brilliance and clarity of the central ruby. Said it was one of the finest he'd ever seen."

"Do you have records on it?" Eleanor asked eagerly.

"Certainly. It shouldn't take me but a few minutes." He went to the cabinet behind him and, after sifting through a row of ledgers, finally extracted one. "My, my." He shook his head as he opened it. "This really takes me back."

Eleanor could barely contain her rising impatience as he slowly leafed through the ledger. Just when she was about to grab it out of his hands and look herself, he found the entry.

"It was '87. June 13, to be exact. We cleaned the necklace and furnished a written appraisal. Mr. Bromley picked up both items four days later."

"How much was the appraisal for?" Eleanor asked.

"Ah, let me see. Forty-six thousand pounds."

"Forty-six thousand pounds!" Eleanor gasped.

Mr. Bridge nodded majestically. "Yes, indeed. As I said, the stones were particularly fine. Of course, today it would be worth quite a bit more. It might fetch as much as sixty or seventy thousand at auction. I can think of several collectors who might pay that much for it."

"Have you seen it since then?" Ryland asked.

"No, more's the pity."

"And you haven't seen any other pieces of jewelry that had stones that looked like the ones in the necklace?" Eleanor persisted.

Mr. Bridge shook his head emphatically. "No, Miss Wallace. Stones like the ones in that necklace are distinctive. Just as individuals are. It wouldn't matter what setting they were put into, they would be immediately recognizable."

"I see." Eleanor's voice fell in disappointment. "Thank you very much for your help."

"It is always an aim of Rundell and Bridge to be of service to the Bromley family, Miss Wallace," he told her as he personally ushered them out of the shop.

Eleanor silently climbed into the curricle, breathing a sigh of relief when Ryland gave his groom a guinea and told him that he wouldn't be needing him for the rest of the afternoon. She wanted to discuss this latest development with Ryland. Something she couldn't do with his groom listening to every word.

Ryland vaulted up into the curricle and deftly steered the vehicle into the teeming traffic. Once he had reached Hyde Park, he turned the horses onto a deserted side pathway and slowed them to a walk.

"I can't decide whether to be angry or amused," Eleanor finally burst out.

"I hope I'm not the focus of either feeling."

"Not you, my grandmother. If what Mr. Bridge said was correct—"

"I think we can safely assume it is. There would be no reason for him to lie. After all, it's an easily ascertainable fact. Besides, it fits."

Eleanor frowned at him. "What fits?"

"Her becoming such a high stickler. Haven't you ever noticed that those who have the most reason to be compassionate are often the most rigid in their prejudices?"

"Not really," Eleanor said, realizing just how limited her actual experience with society was. She might have been her father's hostess, but he hadn't entertained much, and then only business associates. Her grandmother and people like her were entirely outside her own limited experience.

"I shouldn't think the necklace was ever insured," Ryland said slowly. "But it should be easy to find out. I'll have my secretary check with the insurance agents tomorrow."

"Thank you." Eleanor smiled gratefully at him, and Ryland felt as if a band were being drawn around his chest, constricting his breathing. Compulsively his eyes were drawn to her soft, pink lips. To their luscious fullness. He wanted to press his own mouth against them. To explore their exact taste and texture. To revel in their sweetness. He forced himself to look up, away from the tantalizing promise of her mouth. Up into her bright brown eyes. His attention was captured by the way the sunlight filtered through her thick eyelashes, adding a reddish hue to them.

Eleanor ran the tip of her tongue over her lips, and he felt the band around his chest tighten almost painfully. His need to kiss her was rapidly approaching a compulsion that recognized neither social convention nor their present lack of privacy. She was so desirable. And not only physically. With her intelligence and compassion, she'd make a wonderful mother. She'd never abandon her children to follow the giddy social whirl, as so many of the women of their class did, he thought with conviction. Eleanor would love and care for her children. He felt desire slam through him with the force of a blow, hardening his body at the tantalizing thought of making love to her. Of being the father of her children.

"There is one facet about this whole thing that bothers me," Eleanor said. "Who does the necklace really belong to?"

Ryland dragged his mind away from his provocative thoughts and forced himself to concentrate on what she was saying.

"Belong to?" he repeated blankly.

Eleanor nodded thoughtfully. "Yes. I'm sure that my aunt said that Grandfather Bromley left everything he had to Uncle Henry. If he won the necklace in a card game, wouldn't it belong to Uncle Henry?"

"An interesting point," Ryland conceded. "I would think so. It would depend on the wording of the will. But it may also be a moot point, since we aren't any closer to finding it than we were.''

"I know." Eleanor's lower lip drooped, and Ryland watched it in fascination. He wanted to kiss her unhappiness away. To put his arms around her and protect her from all her worries—now and in the future.

Almost without conscious thought, he pulled the horses to a stop and leaned toward her and gently—ever so gently—touched his lips to hers. Her mouth seemed to cling. To grow warmer and fuller, sending ripples of sensation through him. He pressed harder, trying to intensify the intoxicating feeling. To his delight, Eleanor made no effort to withdraw. Instead, she reached up and rubbed the palm of her hand over his cheek.

He shuddered at the sensation that spiraled through him, turning his bones liquid with desire. Blindly, he transferred the horses' reins to his left hand and grasped the nape of her neck in his right, pulling her closer and kissing her with compulsive need. The very faint fragrance of lilacs filled his nostrils, evoking a flood of memories about the joy of springtime after the dreary chill of winter. Eleanor Wallace was his springtime, he thought distractedly. His promise of life to come after the death of this past year.

He wanted to marry her. The truth bubbled to the surface of his confused thoughts. But it was too soon to declare himself yet. He stifled his impulse to say something to her. She needed time. Time to get to know both him and England better. While he needed . . . His eyes focused longingly on her soft, quivering lips.

But not now. He controlled his urge to kiss her again with a monumental effort. Not here in the park, where anyone could see them and subject her to damaging gossip. He needed privacy to kiss her properly. To caress her. To explore the creamy perfection of her small, perfect breasts. He lifted his head and stared down into her unfocused eyes.

She blinked several times, as if trying to bring the world back into perspective. "I think I must be depraved," she said.

"Depraved!" He stared at her in surprise. "You wouldn't recognize depraved if—"

"My dear sir, you forget, I have studied the classics."
Eleanor worriedly nibbled on her lower lip.

He bit back an impulse to laugh when he realized she was
serious. "I stand corrected. You are an authority on de-
pravity. May I ask why you are worried?"

Eleanor looked at him uncertainly for a long moment and
then said, "Because I very much fear that I am far too fond
of kissing you. I don't think women of our class are supposed to enjoy—"

"Of all the damned gammon!" Some of Ryland's sexual
frustration spilled out. "The Romans never tried to convince their women that they had no feelings from the neck
down."

"Your Grace!"

"Well, you were the one who brought the subject up. And
they didn't."

She unexpectedly chuckled. "To be frank, I don't think
they tried to convince them of anything, because they didn't
care what they thought."

"That's slander, and inaccurate slander besides. I have a
book you can read about the real facts. I'll have my stew-
ard post it down from Cumberland." He snapped the reins
and the horses started forward again. "And my name is
James," he added.

James. Eleanor explored the gift of his name and decided it fit him. Perfectly. She felt some of her tension ooze
away. Ryland didn't think she was depraved. And while his
giving her yet one more weighty tome to wade through was
disheartening, that was overshadowed by the knowledge
that he intended to continue to see her. The world suddenly
seemed like an exciting place. A place that she was free to
explore, now that she'd fulfilled her obligation to her father's memory.

Chapter Twelve

"Such a lovely afternoon, isn't it, dear?" Maria smiled warmly at Eleanor, who was sitting on the sofa across from her, pretending to knit.

"Yes, Aunt Maria." Eleanor obediently glanced out the window at the bright sunlight. It really was a beautiful day. In fact, it would be a perfect day, if she didn't have incriminating papers hidden in the library, she thought nervously. She bit on the inside of her soft lower lip as she speculated for at least the hundredth time on Connal's whereabouts. It had been two days since she'd stolen the notes. Two interminable, nerve-racking days, and Connal still hadn't called.

Nor had he put in an appearance at any of the four parties she'd attended during the last two evenings. Nor had she seen the Frenchman, De Selignac. A fact for which she was exceedingly glad. He made her nervous. Very nervous, and ever so slightly afraid. Eleanor shivered at the memory of his cold, flat eyes, which had chilled her when she'd met him at Lady Jersey's ball.

"Yes, dear, I agree. It makes me nervous, too," Maria said.

Eleanor stared apprehensively at her aunt, thinking for one awful moment that Maria was referring to the stolen plans. But then common sense came to her rescue. There was no way that Maria could possibly know what she'd done. No one knew. Not even Connal. Yet.

Maria sighed. "It just will not do."

Eleanor followed her aunt's gaze and realized that Maria thought that she had been reacting to the sight of Bertrem and Drusilla with their heads together, talking in low whispers.

"If Esme should return . . ." Maria murmured, with an uneasy glance at the deserted square outside.

"I think we're safe for at least another hour," Eleanor said soothingly. "You know how Grandmama loves to gossip with Mrs. Scudthorpe. I doubt that she'll be able to tear herself away much before four."

"You're probably right." Maria brightened perceptibly. "I hope so. Mother Bromley has been so irritable lately that I despair of ever pleasing her."

Eleanor eyed her aunt sympathetically. "You mean, since I came to stay?"

"This is your home now that your poor papa has passed to his eternal reward," Maria said earnestly. "Where else would you go but here?"

As far as her grandmother was concerned, virtually anywhere else, Eleanor thought.

"Besides, dear, it isn't all your fault. In fact, I really think she likes having you here."

Eleanor chuckled. "Allow me to inform you that you are all about in your head, Aunt Maria."

"No, dear. You see, since you had to come back here to live, it made Mother Bromley feel that she was right about your father's inability to provide for her daughter," Maria said on a surprising flash of insight.

"So you see, Eleanor, you aren't the real problem. The real problem is that she isn't having any success at forcing an engagement between Drusilla and Ryland. And after bragging to all her friends . . ."

Eleanor frowned. "Aunt Maria, why did Grandmama's fancy land on Ryland? He and Drusilla have absolutely nothing in common. He's very active in government policy circles and scholastic pursuits, while Drusilla . . ." Eleanor gestured impotently.

"He's a duke, dear," Maria said simply. "A very wealthy duke. In fact, other than Devonshire, who is sadly hard of hearing, he's the only duke on the marriage mart this season."

"But it's the man that Drusilla would have to live with. What would they even talk about?"

Maria heaved a heartfelt sigh. "I'm beginning to share your concerns, dear, but if Drusilla doesn't marry as her grandmother wants, then she won't get to marry anyone, and nothing could be worse than to dwindle to an old maid."

There were plenty of things worse than being an old maid, Eleanor thought tartly. Not the least of which was being trapped in a marriage with a man with whom you had nothing in common. With no points of shared interest to build on. A fleeting vision of Connal's face floated through her mind.

"Perhaps something will happen..." Maria suggested with a hopefulness that Eleanor felt was entirely misplaced. "Why, just this morning at breakfast, Drusilla mentioned that Mother Bromley had taken a couple of nasty turns while they were out together this past week."

Eleanor eyed her aunt in unfeigned shock. Drusilla couldn't really be trying to lay the groundwork for poisoning her grandmother, could she? She glanced over at her cousin, who was smiling sweetly up into Bertrem's round face. Drusilla had promised to wait until the Season was over. But would she keep her word? For that matter, was she really contemplating poisoning Esme? It seemed inconceivable, but then, two months ago Eleanor would have said that it was inconceivable that she would take up spying.

Despite the fact that she preferred to wait until her visit was over to announce her intention of giving Drusilla a dowry, she might not have that luxury, she conceded. Either her grandmother or Bertrem's father or Drusilla herself could force her hand, and that being the case, she'd better do as much of the groundwork as possible now. Perhaps this afternoon she could find time to see her uncle's man of business. Something she'd been meaning to do anyway.

Maria nodded, completely misunderstanding Eleanor's worried expression. "I don't doubt the news gave you a turn, dear. It did me, too. I mean, I know Mother Bromley is well into her seventies, but she's never shown any signs of slowing down before. But there's no denying it would be so providential if she were to..."

"Quite," Eleanor said, unexpectedly feeling sorry for her grandmother. How incredibly sad that one's own family would like nothing better than to have you dead. Although, in her grandmother's case, it was certainly understandable.

"Oh, look, there's a carriage pulling up." Maria pointed out the window. "Drusilla, dear, who is that?"

Eleanor sent up a silent prayer. Please let it be Connal. She wanted to give him the copied plans and be done with her part of the spying. The sooner the better.

Heaven, as it seemed to be doing with increasing frequency lately, turned a deaf ear to her plea.

"It's the duke of Ryland." Drusilla might have been announcing the arrival of the hangman.

Eleanor instinctively straightened as a sparkling shower of excitement skittered along her nerve endings.

"And he has someone with him." Drusilla sounded uncertain. "A strange-looking little man."

"Don't stare, dear," Maria ordered. "We don't want the duke to think we're vulgar."

If her grandmother's attempts to leg-shackle him to Drusilla hadn't already convinced him, then nothing ever would, Eleanor thought wryly. It was strange, but despite the fact that she'd only known Ryland a matter of weeks and her relatives had known him all their lives, they didn't seem to have the vaguest idea what he was really like. What he thought or wanted. It was as if they had never ventured past his title to explore what kind of man wore it.

"His Grace, the duke of Ryland, and..." Walker looked down his nose at the small, grubby man standing behind Ryland.

"Jeffers, guvnor," the apparition announced belligerently. "I be Jeffers."

Walker shook his head and, muttering under his breath, left.

"Good morning, Your Grace," Maria said brightly. "Drusilla, say good morning to His Grace."

"Good morning, Your Grace," Drusilla parroted weakly.

"Good morning, Your Grace," Bertrem echoed.

Ryland gave them a polite nod and walked over to Eleanor. He gestured Mr. Jeffers into the chair across from her and sat down on the sofa beside her.

"Mornin', missus," Jeffers offered to Maria, who was staring at him curiously.

"Good morning, Mr. Jeffers. Are you a friend of Ryland's?"

"What, me?" Jeffers laughed, showing a row of rotting teeth. "That's a rare un." He slapped his knee gleefully. "Me, a friend of a bloomin' dook!"

Maria stared blankly at him, obviously uncertain as to what was expected of her in the circumstances. She fell back on that old standby—tea. "I'll just see Walker a moment about a tray." Maria gave Eleanor a helpless look and then hurried out of the room after the butler.

Ryland immediately gestured toward the large portrait above the mantel. "That's the necklace, Jeffers. Take a good look at it."

"Hmm..." Jeffers stared up at it intently.

Ryland glanced over at Drusilla and Bertrem, but they'd retreated back into their private conversation and seemed oblivious of what was going on around them.

"What kind of colleague is Mr. Jeffers?" Eleanor whispered to Ryland.

Ryland chuckled. "One it's best to keep at a distance. A friend of mine suggested him when I mentioned that I was trying to locate a necklace that had disappeared years ago."

Eleanor studied Jeffers' absorbed expression a moment and then asked, "He recovers stolen jewels?"

"No, not to wrap the matter up in clean linen, he helps them disappear."

"Really?" Eleanor turned to study the little man with renewed interest. "Is he any good at it?"

"The Crown's never managed to prove anything. So one would conclude that he's very good or very lucky."

"Or that the Crown's inept," Eleanor added.

"A distinct possibility," he conceded. "By the way, my secretary was able to find out that the necklace was never insured."

"Sorry, dook." Jeffers shook his head mournfully. "Wish I could help ya. Really I does. But them sparklers, I ain't never seen 'em afore."

"Think back, man," Ryland ordered. "They disappeared over twenty-five years ago."

Jeffers drew himself up to his full four-foot-ten and said, "I knows m'business. If'n them sparklers was prigged, then whoever done it has still got 'em." He nodded emphatically. "Ain't never seen nothin' quite like that there ruby." He turned and gave it an admiring glance. "Like somethin' from the bloody crown jewels, 'tis."

"Well, thank you anyway, Jeffers." Eleanor tried to keep her disappointment out of her voice.

"We appreciate your help," Ryland added, pulling a more tangible expression of his gratitude out of his waistcoat pocket and flipping it to him.

Jeffers quickly pocketed the golden guinea and gave him a conspiratorial wink. "Thanks, Yer Worship. Right sportin' of ya. If'n I can help ya again..." He began to edge toward the door.

"Won't you stay for tea?" Eleanor asked.

"Tea!" He looked thunderstruck. "Don't mess with that maudlin stuff, miss. It'll muddle yer insides, it will. Ale's t'only proper drink fer an Englishman."

Eleanor watched him slide out the salon door. A moment later he appeared on the street outside and quickly disappeared from view.

"It was a good idea anyway, James," Eleanor said.

"Unfortunately, it might as well have been a bad one for all the results it got." Ryland shot a frustrated glare up at the painting. "I am fast reaching the conclusion that whoever stole the necklace still has it."

Eleanor sighed. "If that's the case, then we'll probably never find it. I originally thought that my grandmother wouldn't have the willpower to possess it and not wear it, but..."

"No, I still think you're right," Ryland said thoughtfully. "But, unfortunately, I don't have time to try to plot a new line of attack today. I have to give a speech, and I'm already running late."

"Where?" Eleanor was caught off guard by the sense of loss she felt as he got to his feet. Her anticipation of the afternoon began to seep away, leaving the world a rather boring place.

"In the House of Lords." He glanced over at Bertrem and Drusilla, who were still whispering in the corner, shrugged and, with a quick smile at Eleanor, hurried out.

Eleanor watched through the window as Ryland ran down the front steps and vaulted into his waiting curricle. She didn't want him to leave. She faced the fact squarely. She wanted him to stay and discuss the missing necklace with her. Stay and discuss anything, even his boring old Romans, as long as he stayed. It seemed as if he had taken all her pleasure in the day with him.

"But where did Ryland and his acquaintance go, dear?" Maria said as she hurried back into the room.

"They couldn't stay for tea, Aunt Maria. Ryland said something about a speech in the House of Lords."

"Yes. Henry mentioned this morning at breakfast that they're having a debate about the need to adequately support the troops for the final offensive against Napoleon. He expects it to be a close-run thing. They'll need Ryland to influence the ones wavering." Maria shook her head. "Poor Henry, he gets so discouraged sometimes. He says that far too many of the English can't see beyond their own pocketbooks."

"A common failing," Eleanor said sympathetically.

"Well, I for one don't mean to let it cast me into the dismals," Maria said. "Men will do exactly as they please, they always do."

Eleanor grimaced. "It certainly seems so. Aunt Maria, do you suppose I could go for a walk around the square? I feel so restless."

Maria cocked her graying head to one side as she considered Eleanor's request. "It's not what one usually does, but it should be all right if you take a maid with you."

Eleanor bit her lip, feeling guilty about lying to her aunt. But it was imperative she visit her uncle's man of business as soon as possible to find out what the financial cost of rescuing her uncle's family would be. And she didn't dare risk using one of the family carriages to go. The groom might mention where he'd taken her, and it could get back to her grandmother, who would demand all kinds of explanations. Explanations Eleanor didn't want to make.

Daisy, on the other hand, gave every penny of her salary to her widowed mother. The gift of a coin would erase all memory of the trip, as far as the young maid was concerned.

"I think I'll go for my walk now, and then, when I return, I'll read in my room until dinner," Eleanor said, hoping that if she was detained, Maria would simply assume that she was in her room, reading.

Eleanor found Daisy shelling peas in the kitchen, and ten minutes later they were briskly walking toward one end of Grosvenor Square.

"I ain't that partial to walkin', miss," Daisy gasped as she struggled to keep up with Eleanor.

"We aren't going to be walking long, Daisy. Just as soon as we're well out of sight of the house, we'll hail a hackney cab."

"Really?" Daisy eyed Eleanor with sudden interest. "We goin' t'meet yer beau?"

"No. I'm going to see Mr. Potter. I want to know about my grandfather's will." Eleanor gave Daisy just enough information to allow her to draw the wrong conclusion.

"Oh." Daisy nodded sagely. "Ya be wantin' ta see if'n your grandpap left ya anythin'. Oh, there's one now." Daisy waved wildly at the hackney's driver, and he obediently pulled his plodding horse to a stop.

Eleanor gingerly climbed into the ancient carriage and gave the bored-looking driver their destination. Fifteen minutes later the horse lurched to a standstill in front of a plain brownstone building in Lombard Street.

"Here you be, miss," the man announced. "You want I should wait?"

"No, thank you." Eleanor paid him his three shillings and got out, trailed by the curious Daisy. Trying to look more assured than she felt, Eleanor walked up to the door and rapped the gleaming brass knocker.

The door was opened almost immediately by a young man wearing a spotless brown coat and a well-polished face.

"Good afternoon?" He looked taken aback to find two women on his doorstep.

Visiting a man of business was undoubtedly one more of the seemingly endless list of things that women didn't normally do in England, Eleanor thought in resignation.

"I am here to see Mr. Potter." Eleanor borrowed her grandmother's imperious tone.

"Certainly, ma'am. And what name should I give him?"

"Miss Wallace."

"She be Mrs. Bromley's granddaughter from 'merica," Daisy added helpfully.

The young man bobbed an awkward bow and scurried away. He returned a few minutes later with a thin, balding middle-aged man.

Eleanor critically studied Mr. Potter, mentally approving of his well-cut blue coat, his spotless linen, and especially the warm smile on his long face.

"Ah, Miss Wallace. Allow me to offer you a belated welcome to England." He gave her a firm handshake, which increased Eleanor's sense of approval. "Edward, find a chair for Miss Wallace's maid." He ushered Eleanor into his office and, closing the door behind them, motioned her into a green leather chair in front of his desk.

Sitting down across from her, he studied her for a moment and then unexpectedly sighed. "My, how you do take me back. I remember your dear mother. She was so beautiful, like a fairy princess from out of a nursery book." He shook his head as if dislodging the memories and said, "How may I be of service to you?"

"By first giving me your word that what I discuss with you won't be divulged to anyone else."

"Certainly not!" he said emphatically. "A man of business who gains a reputation for gossip will soon find himself without clients."

"Very well, then," Eleanor said. She decided to follow her instincts and trust him. "I don't know what you've heard about me..."

"That your father recently died and that you have returned to live with your only surviving family," he said promptly.

"And I believe the gossip has it that I'm penniless, as well as fatherless?"

He nodded. "It's hardly to be wondered at. A new country, and your father's expertise being in learning, not commerce."

"Mr. Potter, I have not told anyone, but the fact is, my father left me an estate of about three-quarters of a million pounds," Eleanor said baldly.

"Three—" He gulped several times and peered uncertainly at her over the rim of his steel-framed spectacles.

"Give or take a few thousand. I came to England for a variety of reasons, and I felt that my interests would be best served if no one knew about my wealth. The situation here in London with my mother's family is . . ." Eleanor groped unsuccessfully for a word.

"Regrettable?" Mr. Potter offered.

"That's one way of putting it. To cut to the heart of the matter, what I need from you is information. It's difficult to find out exactly where matters stand financially without running afoul of my grandmother. Will you tell me what I want to know?" she asked bluntly.

Mr. Potter frowned, staring out the window as if seeking enlightenment there. Finally he asked, "What do you intend to do with the information?"

"Give my uncle's family a measure of financial independence."

"That's certainly an admirable goal. May I ask why?"

Eleanor shrugged. "Because I like them. Because they're all the family I have left in the world. Because I can easily afford to. Because it would annoy my grandmother . . ."

Mr. Potter permitted himself a small, satisfied smile. "In that case, I will help, if you in turn will promise not to divulge the source of your information."

Eleanor nodded. "Agreed. Would you tell me exactly how my Grandfather Bromley's estate was left?"

"Everything he possessed was left to his sole surviving son, your uncle Henry. The problem was that Mr. Bromley didn't have much to leave. Just the family estate in Lincolnshire, and it's in very bad heart. The rents barely bring in two hundred pounds a year." Mr. Potter shook his head. "It's a shame, because it's prime land that could bring in thousands. Unfortunately, before that is possible, someone must invest substantially in it."

"Mr. Potter," Eleanor said slowly. "A few months before my grandfather died, he won a very valuable necklace in a game of chance from a nabob recently returned from India."

"I wasn't aware of that, unless..." He looked thoughtful. "Would that be the one that Mrs. Bromley accused your father of taking?"

"Yes, but he didn't," Eleanor said vehemently. "What I want to know is, who would it belong to if I were able to find it."

"Clearly your uncle."

"Grandmama couldn't claim it?" Eleanor persisted.

Mr. Potter shrugged. "What she might do is problematic. But legally she has no redress. If the necklace can be located, it belongs to your uncle."

"I see. As for Uncle Henry's estate, do you have any idea of how much it would take to right the situation?"

"An excellent start could be made for about fifteen thousand pounds. That amount would produce added revenues, which could in turn be reinvested."

"I see," Eleanor said. "And my cousin Drusilla's dowry?"

"Is totally dependent on your grandmother's goodwill," Mr. Potter said.

"What would happen to Drusilla's dowry if Grandmama were to die before she married?"

"Mrs. Bromley makes no secret of her will. It specifies a sum of ten thousand pounds to Drusilla. Henry receives the remainder, which would be about seventy thousand pounds in the funds, and all her personal property. No one else is mentioned."

"There is one other thing that I want to know...." Eleanor paused, trying to decide how to best phrase her question. "You are perhaps aware that my grandmother has plans concerning my cousin's marriage...."

Mr. Potter allowed himself a discreet snort. "The whole of London knows of her plans, Miss Wallace. She has told everyone."

"She should have tried telling Ryland," Eleanor said dryly. "I very much suspect that in his way he's even stubborner than Grandmama. He's just a lot more reasonable about what he wants."

Mr. Potter gave her a small smile. "Ah, yes, the duke of Ryland. It will be quite a feather in the cap of any young woman lucky enough to marry him."

"Perhaps, but the duke's marriage plans are not my concern." Eleanor ignored her feeling of loss at the thought of James married to someone and unavailable to talk to. "However, my cousin's are. She is deeply in love with a neighbor from Lincolnshire...."

"Young Arylesworth." Mr. Potter shook his head. "Sad case, that. So many of our old country families have found themselves in the basket, what with the taxes for the war and the falling price of grain...."

"How badly dipped is his father?" Eleanor asked.

"Not as badly as he could be," Mr. Potter said, hedging. "Your cousin's ten thousand would pay off all the outstanding mortgages and allow a little capital for emergencies. Unfortunately, your grandmother has set her face against the match, and young Arylesworth's father is determined to marry his son to an heiress and solve all his financial problems in one fell swoop."

"But what about his son's happiness?"

"Miss Wallace, I don't know about Boston, but here in England, marriages among the ton are rarely contracted for love."

"Perhaps not, but would not a wealthy young heiress be able to look higher than Bertrem for a husband?"

Mr. Potter shrugged. "In this case, the girl is not particularly genteel, the father wants to see his daughter settled this Season, and Bertrem is available. Or so Mr. Arylesworth claims. The two fathers are in the process of negotiation."

"Don't you think Bertrem should at least meet this girl before he's expected to propose?" Eleanor asked.

"I was not asked my opinion in the matter. Squire Arylesworth feels his affairs are such that he doesn't have the option of waiting until next Season."

"I see. Mr. Potter, I will be blunt with you. My cousin, for reasons best known to herself, wants to marry Bertrem. I am willing to give her a dowry equal to the ten thousand that Grandmother had promised."

"You are very generous, Miss Wallace, but I doubt it would answer. The merchant is willing to pay more. Almost twice as much."

"I am not concerned with Bertrem's father's greed," Eleanor said flatly. "Ten thousand is fair, and if my cousin is willing to see her dowry used to rescue her father-in-law, that is her choice. But I am no pigeon to be plucked."

"No." Mr. Potter eyed her with respect. "It would appear that you aren't. Tell me, Miss Wallace, what is my part in all this to be?"

"You've already played it, Mr. Potter." Eleanor got to her feet.

"Please be assured that you may command my help at any time, if you should need it," Mr. Potter said as he walked her to the door.

"Thank you." Eleanor shook his hand and, motioning to Daisy, left his office.

The door had scarcely closed behind them when Daisy demanded, "Any chance of a honey fall fer ya?"

"No." Eleanor began to slowly walk to the corner, her mind on what she'd learned from Mr. Potter. She now knew what the price of rescuing her uncle's family would be, and it wasn't excessive. As she saw it, the biggest problem could well be Bertrem's father's attempts to force a quick marriage on his son.

Bertrem would simply have to continue to stall until the Season was over and she was ready to return to Boston, Eleanor finally decided. Then she'd give Drusilla her dowry and immediately sail for America. That way, she would have the visit to remember, and her uncle's family would have their independence.

"Say, isn't that there the man what give me the shillin' to give ya that note?" Daisy asked.

"What?" Eleanor shook off her faint feeling of sadness at the thought of leaving England.

"That man what give me the note. Remember, ya was that upset about it." Drusilla gestured toward the street. "I'm sure that's him in the carriage."

Eleanor looked where Daisy was pointing and found herself staring at Connal.

Botheration! Eleanor thought in frustrated annoyance. Connal had finally appeared, and the purloined notes were back at her uncle's house.

"Ah, Miss Wallace." Connal pulled his trim-looking bay horse to a halt and raised his hat politely, ignoring the gaping Daisy.

"Mr. Gunn." Eleanor nodded.

"Pray come for a drive with me through the park?" The offer was couched as a question, but Eleanor had no trouble discerning the underlying order. "You there, girl." Connal's voice hardened perceptibly. "Your mistress is going driving with me. Get yourself home at once."

"And how is she to do that?" Eleanor asked reasonably. "We're miles from Grosvenor Square."

"She'll walk, of course."

"Nonsense, it's too far," Eleanor said, remembering how Ryland had so casually tossed his groom a coin for a hackney and a pint of ale, as if looking out for his dependents' well-being were a deeply ingrained habit.

"You want me to waste money for a servant to ride?" Connal demanded, as if he couldn't believe his ears. "You'll spoil her."

"Ha!" Daisy muttered under her breath. "No chance of that, in Mrs. Bromley's house."

Eleanor gave up the argument. Reaching into her own reticule, she pulled out four shillings and gave them to the delighted Daisy. "Don't dawdle on the way home, and if anyone should ask, tell them I accepted a ride from Mr. —"

"Baron," Connal said tightly.

"Baron Gunn," Eleanor repeated as she scrambled into his carriage, pretending not to notice the hand he held out to assist her.

"You're going to have to try harder to remember that I am a baron." Predictably, Connal started off with a complaint. "And what are you doing here in Lombard Street?"

"What are you doing here?" Eleanor countered.

"I paid a boy to watch the house and follow you when you left. He trailed you here and then came to tell me."

Eleanor swallowed her sense of outrage at Connal's invasion of her privacy and focused instead on finding out why he'd done it.

"You went to so much trouble to set yourself up a false identity so you could visit the house, so why are you still setting up clandestine meetings?" she asked.

"Think, Eleanor." He gave her a long-suffering look that made her want to box his ears. It was a feeling she had a lot when she was around Connal, she suddenly realized. Even when she agreed with him on his goals, such as freeing America from England's domination, he still annoyed her. Had he always done that? Or was it something that had just started to happen since she'd come to England?

"Would you pay attention?"

"And would you make up your mind?" she replied. "You just told me to think, and that's what I was doing. And what I think is that I don't like being followed like a common felon."

"I wanted to talk to you without the risk of being overheard. This seemed like the easiest way," Connal said, defending himself. "Now, if you have finished with all the questions, tell me, did you manage to discover anything?"

"Yes." Eleanor choked the word out.

"You did!" He jerked on the reins in his excitement, and the horse sidled nervously to one side, scraping the carriage wheels against the curb. "What?"

"Uncle Henry's notes for the spring offensive to be launched along the Canadian border," she said reluctantly, unable to shake the feeling that what she was doing was wrong. Terribly wrong.

"Give them to me." Connal held out a hand that shook with eagerness. Eleanor stared down at the pale brown leather driving glove reaching so greedily for her and felt nothing but revulsion. Her father, she reminded herself. Her father had wanted America to be free, and her information could help.

"I don't have the papers on me," she finally said.

"Damn!"

"Carrying stolen military plans around is hardly the action of a rational person," Eleanor insisted.

"Then where are they?"

"Safely hidden back at the house."

"I'll get them when I take you home," he planned. "What about Ryland?"

"What *about* Ryland?" Eleanor asked, deliberately being obtuse.

"You were going to see if you could find out anything about what his group is planning for the final offensive on the Peninsula."

"No, you *told* me that I was to do it," Eleanor pointed out. "I certainly didn't agree to it. I don't see why you want to know—"

"France has been a good friend to America, and if we could help them—"

"Napoleon is a good friend to Napoleon and only to Napoleon," Eleanor said, repeating her father's opinion.

Connal gave her a quick sideways glance, his eyes taking in the compression of her lips.

"I can hardly expect a woman to understand the ramifications of world politics, now can I?" He seemed to Eleanor's critical ears to be deliberately instilling a soothing note into his voice. He guided the horse into Hyde Park.

No, but he could expect said woman to risk her neck spying for him, Eleanor thought angrily.

"We'll leave the subject for now. I think when you see how well we do with the information you've already gotten for me, you'll be only too eager to see what you can learn from Ryland."

Eleanor blinked, not understanding the reference, but not wanting to prolong the conversation by asking.

Connal returned to his original question. "You still haven't told me what you were doing in Lombard Street."

Even though she resented his questioning her movements, she decided in the interests of peace to tell him. "I was seeing my grandmama's man of business."

"Why?"

"I wanted some information about my uncle's financial state, as well as to find out how my grandfather's will read."

"Did he leave you anything?" Connal's voice had sharpened.

Eleanor frowned. "Who?"

"Your grandfather. He must have been pretty well inlaid, considering that everything about your grandmother is of the first stare."

"Not her manners, nor, I suspect, her morals!" Eleanor said tartly. "And no, he didn't leave me anything. He didn't have anything to leave. All the money already belonged to his wife."

"I see. Did you find out how her money is left?"

"It all goes to Uncle Henry." Eleanor took great delight in shattering Connal's hopes. He knew she was rich enough to buy an abbey, and yet he still wanted more.

Obviously sensing her distaste, Connal gave her a rueful smile. "I didn't mean to sound greedy, my dear. It's just that I'm ambitious for you. You certainly deserve something from the old woman. You're every bit as much her granddaughter as your cousin."

"True. But poor Drusilla has had to suffer Grandmama's company her entire life. My acquaintance has, mercifully, been much shorter."

"That is not a proper way to talk about your grandmother," Connal rebuked her.

Eleanor stared at him, dumbfounded. "Connal Gunn, you can't be telling me one day to steal state secrets from my uncle and then on the next tell me that I'm not being respectful to my grandmother."

"Shh..." Connal glanced nervously around the park road. To his relief, no one was near enough to overhear. Deciding not to take any chances, he turned the horse onto a deserted byway.

"You never used to be this outspoken," he complained. "In America you were always so docile. So feminine."

Was docile Connal's definition of "feminine"? Eleanor wondered uneasily. She wasn't docile. She never had been. She simply had excellent manners, and since Connal had only seen her as a guest in her father's house... Eleanor stifled a sigh. It was no wonder that Connal had an entirely erroneous idea of her character. And it wasn't all his fault, she admitted.

"Once we return to America and are married—" Connal began.

"I haven't promised to marry you," Eleanor reminded him.

Connal's dark brows drew together into a straight bar, and he looked furious. Why? Eleanor wondered. Because she wouldn't agree to marry him, or because she was opposing his will?

"Your father wanted you to," he insisted. "You know full well he did."

"Yes," Eleanor conceded. "And it's because he wanted our marriage that I haven't flatly refused."

Connal pulled the carriage to a stop under the shade of a huge oak tree and, taking a quick glance around the deserted pathway, scooted closer to her on the narrow carriage seat.

"You're just on edge." Connal put his arm around her shoulders and pulled her nearer. It was all Eleanor could do to keep from jerking away. She didn't want him this close to her. It made her feel threatened.

"I'm sorry to be putting you through all this, my dear." Connal's voice oozed concern, but his eyes were watchful, as if he were waiting to judge her reaction to his words.

"I know that women don't have the constitution to do what you're doing, and I wouldn't ask you if there were any other way. But there isn't, my sweetling. You're the only one with access to your uncle's study."

Eleanor tried to lurch away from him. To her dismay, his grip tightened and, with another of the furtive looks around, he lowered his head, clearly intending to kiss her.

Eleanor swallowed uneasily and prepared to endure it. His firm lips met hers with a steady pressure that hinted at a great deal of experience at kissing. A fact that bothered her not at all. She didn't care who Connal kissed, as long as it wasn't her.

But why? She tried to analyze her sense of revulsion. His embrace wasn't uncomfortable. Nor was it physically threatening. His scent was pleasantly fragrant, without being overpowering, and the underlying aroma was one of cleanliness. And she knew that her father had approved of Connal, even if he wouldn't have approved of him kissing her in a public park. So why did she feel no other reaction than a burning desire to escape?

When James kissed her, she'd wanted it to last forever. She'd been unable to think of anything other than the feel and the taste and the smell of him. She had been so totally wrapped up in his embrace that the world could have ended and she wouldn't have noticed. Or cared. What was the difference between the two men's kisses?

Her train of thought was rudely interrupted as Connal's wet tongue pressed against her tightly closed lips, and she jerked back in revulsion.

"I thought I heard someone," she improvised at his annoyed expression.

Connal hastily looked around the still-deserted park and grimaced. "Undoubtedly an animal in the trees, although it's just as well." He gave her a self-satisfied smile. "Kissing you is very heady business. I can hardly wait until I have the right to embrace you whenever I like."

But what about when she liked? Eleanor thought uneasily. What would she like? And with whom would she like it?

Chapter Thirteen

Eleanor gently traced her forefinger over the miniature of her father as she studied it in the late-afternoon sunlight filtering in through her small bedroom window. It wasn't a very good likeness. The artist had been an itinerant limner of mediocre talents. But Eleanor cherished the miniature, because it reminded her of happier times.

It had been painted almost five years ago, when the future had seemed to stretch before her like a smooth, unending pathway winding through days of quiet happiness and peaceful contentment. She sighed. Now that same pathway was strewn with uncertainties and ethical dilemmas.

"Papa," she murmured, "I did what I know you would have wanted me to do."

Eleanor closed her thin fingers around the chill ivory oval with a sense of acute frustration. If she'd done what her father would have wanted, then why did she feel so badly about having done it? She should be happy, she tried to convince herself. Connal certainly was. Connal was in alt over the information she'd managed to steal. So why wasn't she?

Eleanor slowly walked over to the window, which looked down on the mews at the back of the house. She rested her forehead against the cool pane and tried to think. To analyze the empty feeling inside her. Maybe the basic problem was that in order to be true to her father's principles, she'd had to sacrifice a few of her own. Such as having taken appalling advantage of her uncle's kindness in offering her a home. She'd not only abused his hospitality, but she'd betrayed his trust.

Her uncle had done nothing to deserve such deception. But she'd done it all the same. She'd sacrificed her uncle's interests for her father's. Eleanor gnawed unhappily on her lower lip. The fact that she loved her father far more than she liked her uncle didn't justify her actions—even in her own mind.

Restless under the prod of her guilty conscience, Eleanor wandered over to her bed and plopped down on it, heedless of the fact that she was wrinkling her amaranthus jaconet dress.

Perhaps her sense of guilt was intensified by the fact that the cause that she'd sacrificed so much for was far more her father's cause than her own, she considered. Not that she didn't believe that America should be free, because she did. But she didn't believe that no price was too great to pay for that freedom. Maybe it was because, as a woman, she wasn't as free as men were. Women were forever being hedged in by social custom and prohibitive laws that all too often relegated them to being little more than their husband's property. In that regard, at least, she'd seen precious little difference between her father's America and her uncle's England.

No, Eleanor thought. She was never going to feel as passionately about independence as her father had, because as a woman she was never going to be truly independent. The things of vital importance to her were less empire-shaking concepts, such as loyalty to friends, consideration for one's host, and returning good for good.

But however hard she found it to reconcile her spying with her conscience, it was over, she told herself. Over and done with. She couldn't change what had happened, and that being the case, it was time to put the episode behind her and get on with her life.

Eleanor looked down at the miniature in her hand, and a feeling of sadness twisted through her. Sadness mingled with a sense of inevitability. "I'll always love you, Papa," she murmured. "But I'm me, and I have to live my own life as I think best."

Eleanor opened her bureau drawer and gently replaced the miniature in her silk sachet case. As she did, her father's final letter to her fell out. She picked it up and stared down at it. When the lawyer first gave it to her, immediately after her father's death, she had been so grief-stricken that she didn't question the wisdom of what her father had wanted. It had been enough that it had been his last wish that she marry Connal.

It was no longer enough, she finally admitted. Her father's wishes were no longer a good enough reason for her to put herself within Connal's power. She shivered violently as she remembered the revulsion she'd felt at his kisses. But what she found even more appalling was the fact that Connal hadn't even realized how she felt. He had never made an effort to get to know her well enough to be able to read her reactions. And he hadn't made the effort because he didn't care what she thought or felt. Eleanor forced herself to face the unflattering truth. To Connal she wasn't a unique individual with wants and needs of her own. She was simply a woman, and a woman's role was to fall in with her husband's wants and needs. All Connal expected—indeed, all he wanted—was her immediate and total acquiescence to his every wish.

Eleanor stared blindly down at the chipped top of her bureau. If Connal had seen no need to make the effort to get to know her as a person before their marriage, then it was highly unlikely that he would bother afterward. Thanks to her father's will, she wouldn't be dependent on Connal financially. But what kind of life would she have if she were constantly fighting with him over the use of her own money? And what would be the effect of those fights on their children?

She frowned consideringly. What kind of a father would Connal make? Not one she'd care to have, she admitted. A child growing up in his household would quickly learn the advantages of the old adage that children should be seen and not heard.

James wouldn't be that kind of a father. The thought unexpectedly flittered through her mind, and the tenseness in her muscles eased fractionally. From every indication she'd

seen, James would be a loving, indulgent father. A sad smile curved her lips. Of course, he'd undoubtedly stuff their heads full of all kinds of classical nonsense, but he'd also allow them the privilege of thinking for themselves. Of making their own decisions. Yes, James would be by far the better father. And as for creating those children with him...
A flush skated across her cheekbones, and a tightening sensation coiled through her abdomen. Giving James children wouldn't be a duty. It would be a sensual experience of unlimited proportions, she thought dreamily.

But she wasn't choosing between James and Connal. She pulled her rioting imagination up short. James had never intimated that he thought of her as more than a friend. Nor was he likely to. Even she knew that wealthy English dukes didn't marry provincials. She hadn't needed her grandmother to tell her that. Besides which, she thought unhappily, her father would have hated her marrying a member of the English aristocracy. He would have seen it as a direct betrayal of everything he believed in.

But if she didn't marry Connal, then whom could she marry? Eleanor mentally sifted through her bachelor acquaintances back in Boston. She couldn't think of one who would make her an acceptable husband. They all had major flaws. Such as Clevis Thornapple, who at thirty had already buried three wives. Eleanor shuddered at the memory of his small eyes and tightly compressed lips. Maybe all three had been sickly, as he claimed, but she certainly had no intention of getting close enough to the man to find out.

Of course, she didn't have to return to Boston. She considered the idea, which had been skirting around the edge of her mind for days now. There was no reason she couldn't stay in England. There was much here that appealed to her. Here she had her uncle's family for company, and eventually she'd have Drusilla's and Bertrem's children to dote on.

"Miss Eleanor?" Daisy's harried voice called through the door. "Be ya in there? Your aunt, she said t'tell ya that tea's bein' served in the salon."

Eleanor hurriedly shoved the letter back into the drawer and closed it, grateful for the distraction Daisy had provided. Lately she seemed to spend far too much of her time agonizing over what she should or shouldn't do. At least making polite conversation to visitors was something that required no heartburnings. And maybe, she thought with a sparkle of anticipation, maybe Ryland would be there.

She hurried downstairs, only to find the salon empty of visitors. Even Bertrem had not as yet put in an appearance.

"Good afternoon, Aunt Maria, Drusilla, Grandmama. How are you keeping?"

Esme ignored her, but Maria smiled warmly at Eleanor. "Fine, thank you, dear."

"Me too," Drusilla added. "But I think that poor Grandmama is feeling sadly out of curl."

"Ha! Much the lot of you would care if I were to pop off." Esme reached for another macaroon. "Bunch of care-for-naughts."

"That's not true, Grandmama." Drusilla's sincerity was unmistakable.

"Bah! Fools, the lot of you. Sit down." She pointed a pudgy finger at Eleanor.

Eleanor sat. Now what? she wondered. Conversation lately had become even more hazardous than normal. What with herself plotting espionage, Drusilla plotting murder and Esme simply plotting... Eleanor sighed.

"I'll have none of your die-away airs played off in this house, missy," Esme ordered.

"The duke of Ryland." Walker's words sent a delectable cascade of shivers through Eleanor. Her sense of excitement quickened as she watched James cross the room. Her gaze swept over the polished gleam of his Hessians and up over the pale biscuit pantaloons that molded his muscular thighs like a second skin. Up over his flat stomach, to be caught and held by the black velvet sack he had carefully cradled in his hand.

"Why, Your Grace..." Esme beamed at him, her good humor owing nothing to artifice. "I declare, we do seem to be seeing you more and more in our drawing room." She looked at Drusilla, who seemed to shrink back into the rose silk cushions of her chair.

"I had mentioned to Miss Wallace at the Jerseys' ball some Roman artifacts that I found on my estate in Cumberland, and it occurred to me that she might like to see them," he said.

Ryland crossed the room and, to Esme's imperfectly concealed annoyance, sat down on the sofa beside Eleanor.

Eleanor swallowed uneasily as she felt his weight sink into the soft cushions, tipping her slight frame toward him. For a moment, she was incredibly tempted to simply relax and allow her body to sag against him. To feel his hard muscles pushing against her. To breathe in the clean scent of his clothes and the far more tantalizing fragrance of his skin. But sanity prevailed, and she pushed the tips of her small satin shoes into the thick carpet to hold her steady.

She looked up into James' gleaming eyes—eyes that were gleaming, unless she very much missed her bet, with the unmistakable glow of fanaticism—and she felt her heart contract with tenderness. He was so serious about his broken bits and pieces, and so determined that she appreciate them, too. Like a small boy with his box of dusty treasures that no one else would ever bother with.

"Have some tea, Your Grace." Maria poured him a cup.

Ryland gently set his precious sack down on the sofa table and accepted it.

"Poor Grandmama is feeling a bit knocked up this morning," Drusilla said, adding another strand to the web of lies she was building.

"Nonsense! No such thing. Just a little off-color," Esme muttered. "Barely noticed it myself. Drusilla was concerned enough to worry." She shot Eleanor a venomous look. "Not like some I could mention. But what is it you brought to show us, Your Grace?" Esme stared down at the velvet sack on the table.

"Some fascinating finds that one of my farmers uncovered last month, when he was repairing a rock fence."

Ryland reverently pulled an object out of the sack, and Eleanor almost giggled at the confused expression on her grandmother's face. Clearly Esme was determined to admire anything Ryland found of value, and just as clearly she was having a hard time maintaining the effort.

"Umm, what is it, Your Grace?" Maria asked, looking closer at the brown fragment.

"An artifact from the Roman occupation." He carefully handed it to her.

"A pottery shard," Eleanor elaborated as her aunt turned the small piece first one way and then another, as if looking for some hidden significance.

"That's right." Ryland nodded approvingly at Eleanor. "It's probably from the neck of a water jug. Notice, the design is reminiscent of Panticapaeum."

"Panti..." Maria blinked.

"Capital of the Pontic Empire, on the Black Sea," Eleanor told her.

"Why not just buy yourself a Roman pot, if that's what you want?" Maria suggested. "Like Lord Elgin and his marbles."

"But this proves that the Romans really were on my estate," Ryland said, trying to make her understand.

"The Romans were everywhere but in Rome, where they belonged," Eleanor said tartly. "I'm sure that if you keep looking you'll also find the bones of some poor souls they murdered. They never could resist the impulse to wreak havoc."

"Oh?" Drusilla suddenly looked up. "How did they murder people?"

"In as messy a manner as they could devise," Eleanor said.

"Lamentable, but true," Ryland conceded. "It was the Greeks who showed a great deal of finesse in their assassinations."

"What else is in that sack?" Eleanor changed the subject, not liking the gleam of interest in her cousin's eye. Next Drusilla would be wanting the names of poisons.

"A gold coin." Ryland pulled out a small dented circle, which he handed to her. His fingers brushed against her palm as he placed the coin in her hand, and Eleanor felt a tremor of sensation penetrate her skin. Why did she react to his touch like that? she wondered uneasily. Even in company, with everyone looking on, she still felt a surge of desire when he touched her. Her body reacted to James entirely independently of her mind. Not that her mind wasn't also intrigued by the man, she realized.

"Notice the excellent state of preservation," Ryland pointed out.

"Can you spend it?" Drusilla asked.

"Spend it?" Ryland stared at her in unfeigned horror. "It's very old."

"It is that." Eleanor absently studied it. "It looks like one of the coins Coelius Caldus issued about 100 A.D. My father had several of them from a ship captain who used to trade in the Aegean Sea."

If Daniel Wallace had collected gold Roman coins, then he must have been a man of substance at some point during Eleanor's life. Ryland filed the information away in the back of his mind.

"Don't be trying to give yourself airs here, missy," Esme snapped. "A ne'er-do-well collecting gold coins, indeed!"

Eleanor bit her lip at her inadvertent slip. Gold coins were not the sort of thing that penniless schoolteachers were supposed to possess.

"Well, even if one can't spend it, it would make a lovely piece of jewelry." Maria hurried to fill the silence. "Perhaps a brooch?"

"Or, if one had two, you could make a pair of earbobs," Drusilla suggested helpfully, and Eleanor giggled at Ryland's incredulous expression.

"And what else have you brought to show us?" Esme had lost interest in the small coin.

Ryland pulled a thin marbled-covered book out of the sack. "My mother sent this along for Miss Wallace."

"Her Grace?" Esme looked chagrined, as well she might. Ryland's mother had been avoiding her for years, and now for the duchess to notice her least favorite granddaughter...

"A book?" Eleanor asked cautiously, still remembering his own overly long, infinitely boring offerings.

His lips twisted in a wry grin. "This one you'll like. Mama does not share my fascination with the past."

"Oh?" Eleanor gingerly accepted it and glanced down at it. *"The Children of the Abbey?"*

"If I am to understand my revered parent, it is guaranteed to interfere with your sleep for at least the next fortnight."

"How lovely." Eleanor smiled in genuine anticipation.

"Oh, Eleanor, my particular friend Miss Hampton read it, and she said it was positively scarifying. Please, may I have it after you?" Drusilla begged.

"And I will read it next," Maria happily planned. "I do so like being frightened by things that you know aren't real."

"I suppose, since His Grace's mother gave it to us..." Esme began grudgingly.

"Baron Gunn," Walker's deep voice intoned, and Eleanor felt her shoulder muscles tighten painfully, as if a heavy weight had suddenly been dropped on them. Reluctantly she turned toward the door. It was Connal, all right. A Connal in rather high spirits, too. Eleanor noticed the glow of suppressed excitement emanating from him with a feeling of foreboding. Now what? The last time he'd been this pleased with himself, he'd pitchforked her into spying.

But not again. She unconsciously straightened her shoulders. She'd paid tribute to her father's dream. She'd paid with her own sense of honor. And now it was done. It was over. If Connal wanted someone to spy on her uncle, he could hire a housebreaker. In fact, he could just go away and leave her alone. She didn't even want to see Connal, she suddenly realized. The secret that they shared didn't create a bond between them. It made her feel guilty every time she saw him, because Connal knew what she'd done.

"Good afternoon, Baron Gunn," Maria offered. "Would you like a cup of tea?"

"No, thank you, Mrs. Bromley." He gave her a bright, practiced smile. "I simply couldn't resist stopping by to see you lovely ladies. Your Grace." Connal nodded to Ryland. "Such a delightful spring day, isn't it?"

"Grandmama is feeling a little out of curl," Drusilla commented.

"She was earlier—" Eleanor frowned at her cousin "—but now she's feeling much better."

"Ha! Much you'd care about my health!" Esme snapped, eyeing Connal with frustration. She was almost sure that he wasn't anyone worth knowing, but until she was absolutely certain, she didn't want to irrevocably offend him. Besides, this baron no one seemed to know anything about might be just the man to take her unwanted granddaughter off her hands.

"I was noticing the lovely carving on your stairs," Connal offered into the silence. "It's an example of Grinling Gibbons, isn't it?"

"So my husband says," Maria answered.

"Since you're interested in it, Baron, Eleanor can show you the full extent of the carvings." Esme had issued what was clearly an order, and Eleanor felt her spirits sink. She didn't want to show Connal anything but the door. Particularly when James was here.

"How lovely. I'd very much like to see them," Connal agreed, with a promptness that depressed her even further.

Ryland noted the flicker of dismay in Eleanor's eyes with interest. It appeared that she didn't want to go with the baron. Nor did he want her to, Ryland admitted. He still didn't know what the relationship between them was, if indeed there was a relationship, but he did know that he didn't want Eleanor to be alone with the man. He didn't trust Gunn. Not even as far as the front hall.

"The carvings sound fascinating," Ryland said. "Why don't we all examine them?" He felt a flare of satisfaction at the annoyed expression that flittered across Connal's face. Unfortunately, his satisfaction was short-lived. Esme, with her usual high-handedness, vetoed the idea.

"Drusilla can show it to you later if you're interested," Esme said. "Right now you can tell us more about that bit of broken pottery you brought."

Ryland held on to his temper with an effort. What he really wanted to do was to tell Esme exactly what he thought of her, but he knew his honesty would rebound on Eleanor. So he forced a smile and took his revenge by launching into a detailed lecture on the intricacies of Roman pottery.

Knowing that there was no way to get around going with Connal, Eleanor slowly got to her feet and headed toward the hallway, reluctance visible in every line of her slender body.

"Did you need something, Miss Eleanor?" Walker came out of the library as she and Connal emerged from the salon.

"No, nothing," Connal said shortly.

Eleanor smiled at the old man. "The baron has expressed an interest in the Gibbons carvings on the stair rails, and my grandmother requested I show them to him."

"I see." Walker disappeared behind the baize door.

"Old fool," Connal muttered.

"He has excellent hearing," Eleanor warned.

"So? He's a servant. What he thinks is irrelevant."

"Tell me, have you ever heard of the French revolution?" Eleanor asked tartly. "A lot of the so-called aristocracy lost their heads to their servants."

He frowned at her. "Will you keep your mind on what's at hand," he ordered. "I don't know how much time we'll have."

"It would be easier if I knew what you wanted."

"I came to tell you what we got for your information," he announced, with an air of suppressed excitement.

"Got?" Eleanor repeated uncertainly. "I sincerely hope that what we got was something to bargain with at Ghent."

"Not that," he said impatiently. "From the American government." He paused, as if to give added importance to his words, and then announced, "In exchange for your information, Congress has awarded our shipping line an exclusive contract to deliver the supplies to our troops up and down the entire coast." He grinned at her and rocked back on his heels, obviously expecting her to share his excitement.

Eleanor stared at him in disbelief as the words slowly burned themselves into her mind. She shook her head, trying vainly to dislodge them. She must have misunderstood, she tried to tell herself. Connal couldn't possibly have meant that he'd sold the information she'd stolen to their own government.

"I don't doubt you're speechless," he said smugly. "I was able to get even more than I had hoped."

Eleanor closed her eyes, slowly counted to ten and then carefully asked, "You actually sold the information that I took from Uncle Henry?'' Despite her attempts to remain calm, her voice rose slightly.

"Shh..." He glanced worriedly toward the salon. "I know you're excited, but—"

"No." Eleanor shook her head. "You mistake the matter. I am not excited. I am appalled. I spied in order to help the Americans' cause. A cause that my father passionately believed in. I did it as a final tribute to my father's memory, and then to have you turn around and demand payment..." She stared at him in impotent frustration. By making a profit from her information, he had reduced her actions to the sordid. Something without even a semblance of honor.

"I thought you'd be pleased." Connal looked confused by her reaction.

"You thought wrong! What you did was despicable!"

An annoyed flush darkened the skin along Connal's cheekbones. "You simply don't understand how these things work."

"I understand treachery! And self-serving actions!"

"Eleanor," he began tightly, "you aren't thinking. The government needed that information. They also needed someone to handle the shipping. It was an even trade. We'll do a good job for them, so why are you angry? No one lost a thing."

"I lost my sense of honor!"

"Don't be melodramatic," he said patronizingly. "Honor is for men, not women."

"You don't even know what I'm talking about, do you?" she asked in dismay.

"I know you're talking arrant nonsense. You let me worry about the ethics of the situation."

Eleanor stared into his dark features. Connal truly didn't understand why she was so upset, she realized in shock. Their concept of right and wrong were simply so different that he really didn't understand.

She couldn't marry him. The inescapable conclusion flooded her mind, bringing in its wake a sense of peace. She couldn't marry Connal Gunn. The words sounded even better the second time around.

"You must allow me—" Connal began pompously.

"No," Eleanor said. "I will not. Not now, or at any time in the future. I will not marry you."

Connal's features tightened angrily. "We've been through this. Your father—"

"I don't care if the archangel Gabriel comes down from heaven in a flaming chariot and presents me with a signed document from God," Eleanor said flatly. "I refuse to marry a man I cannot respect. We would not suit."

"You will—" Connal attempted irately, only to have to swallow his ire when the knocker sounded and Walker promptly appeared to answer it.

Walker ignored the obviously seething Connal with a majestic calm that Eleanor could only envy. He opened the door to reveal Bertrem.

"Good afternoon, Bertrem." Eleanor smiled at him with genuine relief. Bertrem was no threat to her, or anything she believed in. "So good of you to call. You do remember Baron Gunn, do you not? He was just leaving."

"I—" Connal said with a scowl at Bertrem, who totally missed the undercurrents swirling between Connal and Eleanor.

"It was good of you to call, Baron," Eleanor lied, breathing a sigh of relief when Connal, with one last, frustrated glare, stalked out.

"The Scots are so volatile," Walker murmured as he closed the door behind him.

"Volatile" didn't begin to describe that particular Scot, Eleanor thought grimly. Not that it mattered anymore. Her contacts with him over the future of their jointly owned shipyard could be handled through a third party. A feeling of light-heartedness swept over her. She was free of Connal. The words seemed to dance through her mind with a joyous litany. She hadn't realized just how much the thought of having to marry him had depressed her spirits. And now she was free.

"Eleanor?" Bertrem's worried voice recalled her to the present. "Is your grandmother here?" He looked fearfully toward the salon.

"I'm afraid so. She was the one who sent me out into the hallway to show Baron Gunn the Gibbons carvings."

"The what?" Bertrem looked confused.

"The carvings on the staircase." She pointed to the elaborate swags of fruit and grapes. "Baron Gunn admired them."

Bertrem stared at the railing in disbelief. "He did? Rum thing to admire, but then, he's Scots, you know."

Eleanor giggled happily. "No doubt that would account for it."

"What are you doing out there?" Esme called from the salon.

Bertrem instinctively inched closer to Eleanor, and she felt like patting him on the head and assuring him she'd protect him. At the moment, she felt more than a match for anyone. She'd managed to face down Connal. After him, her grandmother was nothing more than a domestic bully. She went into the salon, with Bertrem hard on her heels.

"The baron had to leave, Grandmama, but Bertrem has come to call."

"Again?" Esme demanded. "What do you want?"

"Nothing from you," Bertrem hastily told her.

"Bah! Fool!" Esme stood with some effort and glared at Bertrem, who shrank slightly, but managed to hold his ground. "I'll take my leave of you. Not feeling at all the thing." For a moment, Esme sounded old and tired. "Be in my room. Good afternoon, Your Grace. So good of you to honor us with a visit."

Eleanor watched her grandmother leave, feeling sorry for her. Apparently Maria felt the same, for she put down her netting and stood.

"I'd better make sure that she doesn't need anything. Have a comfortable coze," Maria said as she hurried after her mother-in-law.

"Comfortable!" Bertrem moaned. "I doubt that I'll ever be comfortable again."

"What's wrong, Bertrem?" Drusilla asked. "Is it a secret?"

"Secret! It'll be all over London shortly." Bertrem looked pitiful. "Next thing you know, m'father'll be puffing it up in the papers, and then we'll really be in the basket."

Drusilla clasped her small hands together and fixed an imploring eye on him. "Oh, Bertrem, tell me it isn't so."

Ryland glanced over at Eleanor and murmured, "Do you know what they're talking about?"

"Catastrophe!" Bertrem answered him. "M'father's come t'town. He sent for me to meet him at Mr. Potter's. Told me that I was to go propose to her."

"Her?" Ryland looked confused. "What her?"

"Miss... Don't even know what her first name is." Bertrem looked appalled at the thought. "Don't see how Papa can expect me to marry a female whose first name I don't even know."

"Certainly not," Ryland promptly agreed. "Marriage is enough of a shock to a man's constitution. Why, only think what your feelings might be if you were to agree to wed a female and then find out that her name was Opedia or Hezecala."

"That's right." Bertrem nodded vigorously. "Why, I might not find out until we was at the altar. Think of the horror."

"Bertrem isn't going to marry anyone but me." Drusilla looked reproachfully at Ryland.

"I take it that your father and the candlemaker have agreed on a settlement?" Eleanor asked.

"Gas is the future," Ryland unexpectedly offered. "I own quite a few shares of the Gas Light and Power Company myself."

Bertrem blinked. "Really? Miss Wallace said the same thing. Must be something in it, if you both say so, too."

"Never mind the gas company," Eleanor ordered. "Just answer my question."

"Yes. And I did just as you told me to do." Bertrem looked hopefully at Eleanor. "I told m'father that I couldn't entertain the idea of becoming engaged to a female I hadn't met."

"And?" Eleanor persisted.

"Said nothing could be easier," Bertrem said gloomily. "Said she'd be home all afternoon, waiting to meet me. Fair bowled me out."

"A leveler," Ryland agreed.

"But not an insurmountable one," Eleanor said slowly. "We shall all go to visit your intended."

"Don't call her that," Drusilla muttered.

"We have to call her something, since we don't know her name," Ryland pointed out, thoroughly diverted. Bertrem's affairs had all the drama of a Drury Lane farce, and about as much coherency.

"True," Bertrem conceded. "But I'm not sure that you was all invited. Mean to say, Mr. Potter said she was expecting an offer. Stands to reason that if'n you're about to make an offer, you don't take another female."

"No, not one. That would look odd," Eleanor said. "But two other women and a duke would be unexceptional."

"I do not visit strange candlemakers' daughters who don't have a first name," Ryland said, declining the treat.

"No doubt she's got one, Your Grace," Bertrem reminded him in all seriousness. "It's just that we don't know it."

Ryland glanced from Drusilla's tragic expression to Bertrem's pathetic one before coming to rest on Eleanor's. Her brown eyes gleamed with interest—and some plan. And that worried him. Eleanor was very intelligent, but also very naive about society. If he wasn't there to guide her, who knew what social solecism she might inadvertently commit. And it would prolong his afternoon with her, he decided.

Perhaps he could find a way to subtly question her about what Gunn had wanted to say to her badly enough to engineer that ridiculous excuse of looking at carvings. Whatever it was, it had certainly pleased her. She'd seemed different when she came back after seeing him. Happier. More lighthearted, somehow.

But why? She certainly hadn't wanted to go with him in the first place. What had Gunn told her or not told her to cause her change of heart?

He'd accompany her to visit Bertrem's unintended, and, if he was lucky, maybe he'd be able to find out.

Chapter Fourteen

"Well, Drusilla, I understand congratulations are in order."

Eleanor looked up from the dinner she'd been rearranging on her plate and peered cautiously at her grandmother. Esme had sounded…almost jubilant. And that worried her. Anything that brought a smile to her grandmother's face was bound to have been bought at the price of someone else's peace of mind.

"Congratulations?" From the wary sound of Maria's voice, it was obvious that she shared Eleanor's concern.

"Why, yes." Esme gave Drusilla a smile that owed nothing to humor. "I received a letter today from the vicar's wife at Little Heythorpe, and she had the most interesting news." Esme took a bite of turbot to prolong the suspense.

"Interfering old busybody," Henry muttered. "The woman's tongue runs on like a fiddlestick."

"But this time to some purpose," Esme said complacently. "According to Mrs. Archer, she had tea at the Arylesworths', and you'll never guess what the squire told her."

Despite the fact that no one asked to be enlightened, Esme told them anyway. "Squire Arylesworth told her that he had accepted an offer from a candle manufacturer who wants to marry his daughter into the ton. Bertrem and the creature are to be wed at the close of the Season," she finished triumphantly.

"Don't count your chickens before they're hatched," Eleanor said.

Esme glared at Eleanor. "The squire accepted," Esme repeated, "I, for one, have no intention of receiving his bride. I have given Walker orders that he is to deny Bertrem the door." She glanced down the length of the table, daring anyone to object. No one did, although Henry was clearly upset and Maria glanced anxiously at Drusilla, who looked as if she were about to burst into tears.

"Considering your own background in trade, Grandmama, I should think that you would be the one to proclaim yourself the girl's champion," Eleanor said, attempting to shame Esme into decent behavior.

"Why, you ungrateful..." Esme sputtered, her fat jowls wobbling in fury.

"Grandmama, why do you torment the very people you should love?" Eleanor persisted, even though in her heart she knew it was a lost cause. "You know that Drusilla loves Bertrem, and you also know that Ryland hasn't the slightest intention of offering for Drusilla."

"Bah! Love!" Esme snorted. "What, pray tell, is love?"

"Love is putting the welfare of others above your own selfish desires." Eleanor made one last attempt to make Esme understand. "Grandmama, all you have to do is give Drusilla the dowry you've already promised. It won't cause you any hardship."

"No hardship!" Esme exclaimed. "Why, I'd be the laughingstock of the ton if Drusilla were to throw herself away on that... that country bumpkin."

"Bertrem is not a country bumpkin!" Drusilla was driven to object. "He's a good, kind man, and I love him."

"You'll do as you're told, missy! You think Bertrem's father will welcome you without my money?" Esme demanded.

"Mama," Henry began hesitantly, "surely you want to see Drusilla happy?"

Eleanor stared down at the congealing droplets of fat on her plate as she reluctantly faced the fact that the time had finally come when she was going to have to reveal just how rich she really was. And it was impossible to foretell just what the results of her revelation would be.

Her grandmother could throw them out of the house for daring to oppose her will. And if that were to happen, her uncle would probably go back to his estate in Lincolnshire immediately and oversee the needed renovations. If he were to do that, then she wouldn't see James again this Season. She might never see him again before she returned to Boston. A feeling of panic nibbled at her composure. But then, even if she were to decide to remain in England, she might never see him again on a regular basis, she conceded. James was only living in London now because of the Peninsular War, and everyone agreed that it was just about over. Once that happened, James would undoubtedly return to his estate in Cumberland and go back to his excavations.

Maria unexpectedly spoke up. "You cannot refuse Bertrem the door. We would never be able to hold up our heads again at Little Heythorpe."

"Since I haven't been near the place in years and don't ever intend to go back, that's of no concern to me," Esme retorted. "There will be no more discussion of the matter. I have made up my mind." She picked up her fork and stabbed another piece of the turbot. "All that remains is to figure out how to compromise Ryland so that he'll feel obligated to make Drusilla an offer."

"No!" Drusilla jumped to her feet and hurled the denial at her startled grandmother. Drusilla's pale skin was stained by two large blotches of dark red, and her blue eyes glittered with unshed tears. "I will not trap Ryland into marriage!"

"You'll do as you're told, missy!" Esme pounded on the table to emphasize her point.

"I won't marry the duke!" Drusilla repeated fiercely. "And if you attempt to deny Bertrem the door, I'll stand on the stoop and talk to him."

"Henry!" Esme screeched at her son, who looked as startled as Eleanor felt at Drusilla's outburst. "Tell your daughter to keep a civil tongue in her head, or she can go back to your broken-down estate and watch Bertrem and his new wife next door."

"You are an evil, evil woman!" Drusilla cried. "I hate you!" She raced out of the room.

"You will apologize to me at once, do you hear?" Esme shrieked after her.

The only response was the muffled echo of Drusilla's bedroom door slamming.

Esme flung her napkin down on the table and glared at Maria. "This is all your doing, madame. If you had raised her to show the proper respect for her elders—"

"It's love one gives unconditionally, Grandmama. Respect has to be earned." Eleanor got to her feet. Reluctant as she was to reveal her wealth, she couldn't allow Drusilla to go on believing that she was about to either lose Bertrem or condemn her parents to a life of genteel poverty on their tumbledown estate.

"Eleanor's right, you know," Henry said heavily. "No one respects a tyrant."

"Why, you miserable mawworm..." Esme sputtered.

Eleanor tuned out the familiar sounds of her grandmother's hectoring voice as she hurried out of the room after her cousin. In a way, it was ironic, Eleanor thought. Esme had bullied her family all their lives, and when they'd finally found the courage to stand up to her, they'd done it without the knowledge that Eleanor could and would rescue them from the consequences.

Eleanor knocked gently on Drusilla's bedroom door. When there was no response, she called, "Drusilla, it's just me. Eleanor. I need to talk to you."

The door opened a crack to reveal one of Drusilla's blue eyes. The eye blinked and looked beyond Eleanor, down the empty hallway. Seemingly satisfied, Drusilla stepped back and opened the door.

"Come in, Eleanor. I want to talk to you, too." Drusilla wrung her hands together in agitation. "I just don't know what to do. If I marry Bertrem, Mama and Papa will have no place to live. But if I don't marry him, I'd rather be dead.

"Eleanor, I know you said that we shouldn't poison Grandmama, but I can't think of anything else to do." Her voice rose on a wail.

"Fortunately, I can. I'll give you a dowry equal to what Grandmama promised you," Eleanor stated, breaking into Drusilla's unhappy monologue.

Drusilla frowned at her in confusion. "But how can you do that? You haven't any money. You said so."

"I lied," Eleanor said succinctly.

"But why?"

"Would you want Grandmama to know if you had independent means?" Eleanor asked.

"She'd know, because I'd move out the minute I got them. But you moved in. That doesn't make any sense."

"Well, I was all alone in the world, and I wanted to meet my mother's family." Eleanor gave her cousin part of the truth. She didn't want Drusilla probing too deeply into her motives. Some of them couldn't bear too close scrutiny.

"And if you'd come to London by yourself, Grandmama would have refused to receive you," Drusilla concluded. "But, Eleanor, can you really afford to give me a dowry?"

"Yes, and I also intend to give your father enough to bring his estate around."

"You have that much money?" Drusilla's eyes widened in wonder.

"Yes," Eleanor repeated. "But I should warn you that Bertrem's father will probably still prefer the candle-maker's daughter, because her father offered more."

"Bertrem loves me. He was going to marry me without any dowry, you know, if it came to that. The only problem was what to do about Mama and Papa. But this way, they'll be fine, and Bertrem will be able to settle the mortgages for his father. If that isn't enough for the squire, then that's too bad." For an eerie second, Drusilla sounded like her grandmother. "Besides, the squire should be happy to marry into the Bromley family, and when you marry Ryland, he'll be very well connected indeed."

Drusilla's words hit Eleanor with the force of a blow. She felt a heavy weight settle on her chest at the tantalizing thought of marrying James. Of being able to kiss him whenever she wanted to. Of being able to touch him and caress him and—

Stop it! She brought her imagination up short. James had said nothing to make her think that he wanted to marry her. Granted, he'd kissed her. Several times, in fact. But then, she hadn't objected to those kisses. And she certainly hadn't put a price tag on them. Not of marriage, or of anything else. To do so would be to reduce them to the sordid.

"I'm not going to marry the duke." Eleanor forced the words out. It would be humiliating in the extreme if Drusilla were to say something to Ryland that would make him think that she expected an offer from him.

"Not going to marry him?" Drusilla stared at her in surprise. "And the pair of you smelling like April and May? Don't be silly. Of course you are. I don't understand why you like him so much, but it's clear you do. And as for Ryland... He's different with you. When you're there, he doesn't seem so... so bored." Drusilla struggled to put her impressions into words. "It's like he's interested in what you have to say. He listens to you. But when he talks to me, it's as if he isn't really there. As if he's gone away in his mind, and nothing I could do will bring him back. You just wait, Eleanor. I'll dance at your wedding yet." Drusilla blinked uncertainly. "Do you suppose Grandmama will forgive us if you marry him?"

"Thank you for the warning. If Ryland should ever propose, I'll remember that the offer probably comes with Grandmama. That way, if I should forget the unsuitability of his marrying a Colonial, the threat of having Grandmama around will depress all my pretensions." Eleanor tried to sound carefree. Later, she'd examine what Drusilla had said, but this wasn't the moment to be dwelling on her own desires. Now that she'd spoken to Drusilla, she needed to relieve her uncle's mind.

Eleanor left Drusilla dreaming of a blissful future and went to find her uncle, fearing he must be frantic by now, worrying about how he was going to support his family. At least she could remove that worry, she thought in satisfaction. That would partially atone for her spying on him. She would also give to charity every penny that she earned from that infamous contract Connal had arranged, she vowed. She didn't want his blood money.

She frowned at the thought of Connal. She had expected him to try to see her today. Not that she was under any illusions that he was suffering from a broken heart at her

emphatic refusal yesterday to marry him. Or even a bruised
one. But he was a very canny man, and she had a great deal
of money. Money that he clearly had begun to think of as
his own. It was very unlike him to accept defeat so easily.

But then, what could he do about it? Eleanor worried the
question around in her mind. He'd already played his trump
card—her father's wish that she marry him. In fact, she
thought as she reached the bottom of the staircase, he'd
overplayed it.

Connal was the past, she assured herself. Think of the
future. Think of Drusilla, and how happy she was going to
be. Or Uncle Henry and Aunt Maria, and how free they
were going to be.

Eleanor cautiously glanced into the dining room, but it
was empty.

Her uncle was probably hiding in his study, if he hadn't
already escaped to his club, she decided. She hoped he
hadn't left the house yet. She wanted to set his mind at rest
now, so that he wouldn't worry all night long.

The study door was very slightly ajar. Eleanor listened for
a second to make sure that no one else was in the room before she gave a perfunctory knock, pushed the door open
and walked in.

"Uncle Henry, I—"

"Eleanor!" Henry jerked around at the sound of her
voice, an appalled expression on his face as his gaze swung
guiltily back to his desk.

Eleanor's eyes followed his glance, and a cold chill invaded her body when she saw the pile of gems lying in the
middle of his desk. Mesmerized, she watched as the light
from the argand lamp was splintered into thousands of tiny
rainbows by the diamonds, while the deep red glow of the
huge ruby flamed like a malevolent eye. Like something
from beyond the grave. The chilling phrase from one of her
favorite Gothics echoed through her stunned mind.

Slowly, as if drawn by the glittering gems, Eleanor moved
toward the desk.

"Umm, Eleanor, I..." Henry fumbled in his waistcoat
for his handkerchief and mopped his damp brow with a
trembling hand.

Eleanor barely noticed him. She was bewitched by the incandescence of the gems. Tentatively, almost afraid it might disappear if she tried to touch it, Eleanor reached down and picked up the necklace. The brightly scintillating jewels were cold. Icy-cold, and heavy. As if they were weighed down by the cupidity of the people who had coveted them. She studied the necklace closely. It was definitely the one in the portrait. The ruby was unmistakable.

Eleanor dropped the necklace back on the desk in sudden revulsion. That thing had haunted her father all his life. The desire to clear his name had been a compulsion that had grown into an obsession as the years went by. An unquenchable obsession. And all the time it had been here. In Uncle Henry's study. But why?

She hadn't realized she'd asked the question aloud until Henry lifted his head and stared at her from faded blue eyes that appeared sunken in his pallid skin.

"Why?" he repeated with a dejected sigh. "So many whys, and none of the answers have even a tinge of honor to lend them credence." He ran his fingers through his thinning gray hair.

"It seems so long ago. Almost a different lifetime. But, Eleanor, you must believe me. I never meant for your father to be blamed." He grimaced. "I never thought that far ahead. I was, as I so often was in my salad days, castaway when it happened."

"When what happened?" Eleanor asked when he lapsed into silence, staring blindly down at the necklace.

Henry blinked as if breaking free from a spell and said, "I'd been sent down from Oxford for some rig or another we'd run, and m'mother combed my hair in public over the matter. So I went out and got foxed. When I came back that evening, I found the necklace lying on the sofa in the salon. M'mother had thrown it there after a fight with m'father. In my state it seemed like a gift from the gods.

"You see, in those days, all I wanted was a commission. In the Hussars, no less." He laughed self-mockingly. "M'father didn't care, because m'brother was alive then. But Mama, she wouldn't hear of it. She said she wasn't about to waste her blunt on such a demmed foolish notion.

"I took the necklace with some vague idea of selling it and buying my own commission." He shrugged. "But, like most of my ideas, it came to naught. When I woke up the next morning, it was to find the house in an uproar. Mama had discovered the necklace missing and was threatening Daniel with arrest."

Henry shook his head. "I'll never forget how your father stood there and looked at her as if she were a worm that had just crawled out of his apple. He called her a vulgar old harridan and said she'd hidden it herself to try to drive a wedge between him and m'sister. She probably would have, too, if'n she'd have thought of it," he added reflectively.

"The humiliating truth, Eleanor, is that I lacked the moral courage to confess. I was afraid. Afraid that she'd cast me out entirely if I admitted what I'd done. And I was afraid to sell it, for fear she'd find out, and I was even afraid to keep it, for fear someone might find it."

He leaned back in the chair and expelled his breath in a long rush. "I deserve whatever censure you feel. But you can't blame me any more than I've blamed myself all these years. The plain truth, my dear, is that I'm a coward—a man without honor." He looked infinitely sad, and Eleanor felt her heart contract with pity. Her uncle's life had not been an easy one.

She knelt down in front of him and took his cold, trembling hands in hers.

"You are not a coward, Uncle Henry," she said earnestly. "You sent me the money for my passage, knowing full well what your mother would say when she found out. What you were when you took the necklace was young and foolish and afraid. And from what I've seen of Grandmama, you had good reason to fear her. Besides—" she smiled teasingly at him "—if you hadn't forced the issue, Mama might not have run away with Papa, and I'd never have been born."

Henry chuckled weakly. "I wish I could have known your father better, because he must have been like you. No one else in this family has so much heart. You are a credit to him."

"Thank you." Eleanor swallowed the lump in her throat at the guilty feeling that washed over her at her uncle's tribute. She let go of his hands and got to her feet. She didn't deserve his praise. She wasn't honorable. She was nothing more than a spy. A Judas goat who repaid kindness with treachery.

"I'm not sure what we're going to do now...." Henry said slowly. "When your grandmother finds out what I did, it's bound to set the final seal on her anger. But I want you to know, Eleanor, you'll always have a home with your aunt and me."

His words shook Eleanor out of her unhappy thoughts, and she hastened to reassure him.

"Uncle Henry, it doesn't matter what Grandmama says. When I was looking for the necklace—"

"I thought you might be when you moved that picture of Mama into the front salon, because no one would choose to have her glowering down on them in the normal way."

Eleanor smiled. "Quite true. Anyway, I found out that Grandfather Bromley won that necklace in a game of chance."

Henry nodded. "I know. One of the few lucky nights he ever had."

"And according to Mr. Potter, winning it makes it his personal property, and since he left all his personal property to you..."

Henry's eyes seemed to grow too large for his head, and his face went first chalk white and then bright red in excitement. "Truly?" he gasped. "He said that?"

"Yes," Eleanor assured him. "He says it belongs to you. And Mr. Bridge says that it's probably worth a great deal of money."

Henry closed his eyes as if in prayer, opened them, took a deep gulp of air and said, "If only you knew how I've longed to be my own master. But with Maria and Drusilla to provide for..."

"Well, now you'll be in a position to provide for them yourself," Eleanor told him encouragingly.

"And you," he insisted. "You'll have a dowry, the same as Drusilla. And all the pretty furbelows you gels want when they're trying to catch some unsuspecting male in parson's mousetrap."

"That's very kind of you, Uncle Henry, but unnecessary."

Henry frowned uncertainly at her. "Unnecessary?"

Eleanor nodded. "The reason I came to see you was to tell you that I was willing to give Drusilla a dowry and you the funds to refurbish your estate."

Henry looked confused. "But how?"

"Well, the word with no bark on it is that I'm rich enough to buy an abbey," Eleanor said bluntly.

"Rich?" Henry seemed to be having trouble understanding the concept.

"Mmm... Papa turned out to be every bit as good a businessman as he was a scholar. I just didn't say anything before because..." Eleanor groped for a reasonable explanation, but she needn't have bothered. Henry had spent most of his life lying to his mother. He had no trouble believing that Eleanor would follow the same course.

"I'm going to go tell Maria about our good fortune, and then I'm going to find Mr. Potter, and then..." Henry jumped to his feet, looking twenty years younger.

"First, I hope you intend to put that thing back wherever it was." Eleanor eyed the glittering mound of jewels with distaste. "If someone should steal it..."

Henry chuckled. "You mean besides me? But you're right, of course." He scooped it up and carelessly tossed it back into the wall safe behind the Turner painting and then closed it.

"Things are going to be different. You'll see." He nodded in satisfaction. "Very different."

The first evidence of that difference surfaced after breakfast the next morning, when Henry told his mother that not only had he found the necklace, but he had no intention of giving it to her. He then muttered something about a meeting at Whitehall and escaped, leaving his wife, daughter and Eleanor to bear the brunt of Esme's fury. A fury that Esme proceeded to indulge to the fullest.

Eleanor scrunched a little deeper into the sofa as the shrill sound of her grandmother's voice battered against her abused eardrums.

"Rank ingratitude!" Esme sputtered for at least the tenth time. "To think that my own son, my only surviving son, should steal the last token of love from my dear departed husband . . ."

Eleanor finally spoke up. "Doing it much too brown, Grandmama. You loathed your husband. You said so repeatedly."

Esme eyed her in dislike. "This is all your fault. If you hadn't come here, with your encroaching ways—"

"You forget, Mother Bromley," Maria said, entering the fray, "Eleanor had nothing to do with the disposition of the necklace. It was Henry's own dear papa who gave it to him."

"Giles meant me to have that necklace," Esme insisted.

"You're beating a dead horse, Grandmama," Eleanor said. "We all know he didn't."

"But—" Esme began.

"Grandmama, the old order has changed," Eleanor said. "No one will dance to your tune anymore."

"Ha! You think that simply because Henry has stolen the necklace from me that he'll provide you with a dowry—"

"No." Eleanor took an immense pleasure in telling her the truth. "My father provided me with a dowry."

"Bah! A miserable schoolteacher's savings."

"He hadn't taught school since he left England. He owned businesses. Lots of businesses. When he died, he left me a considerable heiress, Grandmama."

Esme audibly ground her teeth, and Eleanor smiled, feeling that her father had at long last been vindicated. Finally Esme had been forced to acknowledge that not only had her father not stolen her gaudy necklace, but that, contrary to her prophecies, Daniel had provided very well for his family. Far better than any Bromley had ever done.

"No amount of money soiled by the shop will ever make you acceptable to Ryland, missy," Esme responded. "He'll look higher than that for a bride."

"That will do, Mother Bromley," Maria said firmly. "Who Eleanor does or doesn't marry is no bread and butter of yours."

Eleanor kept her face expressionless with an effort. Pride demanded that she not let her grandmother know that her shaft had struck home. Eleanor was only too aware of the fact that wealthy English dukes didn't marry Colonials, no matter how wealthy the Colonial might be.

"Mr. Arylesworth." Walker's announcement provided a welcome distraction. Especially for Drusilla, who bounded to her feet and rushed to meet him.

"Bertrem, have you heard yet?" she demanded.

"Wonderful news!" Bertrem caught her small hands and squeezed her fingers in his excitement. "Just this minute left your father! He was on his way to see Mr. Bridge to arrange to sell the necklace!"

"Sell my necklace!" Esme howled.

Bertrem eyed her nervously. "So he said."

"I take it that you and Henry were able to come to some equitable agreement, Bertrem?" Eleanor asked.

"Equitable..." Bertrem looked confused.

"Reach an understanding?" Eleanor rephrased her question, wishing James were here. Things were much more fun when he was there to share the humor.

"Ah, yes." Bertrem nodded emphatically. "Mr. Bromley will pay off m'father's mortgages, and he's going to refurbish the dower house at his estate, so Drusilla and I will have our own place." He smiled at Drusilla, who blushed a bright red.

"You needn't think you're going to billet yourself on me during the Season!" Esme snapped.

"With you?" Bertrem's eyes bulged at the very idea. "No, no, ma'am. Assure you. Rather starve in the gutter."

Eleanor was hard-pressed not to laugh at Bertrem's horrified expression.

Before Esme could give vent to the acid reply burning her tongue, Walker reappeared. "His Grace, the duke of Ryland."

Eleanor, conscious of her grandmother's malicious eye, was careful only to smile politely at him. A smile that seemed to widen of its own accord when he grinned back.

"Good morning, Mrs. Bromley," Ryland greeted Esme. "Please forgive me for calling so early, but Henry just told me the necklace had been found. It must be a source of great satisfaction to you to realize that Eleanor's father was in no way connected with its disappearance. I imagine you must feel badly to have so misjudged his character," he added, to Eleanor's delight.

Esme snorted, but refrained from saying anything.

"Grandmama, feel badly?" Drusilla looked dumbfounded at the idea.

"And I understand from your father that best wishes are in order, Miss Bromley," Ryland continued.

"That's right." Bertrem nodded happily. "'Course, we aren't puffing it up yet in the papers, till I can write m'father. Can't tell you how happy it makes me, though, to be able to claim my bride."

Yes, you could, because it would be exactly how I'd feel if Eleanor were to agree to marry me, James thought with a surreptitious glance at Eleanor. The sunlight streaming in through the window seemed to paint each individual strand of her brown hair with a reddish glow and add a golden patina to her satiny skin. She looked exquisitely beautiful and eminently kissable. He wanted to spirit her away somewhere where they could be alone. Where he could indulge his love for her to the fullest.

He'd intended to wait until after the Season was over before asking her to marry him, but he no longer had that luxury. Not with Henry talking about returning to Lincolnshire to supervise the renovations to his estate. Eleanor would undoubtedly go with him, and James couldn't bear the thought of waking up each morning without at least the possibility of spending a few minutes of his day with her. Of listening to her sage observations on the people and events around them. Eleanor Wallace lent a stability and sanity to his world that he couldn't afford to lose, even temporarily.

He'd spent the short drive here trying to decide what would be the best thing to do, and he'd finally come up with the rather unimaginative idea of inviting her and her family to Ashdean, his estate in Kent, this weekend. Once he had her alone, away from the myriad distractions of London, he'd propose. Then he'd get a special license and marry her as soon as it could be arranged.

"Would you care for a cup of tea, Your Grace?" Maria offered.

"No, thank you." He sat down on the sofa beside Eleanor.

Eleanor swallowed against the sudden dryness in her mouth. She could feel the warmth of his body sending out elusive tendrils to ensnare her senses, and she wanted nothing so much as to lean against him. To luxuriate in the intoxicating feel of his body.

"Actually." James' deep voice shattered the sensual spell that had held her in thrall. "I came to invite you and your family to visit Ashdean this weekend, Mrs. Bromley." He addressed the invitation to Maria.

Eleanor's breath caught in her throat in an agony of longing. A whole weekend with James. A weekend in the same house with him away from the distractions of London and his work at Whitehall. Please say yes, Aunt Maria, she prayed fervently.

"This weekend?" Maria asked uncertainly.

"Yes. It's barely a two hours' drive from London."

"We promised the Buxteds we'd be here for their ball," Esme said, knowing that her only hope of saving some face in the fiasco of Drusilla's marriage to Bertrem would be to claim that she had been the one to turn off Ryland. Something no one would believe if it became known that they had visited his estate after Drusilla's engagement was announced.

"That isn't until Tuesday evening," Maria pointed out.

Esme sniffed. "I dislike scrambling affairs. Perhaps later in the year—"

"I'm sorry you don't feel able to go, but I see no reason why the rest of us can't." Maria had made up her mind. She didn't know why Ryland was inviting them on such short notice, but if there was the slightest chance that it was because he wanted to further his acquaintance with Eleanor, then she intended to make sure he had the opportunity. No matter how inconvenient the visit was.

"Well!" Esme declared in an awful voice. "What is this world coming to, when children set themselves up in opposition to their parents?"

Eleanor barely noticed her tantrum. She was light-headed with pleasure at the thought of the upcoming weekend. A pleasure that dimmed somewhat when she noticed the dejected-looking Bertrem. Catching James' eye, she glanced significantly at Bertrem. James followed her gaze.

"I hope you'll be able to join us, Mr. Arylesworth." James did what he thought Eleanor wanted. It was. The brilliance of her rewarding smile played havoc with his composure.

"Be pleased to. Mean to say, never visited a duke's estate before. M'father'll be that impressed," he said ingenuously.

"Baron Gunn." Walker's announcement caught Eleanor by surprise. In all the excitement over finding the necklace, she hadn't given Connal a thought.

Eleanor forced herself to smile politely at Connal when what she wanted to tell him was to leave. To go away and not to ever come back. That no matter what he said, she had no intention of marrying him. Not now. Not ever.

"Good morning." Connal gave them an encompassing smile, his gaze lingering on Eleanor, who after one brief look refused to meet his eyes. "Such lovely spring weather we're having. It makes me want to invite you all to drive out for a picnic this weekend."

"Thank you, Baron," Maria answered him. "But this weekend we've accepted Ryland's invitation to visit Ashdean in Kent."

"Ah, how I envy you. A visit to Kent is by far the better way to enjoy the weather."

Eleanor listened to Connal's blatant hint with a feeling of dismay. She fervently hoped that James wouldn't extend the invitation Connal was angling for. The weekend would be spoiled if she had to spend her time trying to avoid being alone with Connal. To her infinite relief, James merely smiled politely.

After a small, awkward pause when it became obvious that no invitation was forthcoming, Connal changed tactics. "Actually, I came by to see if I might tempt Miss Wallace to come for a drive with me."

Eleanor had just opened her mouth to hastily disclaim any inclination to go anywhere with him when Esme, correctly assessing her reluctance, took what revenge she could by accepting for her.

"Of course she'll go with you, Baron," Esme said with a nasty smile at Eleanor.

Eleanor bit back the denial hovering on her lips. To refuse to go after Esme had accepted would be bound to occasion precisely the kind of speculation she wished to avoid. She could hardly give the real reason she was avoiding Connal. No, Eleanor thought as she reluctantly rose to her feet. It would be better if she was to go with Connal and this time make her lack of interest in marrying him absolutely clear.

"What were you thinking of?" Connal demanded as soon as they had reached the relative isolation of Hyde Park. "Why didn't you second my attempt to get an invitation to Ryland's house party? All you'd have to do was to say how nice that would be, and he'd have had no option but to invite me."

"I think you underestimate him," Eleanor said dryly. "Besides, I don't think it would be nice. I don't want you to come. I've already told you that I'm not going to marry you."

"We'll discuss that later." Connal dismissed her words with a casualness that she found infuriating. "What we've got to do now is to get hold of the plans for the final offensive against Napoleon. De Selignac will pay fifty thousand pounds for them."

"He can pay fifty million pounds for all I care!" Eleanor replied. "It's blood money, when all's said and done. And I won't be party to helping to kill more people."

"Soldiers die," Connal insisted.

"Murdered by people who spy."

"As you did."

Eleanor grimaced. "As I did. But what I did I did for my father, not for financial gain. I won't help you, Connal. In fact, I sincerely hope that I never have to see you again."

Connal laughed, and the sound scraped menacingly through Eleanor's mind.

"That's going to make for a very strange marriage, my dear."

Eleanor held on to her temper with an effort. "Connal, for the last time, I will not marry a man without honor."

The flush that burned across his cheekbones was the only sign that her thrust had gone home.

"Your opinion of me is of no concern. What does concern me is the information you can get from Ryland. For some reason, he seems to like you. Not, of course, that he'd ever stoop to marrying you," Connal gibed.

"Perhaps not." Eleanor tried not to let her growing sense of anger show. She was becoming very tired of everyone telling her that James wouldn't marry her. "But on the other hand, he'd also never stoop to asking me to spy for him."

"I have borne enough of your insolence!" Connal declared. "You will do exactly as you are told, or—"

"Or what?" Eleanor asked contemptuously.

"Or I will tell both your uncle and Whitehall what you did," he threatened. "And since I have the original notes in your own hand, I rather think they'll believe me." He gave her a thin- lipped smile. "Don't you?"

Eleanor swallowed against the confusing jumble of fear and anger and hatred that engulfed her. She looked down at the ground, focusing on the yellow flowers by the side of the pathway. Instinctively she knew she couldn't let Connal see just how badly his threat had shaken her, because he'd use that knowledge to his own advantage. She had to make him believe that his threat was of minimal concern to her.

"Yes, I rather think they would believe you. If you were foolhardy enough to tell them," she said, with a calmness at complete variance with the scalding emotion percolating through her veins. She wanted to smash Connal's smiling face. She wanted to bring him to account for what he was doing, but she knew she didn't have the power. The best she could hope for was to stop him from doing any more damage.

"However," she continued in that hard-won tone, "if you were to tell them what I did, you'd also have to admit to what you did. And since you were the one who actually sold the information..."

Eleanor forced an insouciant shrug. "I shall simply claim that I didn't have the slightest idea what I was copying. That you told me it was about our shipping business and begged me to take notes. That I did as you asked because I felt I owed it to you, since you had been my father's partner. It might be interesting to see which of us they believe."

Connal looked disconcerted at her response. "And what would your uncle think?" He tried a different tack.

"I rather imagine he would despise me, but since I intended to leave England after the Season anyway, what does it matter what he thinks? I'm also certain that he'd do his best to shift the blame onto you, since my having stolen the plans would reflect badly on him. In fact, by the time my uncle and his cronies at Whitehall get through, you'll be the villain and I'll just be another foolish, credulous woman."

Eleanor watched as Connal's fingers tightened on the reins. She could almost see his mind examining what she'd said. Looking for flaws. For a way to turn the situation to his own advantage.

"My dear Eleanor," he said, switching tactics, "your trip to England has unsettled you. Once you're back in Boston, you'll see that I was right."

Eleanor focused on the rhythmic movement of the horses' flanks as they walked, and did not even bother to dignify his comment with a response. She would never change. In fact, as soon as possible, she intended to sell her portion of their shipbuilding business. She didn't even want a business partnership between them.

Connal reached over and, picking up her hand, squeezed her fingers in what was obviously supposed to be a comforting gesture.

"You're simply feeling out of sorts," he said. "We'll discuss this later."

Eleanor held on to her temper with a monumental effort. Thanks to Connal's duplicity and her own stupidity, her time in England was fast dwindling down to a few precious days. But she'd have those days to remember, she vowed grimly. No matter what, she would have the memories of the visit to James' estate to remember in the long, sterile years that loomed in the future.

Chapter Fifteen

Eleanor finally gave up all pretense of reading her Gothic and tossed it down on the sofa beside her. Impatiently she stared at the carved oak doors of the library. Like everything else at Ashdean, they were oversize. As if James' Elizabethan ancestor who had built the house had somehow been larger than life. She shifted restlessly on the leather sofa, straining to hear the muffled sounds filtering through the thick doors.

"I wonder when Papa and Ryland will be done." Drusilla echoed Eleanor's growing impatience. "It was too bad of that fusty old minister to send them something that has to be done over the weekend."

"They should be finished shortly," Eleanor said, more in an attempt to convince herself than to persuade Drusilla. She wanted so badly to see James. To talk to him. To bask in the infectious warmth of his smile. To believe that this was nothing more than a normal house party. The first of many such to come.

But she knew it was all pretend. Just as she knew that seeing James wouldn't solve her problems. As far as she could see, nothing but an act of God could do that. During the past two days, she'd gone over her last, disastrous conversation with Connal a thousand times. She'd dissected his every single sentence into its individual words, thoroughly examining each one in an attempt to find a different meaning from the one that was so indelibly imprinted on her soul. But the words and their meanings had remained exactly the same. A meaning that effectively destroyed any hope she might have had for a future in England.

Eleanor swallowed against an urge to burst into tears at the thought. She didn't want to go back to Boston. She felt at home in England, and she was very fond of her uncle's family. And then there was James...

What exactly did she feel for him? For the first time, Eleanor deliberately examined her feelings about James. Fighting past the enveloping sensual haze that fogged her mind whenever she thought of him, she tried to identify specifics. She began a mental list. She respected him for his intellectual abilities. She admired his tireless efforts to defeat Napoleon, as well as his care for his dependents' well-being. She felt a deep empathy with him over the loss of his brother. She was intrigued by his dry sense of humor. She felt a sense of tenderness when he mounted his hobbyhorse about the Romans. And she craved his kisses, she concluded on a flash of honesty.

So what did all that add up to? she asked herself. Friendship? No, it was more than simple friendship. More even than a deep and abiding friendship. Far more. It was...love. The word exploded in her mind sending shock waves of dismay through her as she struggled to adjust to the unwelcome insight.

Falling in love with James Wolfe had to be the classic example of an exercise in futility, she thought in despair. There was absolutely no future in it. Even without Connal's threat hanging over her head like the proverbial sword of Damocles, it would be highly unlikely that James would ever marry her. In England, the aristocracy married the aristocracy. And the higher their place in that aristocracy, the more likely they were to adhere to the rules.

But James was different. A small, fugitive hope wouldn't quite die. James was a very unusual member of the English aristocracy. He saw nothing wrong with the Romans stealing their brides from the Sabines. But he'd see plenty wrong with his bride stealing state secrets, she conceded. Unfortunately, there was no parallel in Roman history that she could use as a mitigating circumstance. In fact, one of his precious Roman women would probably have chosen a gory death before stooping to spying, she thought glumly.

But even if he would never have married her, he would have been her friend. A sense of loss weighed her down. She would have seen him occasionally over the years. Talked to him. Laughed with him. Shared ideas with him. Argued with him. He would have respected her and liked her as a person, if not as a lover.

But once Connal made good his threat... And he would. Eleanor didn't doubt it for a moment. Connal was spiteful, and if he couldn't have what he wanted, he'd make sure she didn't get what she wanted.

And the end result of Connal's revenge would be that she would wind up with nothing that mattered. Not a life in England. Not the love of her uncle Henry's family, and, most importantly, not James. The only real question was how long she had before Connal told the authorities about her spying.

Eleanor took a deep breath in a vain attempt to quell her rising sense of panic long enough to think logically. Connal probably wouldn't tell anyone while he was still in England, because then he'd have to explain his part in the affair, and he wouldn't be any too eager to do that.

So it was probable that he'd wait until he'd left England and send an express to Whitehall. But when did he plan to sail? She searched her mind, but couldn't remember if he had ever said. She didn't think he had.

There was also the fact that Connal was a very greedy man, and the money the French were offering him to steal the plans for the final offensive had to be a powerful temptation. As long as he thought there was any chance that he could coerce her into helping him, he wouldn't expose her.

But there was a wild card in all this, Eleanor thought uneasily. Connal's coconspirator, De Selignac. When Connal had introduced the Frenchman to her, her skin had crawled. There was something about the man's eyes.... Eleanor shivered. They were flat, cold, and entirely pitiless. It was as if the villain from one of her Gothics had suddenly been imbued with life. But Eleanor knew that in real life, unlike her beloved Gothics, simply because the heroine was pure of heart didn't mean she was going to triumph in the end. Besides, she wasn't pure of heart. She was up to her neck in spying.

Eleanor sighed despondently.

"What's the matter, Eleanor?" Drusilla asked.

"I'm just bored," Eleanor lied.

"You can help me, if you like. I'm planning my wedding." Drusilla smiled dreamily.

Eleanor tried to ignore the sharp stab of envy she felt. Drusilla deserved her happiness, she told herself.

But did she deserve the mess she was in? She might have spied, but her motives had not been self-serving. She'd been trying to be loyal to her father. She grimaced. At least she'd learned one invaluable lesson from all this, and that was that first and foremost one had to be loyal to one's own beliefs. If she had listened to her own conscience, Connal would have absolutely no hold over her now.

Eleanor's muscles clenched in sudden anticipation as the library door opened, and then promptly sagged in disappointment when she saw Bertrem.

"Bertrem!" Drusilla said in delight. "I wondered where you were."

"Been looking for you." He glanced around the huge room, with its ceiling-to-floor shelves of books. "Deuced strange place to find a couple of females."

"My fault," Eleanor said. "I wanted to read my Gothic, and where better to read than in a library?" And here she had felt closer to James, in spirit, if not in body, she admitted.

"Wouldn't know," Bertrem confessed. "Don't read. Came to see if you wanted to walk in the rose garden." He looked hopefully at Drusilla, who promptly bounded to her feet and hurried over to him.

"Oh, yes. Would you like to come, Eleanor?" she asked politely.

"No, thank you," Eleanor said, trying not to take the identical expressions of relief that crossed their faces personally. She didn't blame them, she told herself as she watched them hurry out as if afraid that she might change her mind. If she had the opportunity to spend some time

with James, she wouldn't welcome a third party tagging
along. No matter how fond she happened to be of them.

Determinedly Eleanor picked up her book again. She
would not sit here and daydream about the man, she vowed.
She would—

Her thoughts were suddenly sucked down into a confused caldron of emotions as James appeared in the open
doorway. Love, guilt and desire all swirled together through
her in a bewildering mixture. Hungrily she stared at him, her
eyes skimming over his gleaming Hessians and biscuit-
colored pantaloons to linger on the narrow green stripes of
the waistcoat that covered his broad chest.

What would he look like without his clothes? The fugitive thought popped into her mind. Would his chest be covered with hair, or would it be smooth and muscled, like
those of the Indians who had occasionally walked through
Boston? Her palms tingled at the thought of rubbing them
over his skin. Of exploring the nuances of its texture. Disconcerted by the explicitness of her wayward thoughts,
Eleanor forced her eyes upward. Momentarily she focused
on the half smile that curved his lips before moving upward
to his bright, sparkling eyes. They were smiling, too. As if
his pleasure at seeing her encompassed his whole being.

Eleanor stared yearningly at him. She wanted nothing so
much as to throw herself into his arms and confess the whole
sordid mess. To try to make him understand why she'd done
it. To warn him what Connal wanted to do.

But if she did that, James' smile would fade, and the
laughter in his eyes would freeze with icy disapproval. Even
if he didn't turn her over to the authorities, nothing would
ever be the same again. Always the memory of her treachery would lie between them. No, she rationalized. It would
be better to send him a letter after she left England. That
way, he would be warned about Connal and De Selignac,
and she would be spared seeing his friendship turn to con-
tempt.

"Good afternoon," James offered at her continued silence. "Seeing me can't be that much of a shock. I do live
here."

"Good afternoon." Eleanor made a conscious effort to throw off her worries and enjoy what little time she had left with him.

"What are you reading? I have an excellent collection of Greek and Roman writings." He sat down beside her on the sofa and picked up her book, frowning when he saw the title. "I would have thought you'd have had your fill of these by now."

"Have you had your fill of all those musty old tomes full of facts about a lot of dead people who were no better than they should be?"

"That is different," James objected. "Besides, you can't judge an historical time period out of context."

Eleanor smiled happily, exhilarated to be arguing with him again. "Of course I can. I just did."

"I meant you shouldn't. And as for this trash—"

"Tell me, have you ever read any of my Gothics?"

"Certainly not!"

"Then how can you, who profess to admire the logic of the Greeks, possibly object to something you know nothing about?"

"One doesn't have to eat spoiled meat to know it's gone off. The smell is sufficient."

"Ha!" Eleanor looked down her small nose at him. "Descending to generalities to buttress an argument because you haven't got any specifics is specious reasoning."

"Specifics? You want specifics?" James flipped open her book and began to read at random. "'He chased her screaming through the house, finally trapping her against the locked door to the attics.'" James grimaced. "And then what does he do?"

"I don't know. You're the one with the book."

"'He begins to importune her virtue. At great length, I might add."

"Then he must be Cyril Verton, the villain, and villains are supposed to importune the heroine's virtue."

"Sounds to me as if the villains get the better role, but that wasn't what I was objecting to. Didn't it occur to you that if he's been chasing her all over the house, he might want to pause and catch his breath, instead of breaking into a speech that goes on for..." James flipped through the pages. "Three full pages, and part of another. The man must have a constitution of iron."

Eleanor frowned at him. "You are going a long way to ruining what was a very good book."

"And another thing—if I were to chase you through the house with you screaming, 'Save me, save me,' I guarantee you that every servant in the place would be there to see what was going on," James said in disgust.

But would I scream for help? Eleanor wondered as her eyes lingered on his firm lips, remembering the feel of them against her skin. Their warmth...their pressure...their intoxicating taste. No, she wouldn't scream to be rescued, she admitted. Far more likely she'd simply stop in a convenient alcove and allow him to have his way with her.

"The villain had his servants cowed." Eleanor felt obligated to defend her book.

"Well, I wish he'd tell me how he did it," James said ruefully. "I've been trying to snub some of mine for thirty years, and they simply ignore me.

"But that's not the worst of it. Listen to this. 'He pushed her against the wall and covered her mouth with his, cutting off her screams.'"

"Yes?"

"That wouldn't do it."

"Wouldn't do what?"

"Silence her."

"Yes, it would," Eleanor objected.

"Would you care to put your theory to the test?"

Eleanor blinked uncertainly. "What are you talking about? Those are imaginary characters."

James leaned closer, and the warmth of his body tugged at her senses, subtly drawing her to him. The very faint aroma of sandalwood drifted into her lungs, making it difficult for her to breathe. Eleanor swallowed uneasily and glanced down, focusing on his hand, outlined against the dark blue marbled cover of the book he was holding. Her eyes traced over his long fingers, imagining them against her bare skin. Slowly stroking...

Instinctively she glanced toward the door. James had closed it when he came in. They weren't likely to be disturbed, Eleanor thought on a rising tide of excitement as she looked into his eyes, which were gleaming with laughter, and something else. Something that sent a quiver of anticipation through her. She didn't know why James seemed to steal every opportunity to kiss her, nor did she really care. All too soon she was going to have to return to the emotional sterility of her life in Boston. What harm could it do for her to enjoy the kisses of the man she loved while she had the chance?

Shivers of longing chased over her skin as James grasped her chin in his hand and lifted her face. She could feel his fingers pressing into her soft flesh, burning into her senses. She watched in bemusement as his face came closer and closer, until it filled her entire field of vision. The warmth of his breath heated her skin until it tightened unbearably across her cheekbones. Desire coiled itself around her heart, sending it hammering violently in her chest.

"But you said if I screamed all the servants would come running," she whispered against his lips, which were a scant inch from hers.

"Scream softly." James closed the gap between them, and his mouth captured hers with an avid hunger he made no effort to hide.

The pressure of his lips sent tiny pinpricks of desire skittering madly along her nerve endings. Eleanor instinctively leaned forward, her only thought to intensify the alluring sensation. At her yielding gesture, James wrapped his arms around her and pulled her closer, molding her pliant body against his. Eleanor gasped at the heavy throbbing that pulsed through her breasts. Their soft flesh seemed to swell with desire, and she pressed harder against his broad chest.

The hot tip of his tongue traced boldly over her lips, and her mouth eagerly parted beneath their seeking. His tongue surged into her mouth. Eleanor moaned, craving more. She craved the feel of his warm, supple skin. Impatiently her fingers grasped his nape, and she rubbed her fingertips over his neck, trembling as the scratchy feel of his hairline scraped abrasively over her sensitive skin.

James shoved his fingers through her short, silky hair, grasping the back of her head. Holding her steady, he began to nuzzle the soft, tender skin beneath her ear.

Eleanor gasped and arched her head back at the exquisite sensation. Slowly, sensuously, he rubbed his lips along her jawline, planting teasing kisses at the corners of her parted mouth. A burning heat scorching over her skin raised her temperature to the boiling point.

"Damn!" James' hoarsely bitten-off exclamation penetrated the sensual daze that had ensorcelled her a second before she heard the sounds of someone fumbling with the door handle.

He jumped up and, hastily retrieving the book from the floor where it had fallen, dumped it in her lap before he retreated to the other side of the fireplace. Disoriented, Eleanor watched as he picked up a poker with fingers that shook and began to wreak havoc on the blazing fire. She understood his sense of frustration perfectly, because that was exactly how she felt. As if someone had wound her up too tightly.

A second later, the door opened and James' butler announced four strangers, neighbors who had come to call now that he was in residence, she discovered when James introduced them.

It was all Eleanor could do to respond coherently to their conversation. She felt as if her emotions had been shattered into a thousand pieces and the only thing that could glue them back together again were James' kisses. Something that was impossible now that the outside world had intruded.

What James thought about the interruption wasn't so apparent. Eleanor studied him from beneath her lashes as he politely responded to the young woman's blatant flirtation. A burning sensation scalded her mind. A sensation she was reluctant to admit was jealousy. She probed the feeling like a sore tooth. It wasn't any more bearable on closer inspection. She simply didn't want other women flirting with James, even if he himself seemed totally oblivious of the fact. What she really wanted to do was to post No Trespassing signs around him and banish all female visitors. It was a lowering thought.

"Isn't that right, Miss Wallace?" the young woman's father asked, and Eleanor nodded, not having the slightest idea what she was agreeing with. And not caring. There wasn't room in her mind at the moment for anything but the emotions James had raised in her. She wanted to examine their kiss in privacy. To relive each and every nuance of it.

"So unusual for His Grace to be in residence at this time of the year," the man continued, and Eleanor forced herself to concentrate on the conversation. If she wasn't careful, James was going to realize just how shattered she had been by his kiss, and she didn't want him to know that. Now she'd concentrate on being polite to his neighbors. Later she'd figure out a way to get him alone again. Perhaps she could ask him to show her his diggings, she decided. Even a hole in the ground would be fun with James to share it.

But her plans came to naught. A steady stream of visitors from the surrounding area filled the remainder of the afternoon, and after dinner the entire family gathered in the salon and listened while Drusilla sang one mournful ballad of death and destruction after another. All the while smiling besottedly at Bertrem. When she had finally run through her entire repertoire, James and Henry immediately excused themselves to return to their work on the dispatch Whitehall had sent down. Frustrated, Eleanor went to bed.

The next morning, Eleanor decided to try to lure James out to his diggings right after breakfast before any more of his neighbors could call. Unfortunately, her plan was derailed when James' bailiff appeared at breakfast with a pile of account books and begged James for just a few minutes of his time. The few minutes stretched into half an hour, then an hour, and became two before Eleanor's sense of pride finally reasserted itself. She might love James to distraction, but she refused to wait outside his study door like a faithful spaniel.

Determinedly she went looking for someone to pass the time with. She found her aunt in the main salon.

"Ah, Eleanor, my dear," Maria greeted her. "I wondered where you were. Do come in."

Eleanor crossed what seemed like acres of pale blue-and-cream Aubusson carpeting and sat down on one of the cream damask sofas, slowly sinking into its down-filled cushions. She wiggled into a comfortable position.

"I was thinking about what we could do this afternoon," Maria said. "His Grace told me there is a very old church in the village that dates from the time of the Saxons. It should be a worthwhile sight."

The only sight she really wanted to see was that of James' face, Eleanor thought wryly. Something she was hardly likely to do if she was to go look at an old church. Although...

"Perhaps you ought to ask Ryland if he would show it to you?" Eleanor suggested.

"His Grace?" Maria looked uncertain.

"Certainly. He is your host, after all. He should be entertaining you. Besides which, he really likes old things," Eleanor assured her.

"There were all those broken little bits of pottery," Maria remembered. "Perhaps he would—"

"Baron Gunn." The butler's sonorous tones echoed sinisterly through Eleanor's mind. It can't be, she tried to tell herself, afraid to turn and look. She'd misheard. She'd been so worried about Connal that she was only imagining she was hearing his name. Please, God, let that be it.

She took a deep breath and forced herself to turn. She immediately wished she hadn't. It really was Connal crossing the room toward her.

Eleanor stared at him, torn between anger that he had dared to follow her here and fear of just what his arrival might portend. She had so counted on having this visit with James to remember, and Connal's arrival could ruin everything.

"Why, Baron Gunn, what a surprise to see you. Whatever brings you into Kent?" Maria gave Eleanor a significant look, obviously thinking that the lure was her niece.

Poor Aunt Maria, she couldn't be more wrong, Eleanor thought drearily. The only thing likely to motivate Connal was money. And, perhaps, power. Her charms not only hadn't registered on him, she wasn't even sure that he thought she had any to register.

Connal gently shook the hand Maria held out to him. "Would you think better of me if I claimed it was in the hopes of seeing you?" He gave her a practiced smile. "Alas, I can't lie...."

He shot Eleanor a steely glance when she suddenly choked.

"Sorry," she muttered. "Pray excuse me."

"It's probably a tickle in your throat from the weather," Maria said, worried. "It did rain yesterday morning, and you would go walking in it and get your feet wet."

"I'm fine, Aunt Maria. Now then, you were telling us how you couldn't lie to us...Baron?" Eleanor ever so slightly emphasized his purloined title.

Eleanor watched with a slight feeling of satisfaction as the muscles in his jaw clenched angrily at her gibe. Aunt Maria might not have a clue what she was talking about, but Connal did. And he couldn't retaliate. Not at the moment.

"My friend, Monsieur De Selignac, drove down to visit an ailing cousin of his at Bexley. I came along to keep him company, but I, of course, didn't want to intrude on the family scene..."

"Very proper of you." Maria nodded approvingly, and Eleanor wanted to scream. Why couldn't her aunt see Connal for what he was? A self-serving opportunist. She'd wager her not-inconsiderable fortune that the closest relative De Selignac had was in France, and that the trip to Kent was simply a ruse to call on her. To try to force her to spy for him. But why now? she wondered. Why not wait until she returned to London? Her aunt might believe the taradiddle about ailing relatives, but James or Henry would be bound to suspect. Although, Eleanor admitted with a sinking feeling, they might also believe that the lure had been her.

"And then I remembered that Miss Wallace was to visit Ryland this weekend, and I felt rewarded."

"Why don't you take the baron for a walk in the duke's rose gardens, dear?" Maria smiled at Eleanor, obviously feeling that she was aiding the cause of love.

Eleanor smiled weakly back. "I wouldn't dream of leaving you here alone, Aunt Maria," she tried.

"Nonsense, dear. I was about to go and find Henry when you came in."

"I'd very much like to see the rose gardens, Miss Wallace," Connal hastened to insert.

Liar, Eleanor thought in impotent anger. Connal didn't dare expose her, but by the same token, neither could she expose him.

Giving in to the inevitable, she got to her feet. Maybe it would be better to show him the garden, listen to his pleas and threats, and then flatly refuse. Or, perhaps, she'd get lucky and Drusilla and Bertrem would already be in the rose garden, which would forestall any importunings on Connal's part.

As it seemed so often lately, Lady Luck had deserted her. The rose garden was empty of everyone, even a gardener.

"Well?" Connal demanded. "Have you come to your senses yet? This is of vital importance. It's a time for action."

Eleanor grimaced. "You sound like you've been reading one of those infernal Roman generals' memoirs."

Connal frowned at her. "What are you talking about? I don't read Latin."

"You don't?" Eleanor eyed him consideringly. "That should have been a point in your favor, but then, I suppose that there are so many points against you that it doesn't matter."

"Will you pay attention?" Connal glanced hurriedly around the empty garden. "Someone might come."

"Hope springs eternal," Eleanor muttered.

"De Selignac has discovered something," Connal announced. "Something of outstanding importance. The plans for the final offensive were brought down from London yesterday so that Ryland and your uncle can check them over before they're sent directly on to the English command on the Continent."

"If that's so, why don't you and your fellow spy—"

"Hush!" Connal ordered. "Someone might hear you."

"When a man is afraid of the truth about his actions being overheard, then it's time for him to reassess his way of life," Eleanor replied.

"This isn't my way of life," Connal protested. "I'm simply a businessman trying to take advantage of a once-in-a-lifetime opportunity. Once we've managed to get our hands on the plans, then I'll give them to De Selignac, collect our money and book us passage on the first boat home, and that will be the end of it."

"No." Eleanor shook her head. "The end of it will be the countless young men like Ryland's brother who will die because of what you did. I'll have no part of it."

"Your sensibilities do you credit, my dear, but I've already told De Selignac you'll copy the plans."

"Rather premature of you. I'm sorry, but I have done my last bit of spying for you."

"But—"

"No." Eleanor shook her head. "I want no part of spying nor of you. Please leave."

"Now see here . . ." Connal blustered.

"I have already seen far more than I want to. We can discuss how best to dissolve our partnership in the shipyards when I return to Boston, which will be as soon as this house party is over. Now get out. I want to spend these last few days with my aunt and uncle."

"You haven't heard the last of this. I won't give up this easily when there's so much at stake!" Connal turned on his heel and stalked around the side of the house.

Eleanor released her breath on a long sigh and sagged down on a stone bench at the edge of the path. She didn't doubt for a minute that Connal meant what he'd said. How could she have gotten into so much trouble, when her motives had been so good? she wondered in despair. What was it that Scottish poet her father had been so fond of had said? Something about the best-laid plans of mice and men . . .

Chapter Sixteen

"It's been such a lovely day." Maria leaned back on the sofa in James' salon and smiled contentedly. "And now that Henry has the funds to renovate our estate, we'll be able to remove to Lincolnshire, so I won't have to..."

"Put up with Grandmama's tantrums," Eleanor finished, trying not to let her own sense of loss at leaving England and James spoil her aunt's pleasure at finally getting to be mistress of her own home. She'd tell Maria that she wouldn't be going to Lincolnshire with them just as soon as she'd actually booked passage, she decided.

"Well, dear, I certainly hope that I will always value dear Henry's mother the way I should, but I must admit that it will be much easier to do it when I'm not living in the same house with her," Maria said.

"Yes, indeed," Drusilla muttered, furtively sticking her head out of the salon and peering down the hallway.

"Drusilla, do come away from the door. Whatever will the men think if they come out of the dining room and see you?"

"They aren't going to think anything, because they aren't ever going to finish their port!" Drusilla wailed. "What can be taking them so long? We finished dinner hours ago."

"Nonsense," Maria said placidly. "It can't have been more than twenty minutes, and you know what men are like over their port. They start exchanging the most unlikely tales, and lose all track of the time."

Eleanor shifted restlessly on the sofa, sharing Drusilla's impatience for the men to rejoin them. Her time with James was dwindling down to a few precious hours, and she didn't want to waste one single moment of them. She wanted to hoard each conversation. Each smile.

Eleanor's eyes strayed to the door Drusilla was watching so fixedly. Much as she wanted to see James, a tiny part of her dreaded his appearance, because she knew she should tell him that Connal wanted to steal the dispatch from Whitehall. But did Connal still intend to try, now that she'd categorically refused to help him? Breaking into Ashdean without someone on the inside to help would be a very risky undertaking. Connal might be greedy, but he wasn't stupid. He wasn't about to do anything that would put his own future in jeopardy. His common sense should tell him that his only viable option was to abandon his plans and return to London.

Eleanor unconsciously gnawed on her lower lip. The one imponderable in this whole equation was De Selignac. From various things Connal had said, it almost seemed to her as if the Frenchman were the one making the decisions. As if Connal were merely a well-paid dupe. If that was true, then the real question was, what did De Selignac intend to do? What might he feel driven to do, with the fate of Napoleon hanging in the balance?

Eleanor squinted at the crackling fire as an image of De Selignac's malevolent eyes seemed to flicker in the depths of the flames. He wasn't a man to give up easily, she thought nervously. He would make at least one attempt to get a look at the plans. But how? By housebreaking? Or by trying to convince her to change her mind?

But if she didn't tell James, and the Frenchman did somehow manage to copy the plans, then would she not be guilty of a greater betrayal than the one she'd already committed?

She rubbed her head, which was beginning to ache. If only she were sure what was the best thing to do. No, she amended honestly, she knew what was the best thing to do. What was the honorable thing to do. What she didn't know was where to find the courage to do it.

She glanced up as Drusilla came scurrying across the room and dropped onto the sofa nearest the fire. "The door to the dining room just opened," she explained at Maria's astonished look.

Eleanor felt her stomach flutter as she heard voices in the hallway. She stared at the door, her emotions a confusing blend of anticipation and dread while she waited for James. First her uncle appeared in the doorway, a wide smile wreathing his round face. He seemed to have shed years overnight, now that he was no longer dependent on Esme's chancy benevolence. At least she'd done that for him. Eleanor tried to find some comfort in the thought.

Bertrem was right behind him. He quickly scanned the room and, finding Drusilla, immediately headed toward her.

Eleanor's breath caught in her throat as James finally appeared.

He smiled warmly, intimately, at her, as if they shared a secret no one else knew. Her heart seemed to skip a beat at the glow that lit his eyes. He really liked her, she thought joyfully. But for how long? Her sense of guilt momentarily gained the upper hand. How long would it be before that warmth withered and died?

James greeted Maria, nodded at the oblivious Drusilla, and then sat down next to Eleanor.

She gave James a quick, nervous smile that sent a flicker of unease through him. Eleanor wasn't the nervous type. In fact, one of the things he liked about her was her matter-of-fact, no-nonsense approach to life. Unless ... Could she somehow suspect that he had invited her to Ashdean to propose? Could that be making her nervous? It didn't seem likely. She'd never been nervous in his company before, and she must have realized that he would make her an offer after those kisses they had shared. Or maybe she was nervous because he hadn't declared himself yet? He didn't know. What he did know was that he wanted to get the formalities over with.

Soon, he promised himself. Soon they would be married, and he could spend his nights making slow, intoxicating love to her, instead of having to settle for snatched kisses in out-of-the-way corners. And soon Napoleon would be nothing more than an annoying footnote to history, and his part in the war effort would be over. Then he'd be able to take Eleanor home to Cumberland.

They could excavate for artifacts together. A deep feeling of contentment filled him. Just a few months ago, his world had been a bleak place, offering little solace from the pain and loneliness of his brother's death. Now, while the loss of Paul would always leave a rent in the fabric of his existence, he felt as if he had a future again. A future that promised happiness.

"Ashdean is so peaceful, Your Grace," Maria offered.

"Not too peaceful, I hope. What would you like to do this evening?" James asked, recalling his duties as host.

"What I'd like to do is not what I'm going to do, Ryland," Henry said. "Dealing with that dispatch from Whitehall has set me back. I still have some work to do on a memo for the American campaign I brought with me. It has to be ready to return to London with the courier tomorrow."

"And I intend to retire to my room with a book," Maria said. "I don't know what it is about the country, but the air always seems to tire me out so." Gathering up her netting, she followed her husband from the room.

If James wanted to entertain me, he could kiss me, Eleanor thought dreamily. That was the most entertaining experience she'd ever had. He could put his arms around her and pull her close to him. So close that she could feel the scratchiness of his neckcloth and smell the fresh, clean scent of it. So close that she would be able to feel the hardness of his muscles as they held her a willing captive against him. Eleanor swallowed against the sudden dryness in her mouth. That would certainly be entertaining. Of course, to do it, they'd first have to escape from Bertrem and Drusilla, and then find a dark corner where none of the servants would be likely to disturb them.

Which would leave the way open for Connal to sneak into James' study. If he and De Selignac had decided on housebreaking. The appalling thought effectively shattered Eleanor's sense of euphoria. If she couldn't bring herself to tell James what she'd done, then the very least that she could do would be to make sure that Connal couldn't do any more harm. But how?

Unless . . . Connal couldn't steal the plans if he couldn't get to them. She knew they were in the safe in James' study, because her uncle had worried out loud at dinner about how secure they were there. So, if the four of them were to spend the evening in James' study, Connal wouldn't have an opportunity to get to them. She shivered nervously, knowing that her plan was full of holes, but it was the best she could do on the spur of the moment.

James frowned at her involuntary movement. "Cold?" he asked.

The concern in his voice gave her an idea.

"Yes," she said. "I am cold. Would you mind if we all went to your study? It's much warmer in there." She tried her best to make the request sound commonplace, even though she was perfectly aware that guests did not normally request to be entertained in particular rooms. Ah, well, she thought, far better that James should suspect she was rag-mannered than that he should know she was a spy.

James blinked in surprise. "My study?"

"With Drusilla and Bertrem, and play whist," she said, hoping that James wasn't aware she loathed the game. Especially with her cousin, who could never seem to keep the rules in her head.

"A rubber of whist in my study it is," he agreed.

"Drusilla," Eleanor said, "we're going to go play whist in his grace's study."

Drusilla tore her fascinated gaze away from Bertrem's face and looked uncertainly at Eleanor. "We are?"

"Yes," Eleanor said firmly. "It will be fun."

"But you said the last time we played whist that nothing on this earth could ever induce you to—"

"I was a little upset that you trumped my ace," Eleanor said, interrupting her. "I got over it."

"But I don't like—" Drusilla began.

"You can have Bertrem as a partner," Eleanor offered.

Drusilla looked unhappy about the projected use of her evening, but, fortunately, her good manners prevented further complaints. Reluctantly she got to her feet and, trailed by Bertrem, followed Eleanor and James to his study.

"So many books, and it ain't even the library," Bertrem marveled as he took in the bookshelves that lined two of the study's four walls.

Eleanor was totally unmoved by the books. What caught her eye was the set of French doors that opened onto the garden. A determined thief would have very little trouble prying them open. Eleanor stifled a sigh. If it weren't French doors, it would probably be an oversize window, she tried to tell herself. And whatever the room's architectural deficiencies, Connal and De Selignac couldn't do anything about it while the four of them were in the room.

Eleanor organized her unenthusiastic audience. "Bertrem, you sit there, and Drusilla, you sit here."

Taking the deck from James, Eleanor sat down across from him and started to shuffle, managing to scatter the cards all over.

"Here. Allow me." James picked the cards off the table, while Bertrem scrambled around on the floor, retrieving the rest of them.

"Females and cards don't mix," Bertrem gravely told her.

"I must mention your theory to my grandmama sometime," Eleanor said, and then felt a stab of guilt when Bertrem paled.

"Although, on second thought, I probably won't see her again," Eleanor said, trying to make amends for taking her own worries out on Bertrem.

"Why not?" James asked sharply.

"Grandmama said that if Papa sold his necklace instead of giving it to her, then we were to leave and never darken her door again. She sounded just like the villainess from *The Dungeon of Fear*," Drusilla related.

"True." Eleanor chuckled. "However, the situation might not have disintegrated so rapidly into a shouting match if you had refrained from mentioning that fact to her."

"It just popped out," Drusilla said, defending herself. "Besides, I think it was all for the best. If I hadn't annoyed her so much, she might have forgiven us." Drusilla's eyes widened in horror at the thought. "And we might have had to have gone on living with her."

"Not you, my dear." Bertrem smiled besottedly at her. "You're going to marry me and live in Little Heythorpe."

"Yes." Drusilla heaved a happy sigh as she returned his smile.

Eleanor looked from one face to the other, trying to understand what they felt for each other. She loved James. Loved him with every fiber of her being. She loved his sharp mind, his concern for his dependents, his kindness, his sense of humor, the incredible way he made her feel when he kissed her. She loved him with a depth and scope that seemed to have no limits. But despite her overwhelming feelings for him, she wasn't oblivious of his faults. She knew perfectly well that he could be extremely aggravating on the subject of his artifacts. Her love might have made her very tolerant of that aggravation, but it didn't blind her to it, the way Drusilla seemed to have been blinded to Bertrem's many faults. Did that mean that she didn't love James as much as Drusilla loved Bertrem?

Her eyes strayed to James, who was shuffling the cards. With far more competency than she had shown, she noticed. She watched as his lean fingers began to deal them out. Unconsciously she ran the tip of her tongue over her lips as she remembered the feel of those fingers on her skin. Softly stroking. Bringing her to a frenzy of excitement that had seemed to teeter on the brink of something more. Something fantastically wonderful. Now she'd never get to explore the depths of that feeling, she thought sadly. Once this house party was over with, she'd have to leave England, and in all likelihood she'd never see James again. A surge of grief ripped through her.

"Eleanor, are you all right?" Drusilla asked anxiously. "You've gone all pale."

"Umm, yes. It's just a little stuffy in here," Eleanor muttered. It was the first excuse that came to mind.

"I'll open the doors for you." Eager to be of help, Bertrem sprang to his feet.

"Oh, no, don't bother," Eleanor said sharply, not wanting the doors open. Who knew what might happen?

"No bother at all," Bertrem assured her. "Besides, you're going to be m'cousin," he said, with another smile at Drusilla, who gave him a trembling smile in return.

Eleanor looked up to find James watching her with a narrowed intensity that made her very uneasy. Act naturally, she ordered herself. What this situation most emphatically didn't need was for James to become suspicious. Become any more suspicious, she amended. He must already be wondering about her request to play whist in his study, and then her dropping the cards all over the floor in such a distracted manner.

She was so enmeshed in a web of half-truths and outright lies that she felt as if she'd never escape them. Maybe that was her punishment for the spying she'd done. To spend the rest of her life regretting it. It was too bad that one didn't get to rehearse life first, before one actually had to live it, she thought sadly. So much unhappiness could be avoided.

"Your turn, Eleanor," Drusilla told her, and Eleanor carelessly threw a card down. James' hastily stifled exclamation recalled her, and she made a valiant, if ineffectual, effort to pay attention. She simply couldn't keep her mind on the game. Her eyes kept straying to the open French doors as she strained to hear any noise from outside. Anything that sounded like footsteps, or someone moving through the shrubs. But the only sounds she heard were the normal ones of an early-spring night. But even so, Eleanor didn't feel any easier in her mind. It only made her strain all the harder.

As a social event, the evening was an unmitigated disaster. Eleanor's mind was clearly not on the game, while Drusilla's was firmly focused on Bertrem and his on her. The only one who was paying attention to the cards was James, and it wasn't doing him much good, as Eleanor was showing an alarming tendency to throw cards at random.

"That's the rubber." James added up the column. "We win."

"How nice," Drusilla muttered, with a vacuous smile for Bertrem.

"Let's play another rubber," Eleanor hurriedly suggested with a sideways look at the curtains blowing in the gentle breeze.

"Let's not!" James said emphatically.

"No," Drusilla agreed. "I never was very clever at cards."

"You don't have to be clever," Bertrem assured her. "I like you just the way you are."

James caught Eleanor's eye and, despite all her worries, she almost burst into laughter at the wicked laughter glinting in his eyes.

"The tea tray should be here shortly," Eleanor said, scrambling for an excuse to prolong the evening.

"None for me, thank you." Drusilla got to her feet. "I think I'll retire."

"That's the ticket. Get a good night's rest," Bertrem agreed. "Tomorrow's another day, an' all. I'll see you to your room."

Eleanor watched in frustration as they left.

Once they were gone, James turned to Eleanor. "What's wrong?"

Eleanor's stomach muscles clenched nervously. "Wrong?" she stalled.

"Cut line, woman. You've been nervous as the devil all evening. It isn't like you. What's wrong?"

"Umm, well..." Eleanor absently waved her hand at a moth that had flown into the lighted room as she frantically searched her mind for a plausible excuse, but it remained discouragingly blank. Finally, she muttered, "I'm not used to the quiet of the countryside. It makes me nervous."

"Lies make me nervous." James stood and walked over to the French doors to adjust the curtains, which had parted to allow the more adventurous bugs inside. Satisfied, he turned and stared at her for a long moment. "And you, my dear, are lying. Why?"

The very faint hint of pain in his voice was Eleanor's undoing. She hadn't wanted to tell him what she'd done, for her own sake. So that she would have the memories of these last few days with him to remember. To hoard against a lonely future. But postponing telling him wasn't giving her good memories to store up. In fact, she'd never spent a more nerve-racking night in her life. And as if that weren't bad enough, now she was hurting James with her evasions and half-truths. She was going to have to tell him. She had to spare him any more pain. She glanced down at her hands, trying to find the words to begin.

There was always the forthright approach, she considered. Something along the lines of, yes, James, you're right. I'm nervous because the man I spied for is now trying to force me to steal your plans for the final offensive against Napoleon. No, that was too forthright, she decided. Maybe she should start by telling him about her father and how much he'd loved the Colonies and what desperate straits they were in and how she'd just wanted to be loyal to her father's memory?

There was a muffled thump, and she looked up, her eyes widening in shock as James slowly crumpled to the floor. Horrified, she jumped to her feet, only to freeze as Connal strode boldly through the French doors and stared down at James' unconscious body.

Eleanor felt a surge of fury at Connal's smug expression. A red haze glowed in her mind, and her hand crept toward the oversize millefiori paperweight on the desk. She wanted to smash him. To beat his smug smile into oblivion, and Connal along with it. But an icy splinter of fear pierced her mind, stilling her hand as a second man invaded the room. De Selignac.

Think, she ordered her sluggish mind. Anger wouldn't help James now. There was no way she could overpower both Connal and De Selignac, but she might be able to out-think them.

Purposefully, she kept her eyes averted from James' body, praying he'd stay unconscious. Awake, he was a threat to them. And while she wasn't precisely afraid of Connal, De Selignac was quite another matter. She didn't trust him an inch. With anything. About anything. She didn't have the slightest doubt that if either she or James were to prove to be a problem, he'd slit their throats without a second thought. And she very much doubted that Connal would be able to stop him. Or even that he'd try very hard.

"Splendid, Eleanor," Connal said approvingly. "I would never have thought of luring Ryland in here so that we could overpower him away from witnesses. And in the same room where our contact tells us the plans are stored, too."

"You did well, *mademoiselle*. I personally will inform the emperor of your resourcefulness." De Selignac smiled at Eleanor, and she felt as if she'd just been touched by something unclean. "But we have little time. Someone might bring that tea tray you mentioned. Close the door." He barked to Connal, who hastened to do his bidding with a promptness that frightened Eleanor. It was as if Connal were little more than a servant. Clearly, he would have no voice in how events unfolded.

De Selignac headed toward the landscape painting on the wall, which he quickly removed to reveal a safe. Eleanor watched as he fiddled with the lock. "Umm," he grunted in satisfaction as he managed to open it. "My contact was right. This safe is very old, and very easy to break into."

"But what good is stealing the plans going to do?" Eleanor asked. "The English will simply make more."

"Ah, *mademoiselle*." De Selignac grinned at her, sending a shiver of apprehension slithering down her spine.

"You are to be congratulated on your grasp of the situation. Your fiancée is a pearl above price, Monsieur Gunn."

Eleanor bit back her instinctive denial of any relationship with Connal. This was not the time to make either of them angry. There was no telling what the results might be. Since they refused to respond to logic, she'd simply let them steal the blasted things and then tell James who had taken them. He'd issue an alarm, and the command would have to redesign the plans. They wouldn't like the extra work, but it could be worse, she told herself.

She was right. The situation not only could be worse, but it proceeded to become so almost immediately.

"They won't know, *mademoiselle,* because I will not steal the plans." De Selignac smiled condescendingly at her. "I assure you that Napoleon's agents are not so inexperienced. Rest easy. I will copy the notes, return them to the safe, and no one will ever know."

"Ryland is going to have a lump on his head the size of a goose egg, and you think he isn't going to figure out that something's amiss?" Eleanor asked incredulously.

"Ah, but the lump will not bother him, because he will not feel it. You see, *mademoiselle,* it is necessary for le Duc to be dead. That way, if the safe is still intact, the authorities will assume that our host surprised a housebreaker and..." De Selignac shrugged. "Such a shame, but the fortunes of war, you understand."

"You didn't say anything about murder." Eleanor stared disbelievingly at Connal as icy tendrils of fear snaked through her body, making her feel weak. As if she were going to faint. Not now, she told herself. This was not the time for missish behavior, no matter how extreme the provocation.

"Ah, do not despair, *mademoiselle.* I have already given your fiancé more money for the added risk."

Eleanor looked away from Connal, trying to contain her sense of revulsion. She'd already known he was a greedy, self-serving man, but to kill a defenseless man for money...

"You're a woman. You don't understand," Connal said defensively. "We are at war with England. People die in wars."

"And it was a lot of money," she muttered.

"A very lot of money," De Selignac said dryly. "Enough that I think that you can help me copy these plans, *monsieur. Vite!*" he snapped when Connal hesitated, his eyes still on Eleanor's pale face. "We must hurry and be gone before a servant returns and discovers us."

For a moment, Eleanor hoped Connal might be having second thoughts about cold-blooded murder. A hope that died when he set the pistol he'd been carrying down on the edge of the desk. Pulling up a chair, he began to write.

Eleanor stared down at the floor, panic and dread swirling through her benumbed mind. James couldn't die. She focused on that single, immutable fact. He mustn't die. She had already come to terms with the fact that she couldn't marry him, but she'd found comfort in the knowledge that he would be alive in the world. Alive and healthy and, hopefully, happy. The very thought of him dead... of his laughing eyes forever dimmed...

Eleanor swallowed against the sour taste of panic in her throat.

She couldn't bear the thought of a world without James in it. And to know that she was the one who had set into motion the events that had led to his death was too great a burden to have to live with. If James were dead, then she would prefer to be dead with him rather than alive with Connal. Her decision helped to calm her frantic thoughts, making it easier for her to think more clearly.

Trying to scream for help would do no good, she concluded. At this time of night, the servants were either in their own quarters or in the servants' sitting room, off the kitchens. They'd never hear her, because De Selignac would throttle her before she could get out more than a shriek or two. No, there was no outside help to be had. It was up to her to rescue James from the situation she'd inadvertently embroiled him in.

Eleanor glanced over at the desk where the two men were hurriedly copying. Her eyes were drawn to the silver-and-black gun. Somehow, she had to get her hands on it. That gun would go a long way toward equalizing Connal's and De Selignac's superior physical strength. But how could she get close enough to grab it?

She allowed herself to peek at James, and to her horror she saw that his eyes were open. She gave him an agonized look, praying he wouldn't move. If De Selignac saw that James was conscious, he might decide to kill him now. Not later.

To her infinite relief, James winked at her and then feigned unconsciousness again.

Eleanor closed her eyes, waiting for her pounding heartbeat to slow, and then opened them again. A slight frown creased her forehead as she found herself looking at the serene features of a Sevres shepherdess. They were going to blame James' death on a housebreaker, she suddenly remembered. That was how she'd get close enough to get her hands on the gun. She felt a burst of energy flood her trembling limbs as a plan seemed to spring full-blown into her mind.

She took a deep, steadying breath, sent up a silent prayer for James' safety and then picked up the Sevres piece. She walked across the room and carefully placed it on the desk, trying to appear casual. Then she gathered up a Ming figurine and a jade carving. She set them down beside the shepherdess.

Connal looked up from his copying and frowned at her. "What are you doing?"

"I rather like those pieces," she said.

"So?" Connal demanded.

Eleanor shrugged, hoping the tension she was feeling wasn't visible in her face. "You said that you were going to blame everything on a housebreaker. And a housebreaker would steal something. You can carry the pieces away with you. And mind that you don't break them. That Chinese stuff is very valuable."

Connal grimaced, but De Selignac chuckled appreciatively. "Ah, *mademoiselle*. You have the soul of a Frenchwoman."

Eleanor bit back the urge to tell him what she thought about the condition of *his* soul. Instead, she forced a smile and went back to gathering small objets d'art. Carefully, she added first one and then another until, finally, when she was relatively sure that neither man was paying any attention to her, she placed her latest acquisition down on the desk and snatched up the gun.

Jumping back out of reach, she pointed it at the two men.

"Don't move," she ordered, her voice shrill with nervous fear, "or I'll—"

"You'll what?" De Selignac seemed merely curious. "Shoot your fiancé as well as me?"

"He is not my fiancé!" Eleanor bit out the words. "I wouldn't have the miserable, cowardly sneak if he came draped with the crown jewels."

"Eleanor—" Connal took a step toward her "—you don't know what you're saying."

"Stand still." Eleanor leveled the gun at him, hoping she sounded more formidable than she felt. "I know exactly what I'm saying. Your problem is that you never listen to what it is I say."

"A mistake that I shall take great care not to duplicate."

Eleanor heard the sound of James' voice from behind her with an overwhelming feeling of relief. Despite her threats, she wasn't sure that she could really bring herself to shoot anyone at point-blank range. Even De Selignac.

"Here." Eleanor edged sideways and handed the gun to James. As she turned back, she saw De Selignac surreptitiously easing a knife out of his coat sleeve.

"James!" she yelped. "The Frenchman!"

De Selignac yanked the knife free, but before he could throw it, James calmly pulled the trigger. Eleanor watched in stomach-churning horror as a bright red stain sluggishly oozed across the front of De Selignac's white waistcoat. De Selignac looked down at it, a surprised expression on his face, as he seemed to slowly collapse in on himself.

Eleanor swallowed against an overwhelming urge to cast up her accounts and looked away. She looked back, her eyes huge in her chalk-white face, just as Connal sprinted for the open French doors.

"Don't shoot him, James," Eleanor begged. "Don't kill him, too."

"I couldn't if I wanted to," James said tiredly. "This type of dueling pistol only has one shot."

"Connal isn't important," Eleanor said. "He was only doing it because he—" she glanced down at De Selignac's body and hastily averted her eyes "—was paying him. I'll bet any amount Connal will be on the first boat back to America he can find."

James gave her a long, thoughtful look. "I think—"

"Your Grace!" The door burst open to reveal the elderly butler, and a scrawny footman brandishing a poker.

"We heard a shot and—" The butler looked down at De Selignac's sprawled body and frowned.

"Is he—?" The footman gulped.

"Dead," James obligingly supplied.

The butler drew himself up to his full height, frowned at the footman for his impertinence in asking a question and then said, "I'm sure you know your own business best, Your Grace, but might I point out to you that the...man is bleeding all over your mother's prize Chinese rug. I don't know how we'll ever get the stains out."

"No, indeed." Eleanor began to giggle uncontrollably. She was up to her neck in espionage, a man was dead, another was a fugitive, state secrets had been compromised, but all Gretton was worried about were stains on the carpet.

"Stop that, Eleanor!" James ordered. "This is no time for hysterics."

"Oh?" Eleanor bit down on her lower lip, and the resulting pain helped her to partially control her laughter. "When would be a good time for me to become hysterical? I realize that to a Grecophile a few bodies more or less don't signify, but..."

"The dook, he ain't no Grec...what you said." The footman rushed to Ryland's defense. "He's a loyal Englishman, born and bred."

"Thank you for the testimonial, Timothy, but this is also not the time to discuss loyalties," James ordered. "Right now, I need you to ride over to the Two Swans in Bexley, find a Mr. Smythe who's staying there, and ask him to come here as soon as possible."

"Right, Your Grace." Timothy seemed only too happy to escape the scene of the carnage.

"Gretton—" James turned to the butler "—you check and make sure that none of our guests heard the shot. If they did, reassure them with some banbury tale or other."

Gretton straightened his shoulders. "Yes, Your Grace. Might I ask what you wish done with..." He gestured toward the body.

"Have him taken to the stables. Mr. Smythe can see about returning him to London tomorrow. I'll be in the library when he comes."

About to say that she'd be in her room, Eleanor wasn't given the choice. James took her upper arm in a grip that foiled her instinctive impulse to run and escorted her to the library. His fingers seemed to burn into her upper arm like shackles, and she could almost see the scaffold looming in front of her. There was no way that she'd ever be able to convince James that she hadn't been a part of De Selignac's plan, she thought in despair. She wasn't even sure it was worth the effort to try. Even if she did manage to convince him, there was still the matter of the spying she really had done.

But De Selignac hadn't hurt James. She was able to find some comfort in that fact. No matter what happened to her, James was safe.

James closed the oversize oak doors behind him with a thump and turned to face her. "Now then." His brisk voice sounded out of place in the funereal silence of the library.

Eleanor looked at him, her eyes tracing over his clenched jawline and lingering on his tightly compressed lips. James was laboring under some strong emotion and, all things considered, the most likely candidate was anger, she concluded morosely. Pure, unadulterated fury. Eleanor sagged down on the sofa, fighting an urge to burst into tears. James had every right to be livid. Her arrival in England had cost him dearly. And he hadn't deserved it. She sniffed mournfully. Neither had her uncle.

"I would like an explanation," James began.

"I wish I had one to give you," Eleanor muttered despondently. "Unfortunately, I'm none too sure exactly what happened myself."

"Since I already know the end, suppose you start from the beginning." He clipped the words out.

Eleanor stared up at the ornate plaster moldings on the ceiling and tried to think of a logical place to begin. "I guess it all started with my father." She picked up a thread to follow. "I loved him, you see. A lot. And he loved me. I was all he had. And he hated the English, and he loved America. It had been very good to him."

"Yes?" he prodded when she fell silent.

"And when he had his first seizure, he was worried about me handling his money."

"So he didn't lose it all during the war?"

Eleanor grimaced. "He didn't lose anything. Papa was a very canny businessman. When he died, he left me close to three-quarters of a million pounds."

James blinked in shock at the sum. He wasn't sure *he* had that much money. "Then why the masquerade as a poor relation?"

"Because Connal found out from a contact of his in the State Department that Uncle Henry was someone of importance at Whitehall, and he wanted me to come to England and discover something that the Congress could use to make the English modify their demands for peace at the talks at Ghent."

"And you agreed?" he demanded.

Eleanor squirmed beneath his incredulous expression and forced herself to continue, when what she really wanted to do was to hide. The fear that had driven her to rescue James from Connal had dissolved now that the danger was past, taking her energy and stamina along with it.

She sighed. "Not exactly. When my father died, it was as if all the color had bled out of the world. Nothing seemed to matter very much, and everything was such an effort." She struggled to make him understand. "And Connal was pushing me to marry him, and I felt guilty stalling, because I knew our marriage was what my father wanted. Coming to England seemed like a reprieve. I thought it would give me time to think, away from Connal's continual nagging. Time to recover my normal equilibrium."

James nodded slowly.

"Then the situation with the war in the Colonies worsened, and I found out Connal was in England, instead of safely back in Boston, where I thought he was, and I knew my father would have wanted me to help the American cause, and I just didn't see how I could do what he wanted in regard to marrying Connal..." Her monologue slowed to a halt as Eleanor ran out of breath.

"So you did the other thing you knew he wanted, and agreed to spy for America," James said slowly.

Eleanor swallowed the lump in her throat and whispered, "So I spied on Uncle Henry. And felt like the greatest villain unhanged. Then, when Connal wanted me to spy on you..."

"Yes?" James sounded no more than mildly curious.

"I told him no, and he threatened to tell Uncle Henry what I'd done if I wouldn't help him."

"And?"

"I told him to go ahead and tell. That I would be returning to Boston and it wouldn't matter," she muttered, staring down at her fingers, vaguely surprised to find them clenched into fists.

"And that's why you tried to keep us all in the study?" James concluded.

Eleanor sighed. "I thought if we were actually there, they couldn't do anything."

James unexpectedly chuckled. "You proved more than equal to their plots. But I'm curious, my dear—why didn't you just warn me?" He rubbed the lump on the back of his head, and Eleanor was consumed with guilt when he winced.

"I was going to write you a letter when I left," she mumbled.

"But I don't want you to leave," he said calmly. "I very much want you to stay. In fact, I brought you down here to propose to you."

Eleanor's eyes widened, and she stared at him in disbelief, afraid to believe what she'd just heard. Everyone had been at such pains to convince her that James would never marry her that she'd finally come to believe them. And they'd been wrong. He had actually wanted to marry her. But how could he still want to marry her, knowing what she'd done? Not only that, but how could she tell him she loved him with her spying hanging between them. He'd never truly believe her. Not deep down in his heart. He'd think her love was cream-pot love, professed so that she could escape the consequences of her crime. Her lower lip began to tremble with the effort it took her not to burst into tears at the incredible mess she'd managed to make of everything. And the most frustrating thing about it all was that she'd meant well.

James frowned at her reaction. Grasping her chin in his warm fingers, he tilted her head up and studied the diamond glitter of tears on her thick eyelashes speculatively.

"Not tears of joy," he murmured. "Which makes me wonder why. You certainly seemed to enjoy kissing me."

"James!" His comment jerked her out of the morass of self-pity she was drowning in.

"Well, didn't you? It seemed so at the time. But, of course, my perceptions of your reactions were colored by my own intense pleasure," he admitted, looking uncertain. "And I am a duke, and very wealthy."

Eleanor instinctively responded to his uncertainty. It was unthinkable that she allow him to think even for a moment that his enormous attraction for her hinged on either his money or his title.

"I have more than enough money of my own," she reminded him. "And as for your being a duke, that's not an advantage, as far as I'm concerned."

He eyed her dubiously. "I must admit that I've often found the title to be a millstone around my neck, but you're the first woman I've ever met who's felt that way."

"That, my dear sir, is because I am a staunch republican. We don't set much store by titles."

"Am I?" he asked wistfully.

"Am you—" She grimaced. "Are you what?"

"Your dear?"

Eleanor slowly ran the tip of her tongue over her dry lips, mesmerized by the flickering pinpoints of light glowing deep in his eyes. Even if he couldn't or wouldn't believe her, she still owed him the truth. It was all she had left to give him. She took a deep breath and blurted out, "Yes, you are my dear everything. I love you to distraction. In fact, I—"

Her words were abruptly cut off as he grabbed her, pulled her into his arms and covered her mouth with his with a rough hunger that told her his calm was only skin-deep. Below that calm was a seething caldron of emotions—of which passion played no small part.

There was no gentleness in his kiss—just raw, driving need. It was as if his ardor had overridden all other considerations. He pressed harder on her mouth, his tongue boldly demanding entrance. Obediently Eleanor opened her lips, and his tongue surged inside.

Eleanor gasped at the sensations that engulfed her as he meticulously began to explore the inside of her cheek. She felt as if she'd just stepped off the bottom step, and instead of touching the floor as she'd expected, she'd been hurtled into space. She snuggled closer, clutching his head for anchorage. His hair felt soft and silky and his skin warm and supple as she dug her fingertips into it.

A moan bubbled out of her throat as a sense of urgency wrapped itself around her mind, squeezing out all her doubts and uncertainties. Anything that felt this good couldn't possibly be wrong, she thought distractedly.

She gasped, suspended in the grip of a terrible longing as his hand suddenly slipped inside her neckline to find and cup her breast.

His hand seemed to burn into her flesh, heating it to an unbearable level. Eleanor whimpered in mindless desire. As if to reward her, he slowly rubbed his palm over her throbbing nipple. His slightly roughened skin intensified her longing, tightening the coil of desire to a level she wouldn't have thought possible.

Despite her muttered protest, James suddenly yanked his hand away and, with what was probably meant to be a soothing kiss on her forehead, hurriedly turned her flushed face into his coat, shielding her from the sight of whoever was opening the door.

It was Gretton. The butler was becoming so inured to events that he didn't even seem to notice that Eleanor was sitting in his master's lap.

"Mr. Smythe has arrived and awaits your pleasure in the book room." Gretton aimed the words at a point over James' head.

James glanced down at Eleanor's pale face framed by her tumbled brown hair and said, "Tell him I'm coming."

"Who's Smythe?" Eleanor asked when Gretton had left to deliver the message.

"He's really Colonel Smythe. He's the head of the mission that brought the plans from Whitehall and will be carrying them on to the Continent in the morning. We felt that it would be better if people who saw them on the road believed they were civilians. I won't be long. I simply need to tell him about De Selignac."

"Oh," Eleanor muttered, worried about what else he might feel obligated to tell Smythe.

"You wait here," James ordered. "I'll be back as soon as I can."

By the time James returned, some thirty minutes later, Eleanor was a mass of conflicting emotions. She'd traveled from mindless pleasure in James' arms all the way to abject terror at the thought of herself rotting away, unlamented, in the Tower for spying.

"What happened?" she asked apprehensively.

"I gave Smythe an expurgated version of the affair, and he'll have one of his men return De Selignac's body to London tomorrow and inform them of what happened."

"And Connal?" Eleanor asked fearfully.

"Personally, I'd like to see him hang for threatening you, but to bring him to justice would mean that everything else would have to come out. So I just told Smythe that De Selignac had an accomplice who escaped and then gave him a very inaccurate description. But I do intend to make sure Gunn really leaves England."

"It's more than he deserves," Eleanor admitted. "It's more than I deserve."

"As for that, my dear..." James reached for her again, and Eleanor willingly snuggled into his arms. He held her tightly, making her feel safe and protected in a way she never had before. "While I thoroughly disapprove of your spying, I can understand why you did it."

Eleanor sighed. "I wonder if Uncle Henry will?"

"Since we aren't going to tell him, we'll never know."

Eleanor leaned her head back and stared into his beloved features, her eyes lingering on the enticing shape of his mouth. "We aren't?" she asked uncertainly.

"No, we aren't. Confession might be good for the soul, but it often leaves a heavy burden on the person you confess to. Henry deserves his peace of mind and, since it's too late to change what you did, our only viable option is to inform Whitehall that we found out from De Selignac before he was shot that the plans for the spring offensive out of Canada were leaked to the Americans. But I doubt it will make much difference in the long run, since the plans for the Canadian offensive have already been shipped to America."

Eleanor sighed. "I never felt right about doing it, but America really does deserve her chance, James. Declaring war may have been an ill-advised thing to do, but Congress was goaded into it by those infernal orders-in-council of your government."

James chuckled. "You have the makings of an ardent Whig hostess. How unfortunate it is that I'm a Tory. Although..." He rested his chin on her head and stared into the crackling fire for a long moment. "I must admit that it is to England's advantage to settle the war as quickly as possible. America is an important market for our manufactured goods.

"I'll ask Wellington to talk to Whitehall and see if we can get them to soften their demands for an American peace. Old Duro doesn't want to wage a war on two fronts any more than the rest of us do."

Eleanor closed her eyes and felt a sense of peace steal over her at his offer. It represented real, substantial help for her father's cause. A final tribute to his dream of a free and independent America. She could grasp the happiness James was offering without feeling that she'd betrayed her father. Even if James was a member of the English aristocracy, he was also an intelligent, loyal man who embodied all the traits her father would have wanted in her husband. Her father would have liked James, she admitted. She loved James with all her heart, and that love didn't require anyone else's approval.

Eleanor smiled up into his gleaming eyes as a feeling of perfect contentment flooded her. At long last, she knew what her mother had found out all those years ago. That love was more than adequate compensation for giving up one's culture and country, because the rewards were so great.

She smiled seductively as James pulled her tighter into his arms and lowered his head to hers.

"Now then, that seems to have tied up all the loose ends, except for the matter of your accepting my proposal." James' voice was casual, but Eleanor could feel the tension vibrating in him.

"We can get married by special license. I know just how to go about it from reading one of my Gothics," she added smugly.

James chuckled, and the obvious happiness in his face warmed her. "You bring your Gothic, and I'll bring a book

I have, and we can see which is the most useful for a honeymoon."

"Your Romans—"

"It's not Roman, it's French. Very, very French," he said, a second before his mouth cut off all further talk and the room became silent.

In the hallway outside, Gretton stationed himself protectively in front of the door, his mind filled with visions of the pleasures in store. Soon there would be visitors coming and going, house parties, and the laughter of happy children. Many children, from what he had seen so far, he thought. Yes, the future looked a very inviting place at the moment. He sighed in anticipation.

*   *   *   *   *

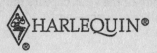 HARLEQUIN®

Weddings, Inc.

The proprietors of Weddings, Inc. hope you have enjoyed visiting Eternity, Massachusetts. And if you missed any of the exciting Weddings, Inc. titles, here is your opportunity to complete your collection:

Harlequin Superromance	#598	*Wedding Invitation* by Marisa Carroll	$3.50 U.S. ☐ $3.99 CAN. ☐
Harlequin Romance	#3319	*Expectations* by Shannon Waverly	$2.99 U.S. ☐ $3.50 CAN. ☐
Harlequin Temptation	#502	*Wedding Song* by Vicki Lewis Thompson	$2.99 U.S. ☐ $3.50 CAN. ☐
Harlequin American Romance	#549	*The Wedding Gamble* by Muriel Jensen	$3.50 U.S. ☐ $3.99 CAN. ☐
Harlequin Presents	#1692	*The Vengeful Groom* by Sara Wood	$2.99 U.S. ☐ $3.50 CAN. ☐
Harlequin Intrigue	#298	*Edge of Eternity* by Jasmine Cresswell	$2.99 U.S. ☐ $3.50 CAN. ☐
Harlequin Historical	#248	*Vows* by Margaret Moore	$3.99 U.S. ☐ $4.50 CAN. ☐

HARLEQUIN BOOKS...
NOT THE SAME OLD STORY

TOTAL AMOUNT	$
POSTAGE & HANDLING ($1.00 for one book, 50¢ for each additional)	$
APPLICABLE TAXES*	$ _____
TOTAL PAYABLE (check or money order—please do not send cash)	$ _____

To order, complete this form and send it, along with a check or money order for the total above, payable to Harlequin Books, to: **In the U.S.:** 3010 Walden Avenue, P.O. Box 9047, Buffalo, NY 14269-9047; **In Canada:** P.O. Box 613, Fort Erie, Ontario, L2A 5X3.

Name: _____

Address: _____ City: _____

State/Prov.: _____ Zip/Postal Code: _____

*New York residents remit applicable sales taxes.
Canadian residents remit applicable GST and provincial taxes.

WED-F

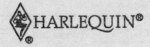

Maura Seger's
BELLE HAVEN

Four books. Four generations. Four indomitable females.

You met the Belle Haven women who started it all in Harlequin Historicals. Now meet descendant Nora Delaney in the emotional contemporary conclusion to the Belle Haven saga:

THE SURRENDER OF NORA

When Nora's inheritance brings her home to Belle Haven, she finds more than she bargained for. Deadly accidents prove someone wants her out of town—fast. But the real problem is the prime suspect—handsome Hamilton Fletcher. His quiet smile awakens the passion all Belle Haven women are famous for. But does he want her heart...or her life?

Don't miss THE SURRENDER OF NORA
Silhouette Intimate Moments #617
Available in January!

This holiday, join four hunky heroes under the mistletoe for

Christmas Kisses

Cuddle under a fluffy quilt, with a cup of hot chocolate and these romances sure to warm you up:

#561 HE'S A REBEL (also a Studs title)
Linda Randall Wisdom

#562 THE BABY AND THE BODYGUARD
Jule McBride

#563 THE GIFT-WRAPPED GROOM
M.J. Rodgers

#564 A TIMELESS CHRISTMAS
Pat Chandler

Celebrate the season with all four holiday books sealed with a Christmas kiss—coming to you in December, only from
Harlequin American Romance!